P9-ELS-861

TO THE RIVER'S END

Look for these exciting Western series from bestselling authors
William W. Johnstone and J.A. Johnstone

The Mountain Man

Preacher: The First Mountain Man

Luke Jensen: Bounty Hunter

Those Jensen Boys!

The Jensen Brand

MacCallister

The Red Ryan Westerns

Perley Gates

Have Brides, Will Travel

Will Tanner, Deputy U.S. Marshall

Shotgun Johnny

The Chuckwagon Trail

The Jackals

The Slash and Pecos Westerns

The Texas Moonshiners

Stoneface Finnegan Westerns

Ben Savage: Saloon Ranger

The Buck Trammel Westerns

The Death and Texas Westerns

The Hunter Buchanon Westerns

TO THE RIVER'S END

WILLIAM W. JOHNSTONE
AND J.A. JOHNSTONE

KENSINGTON
PUBLISHING CORP.

www.kensingtonbooks.com

KENSINGTON BOOKS are published by

Kensington Publishing Corp.
119 West 40th Street
New York, NY 10018

Copyright © 2021 by J.A. Johnstone

All rights reserved. No part of this book may be reproduced in any form or by any means without the prior written consent of the Publisher, excepting brief quotes used in reviews.

All Kensington titles, imprints, and distributed lines are available at special quantity discounts for bulk purchases for sales promotion, premiums, fund-raising, educational, or institutional use.

This book is a work of fiction. Names, characters, businesses, organizations, places, events, and incidents either are the product of the author's imagination or are used fictitiously. Any resemblance to actual persons, living or dead, events, or locales is entirely coincidental.

To the extent that the image or images on the cover of this book depict a person or persons, such person or persons are merely models, and are not intended to portray any character or characters featured in the book.

Special book excerpts or customized printings can also be created to fit specific needs. For details, write or phone the office of the Kensington Sales Manager: Kensington Publishing Corp., 119 West 40th Street, New York, NY 10018. Attn. Sales Department. Phone: 1-800-221-2647.

PUBLISHER'S NOTE: Following the death of William W. Johnstone, the Johnstone family is working with a carefully selected writer to organize and complete Mr. Johnstone's outlines and many unfinished manuscripts to create additional novels in all of his series like the Last Gunfighter, Mountain Man, and Eagles, among others. This novel was inspired by Mr. Johnstone's superb storytelling.

KENSINGTON BOOKS and the WWJ steer head logo are trademarks of Kensington Publishing Corp.

ISBN-13: 978-1-4967-3452-5 (ebook)

ISBN-13: 978-1-4967-3451-8

First Kensington Trade Paperback Printing: October 2021

10 9 8 7 6 5 4 3 2 1

Printed in the United States of America

Chapter 1

"What's on your mind, Luke?" Tom Molloy asked when he pulled up next to Luke Ransom, who had halted his string of packhorses at the mouth of a small stream. The four-man team of two trappers and two camp tenders were on their way to the annual rendezvous at Horse Creek where it joined the Green River. They were following an old Indian trail between the Snake and the Green River that should allow them to strike the Green River a short distance north of Horse Creek.

"Whaddaya stoppin' for?" Charlton Lewis wanted to know as he caught up to them now.

"That's just what I was askin', Luke," Tom answered him.

"I was just studyin' this little stream," Luke explained.

"What for?" Charlton asked. "If you're thinkin' about beaver, forget about it. We checked it out last year, when I was ridin' with Rex Gorden. It ain't big enough to attract beaver."

"Besides," Tom said, "we've got a pretty good yield for our year's work. I'm ready to get on to rendezvous. I need a drink of likker bad. Ain't that what you say, Luke?"

"I reckon," Luke hedged. "But I'm still a little curious about this stream. I remember this stream when we rode outta rendezvous last summer. And when I look at it now, I'm wonderin' why the mouth of it ain't as big as it was. It was bigger'n that last summer. So, I'm wonderin' if somethin's stoppin' it up back toward that ridge—like a beaver dam that wasn't there last time we rode along this river."

"Maybe it's just dryin' up," Tom said, not really interested in investigating it.

"I hope to hell this ain't the rendezvous," Fred Willis called out, just then catching up to them. "I was hopin' for somethin' a sight bigger'n this," he japed.

"It's only Luke havin' one of his notions," Tom said. "He thinks he smells beaver up this little stream."

"Hell, we're gettin' close enough to rendezvous till I can't smell nothin' but whiskey," Fred replied. "I'm goin' on." He gave his horse a nudge with his heels and rode around the other horses. Tom and Charlton fell in behind him.

"I'm gonna take a look up this stream," Luke called after them. "If I don't catch up with you pretty quick, I'll see ya at camp." Without looking around, Tom held his hand up to let him know he heard him.

It was still early in the day. He had time to follow the stream back toward the mountains west of the valley, and he could catch up with the others where they camped for the night. They should make the rendezvous by suppertime the day after tomorrow. If he didn't catch up to them tonight, he'd do it tomorrow night. He guided the big bay gelding he called Smoke along the stream, leading two packhorses. The stream was obviously smaller than it had been last year, but the current was still pretty healthy. He could see no reason why it would dry up. There were no signs anywhere else that there had been a lack of rainfall. So he was not really surprised when he finally saw the dam up ahead of him, after riding less than half a mile. He smiled to himself and muttered, "Yep, I reckon I had another one of my notions." He discovered only one lodge, which didn't surprise him, since the dam and the pond it created were not that old. More than likely, the family all lived in the one lodge. That told him the pelts wouldn't be big, except for those of the mama and papa. Now he had to make a decision on whether or not to set his traps and hope to catch one of the adults—or leave them alone to give the kits a chance to grow up and build more lodges. The problem was, the stream was too close to a commonly used trail, so he doubted they would be left unharmed. *"I'll set just a couple of traps, maybe catch one of the adults,"* he decided.

He took a wide circle around the lodge and the pond created by the dam to leave his horses while he set his traps. After taking care of the horses, he took two No. 4 Newhouse beaver traps and set them, wading down the stream in the water, so he would not leave his scent on the banks near the traps. Working as fast as he could, since it was not the usual time of day when he would normally be setting traps, he set each trap quickly. He placed the cocked trap so that the trigger was about a hand's width below the surface of the water. Then he pulled the chain to its full length and secured it with a sharpened stick he drove into the bottom of the stream. Once the trap was set, he took a willow twig, peeled it, and covered it with "medicine," which was a yellow, sticky substance called castoreum. The trapper gets his "medicine" from the beaver's scent glands. A beaver is a highly territorial animal and each one has a distinctive scent. Luke fixed the willow twig with the castoreum over the trap to bait his trap, knowing a beaver could not resist investigating the stranger's scent.

With his traps set, he went about the business of making a camp for the night. He felt pretty confident in his prospects of adding another plew or two to his total, but it was necessary to stay there that night and check his traps in the morning. Beavers did most of their business during the night. It would not be the first time he had failed to show up for a day or so. Tom and the others were accustomed to his occasional absences. He was well aware of the reputation he had acquired during the years he had worked for the American Fur Company. Tom Molloy, especially, couldn't resist reminding Luke that they trapped for the company and were paid a salary, no matter how many plews they trapped. Fred and Charlton were of a like mind, but they soon learned that it was simply Luke's nature to work as hard as he could to get every last pelt out there.

It was Fred, who worked as a camp tender along with Charlton, who put the idea of quitting the American Fur company in his head. "As hard as you work at it, I'm surprised you ain't quit this outfit and gone free-trappin'," Fred told him. "Hell, they'll buy your pelts, same as they do everybody else's. You'd wind up makin' a helluva lot more money than you're makin', workin' for the company."

Luke had answered the call when William Ashley advertised in the St. Louis newspaper for one hundred men to go up the Missouri River to its source. They were to sign up for one, two, or three years to work there to establish the company in the fur business. Like most of the men, he signed on for three years, to trap the mountain streams for beaver pelts, but the new fur company found itself in a constant war with the Arikara and Blackfoot Indians. A lot of men were killed before Ashley abandoned the upper Missouri and sent his men into the Rocky Mountains to trap the streams and rivers. That was five years ago and now Luke figured he had given the company fair value in exchange for his horse and traps, and it was time to sever the ties and start out next season as a free trapper. This was another reason he had decided to trap this little stream while the others went on to rendezvous. In his mind, he felt he should do the best he could for the company since this was his last year with them. It wouldn't be a prime pelt, since the beavers had likely lost their heavy winter fur this time of the year. But it was one more plew for his employer.

Before sunup the next morning, Luke rolled out of his blanket and went to check his traps. He found a beaver in one of the traps but nothing in the other one. Satisfied that the one pelt was at least worth the trouble, he pulled the carcass out of the water and pulled his traps out of the pond. An adult male, he estimated the beaver weighed about forty pounds. He was not the biggest catch, but his fur was not bad for this time of the year, which told Luke he was still a young specimen. Instead of his usual custom of skinning it right there, he took the beaver back to his campfire and skinned it there. After he stretched the pelt out on a willow hoop to dry for a couple of days, he extracted the scent glands for the medicine and scraped the tail and charred it over his fire. Then he boiled it for a source of butter-like tallow in addition to the tasty meal it provided.

He had finished his breakfast and was packing up his horses when he heard the first shot. He paused at once to listen. It sounded as if it had come from upstream, maybe a mile or less away. His first thought was that someone had shot a deer or a wolf. But then, he heard another shot, followed shortly by a third. *Better take a look,* he decided. *Somebody must be having some trouble.* Since his horses were pretty well hidden where they were, he decided to leave them tied there while he followed the stream up to the top of a high shoulder of the mountain west of the river. He wasn't willing to go out of sight of his horses, but if trouble was on its way to visit him, he wanted to be ready to meet it. And he figured he could get a better look at the top of that shoulder. He pulled his Pennsylvania long rifle from his saddle sling as well as his backup rifle from one of his packhorses. Then with a rifle in each hand, he started up the stream at a trot.

He had not reached the top of the rise before another shot rang out. This time, it sounded as if it was just on the backside of the shoulder he was climbing, causing him to stop and drop to one knee to take a cautious look before proceeding. The mountain was heavily forested, so it was difficult to see very far in front of him. He took another look behind him to make sure there was no one circling back toward his horses before he rose to his feet again and continued up the slope. When he reached the top of the shoulder, he discovered that it leveled out for about fifty yards before rising up into the mountain. He also discovered a small grassy meadow bisected by the stream he was following, and the source of the gunfire.

It took only minutes to size up the situation. A man, obviously a trapper, was under attack by Indians. His attackers, only two that Luke could see, were between him and Luke, giving Luke a clear field of fire. Some movement among the trees off to his left caused him to watch for a few moments until he caught sight of the horses the Indians left there. The trapper had taken cover behind his packhorse, which had evidently been killed by the Indians. One of the Indians had a firearm, a Northwest Trade Gun, which was usually called by the French name, *fusil*. A smooth bore gun, it was a popular weapon with the Indians, more so than the rifle-barreled Kentucky Long Rifle. The Indian raised it and threw another lead ball into the carcass of the dead horse. Luke figured the horse had been shot accidentally, since the Indians were no doubt after the trapper's horses as well as the pelts they carried. He hesitated only long enough to make sure there were no other Indians with the two he was about to assassinate before he acted. When he felt sure, he checked the loads in both his flintlock long rifles, raised one of them and took dead aim on the farthest warrior, and squeezed the trigger. Without waiting to witness the results of the shot, for he was confident of his accuracy, he quickly picked up the other rifle and squeezed off another shot. The rifle ball caught the startled warrior in the chest when he turned to see where the first shot had come from.

Suddenly, the forest was silent for a long couple of minutes while Luke reloaded his rifles. When there was no evidence of any additional threat, Luke called out. "Hello, the camp! You all right?"

The gnarly gray-haired little man, lying behind the dead horse, breathed a tentative sigh of relief when he heard a white man's voice. But hostile Indians weren't the only murderers and thieves in the Rocky Mountains, so there was the possibility his rescuer was an even nastier scoundrel than the redskins just eliminated. "Yes, sir, thanks to you. Come on in," he called back. Then, with rifle in hand, he rose up on one knee to watch his visitor approach. In a few seconds, Luke walked out of the cover of the pines. He paused to make sure the two Indians were dead before continuing. Seeing that he was alone, Jug Sartain got to his feet. "You on foot?"

"My horses are down at the foot of the hill," Luke said. "I didn't even know you were up here, till I heard the shots." Concerned then about his horses, he asked, "Blackfoot, any more of 'em around? Or was there just those two?"

"Didn't see any more," Jug answered. "You on your way to rendezvous?"

"As a matter of fact," Luke said. "My name's Luke Ransom. I work for American Fur Company. I was ridin' with three other fellows, but I decided to stop here to check on a new beaver dam below."

"Well, I'm mighty glad you stopped," Jug said. "I wasn't at all sure I was gonna get away from those two boys you shot. That one with the rifle shot my damn packhorse." He offered his hand. "Jug Sartain's my name and I'm pleased to meet you, Luke."

Luke shook Jug's hand. "They left their horses back yonder in the trees. We can go over and see if one of 'em can take on your packs for ya. Then, if you're of a mind to, we can go on down to pick up my horses and we'll ride on to rendezvous together. I reckon that's where you were headin'."

"I sure was," he replied. "I ain't had a drink of likker in two months. That's when that jug on this dead horse went empty.

Luke smiled at the odd little man, dressed in animal skins from his hat to his beaded moccasins, almost black from the smoke of countless campfires. It was hard to guess just how old he was. His hair was long and gray, as were his whiskers, but his eyes were bright and quick. After the comment he just made, Luke couldn't resist asking a question. "Jug, that's an unusual name. Has it got anything to do with the jug hangin' on your packhorse?"

Jug laughed in response to the question. "Yeah, I reckon it has," he said. "Some boys over at Fort Union hung that name on me a few years back. I did some tradin' there and I always bought whiskey in a jug. When they started sellin' most of the whiskey there outta bottles, I just kept my jug and emptied the bottles in it. I never gave 'em no first name, so they started callin' me Jug, and I reckon it stuck. It's better'n my real name, so I just kept it."

"What is your real first name?" Luke asked, curious now.

"Well, see now, Mr. Luke Ransom, you mighta saved my bacon for sure this mornin', but you still ain't knowed me long enough for me to tell you what my mammy named me. She heard a name somewhere that she thought sounded pretty good, but it just didn't suit me."

Luke shrugged. "Jug it is, then. Let's go round up those Blackfoot ponies, and go pick up my horses."

They found the two Blackfoot horses tied in the trees where Luke had spotted them. Both horses were in good condition. Jug looked them over carefully before deciding the bay was his choice as substitute for his packhorse. The other horse, a paint that Luke figured to be about four years old, would have been his choice and they had a friendly discussion over who the paint should belong to. Luke argued that the two warriors were attacking Jug, so both their horses should belong to him. Jug countered with the argument that he might have gone under if Luke hadn't killed both warriors. And since Luke killed them, all their property should be rightfully his. They were still debating the issue when they got down the mountain to get Luke's horses. It was set aside, however, when they reached Luke's camp and Jug saw the load of pelts Luke was packing. "You trap all them plews, yourself?" Jug asked.

"No, well, most of 'em," Luke answered after a pause to think how much of the load was his. "I was workin' with a team of three other men and one of them was trappin' with me."

"How long you been workin' for American Fur?" Jug asked. When Luke told him, Jug asked, "You ever think about free-trappin'?"

"Well," Luke hesitated, "funny you ask. I've thought about it a lot lately, enough that I'd already decided that this was my last rendezvous as a company man. I wanna part with them on good terms, so that's why I wanna make sure I get this load of pelts to the rendezvous. And I weren't too happy to find some Blackfoot raiders between here and Green River. This bein' Shoshone territory and all."

"I know what you mean," Jug replied, "and it don't seem likely that them two that jumped me was down here all by theirselves. There's always some Blackfeet, and sometimes Sioux, sneakin' around when it comes to rendezvous time to try to ambush trappers on their way to the party. There's most likely a larger party of Blackfoot down this way. Those two just broke off and went huntin' for some lone trapper like me." He paused to tug on his beard, then commented with a grin, "Well, they found me, didn't they?"

"I expect we'd best keep a sharp eye out for any sign," Luke replied, "and just play it like they're somewhere around here for sure."

Chapter 2

The two trappers reached the Green River Valley with no more sign of Blackfoot raiders along the way. There was an abundance of tracks on the trail they followed, however, all heading toward the rendezvous. So, there was no way of telling if they were left by friend or foe. Even though many of the tracks were left by unshod hooves, they offered no useful information to Luke and Jug. Hundreds of Indians friendly to the white man attended the rendezvous to trade for themselves. Shoshone, Flathead, Crow, and Nez Perce would all take part in the annual celebration.

Upon first reaching the upper end of the rendezvous site, they automatically paused to survey the scene in the lush river valley. As far as the eye could see, there were camps of all kinds, fur companies, Indian camps, individual traders, and trapper camps. There were thousands of horses and cattle, as well. It was almost as if a whole city had appeared where there had been an empty river valley in the early part of the summer. It would remain that way until the middle of the summer before disappearing to leave only a few shacks and sheds behind. For both Luke and Jug, it was the yearly event where they acquired the supplies they needed for the coming year without having to travel back east to resupply. They were just two of the five hundred mountain men there for the same reason. In addition to the essential supplies needed to survive the coming winter, there were opportunities to "let the dogs out," as Jug expressed it. Foremost for many was the opportunity to buy whiskey. There was gambling of all kinds, as well as horse races, knife-throwing contests, target shooting, wrestling matches, drinking contests, foot races, and anything else that could offer a challenge.

"Well, we made it with our scalps still on," Jug declared, all thoughts of Blackfoot warriors gone from his mind, replaced by the sight of the empty jug on his packhorse.

"Looks that way," Luke agreed. "I reckon I'll ride down the river a-ways. The American Fur Company is supposed to be camped where Horse Creek meets the river." He was anxious to turn his packs of furs over to the company and set his camp up with the other men.

"If it's all the same to you, I'll ride along with you and maybe set up my camp down that way," Jug said.

"Why sure," Luke replied, "glad to have you. You might wanna make camp with us. The three fellows I work with are pretty good to camp with. Matter of fact, most all the company men will be in one big camp. You won't even be noticed."

"Maybe I'll just set up close by," Jug responded. "I wanna see what some of the other companies are payin', too. Need to get the best price I can for my plews." So they rode on down the river until reaching Horse Creek and the American Fur Company camp. When they reached the tents the company had set up for receiving furs, Jug pointed to another one about seventy-five yards farther with a sign out front that proclaimed it to be a saloon. "Yonder's where I can fill my jug. Maybe I'll just go ahead and let your company gimme a price for my plews. Maybe we can have a drink after you get through." He realized that he was going to miss the strapping young man. In the short time he had spent with Luke Ransom, he could feel the honesty in him and the obvious portion of common sense he seemed to possess. He liked the way he carried himself.

"Good idea," Luke replied. "I'll turn these pelts in and see

where Tom and the others are set up, and maybe they'll join us."
He led his packhorses around behind the trader's tent where he
could see the large stacks of packs stacked. As he pulled his
horse to a stop, he saw Jim Frasier coming out to meet him.

When Jim realized who it was, he stopped suddenly, as if he
had seen a ghost. "Luke," he uttered.

"Howdy, Jim," Luke returned, oblivious of Frasier's open-
mouth gaping. "I reckon you boys have been wonderin' about
the rest of the pelts Tom Molloy claimed he had. Well, here they
are. Is Tom around?"

Jim hesitated before answering, long enough for Luke to start
to repeat the question. "No," Jim interrupted then, "Tom ain't
hardly around, and neither is Fred Willis, and neither are the furs
they was supposed to be packin'."

"What?" Luke responded. "What are you talkin' about?" Jim
just continued to stare wide-eyed at him. "You didn't mention
Charlton Lewis. What about him?"

"He made it here, but just barely. He had to run for it, let 'em
have the furs, and run for his life."

"Tom and Fred dead?" Luke uttered in disbelief. "Let who
have the furs? Blackfoot?"

"That's what Lewis said," Jim answered. "Molloy and Willis
were both shot down. He said he was just lucky to get away."
Stunned, Luke found it hard to believe what he was hearing.
When he said nothing for a long few moments, Jim continued.
"Axel said he asked Charlton Lewis about you, and Lewis said
you dropped out about fifteen or twenty miles before a big party
of Blackfoot warriors came down on 'em."

Still shocked and knowing that Tom Molloy and Fred Willis
would have put up a hell of a fight, Luke wondered if Charlton
Lewis would have done the same before he ran. He didn't know
Lewis as well as he did Tom and Fred, since this was the first
time he had ridden with them. "Where is Axel? He needs to take
the count on these pelts I'm haulin'." He wanted to talk to Axel

Thompson and Charlton Lewis, as well. This business just didn't add up. "How many was in that Blackfoot party?"

"He just said it was a big party," Jim answered. "Axel's in the front, talkin' trade with a free trapper."

Luke stepped down from his horse and walked in the back flap of the large tent where the furs were bought and sold to find Axel Thompson examining Jug Sartain's pelts. "Luke!" Axel exclaimed upon seeing him. "We was wonderin' about you."

"Jim's unloadin' the pelts I brought in," Luke said. "I need to talk to you when you're done with Jug."

"We're just about done," Axel said. "Jug, here, says he's a friend of yours. He's brought in some prime fur, and he's gettin' as good a price as he could get anywhere in this valley for 'em." He nodded toward a small group of men near the other end of the long tent, who had stopped talking and were looking at him now. Luke recognized them as company trappers. "There's some of the boys shootin' the breeze over there," Axel said. "They've been talkin' about what happened to Molloy and Willis."

Luke shrugged. "Right, I'll go chew the fat with 'em till you're done tradin'." He walked over to join the group of trappers. "Howdy, boys," he greeted them, "glad to see you all made it back this year. I just found out about my partners a few minutes ago, and I still have trouble gettin' my head around it. Tom Molloy and Fred Willis, they were two damn good men, best I ever worked with."

His greeting was met with a puzzling silence until a big, heavyset mountain man named Bloodworth responded. "Looks like you made it here without a scratch." His tone was blatantly sarcastic. "Sure was lucky for you when you decided to leave 'em right before they was ambushed by them Blackfoot, weren't it?"

Luke didn't like the tone of his question. It sounded as if there was an accusation attached. He met Bloodworth's intense gaze with one of his own. "I reckon you could put it that way," he responded. "Every man here made it to rendezvous on account of luck."

"Sometimes a man might make his own good luck and that turns out to be bad luck for somebody else," Bloodworth declared.

"You sound like you've got something chewin' on your mind, Bloodworth. Why don't you just spit it out?" Luke suggested.

"All right, Ace, I'll spit it out. Charlton Lewis said him and Molloy and Willis thought it was kinda strange that you just decided to hang back on a little stream that didn't amount to more'n a trickle of water. Talkin' about a beaver dam up the mountain, said you was gonna catch up with 'em after you took a quick look. Only, you never showed up when they stopped to camp that night. And you never showed up when them Injuns jumped 'em and got away with a helluva lot of beaver pelts that rightfully belonged to this company."

"There was some talk about that, Bloodworth," Hiram Jones spoke up at that point. "And it did smell a little bit like a double-cross, but that was before Luke showed up with his share of the pelts. It don't make no sense to show up with the pelts, if he was in cahoots with them damn Injuns."

Not to be dissuaded from the opinion he had formed, and already set to carry it to a physical confrontation, Bloodworth was not willing to concede any ground in his accusations. "Maybe he thinks we're too dumb to see the fur he stole, if he brings a fourth of it in to be counted. And it still stinks to hell that he didn't come to help when his partners was under attack. He's still earned hisself an ass-whuppin' for that."

Luke responded with a tired smile. "And whose job is that gonna be, Bloodworth? Yours?"

The heavy beard on the big man's face twitched upward in reaction to his smug smile. "I reckon I could take it on. I ain't particularly busy right now."

Luke nodded, then turned his attention away from the eager bully to address the rest of the men standing by. "Seems like you fellows have already had a trial for me, and without any witnesses at that. I appreciate the point you brought up, Hiram, but seems like there's still some question about why I never caught up with my partners. Well, it's an unfortunate fact, since a couple of good men lost their lives maybe because of it, but I was busy. And before Mr. Bloodworth gives me my ass-whuppin', I'd like to bring forth a witness that will testify to the truth of my claim for being so late gettin' here." He turned back to Bloodworth. "Is that all right with you, Bloodworth?"

"Yeah," Bloodworth smirked. "I got plenty of time, and it ain't gonna take long once I get started."

Standing back at the counter with Axel Thompson, Jug Sartain had been frozen spellbound upon hearing the informal trial being played out by Luke's fellow trappers. He recoiled slightly when he heard Luke state that he had a witness who would testify that he was too busy to catch up with his partners. He took no more than two steps toward him when Luke made his next statement, stopping him again. "My witness is waitin' out back of this tent. His name is Mr. Beaver, and he's stretched out on a willow hoop, hangin' on my saddle horn. I'd be happy to fetch him, or one of you distinguished gentlemen of the jury can. Any man of you can examine Mr. Beaver and can see that he is almost dried out enough to fold, which oughta give you a pretty good idea what I was doin' when I didn't catch up to Tom and the other boys."

His statement succeeded to cause a pregnant moment of silent amusement to fall upon the small group of men. Before anyone else spoke, Jug strode forward and announced. "I'd like to be another witness, your honors."

"Who the hell are you?" Bloodworth blurted.

Jug cast a look upon Bloodworth that Luke later described as incredulous. "Why, I'm Jug Sartain," he said. "Everybody knows who I am." Of course, no one did, but his boast captured their attention. "Luke didn't mention that after spending the night to trap that beaver, he skinned it and stretched the hide to dry. Then he made breakfast outta him and scraped, charred, and boiled the tail. After that, he took a little time to come into the mountains when he heard a couple of Blackfoot Injuns takin' potshots at a trapper trapped behind his dead horse—that bein' me—the trapper, not the horse. After he sent the two Injuns to Injun Hell, it took us a little more time to round up the Injuns' horses, load all my stuff, then go back and get Luke's horses. So, like he told you, he was busy, and we didn't see no sign of that ambush you said killed Luke's partners on our way to the rendezvous."

"Well, that pretty much satisfies the issue for me," Hiram Jones announced. "We all shoulda known better'n to even think Luke Ransom ain't a genuine mountain man when it comes to helpin' another trapper in trouble." His declaration brought on cheers of agreement—except for one. Bloodworth was all primed to administer a generous helping of pain on one he suspected of cowardly deceit. Being deprived of that pleasure served to cause him to despise the tall, broad-shouldered young man even more.

For Luke, there was still the matter of settling up with Axel Thompson, not only for the pelts he had just brought in, but also for drawing his wages from the company. There was also the promise of having a drink with Jug, so he told him to go ahead and set up his camp and take care of his horses, and he would meet him at the saloon he had pointed out earlier. Jug agreed to that and left him to talk to Axel back at the buyer's station. When all the counting and grading of the firs was completed, Axel decided to pay Luke the bonus price for every pelt he had brought in. He commented that it was a shame that Charlton Lewis would receive only a tiny percentage of the bonus, a much smaller cut than he would have received had all the other pelts they had gathered made it to rendezvous. Luke agreed with him and suggested that the two of them should just split the bonus money fifty-fifty. When they were finished, they shook hands, and Luke told Axel he could strike his name from the payroll because he was quitting the company to try free trapping. Axel said he was really sorry to hear that but wished him luck. "You've been a good man for a good many years, so you can still sell your pelts here, and we'll give you the best price we can," Axel offered. Luke thanked him, knowing Axel was sincere, but also knowing that whatever the market price for prime beaver would be next year, that would be the best price he would get.

People were still pouring into the river valley, but there were still many good spots for Luke to make his camp. He picked a grassy meadow next to the creek where his horses could graze close to water, and there was plenty of firewood available in a stand of trees nearby. He set up his camp close to the trees where it would be easy to make a quick shelter in the event of rain. After his horses were taken care of, he started collecting a supply of firewood to use later on.

"When we gonna have that drink of likker?" The voice startled him. He turned quickly to discover Jug standing a few yards away in the trees. "I swear, you snuck right up on me. I was fixin' to walk over to that saloon as soon as I laid some firewood aside. You camped near here?"

"About thirty-five yards that-away," Jug said and pointed toward the opposite edge of the trees. "I see you know how to pick a pretty good campsite. Better'n mine. If I'da cut around these trees, I mighta beat you to this spot."

"Well, you're welcome to move your possibles on over here with me, if you want to," Luke invited. "From here, you got a clear shot at that saloon, if you were to need one."

"That would suit me just fine," Jug replied at once. "I thought you mighta been campin' with some of the American Fur fellers. Did you quit the company like you said you was gonna do?"

"I did," Luke answered. "So I figured I oughta make my camp somewhere else, but I intend to have a drink with some of the boys. I've known some of 'em since we damn-near got cleaned out by the Rees and the Blackfoot up on the Missouri. I need to see Charlton Lewis for sure. I'd like to hear his account of what happened to them."

"I declare, you mighta oughta been a lawyer," Jug said. "You had me guessin' back yonder when you said you had a witness named Mr. Beaver." He threw his head back and released a loud guffaw. "I don't believe it set too well with that big blowhard that was doin' most of the talkin', though. I think he was wantin' a piece of you."

"Bloodworth," Luke said. "I never did have much use for him, and I reckon he musta known it." He grinned and commented, "I believe it was your witness testimony that swung the jury for me, though."

"I reckon I owed you that for savin' my bacon back on that mountain," Jug said. "I'll go fetch my belongings, then we'll go get that drink."

"Luke!" Charlton Lewis sang out when they walked into the large tent that housed Berman's Saloon. He walked over to meet Luke and Jug. "I swear, I heard you rode in with your string of horses. I was afraid those murderin' Blackfoot mighta jumped you, too." He nodded briefly to Jug before coming right back to Luke. "It was a terrible thing, Luke. They came down on both sides of us. Tom and Fred were ahead of me and they was shot outta the saddle before we even knew they were there. There wasn't nothin' I could do against that many Injuns, so I took the only chance I had and that was to run for it. You understand that, don'tcha, Luke? Tom and Fred were both dead."

It was obvious to Luke that Charlton was concerned that he might think he could have made more of an effort to fight. "I reckon you did all you could," Luke said. "It wouldn'ta made much sense to commit suicide against that many Injuns. How many was there?"

"I don't know exactly," Charlton replied. "Twenty or thirty maybe. They was hid in the rocks and trees on both sides of that creekbank we rode up, lookin' to camp. Rifle balls and arrows was flyin' back and forth like a hailstorm."

"I reckon you were just lucky to get outta there. Guess your number just wasn't up yet. I didn't say anything about it to you and Tom and Fred, but I'd decided to quit American Fur and trap on my own. I already told Axel and settled up with the company. I know you lost a lot of bonus money when all those pelts was stole. So, I told Axel to just give you half of the bonus on those pelts I brought in."

Charlton was pleasantly surprised. "Well, damn, that's mighty sportin' of you. I 'preciate it."

Luke chuckled. "Hell, easy come, easy go, ain't that right, Jug? Say howdy to Jug Sartain." Charlton and Jug quickly exchanged greetings. "We were about to have us a drink. Care to join us?"

"Yeah," Charlton replied, "why don't you come on back in the corner with me? There's a bunch of the AFC boys that'll be glad to say howdy."

"Lead the way," Luke said. "Come on, Jug, we'll drink with some of the company boys." They followed Charlton back to a corner where several tables had been pulled together to accommodate the drinking party.

Several of the men called out a friendly howdy to Luke and offered condolences on the loss of his two partners. There was not a lot of time spent on the tragic killings, however, because it was a common risk in the life of a mountain man. And rendezvous was a time for celebration. Hiram Jones spoke up then. "I see you brought one of your witnesses with you. How come you didn't bring the other one?" His question brought a laugh from those who had been at the buying shed when Luke came in. One who did not laugh, the brute called Bloodworth, continued to stare at him with an accusing eye.

Answering Hiram's question, Luke said, "I left him with Axel 'cause he's a 'made beaver' now." That was the common term for a pelt that had been properly dried and folded, fur side in, to be put in a pack of eighty-nine other made beavers for shipping. His answer brought a few more chuckles to the group of trappers.

"Axel said you up and quit the American Fur Company," Bloodworth commented. "This little party here is for company men. Free trappers usually do their drinkin' down at Boutwell's Tradin' House where the Injuns do their tradin'. That ain't but about a mile from here. Maybe you'd see some of your Injun friends there."

"What you say is true, Bloodworth," Luke replied calmly. "I have decided to go into business for myself. But I worked for the company longer than you have. I think Mr. Berman is open to free trappers and anybody else he wants to sell whiskey to."

"Yeah? Well, you don't work for the company no more, so you ain't welcome to drink with us."

"If all of you feel that way, then Jug and I'll move over to the other side of the room," Luke said. "That all right with you, Jug?"

"Suits the hell outta me," Jug answered. "I don't wanna stick in nobody's craw."

"Now, hold on, Bloodworth," Hiram interrupted. "Luke's got a lot of friends here, and we ain't talkin' about any secret places we're fixin' to trap next season, or nothin' else we don't wanna advertise. Ain't nobody in the company who's got a gripe against Luke Ransom."

"Is that so?" Bloodworth came back, fully worked up by now. "Well, then, I reckon it's just me that's got a gripe against him. I don't like him, and I don't wanna drink in the same place he's drinkin'." He turned to face Luke straight away. "So whaddaya say about that, Ransom?"

"Like you said," Luke replied. "Boutwell's is about a mile down the valley. You can go down there to drink."

Bloodworth didn't say anything for a few moments while he decided how best to deliver his threat. The whole corner of the room was silent as everyone waited to see what was going to happen. As curious as any, Jug was interested to see how his new friend was going to handle the situation that was being forced upon him. After glaring at the seemingly unruffled Luke for what seemed a long time, Bloodworth issued his ultimatum. "If you don't haul your lanky ass outta here right now, I'm gonna break your back for you. And take that little runt with you."

Still calm, Luke took another moment to size up the bully before he responded. "You know, Bloodworth, I mighta left, just to avoid trouble. But then you went and insulted my partner, here, and I can't let you get by with that." He glanced over at Jug. "Partner, we'll have that drink right here."

A smug grin slowly developed on Bloodworth's square jaw. "All right, smartass, what's it gonna be, knives, fists, guns? You name it."

"How about a foot race?" Luke asked.

"You ain't gettin' outta here without fightin'," Bloodworth answered, "unless it's on your knees like a yellow dog."

"All right, if it's a fight you gotta have, we'll fight, but I get to pick, so it's with no weapons, no knives or guns, just your hands and anything you can pick up with 'em. Does that suit you?"

"It's perfect," Bloodworth said, since he felt he had every advantage under those rules. "Let's get started." He pulled his heavy deer hide shirt off to free his arms, which resembled two hams hanging from his massive shoulders. Then he walked out into the middle of the room where the tables and chairs had been hastily pulled aside for the contest. Spectators from the other end of the room, eager to see the fight, dragged their chairs up to form a ring. Bloodworth looked around the ring of spectators, grinning as he pounded a heavy fist into the palm of his hand.

Luke, on the other hand, kept his antelope hide shirt on for the protection it might lend. In his mind, he was in the same situation he might find himself if trapped by a grizzly bear, with one exception. He figured the bear might be smarter than Bloodworth. He took note of the chairs lined up on one side of the ring and the slop bucket being used as a spittoon and receptacle for runny noses and drunken vomiting. *I might need that early on*, he thought. He walked out to face Bloodworth but standing close to the side where the chairs were. "We don't have to do this," he said, making one last attempt.

"The hell we don't," Bloodworth retorted.

"Well, come on, you big blowhard. Let's see what you've got." He was counting on Bloodworth acting in rage, and Bloodworth didn't disappoint. Like the grizzly he resembled, he charged full force at his adversary, meaning to crush him. Luke remained poised in a half crouch as if ready to meet the charge. Bloodworth roared as he built up speed, but just an instant before the impact, Luke deftly stepped aside, leaving one foot trailing for Bloodworth to trip over. The momentum of his charging bulk carried him crashing into the tables and chairs to land on the floor facedown. Luke picked up a chair and stood over him, waiting for him to move. And when he rolled over and started to get up, Luke swung the chair at his head. Bloodworth managed to ward the blow off with his arm, grabbed the chair, and ripped it out of Luke's hands. In a fit of rage, he threw the chair across the room to go bouncing against the bar. He hesitated for just a moment to glare in contempt at Luke's attempt to brain him with a chair. Then he wiped a trickle of blood from his nose, a result of his collision with the floor when Luke tripped him.

"I said your hands and anything you can pick up with 'em," Luke reminded him in defense of his attacking him with a chair.

"Right," Bloodworth responded contemptuously, as he got to his feet, "anything you can pick up." Then, to show his strength, he turned around and raked the glasses off a table where five men had been sitting. With one short grunt, he picked the table up over his head, his heavy arms extended straight up. Impressed by the man's strength, Luke took a few steps to the side to pick up the half-full slop bucket and waited for the angry brute to turn around to face him. As soon as he did, it was to be met with the filthy contents of the bucket in his face, the tobacco juice and vomit stinging his eyes. Barely able to see now, he continued to hold the heavy table over his head while he advanced toward Luke. Spreading his legs wide when Luke threw the empty bucket at his feet, he avoided being tripped. With his legs wide apart, however, he was vulnerable to Luke's quickness and was caught totally by surprise when his tall adversary stepped in and delivered a well-placed foot hard up between his outstretched legs.

In Jug's opinion, it was akin to seeing a tree in the redwood forests chopped down. Bloodworth released a primeval howl as his knees buckled, dropping him to the floor. His arms collapsed, causing the heavy table to come down on his head and shoulders. He rolled over on his side in a fetal position, moaning in pain, as Luke stood over him to make sure he was finished. One of Bloodworth's few friends, Lonnie Johnson, walked over to look at the felled brute writhing in pain. He looked at Luke and said, "That weren't hardly a fair fight."

"I never fight fair when I'm fightin' a grizzly," Luke told him. "And if the grizzly comes back at me again after I run him off, I usually shoot him." Lonnie had nothing more to say, so Luke looked at Jug and said, "Let's go find you a quieter place to have your drink of likker."

More than ready, Jug led him toward the door. As they passed by the bar, Claude Berman suggested, "Why don't you fellers find someplace else to do your drinkin'?"

"That's what we were just fixin' to do, Claude," Luke replied. "We don't wanna cause you no trouble."

"No hard feelin's, Luke," Berman responded quickly. "I've been dealin' with you for quite a few years now at the rendezvous, and we've always got along just fine. But you mighta lit the fuse on that stick of dynamite, and he's liable to break up the rest of my tables."

"No, no hard feelin's, Claude," Luke assured him. "We'll just mosey along down toward the south end of the valley."

When they got outside the tent, Jug had to ask, "You've been with American Fur for a few years. Was everybody always this glad to see you every year?"

"This year was kinda mild," Luke japed. "Last year, they tried to string me up to hang." He didn't express it, but he was a little disappointed not to have visited with some of the men he knew with the company. He would definitely miss Tom Molloy and Fred Willis. They were the best friends he had. He'd drink a silent toast to them tonight—an act that was rare for him. He wasn't much of a drinker.

Chapter 3

"You might wanna set your camp up somewhere else," Luke suggested after two drinks of Boutwell's whiskey. They stood at the bar and watched while Andy Cruze, Boutwell's bartender, filled Jug Sartain's jug.

"That about does it, Jug," Andy commented. "Leaves just enough room for the cork." To Luke's surprise, Jug was well known at Boutwell's, patronizing the trading post every year at rendezvous.

"I was thinkin' about that," Jug said to Luke then, in response to Luke's suggestion that he should move his camp. His attention right back to Andy then, he said, "I make it about a quart and a half. Is that what you got?" Andy said that it was and that it was the same as last time and every time before that. "Don't hurt to check," Jug said. "I mighta left some whiskey in there."

"That'd be the first time if you did," Andy said and winked at Luke.

Back to Luke again, Jug commented, "You oughta be thinkin' about movin' your camp, too. You put a pretty good lickin' on that Bloodworth feller, and he don't strike me as the kind to give you any warnin' next time. So we might as well find us another campsite, a little farther away from American Fur."

"You sure you wanna camp with me?" Luke asked. "It wouldn't

seem right to draw any of my trouble down on you. You'd be better off away from me."

"You told that grizzly back yonder that we was partners," Jug insisted. When Luke looked puzzled at that remark, Jug went on to remind him. "You said you weren't gonna fight, but he went and insulted your partner. That's what you said."

Luke smiled. "I guess I did say that, but I was just . . ." That was as far as he got before Jug interrupted him.

"It sounded to me like you meant what you said," Jug declared. "So, I thought, 'fine by me, partners it is.' You ain't changed your mind already, have you? Before we even give it a chance to see if it works?"

Luke was too surprised to think how he felt about that. He hadn't given any thought about partnering up with anybody. "I thought free trappin' was your style, and you didn't want any partners."

"I'm a free trapper and I ain't ever partnered up with nobody. But that's just because I ain't never run up on anybody I thought I could put up with for a whole year in the mountains. I know some places where there's beaver nobody's been gettin', but it's in Blackfoot country. I've been a little shy about trappin' that country by myself. I can move around the mountains without attractin' no attention 'bout as good as a blame Injun. But if I make one mistake, there ain't much I can do against a whole blame war party." He paused to shake his head before continuing. "Well, I reckon I found out I can make that one mistake when I let them two Blackfoot pick up my trail. And if you hadn't come along, I reckon they'da smoked me out from behind my horse before it was over. I think two of us would jump the odds of us seein' old Andy, here, next summer." He waited for Luke to respond, but when he didn't right away, Jug said, "We'd both be free trappin'. You'd keep any plews you trapped, and I'd keep mine. You interested?"

Luke still didn't answer him right away. Instead, he looked at

Andy Cruze and asked, "What do you think, Andy? Am I interested?"

Andy chuckled and replied grandly, "I expect so. You two could make the kind of legends young folks will be readin' about in their history books."

Looking back at Jug, Luke said, "You heard the man, partner. I reckon we'd best see about movin' our camp down the valley a-ways. And by the way, if Bloodworth shows up on our doorstep again, it'll be your turn to deal with him, partner."

"The hell it will," Jug shot back. "That's a problem you brought with you when you was a company man." They both laughed at Jug's response, but Luke knew it was highly unlikely that he'd seen the last of Dan Bloodworth. Bloodworth had only two assets going for him, his hulking size and his brute strength. Luke had made a fool of him in front of a saloon full of witnesses. He didn't want Jug to suffer any harm in the wake of Bloodworth's pursuit of revenge.

Like a wounded bear, Bloodworth remained there on the floor in his fetal position for over half an hour, spitting blasphemous oaths at anyone who ventured near him. Luke Ransom's blow to his nether regions had landed with serious results, serving to temporarily immobilize him while he waited for his pain to subside. When he began to move his legs gradually from his tucked position, Lonnie Johnson came to stand over him. "You gonna make it, Bloodworth?"

"That son of a . . ." Bloodworth started, but didn't finish because a sharp pain interrupted him when he straightened his leg too far. He looked up at his partner in shameful agony. "He's a dead man, Lonnie. I swear I'll kill him."

"I figured that," Lonnie stated matter-of-factly. "That pain oughta be easin' off pretty soon now, and you'll be back to normal."

"He ain't gonna get away with no tricks next time," Bloodworth stated. "I'm gonna wring his neck like I'd wring a chicken."

"If he's got any sense a-tall, he's most likely already cut out from here," Lonnie said. "You feelin' any better?"

"I'm gettin' there," Bloodworth said and reached up to grab a chair beside him. Then he slowly pulled himself up to sit in the chair. "Tell Berman to pour me a drink of likker. And bring me my shirt." He reached up to feel his nose and his hand came away bloody to remind him of his collision with the floor. "I'll kill him," he vowed again.

Two miles down the valley from Berman's Saloon, Jug led Luke to a vast grassy meadow, bisected by the Green River. There was a string of merchants' shops along the bank of the river, some with elaborate store fronts, and some as simple as a counter constructed in front of a wagon. "This is the place I was lookin' for," Jug said. "You can buy anything you need right here, same as if you was in St. Louie. We'll come back here tonight, after we set up camp and maybe go to The Chinaman's."

Luke paused to look around him at the various businesses, then looked beyond them toward the other side of the river where there were trappers' camps lining the bank. "Free trappers?" he asked, looking at Jug.

"Every one of 'em," Jug answered.

"What's the Chinaman's?"

"A cookhouse where you can get Chinese food," Jug said. "Ain't you ever et Chinese food?"

"Can't say as I have," Luke answered. "At least, if I have, I didn't know it at the time."

"I acquired me a taste for it at the rendezvous on Popo Agie, back in twenty-nine. That was my first rendezvous and the first one for the Chinaman. I told him I hadn't never et no Chinese food, and he said, 'You try, you no like, you no pay.' So I tried it, and I ain't been to a rendezvous since without havin' me some Chinese food. And that includes thirty-one, when they didn't have no rendezvous 'cause the supply train bringin' the trade goods never got there. The Chinaman got there, and he had to turn around and go home, but not before he cooked up a big supper for me and about a dozen other trappers who didn't get the word about the cancellation, neither."

"Like I said," Luke commented, "I ain't ever tried it, myself, but I thought Chinese cookin' was a lotta pork and chicken, fish and stuff like that. Where's this fellow get that stuff to cook? Does he bring hogs and chickens to rendezvous?"

The question stumped Jug for a moment. "I ain't never thought about where he got his food. He fixes beef dishes, too. But he ain't got no chickens or hogs with him. I don't know how he does it. Might be he brings a load of salt-cured pork with him, just like bacon and ham. I wish to hell you hadn't asked me about it. Now I'll be wonderin' where every mouthful came from."

"Well, I reckon I'll have to try it," Luke declared, "if you're sure it won't stunt my growth."

"It ain't had no effect on mine," Jug replied. So they made their camp along the river with the other free trappers, and Jug introduced Luke to several of the men set up closest to them. After that, Jug took him to meet Lee Wong at his eating establishment. A long table set up between two wagons formed The Chinaman's and it afforded an excellent view of an open area that served as an arena for bare-knuckle fighting, knife-throwing contests, step-dancing, and anything else that could invite competition. Luke had to agree with his new partner that the food was tasty, and certainly different from their standard fare. Jug stopped him when he started to comment that it was hard to identify some of the things that were mixed up in the sauces. "I don't wanna know what they are," he said.

When they finished their supper, they walked a couple dozen yards to Red's Saloon. As soon as they walked into the large tent with a bar at one end, Luke realized that they were in the right place. For of the nine men sitting on the benches on either side of a long table, all but one or two knew Jug. "Hot damn!" One of those at the table sang out. "I know the rendezvous is officially

open now. Jug Sartain's here." They all greeted him then. "Who you got with you, Jug? You ain't partnered-up, have you?"

"Howdy, boys," Jug responded. "I was hopin' I could avoid bumpin' into you fellers this year, but you gotta have a little bad luck once in a while." He waited while they all replied with raucous insults of their own, then announced, "This, here, is my partner. Say howdy to Luke Ransom."

"Well, I'll swear," Ike Hopper, the man who had first spotted him, said, "you did partner-up. I was just japin'. I thought I'd never see the day."

"Howdy, Luke," Zeke Singleton greeted him. "I hope you can set your traps with a blindfold on 'cause Jug don't let nobody see where he's trappin'."

That brought a laugh from the group and another voice called out. "That's right. Where you headin' this fall, Jug?"

"Me and Luke been talkin' about that," Jug answered. "We've been thinkin' we oughta see what kinda fur the beavers down in Mexico are wearin'." When that remark brought forth a round of loud catcalls, he added, "You don't never know till you check it out."

"Luke," Ike japed, "it might be worth a little money if you was to let me know where you and Jug are headin' when you leave here."

"I'd be glad to tell you," Luke replied, "but Jug said I have to wear a blindfold. He did say something about Mexico, though."

After another round of chortles, Ike remarked, "I swear, I know I've seen you before. This ain't your first rendezvous, is it?"

Jug answered for him. "Luke's been workin' for the American Fur Company, but we ought not hold that agin' him. And he's the only reason I'm here to shoot the breeze with a wore-out bunch of trappers like you boys tonight."

"Blackfoot?" Zeke asked. When Jug said that was the problem, Zeke said, "I heard about American Fur losin' two men. Was they some of the bunch that hit you?"

"I wouldn't be surprised," Jug answered. "There weren't but

two that came after me, but they was most likely part of that bigger bunch that killed them two American Fur boys. Luke, here, mighta been part of that ambush, but he was busy savin' my behind from two Blackfoot raiders that had me pinned down behind a dead horse." He went on to explain the circumstances that caused him and Luke to meet.

"So, them two fellers was your workin' partners," Ike remarked to Luke.

"Yes, they were," Luke said, "and they were my friends, as well. I trapped with them for the last three years."

"Is that what made you decide to quit American Fur?"

"No, I'd already decided this was my last year," Luke answered. "I had decided to tell the folks at the company when I got to rendezvous that I could do better for myself alone." He chuckled before adding, "And then I went and partnered-up with Jug first thing."

"Well, let me tell you somethin', in case you didn't know it," Ike said, then lowered his voice so Jug wouldn't hear him. "Jug is one helluva trapper, and he don't work with anybody, ever. He musta seen somethin' in you he ain't seen in anybody else. So I wish good luck to you and Jug this season."

Luke thanked him and wished him a good season, as well. The more he heard about Jug, the more he wondered why Jug wanted him to be his partner. He could only imagine that this special territory Jug was willing to share with him had to be up in Blackfoot country, as he had hinted before, and he was hesitant to risk it alone. The risk didn't bother Luke because he was planning on trapping up in Montana Territory before he met Jug, and that was not only Blackfoot country, but Hudson's Bay Company also. He guessed that he and Jug believed in the same simple principle, "If you want to take more hides than the competition, you have to go where they fear to go."

It was two full days before the inevitable meeting between Luke and Dan Bloodworth occurred, which was not unusual con-

sidering the area of the Green River Valley that was covered by the great rendezvous. The valley was alive with the thousands of Indians, trappers, traders, horses, and cows, even curious spectators who had traveled great distances just to witness the event. Just as they might have done in St. Louis, Luke and Jug checked out the prices of several different suppliers. Although flush with the money from the sale of their pelts, they had to buy supplies to last them for a year. And sometimes there was a difference in the price of gunpowder from one trader to another: a dollar-fifty a pound from one source, a dollar-seventy-five from another. It was the same for lead, shot, and flints. The same applied for sugar, coffee, flour, and tobacco. So they rode to the lower part of the valley to see what the prices were like there. When they were done with their shopping, they bought the supplies they needed, planning to leave the rendezvous the following day. With that thought in mind, they figured to have a farewell drink to this year's success and a toast to a better year coming.

After one more supper at The Chinaman's, Luke and Jug walked over to Red's Place to have a drink with the other trappers. There were only four of the gang that Luke had been introduced to on the first occasion. Ike and Zeke were both still there, so Jug asked if the others had already gone. "Yep," Ike replied. "Most of 'em headed out this mornin'. Headin' for Mexico, I think," he japed.

"We told 'em we was waitin' for you, so we could follow you and Luke to that valley you been keepin' secret," Zeke joked, "where the beaver are so thick they're flyin' around in the air, and you can catch 'em with a butterfly net."

"Me and Luke decided we ain't gonna hunt nothin' but buffalo this year," Jug countered. "Beaver didn't bring but three-fifty this year, and it was four dollars last year. Ain't no tellin' what it'll be next year."

Ike's grin froze in place for a few moments before he switched to a sober expression. "You know, we can joke about it, but if the price for a made beaver keeps droppin', we're all gonna be huntin' deer and antelope."

"It's liable to go back up again, too," Zeke commented. "Them folks over in Europe ain't never gonna quit wearin' their fancy hats." He was about to comment further, but he was interrupted by a loud voice near the front entrance to the tent.

"Well, now, lookee here, Lonnie, I do believe we found us one, Mr. Luke Ransom."

"I do believe you're right," Lonnie Johnson said. "Settin' there big as you please. I swear, I thought he had enough sense to be high-tailin' it way up in the mountains by now."

Puzzled by the obvious sarcasm in their tone, the four free trappers sitting at the table waited for Luke's response to clarify the strangers' remarks. "Howdy, Bloodworth," Luke responded. "I would say I'm happy to see you, but I was kinda hopin' I wouldn't."

Grinning like a trapper who had caught a sixty-pound beaver in his trap, Bloodworth walked over to take a commanding stance at the foot of the table where Luke and Jug were sitting with the others. "I've been lookin' for you, Ransom, ever since you walked outta Berman's the other night. I figure I owe you for that."

"Well, it looks like you're movin' all right," Luke replied. "You were lookin' kinda puny and bent over last time I saw you. You looked like you were sufferin' so bad, I thought about puttin' you outta your misery. But I decided there weren't no call for that, and you'd most likely be good as new in a day or two. Now, here you are, rip-snortin' and rarin' to go, come back to tell me there ain't no hard feelin's between two men that worked for the same company. Well, I gotta say it takes a big man to admit he mighta been wrong and comes to make things right."

Bloodworth remained in his aggressive stance, fairly perplexed by Luke's rambling discourse until Luke paused. "In the first place, you ain't no company man no more, and even if you was, I owe you a whuppin' for that lowdown trick you pulled on me. I aim to take it outta your hide, so you choose, fists or knives."

"All right," Luke replied, "since you ain't got sense enough to understand I'm tryin' to save your life, I'll choose. It'll be knives. I'm warnin' you, though, this time I'm liable to kill you. You sure you wanna do this?"

"Oh, I'm sure, all right," Bloodworth said with a smug grin for Lonnie. "Knives it is." Lonnie winked at him, knowing how good Bloodworth was with a knife, and thinking it couldn't have been a better choice for him. Bloodworth looked around the table before him at the astonished witnesses to his challenge. "Everybody heard you agree to face me with knives."

"Right. We'll do it right over yonder where those fellows are dancing—day after tomorrow at noontime," Luke said. "Don't be late."

"No, you don't," Bloodworth came back at once. "We'll do it right here, right now where there's plenty of room and all your friends can watch. You just hand your rifle and that pistol in your belt to that little runt with you. You ain't gonna need nothing but that knife. Lonnie, you keep an eye on his partner. If he shows the first sign of cockin' his pistol, you shoot him." As he had done at their first face-off, he pulled his shirt off to free his massive arms and chest.

Luke shook his head slowly in disgust for the useless duel that he proposed. "Bloodworth, you dumb halfwit, I'm tryin' to save your life. I'm tellin' you, forget about it and walk away."

Certain he had Luke begging to get out of the fight, Bloodworth threatened, "Draw your knife outta that belt and stand to face me. Or so help me, I'll carve you up where you sit." He backed away from the table and waited in the center of the floor, tossing the large skinning knife from hand to hand in front of him.

Luke got up from the table, deposited his rifle and pistol beside Jug, and drew his knife from the sheath on the belt he left on the table. He held the knife in his hand for a few seconds, feeling the balance of it, as if getting reacquainted with it. "All right, Bloodworth, let's get this over with." He walked out to the center of the floor to face his grinning adversary, stopping when they were about twenty feet apart. "Any rules to this fight?" Luke asked. "First to draw blood wins, anything like that?"

"Ha!" Bloodworth blurted scornfully. "There ain't no rules. The one who walks away after it's over is the winner. So you'd better be ready 'cause this time I'm keepin' an eye out for any lowdown tricks of yours." He stood tall and tossed his knife back and forth again, then with his arms spread wide, he motioned, taunting Luke to come to him. At his invitation, Luke took only one step and that was to plant his foot solidly. An instant later, Bloodworth froze. He looked down to see the long skinning knife buried to the handle just below his rib cage. Unable to believe it was real at first, he could only stare at it until a trickle of blood welled up around the blade and ran down his belly. It was then he felt the heavy obstacle in his gut, like a piece of hot steel. He realized he had been stabbed deeply, but still couldn't believe it possible. The shock of seeing the knife handle protruding from his bare belly was enough to cause him to sink to his knees, where he remained in shock for what seemed long minutes.

There was not a sound from any of the stunned witnesses to the sudden ending of the knife fight. No one had anticipated anything other than the typical sparring of the two combatants, thrusting and swiping at each other until one of them was able to slash the other. This fight had ended as soon as it had started. They stood, staring silently at a mountain man so skilled in the art of throwing a knife that he was willing to gamble on his aim and the force he could put behind the throw. If his aim had been inaccurate, or there had not been enough force to inflict a serious wound, he would have been left weaponless to defend himself.

"That ain't fair!" Lonnie Johnson cried out, but Jug immediately reminded him that Luke had brought up the subject of rules. And Bloodworth had insisted that there were none.

Meanwhile, Bloodworth remained in the middle of the floor on his knees, unable to move, his eyes wide and still staring at the handle of the knife, until Luke walked up to him. "I'm gonna be needin' my knife," he said to the dazed brute. With that, he took hold of the handle and, with one forceful move, yanked the blade free of his stomach. Bloodworth cried out in pain and keeled over on his side. Luke turned to Lonnie, who was still in shock, as well. "You'd best get him back to the company and see if there's anybody there to do any doctorin'. He's a pretty strong grizzly. He might make it through this." When Lonnie just stood gaping at him, he said, "I'll help you get him on his horse."

"He'd be better off in a wagon," Red Duncan offered. Like everyone else, the saloon owner had been momentarily stunned. "My boy can take him for you." His son, a sixteen-year-old who worked in his father's business, didn't wait for a direct order, but ran out the back of the tent to hitch up the wagon.

When Red's son pulled the wagon around to the front of the tent, Luke took hold of Bloodworth's boots and Lonnie lifted his shoulders. Together, they carried the wounded brute out to the wagon. Although his eyes darted back and forth while they struggled to shift his heavy body around, he didn't make a sound. Luke walked over to their horses with Lonnie with one final word for him. "I've seen men come back from some bad wounds before, so he might make it. I reckon it'll be up to him, but if he does, I want you to tell him to let this be the end of it between him and me. I've had enough of it. You remind him that I coulda just slit his throat and sent him to hell today. But I didn't because there ain't ever been any reason for us to wanna kill each other, so tell him this is the end of it." He stepped back then, and Lonnie climbed up into the saddle.

Jug walked over and stood beside him as they watched Lonnie ride away, leading the wagon. After a moment, Jug said, "Partner, there's one helluva lot I've got to learn about you."

"Reckon so," Luke replied.

Ike Hopper grinned at the two partners and suggested, "There ain't no better way I can think of to get to know a partner than to spend a winter camp together. You two plannin' to make the winter gatherin', or are you gonna ride it out on your own?"

Luke glanced at Jug before answering. "I don't know, Ike, we ain't decided yet. Reckon it'll depend on where we end up when the time comes." In fact, they had already planned to risk their necks and go it alone that winter. It would depend on what kind of luck they had. If it was as good as they hoped, they wouldn't want to take a chance on leaving a good hunting spot. If their luck wasn't anything to brag about, he imagined they would decide to go to the winter gathering where they would benefit from the safety in numbers. "Come to think of it, I ain't heard for sure where it's gonna be this winter."

"Cache Valley," Ike said. "The winters ain't as bad there as it is in most of the holes in this part of the Rockies."

"I reckon we'll have to see just what part of the country we wind up in when the streams freeze over," Jug said.

"Might have somethin' to do with what kinda huntin' ground you and Luke find. Right Jug?" Zeke Singleton asked. "If it's runnin' over with beaver, and you wanna come to the gatherin', you can just carve your name on a tree and we'll know not to trap there."

"That'ud work," Ike cracked, "or you could just tell us now where you're headin' and we'll be sure and stay away from there."

"I told you, me and Luke are goin' down to Mexico," Jug said. "Matter of fact, just to be fair about it, we'll wait a while and let you boys get a head start. Ain't that right, Luke?"

"Whatever you say, partner," Luke replied, seeing their grins, but also knowing they were still wondering why Jug decided to partner-up, after years of free trapping.

After the customary farewells and wishes of good luck on the night just passed, Luke and Jug broke camp the next morning and started north, following the Green River to its confluence with the Snake. From there, they followed the Snake River to its origin in the place the Indians called Yellow Stones, a place where the water under the ground was boiling hot and sometimes shot up a hundred feet in the air. Luke had heard it called *Colter's Hell*, named for a man who had traveled with Lewis and Clark. He had written about the place, saying there were terrible noises under the ground that shook his feet, and steam and hot water shot out of the ground. Most folks figured Colter was probably out of his head, since he was in the process of recovering from a wound, suffered in a fight with the Indians. At any rate, if there were any supernatural agents at work there, Luke didn't care. He figured as long as they did their business underground, he'd take care of his above ground, and there shouldn't be any problems at all. Jug was not as blasé about it. He was convinced that, if you searched among the many stones long enough, you would eventually find one that could be moved to reveal a stairway straight down to a fiery underworld. It was a mysterious place. And even though Luke had heard it called Colter's Hell, he knew that to the mountain man, Colter's Hell was a mud pot area at the junction of the North and South Stinkingwater Rivers. At any rate, when they came to a big geyser shooting steaming water high into the air, they turned to the west with the intention of striking the Madison River. They figured they'd prefer to follow the Madison to Three Forks where the Madison and two other rivers joined to create the Missouri.

They had been in the saddle for over six days since leaving the rendezvous, having stopped twice to hunt and once to smoke-cure some antelope when they struck the Madison River. Up to this point, they had seen no sign of recent Indian activity, but it was natural to become more alert for the possibility. For they were now in territory that the Crow claimed as their own but was often raided by Blackfoot war parties. They were of like mind regarding their plans for the new year's trapping season. The best territory to find the beaver population plentiful was Montana Territory and north into Canada. While he worked for the American Fur Company, he and his team of trappers could not trap in this territory without starting a war with Hudson's Bay Company. As free trappers, he and Jug were of the opinion they could trap anywhere they wanted, including the moon, if they could find the trail to lead them there. The purpose of the journey they were now on was to search out the best possible places to concentrate their trapping when summer was over, and the fall season began.

As they got closer to Three Forks, they both agreed that the winding course the river took before its confluence with the Gallatin and the Jefferson created an ideal location for the possibility of many beaver lodges. The only problem was that it was well known as one of the best areas for beaver to other trappers, Indian and white. "This river will be overrun by Crow beaver hunters when the fur thickens up, catchin' 'em anyway they can. Clubs, arrows, snares, some of 'em will even be usin' traps that Hudson's Bay give 'em," Jug bemoaned. "What we need to find is a little valley up north of the Yellowstone River that ain't that easy to get into."

"We can go above Three Forks, where the Missouri starts out to the north," Luke suggested. "There's another river breakin' off from the Missouri that heads toward the Big Belt Mountains. Those mountains might have what we're lookin' for. If they don't, maybe the Little Belts, farther to the east might." After talking it over, they decided that the mountain range called the Little Belt might hold more potential for them. Jug had been there before, although never in the winter, but he said they looked to be the perfect mountains for the two of them to trap beaver without being discovered. He said the Judith River's origin was in the Little Belts, offering more potential for beaver. So they headed a little more to the east to the Little Belt Mountains.

Chapter 4

"I think there were only two," Iron Pony said as he shifted through the ashes of a fire, "and they have not been gone long." He and his two companions scouted the small clearing next to the stream where someone had obviously skinned and butchered a deer. They were satisfied that the single rifle shot they had heard that morning had come from the two hunters who had brought their kill here to butcher.

"Maybe Crow," Hears the Wind said. "The hoofprints we've found are not wearing the iron shoes that the white man likes to put on his horses."

"Maybe white man, riding Indian ponies," Two Bears suggested. "They took the meat and the hide and left the rest of the deer."

"What Two Bears says is true," Iron Pony said. "I, too, think this is the kill of white hunters in our territory. Since there are only two of them, I think we should find them. They will have guns and there are tracks of five, maybe six, horses." Part of a larger party of hunters who had spent a week in the northern half of this belt of mountains, these three had decided to scout the southern half of the mountains to see if the game was as plentiful there as it had been in the upper part. Standing Elk, Iron Pony's brother, and the leader of the hunting party, had advised them not to take too long on their scout. They already had almost as much meat as they could carry, and the skies indicated a possible heavy snow on the way.

"I agree with Iron Pony," Two Bears declared. "It would be a good thing if we returned to the village with the scalps of two hunters—white man or Crow, it doesn't matter."

"I agree, too," Hears the Wind said. "And they have guns and a fresh-killed deer." That was enough to inspire their enthusiasm, for none of the three possessed a firearm.

The three Blackfoot warriors scouted the campsite carefully before deciding which way the hunters had gone when they left the clearing. The obvious tracks led into the stream, and apparently, they had led their extra horses in a straight line behind them, for there were no tracks outside the stream. So the Blackfoot warriors rode on either side of the stream, their eyes focused to pick up any sign of a hoofprint, as they followed it down the hill. When they reached the bottom, Two Bears called out, "Here! This is where they came out!" His companions came at once to see. "They tried to come out on these flat rocks, so no one would see, but one of their horses stepped on the soft sand before the rock."

They immediately hurried across the rock ledge to find the trail on the other side, but there was no trail to follow. The ledge was approximately twenty yards square, and they searched around the entire edge of it, but there was no sign the hunters had left it in any direction. "I think the white men have horses that fly like birds," Hears the Wind remarked, half in jest.

"They must have gone back into the stream," Iron Pony said.

"It would be very hard for them to do that without leaving tracks," Two Bears insisted, as he stood looking at the edge of the ledge. "The horses had to step up to get out of the water, but it would be much harder for them to step back down into the stream without dropping their hooves to keep from sliding."

Iron Horse could see that Two Bears was probably right, especially when there were five or six horses attempting it without leaving a track. He turned and looked across the narrow valley, trying to determine a probable direction they might had ridden when they left the rock ledge. "Maybe they rode toward that ravine across the valley," he said, pointing to a narrow cut up a hill on the far side.

"Or the white devils flew over to it," Two Bears added. But with no better suggestion, he followed along when Iron Pony and Hears the Wind rode off the ledge and headed for the mouth of the ravine. Again, they found no tracks, leaving them to puzzle over the unlikely occurrence.

Back on the far side of the hill the Blackfoot warriors had just left, Jug stopped the horses in the middle of the stream and waited. In a little while, he heard a horse splashing in the water behind him. "I hope to hell that's Luke," he mumbled to himself. But just in case, he pulled his rifle out of his saddle sling and turned in the saddle to watch the stream below him. A moment later, he relaxed when he saw the familiar figure of his partner. "Took you a while," he commented when Luke caught up.

"I had to ride all the way down to the bottom before I could find a good spot to leave anybody a track who might be tryin' to follow us," Luke replied. He went on then to tell Jug how he had to get his horse to jump off the flat rock ledge into the middle of the stream. "You weren't worried about me, were you?" he joked.

"Hell, no," Jug replied. "I just didn't wanna have to turn around and go back to get you outta trouble. Let's get on back to camp and start smokin' this meat. I can feel it in my bones, this winter comin' on is gonna be a cold one. We need to get our camp ready 'cause it ain't gonna be long now before this whole mountain range is gonna be froze solid."

Luke had the same feeling about the mountain range they had decided on for their winter camp. It was a short range of probably forty or fifty miles long, running north and south, just above the Judith Basin. But after exploring the mountains, they found that there were many secret valleys to choose from that would be well hidden. When the ponds and streams froze over, and trapping was not possible, there were good spots to hole-up until spring. They had discovered the presence of many beavers in the mountain valleys plus in the fertile creeks along the Judith River. It seemed the perfect base for a pair of fur trappers with plenty of game for food, and fir and pines for cover.

The only thing wrong that had come to trouble them was the sudden appearance of a small party of Indian hunters they discovered sign of in the past few days. It was their misfortune that the Indians had decided to hunt in the same part of the mountains they were set to trap in. When they first discovered they were not alone in their chosen hunting grounds, Luke and Jug had talked about the problem. Since they had selected the little belt of mountains as perfect for their needs, didn't it stand to reason some Indians might think the same? "What sign we have seen ain't been nowhere near our camp," Jug pointed out when they were discussing the prospect of relocating. Like Luke, he was reluctant to move since they had put so much work into their winter home already. With short spades and hand axes, they had dug a cave into the face of a blind canyon, out of the wind, where a small stream came down from the mountain above. They had shored-up the sides and roof of the cave with logs to form a space wide enough for the two of them to place their bedrolls and deep enough to store their pelts. There was plenty of grass and wood for a fire. It was ready for winter, and they both felt it was time to start setting their traps. They had no time to relocate their winter camp. Both of them were of the opinion that the sign they had seen indicated only two or three Indians, Blackfoot or Crow, they could only guess. They decided to deal with them when the time came, if in fact it did. But for now, it was time to set their traps. The weather was cold, there had already been a light snow night before last. The horses were already beginning to look shaggy with the growth of winter hair. And the beaver were waiting. So they took care of the deer Luke had killed, smoking most of it to store for later, and tomorrow, they would set their traps.

*   *   *

They started their first day's trapping at a spot a long way from the Indian sign they had come across before. At a point where the Judith River began, created by the busy streams that fed into the river from the tall mountains above, there was a busy colony of beavers, making their preparations for winter. The streams formed a sizable pond with two lodges, one at each end. Both men carried six traps and they set all twelve in that one network of streams. They worked quickly as they moved from one location to the next, each man with rifle and pistol close by with their possibles bag with powder horn, flints, and rifle balls. In a short time, all traps were set and baited with castoreum, so they returned to their camp to dry off by the fire and cook some of the deer meat they hadn't smoke-cured. "Now, all we got to do is wait till mornin' to see if we know beaver as well as we think," Jug commented.

"I predict a big harvest," Luke japed. "When they get a good look at us, they'll know they ain't got a chance. When we get back in the mornin', we might find the whole colony lined up waitin' to surrender."

"I'll drink to that," Jug replied, and reached for his jug. He took a long pull, smacked his lips, then offered it to Luke.

"Thanks just the same," Luke responded, "but I don't wanna cause you to run short on your whiskey. That jug's gonna run out soon enough without me helpin' you." When Jug started to insist, Luke said, "If we pull a beaver outta every one of those traps tomorrow, I'll take a drink to celebrate that."

"Dad gum it, partner," Jug commented, halfway serious. "I ain't sure what to think about a man that don't take to likker. I'm a-feared you might just start howlin' at the moon one night and go plum loco."

"You might be right," Luke joked. "Ever once in a while, especially if it's a full one, I look at the moon and start in to itchin' all over."

"I wish you'da told me all this back yonder when we was still at the rendezvous," Jug said. Turning serious then, he recalled,

"I never thought about it before, but you ain't ever took a drink outta my jug since we've been on this trip—at least not when I was lookin."

Luke laughed. "I enjoy a drink of likker once in a while, but I reckon I just never got in the habit of drinkin' it all the time. Matter of fact, I came pretty near gettin' really drunk one time in a saloon with some other fellows and I didn't like the way I felt. It was like I didn't have control over my body, or my brain either, and I didn't like it. I reckon it scared me so bad I was afraid to ever have more than one or two ever since."

Jug stared at him in wonder before declaring, "That's the saddest story I think I've ever heard." He shook his head slowly as he thought about it, then said, "I reckon it ain't a bad idea for one of us to be sober all the time, though."

Luke revived the fire, and they cooked some of the deer meat they had left on one side of the fire while they dried their moccasins out on the other side. When the meat had cooked enough to turn color on one side, they turned it over and colored the other side. Then they ate it while waiting for their moccasins to dry, which didn't take an unusually long time. Their moccasins, made out of animal hides, were waterproof. In Luke's case, soles made of stiff, double rawhide buffalo, were sewn to soft, long uppers that had been waterproofed with grease and a mixture of bee's wax. He carried a second pair of moccasins, just as Jug did, but he very seldom wore them unless he had done a thorough job of soaking his favorites. The wetness the two men suffered was confined mostly to their trousers and occurred whenever encountering a hole or step-off when they were wading in the shallow water to set their traps. Since his Creator had outfitted him with short legs, Jug was troubled more than his long-legged partner.

With his belly full of venison, Jug announced that he was going to take a little nap before working on some finishing touches for their winter camp. Luke decided he was going to saddle Smoke and scout the mountain that adjoined the one standing over their camp. He was still somewhat concerned that the Indians they had found sign of might have come across the spot where he and Jug had butchered his deer. All the trouble he had gone to, in order to mislead them, may not have fooled them at all. And he wanted to reassure himself that they had not somehow found the bend in the Judith where he and Jug had set all their traps.

"Don't you want me to go with you?" Jug asked, not really enthusiastic about the prospect. He had just made himself comfortable with his feet to the fire.

"No," Luke japed. "I'd feel better knowin' you were here guardin' our camp."

"You're so full of it," Jug japed back at him. "You go ridin' off . . . How will I know if you're in trouble?"

"I won't come back," Luke laughed. "That's how you'll know."

"Damn it, be careful," Jug said. "I ain't got time to hunt all over these mountains to find your bones."

"Yes, Papa," Luke replied, laughing as he picked up his saddle and went to fetch his horse. He was beginning to believe Jug partnered-up with him just because he was lonesome, after his years of working as a free trapper.

With a feeling of complete freedom, Luke guided the big bay gelding through a forest of Douglas fir, as he sidled around the mountain where he had killed the mule deer. He wondered if he would one day grow tired of his life in the mountains, and long for the companionship found in the towns and saloons. Somehow, he couldn't imagine that day occurring. He felt the chill wind upon his face as it whispered through the fir trees, and he knew that it was a promise that winter was on its way. If they could go by the feeling in Jug's bones, it was going to be a cold one. He pushed Smoke along until they reached the stream where he and Jug had butchered his kill. He turned the bay down the mountain to return to the exact spot. When he reached it, it was obvious that what he had suspected was accurate. The Indians had found it. Their tracks were all around it, testifying to their search of the area. Out of curiosity, he couldn't resist riding on down the stream to the rock ledge and he smiled when he saw the evidence that told him the Indians had ridden all around the ledge before riding off across the narrow valley. "You see that, Smoke," he said to the gelding, "you fooled 'em." He brought his mind back to the purpose of his scout then and nudged the horse into a fast walk, following the trail left by the Indians.

It led straight to a narrow ravine on the opposite side of the valley. He followed it to the mouth of the ravine, then hesitated before continuing. How long did they ride before they realized they were following a trail that didn't exist? He nudged Smoke again, and the big horse took him to the top of the ravine. *This is where they finally gave up,* he thought. What he was interested in seeing now was which way they rode from that point. What he saw was what he had hoped he would see. After obviously lingering there at the top of the ravine while they decided, they then headed down the hill, angling back toward the north. *Good,* he thought, for they were heading in the opposite direction from his and Jug's camp. He rode down the ravine to the valley floor and just as he reached it, he reined Smoke to a sudden stop. Dead still on the other side of the narrow valley, an elk cow stood watching him. His natural reflex was to slowly draw his rifle from the saddle sling and pull the weapon up against his shoulder, but that was as far as he got before hesitating. Literally a sacrifice, she remained there, looking at him, fresh meat, no more than a thirty-five-yard shot. Moving just as slowly as when he raised the rifle to shoot, he pulled it down and slipped it back in the saddle sling. He realized that he could not risk a shot that might be heard by the Indians he was scouting. Evidently losing interest in the strange-looking animal confronting her, the elk suddenly turned and bolted toward the mouth of the valley and the herd gathered by the creek beyond. "And good day to you, ma'am," he muttered to himself, at that moment deciding he had been wrong to quit practicing with a bow. A Shoshone hunter named Rain Dancer at the rendezvous two years ago had let him try his. And when Luke showed a considerable talent in the use of one,

Rain Dancer told him how to make his own bow. But Luke had decided he was better off with his Pennsylvania rifle. "Except right now," he mumbled to Smoke and started back to camp to give Jug his report. He didn't tell him about the elk cow.

They rolled out of their blankets the next morning before sunup and went to check their traps. When they got back to the pond, they left their horses and rifles close by, where they could get to them in a hurry, should that be necessary. Wading into the water again with no weapons other than their pistols stuck in their belts, they made their way around the pond, checking each trap, removing the catch, and resetting the trap. When they had completed the harvest, they were satisfied to have caught ten beavers in the twelve traps they had set. "Not a bad start, I'd say," Jug commented. "I ain't surprised, though, with all the sign we saw." They decided to leave the traps where they were for another day and then move them to the many little streams feeding the river. They skinned the ten they had caught, removed the scent glands, and took the meat and tails of four of them back to camp for breakfast. They would come back that night to check their traps again while the rest of the day would be filled with the scraping and stretching of the beaver pelts. Ordinarily, a little time for hunting for something to eat besides beaver might be available, but they decided against that, for the same reason Luke had spared the lady elk. "I hope to hell those Blackfoot have moved on north. I'm afeared they won't, 'cause the huntin' is too blame good in these mountains. Mule deer, white tail, probably even elk, I expect," Jug allowed.

"Yeah, there's elk," Luke agreed but refrained from telling him why he thought so. "What makes you think those Indians are Blackfoot?"

"'Cause that's what they like to do best," Jug replied. "They was just born to aggravate white men."

"They get along all right with white men who work for Hudson's Bay, though," Luke commented.

"Well, I reckon so," Jug replied. "That's where they get their guns and ammunition."

"You know, if those Blackfoot ain't usin' their rifles to hunt, you know, usin' bows and arrows, they could be closer to us than we know," Luke suggested. He was still thinking about his earlier meeting with the elk. Jug remarked that there was no doubt about that, and it was a good reason why they had to keep alert all the time. Luke went on to tell him what was on his mind. "You ever do any shootin' with a bow?"

"No, I never have," Jug answered. "Never thought I'd be much good with one."

"I did a little bit of shootin' with one, year before last at Cache Valley when they didn't have the rendezvous," Luke started.

"That's when I discovered The Chinaman's," Jug interrupted. "Was you there, too?"

"Yeah, but not for long," Luke answered. "I was with American Fur, with those fellows that got killed this year. There was this Shoshone guide with us and I got kinda interested in his bow, so he took it on himself to teach me how to shoot one." He paused to say, "There ain't much to learn about how to shoot it. He spent most of the time trying to teach me how to make a good one. I got to where I could hit a target with his bow, but I never got around to makin' one." He decided then to tell Jug what started his thinking on the subject. "What I'm sayin' is, I wish to hell I'd had one today." He went on to tell Jug about the elk cow at the bottom of the ravine.

Jug cocked his head to one side and pictured the cow standing still, waiting to be shot. Having hunted many an elk in his life, he found it hard to believe the cow would have stood there, if she could see him. But in the short time he had known Luke Ransom, he had formed the opinion that the young man was not prone to exaggerate. "I do declare," he said, "a good supply of elk meat would carry us a while, wouldn't it? And it'd be handy to have another good elk robe for this winter comin' on. Then we could sell it at rendezvous next summer. I don't know, I mighta just had to risk one shot, if she was standin' as close as you say."

"I figured we had too much ridin' on keepin' our camp a secret," Luke said. "But it was awful hard to pass her up." He
laughed then. "Maybe we'll meet again. We were both eyeballin'
each other like there was something goin' on between us."

They were still talking about it when they left after dark to
check their traps. They found six more carcasses in the pond but
decided to leave only four traps there and set the rest of them in
the streams around the pond and between it and the river. "I'd
hoped we'd do better than that in this pond," Jug complained.
Beaver usually live in family groups of six or more, and the pond
was large enough to have two lodges. Judging by the size of those
they had already skinned, they figured these beavers had been
there a long time. "Hell," Jug decided, "they're just bashful.
They ain't never done no trappin' before."

Jug started skinning the six carcasses they had caught while
Luke finished setting the traps in the streams. He finished in
time to skin the last of the six beaver. All done, they headed back
to their camp, ready to crawl in their blankets for the night but
knowing it best to scrape and stretch the six hides right away.
The six beaver pelts were completely forgotten, however, when
they rode into the blind canyon to find the remains of their camp
scattered about the ground in front of the cave. Their other
horses were gone, along with their supply of ammunition. Even
the beaver pelts they had been drying before folding them to
pack were missing. Contents of sacks holding supplies like flour
and coffee, that the savages had no use for, were scattered about
the ground. The bottoms of logs supporting the lintel over the
doorway were scorched, evidence of an unsuccessful attempt to
burn the log framework they had constructed to support the cave
opening. The scene caused an explosion in Luke's mind at once,
fueled by the realization that it had to have been a result of his
carelessness. Somehow, they must have tracked him while he
was attempting to track them. There was no time, at that point,
to dwell on it, for first, he and Jug had to make sure there was no
ambush waiting for them to ride in.

"Check that side!" Luke exclaimed as he rolled off his horse, pulling his rifle with him, and ran into the trees on one side of the canyon. Thinking the same as his partner, Jug came off his horse and ran into the trees on the other side. The sides were the only realistic places to wait in ambush, and it didn't take long to determine there was no one there. The fact that the raiders had not waited in ambush told Luke that he was right in his estimation that the hunting party was no larger than two or three. And it was his guess that they probably had no guns—either that, or no ammunition. His reaction now was to go after them, but he knew it was too dark to track them, and he felt the total frustration of that fact.

"Ain't that a helluva howdy-do?" Jug commented when they came out of the trees to get their horses. "They snookered us good. I don't know, maybe we oughta be dancin' a jig and hollerin' hoo-ray 'cause we weren't settin' in front of the fire, jawin', when they snuck up on us."

"They wouldn't have found us, if I hadn't led them to us," Luke said. "I was careless somewhere back there when I thought I was tracking them."

"Don't go beatin' yourself up, thinkin' like that," Jug responded. "These ain't no ordinary Injuns. These boys are Blackfoot. Ain't nobody smarter, and we're tryin' to make it in their territory."

"I'm goin' after 'em just as soon as it gets light enough to find a track," Luke said. "We gotta find these coyotes. They know where our camp is."

"That's a fact," Jug replied, "and the only thing they wanted but didn't get, was our scalps. So, I expect they'll be comin' back for them."

"That's what I think," Luke said. "And that's why I wanna get on their trail before they decide to pay us another visit." He thought about it for another minute, then added another possibility. "On the other hand, they mighta just been interested in stealin' our horses and they're figurin' on hightailin' it with the horses they took. And we've got to have those packhorses."

Chapter 5

Luke slept very little during the rest of the night, and with the first light of day, he was saddling Smoke. Jug, also awake early, was reluctant to see his partner ride after the raiders alone. "There's three of 'em," he said, after they had both scouted the ground around their camp. "I think you'd do well to have some help to even up the odds a little."

"Always appreciate your help," Luke replied. "But I think it best if you keep an eye on our traps and anything else we've got left. I just hope to hell these three ain't got any more of their tribe close by. There are three of 'em, but I really think they don't have any guns."

"Yeah, but they stole all our extra ammunition," Jug insisted. "Maybe they hadn't used their guns because they was outta powder and shot."

"Maybe," Luke countered, "but ammunition is the same as money to them, so they'da stole it whether they had guns or not. And if they just have bows, and I do catch up with 'em, I can cut a couple of 'em down before I get in range of their bows." He paused to grin and remind him, "Like I did when I found you lyin' behind a dead horse."

"Yeah, well, you just be damn careful you don't ride into an ambush," Jug warned. "They drive an arrow through your meat sack, it'll hurt just as much as a bullet."

"I will," Luke assured him. "You keep a sharp eye as well, in case they double back on me. They fooled me once, they might do it again, tryin' to steal our traps." He gave him another grin and said, "I don't wanna come back here and find you pinned down behind that big jug of yours and it with a hole in it."

He led his horse to the mouth of the canyon to see if he could pick up a trail. With no one at the camp to shoot at them, it was the logical way out. Any other way would require a steep climb. Their trail was easy to find, as they had galloped out of the canyon and followed the valley to the north. He climbed up into the saddle and followed the tracks to the end of the valley, where he stopped to make sure which way the tracks led then. It was the dark of the night when they had ridden this way, and lucky for him, they were not thinking so much about the tracks they were leaving. They were so obvious that he had to caution himself that he might be riding into an ambush. Their first attempt to disguise their trail came when he came to a wide stream making its way down the steep slope of the mountain he was circling. The trail he had been following failed to appear on the other bank of the stream, so he turned Smoke around and went back into the water. He reined the gelding to a stop and waited for him to drink, while he looked up the stream to try to see where it might lead. About one hundred and fifty feet up the slope, he saw what appeared to be a level ledge and he thought at once that it was where their trail led.

He gave Smoke a touch of his heels, and the bay gelding started immediately up the busy stream. While the horse climbed, Luke imagined what the three Indians were thinking during their ascent of the stream in the pitch-black darkness under the branches of the big fir trees. In spite of his first thought when he came to the stream, he now believed they had no thoughts at that point toward hiding their trail, no more so than when they were galloping away from his camp. When he reached the ledge, he felt doubly sure he was right, for he found that the ledge held a game trail leading toward the adjoining mountain. He paused to look in the opposite direction and saw that it continued along the slope of the smaller mountain. There was no question which way the Indians had taken on the trail, however, for there were plenty of tracks to show that they came out of the water and headed still in a northerly direction toward the larger mountain.

It was time to become a little more cautious, he told himself, as he held Smoke to a fast walk, slowing almost to a halt whenever he approached a sharp turn in the trail. *I don't want to make a sudden appearance at their camp when I come around one of these curves,* he thought. This, even though he felt pretty confident the three raiders he was chasing would not likely be encamped on a game trail part way up a mountain. Halfway around the mountain, the ledge came to an end, but the game trail continued on, descending sharply toward the base of the mountain. At this point, the trail took a little more concentration on his part, for it led out on a grassy valley split by a creek. Still, he found it not too difficult to follow the tracks of the three Indians on horseback, apparently leading his and Jug's packhorses behind them.

Feeling vulnerable to a rifle shot as he rode across the wide valley, he hoped he was right in thinking the three he followed had no rifles. The trail they left angled toward the creek as if they intended to follow the creek up a narrow gorge. He continued on, following the creek past the point where it came out of a thick growth of cottonwood trees at the foot of another mountain. His concentration on the three Blackfoot warriors was so intense that he didn't realize the trees were cottonwoods and excellent horse feed. Otherwise, he might have been surprised to find them amid the fir and lodgepole pines. He was further distracted when he heard a noise ahead, but immediately recognized it as the sound of a waterfall. It caused him to suspect he must be approaching their camp. He was further convinced when he noticed Smoke's ears perk up as if sensing other horses nearby. He reached for his rifle, pulling it out of the saddle sling as he dismounted. The smallest fraction of a second after he dropped to the ground, he felt the arrow pass over his head and heard the dull thunk as it struck the tree behind him. It was followed by the startling cry of alarm released by the Blackfoot warrior charging toward him with his tomahawk raised to strike. Luke pulled the pistol from his belt, it being the quicker choice, cocked it, and put a bullet in Hears the Wind's forehead.

He wasted no time then, for the alarm had been sounded, and reached back to his saddle to get his other rifle. They were both primed and ready, but he only cocked one of them as he ran toward the smoke of a campfire. Due to the bushes between him and the camp, he couldn't see the fire, or the two warriors sleeping beside it until they jumped up at the sound of alarm. He laid his spare rifle on the ground and took dead aim at the biggest target. He squeezed the trigger and Iron Pony stood straight up when the rifle ball struck his chest. Seeing what had happened to him, Two Bears dropped to the ground again and rolled away from the fire before scrambling to his feet, his bow and arrow quiver in his hands.

Not sure where Two Bears had fled to, Luke watched the bushes between him and the fire while he hurried to reload his rifle. Then with both rifles loaded again, he hurried through the trees to find a better location. When he reached a position where he could see into the camp, he knelt beside a tree and scanned the small clearing, looking for his target. With no sign of Two Bears, he made his way deeper into the trees and stopped when he saw the waterfall and the pond it had formed. Beside the pond, he saw the packhorses and the Indian ponies grazing on the grassy bank. Still there was no sign of Two Bears, so he started to move again when another arrow thudded into the tree beside his head. He realized then that the Indian was circling around in the opposite direction, trying to get a shot at him. Without thinking, Luke naturally looked in the direction the arrow had come from in time to see the bushes moving after Two Bears had shot his arrow. He cocked both rifles. Laying one beside him, he quickly fired at the bushes he had seen move. Then, gambling that the Indian would continue to move in the same direction he had been circling in, he picked up his other rifle and aimed it to the right of the bush he had just shot at. His bet paid off because he caught sight of a patch of buckskin moving behind the screen of bushes. He pulled the trigger and heard a cry of pain. Wasting no more time, he immediately reloaded his rifles in case his shot had not been a lethal one. Then he pulled his pistol out of his belt again and reloaded it. He had to check on all three to make sure they were dead. And even though he assumed there were only three Indians, he could have been wrong. So he had to be sure there was no one else to be accounted for.

His first concern was the last one he had shot, for he really couldn't tell if he had guessed right when he fired. He had heard a cry of pain, but that could have been fake, and he might be waiting for him to come to him, with arrow notched and bowstring fully drawn. So, as a precaution, Luke circled around to come up to him from behind. He found Two Bears slumped on the ground, his back against a tree, his war axe in his hand. He was obviously in great pain. He had been gut shot and was bleeding profusely. When he heard Luke behind him, he turned and gazed at him forlornly. Luke paused to look at him, realizing at once the man was going to die. He walked past him, and when he was behind him, he turned back and shot him in the head, thinking he should end the poor devil's suffering. With that done, he then went to the campfire to make sure of the one he shot there. There was no question. As he looked down at the dead Indian, he thought, *Jug was right, they're Blackfoot, all right.* Then he straightened up and looked around him. "And they've got a better spot for a winter camp than we have." He walked over to the edge of the pond and took a long look at the waterfall he guessed to be a hundred feet high. *Good water, good grass, good wood, and protection from the wind,* he thought, and decided to bring Jug there to see if he thought it worthwhile to move their camp here.

After he had put out their campfire and gotten all the horses ready to be led back to his camp, he walked back to Two Bears' corpse and took the bow from his hands. He drew it full to test the strength of it. *Not bad*, he thought. He pulled his quiver of arrows off him and went to compare that bow with the other two. He selected the best two, with the thought that Jug might want to try one, and took all the arrows. Before he left, he pulled the three bodies out of the clearing and dumped them on the ground while he decided what best to do with them. His first impulse was to drag them back beyond the place where the stream came out of the hill, and find a gully or a crevice to dump them in. But he gave it a little more thought and decided it might be worth his effort to carry the bodies farther away from this spot, in case he talked Jug into moving their camp here. The more he looked around him, the better the place looked in comparison to the cave he and Jug had already finished. And if the spot struck Jug the same, and they moved their possibles there, maybe it would be best not to have the three bodies anywhere nearby. If some of their friends stumbled on them, it might not be good to have them so close to the camp.

Jug came out from behind the big rock that stood on one side of the cave they had dug. "I swear!" he exclaimed. "Looks like you found what you was lookin' for."

Luke stepped down from the saddle and the horses he was leading all gathered around him creating a small dust cloud. "I reckon you could say that," he replied.

"You was gone a while," Jug said. "I was thinkin' I might have to go look for you, if you didn't show up pretty soon."

"It took a while to pick up all our supplies they stole," Luke explained. "They didn't wanna give 'em back, but they finally realized they were in the wrong."

"Blackfoot," Jug pronounced in disgust.

Luke couldn't resist japing him. "Oh, they weren't Blackfoot. They were Flatheads."

"I'll be damned," Jug blurted. "There ain't no Flathead over this far. They was Blackfoot." When Luke laughed, Jug knew he

was japing him. "You ain't much of a liar, are you? Was there
three of 'em, like we figured?"

"Yep," Luke answered, "and they had a dandy place to make a
camp. Might be better'n ours. We can take a ride back over there,
so you can see it. You might wanna move over there when the
real cold sets in and we can't trap no more."

"Don't see no harm in it, but I'm satisfied with this'un we
worked on already. 'Course it don't look like it's too hard to find,
does it?" He changed the subject abruptly. "You ain't asked if we
caught any beaver last night."

"That's right," Luke replied, his confrontation with the Blackfoot still occupying his thoughts. "You got there pretty late this
mornin'. What kinda luck did we have?"

"Three of the four traps we left in the pond had beaver in 'em.
I took seven more outta the traps we set in the streams. I was
workin' on those plews when I heard you comin' up the canyon
soundin' like a war party of Injuns and I got behind this rock."

Luke grinned and nodded his head. "That ain't a bad start, is
it? Looks like we picked us a good spot. We'll just keep on
workin' those streams till we get down to the river. What about
the pond? Did you reset those four traps, or do you think we
oughta leave the pond be for a while?"

"I set 'em one more time," Jug answered. "Then I think we
oughta move on toward the river. We'll see what we got tonight.
We can work right on up this mountain range, but I got a feelin'
we'd be smart to work on down the Judith before it starts to get
real winter. Tomorrow, after we check our traps, let's take that
ride over to where you found them Blackfoot. You got my curiosity up."

The days that followed were not as productive in beaver pelts
as the first days in the Little Belt Mountains, but there was not a
day when there was no catch. Luke led Jug to the hidden valley
where the three Blackfoot hunters had made their camp by the

waterfall, and Jug was as impressed by the potential as Luke had been. He was also pleased to see beaver sign in the creek that split the grassy valley before the waterfall. "With that creek and that grass valley, we won't have to hunt for meat. The game will come to us," Jug declared. "Them three Blackfoot musta been sent here to show us this valley was what we needed to make it through the winter."

"I just hope to hell this little hard-to-find valley ain't a favorite huntin' spot for the rest of their village," Luke said, "and come the first hard freeze, they all show up expectin' supper." On a serious note then, he suggested, "We need to see if we've got a back door outta this place, in case we need to leave in a hurry." He paused then while he watched Jug's reactions to all the positive aspects of this hidden camp. Finally, he said, "You ain't said the first thing about that bunch of cottonwood trees where the creek comes off the mountain."

"I saw 'em right off," Jug lied. "Didn't see no reason to say anything about it." It irritated him that he had not noticed something that almost made this valley a perfect winter camp. Cottonwoods meant feed for their horses when the snow covered the grass. When the bark was peeled off the trunks of a felled tree, the horses readily ate it. And they would peel the small limbs and branches themselves. The thing that made this camp unique was the existence of the trees this close to the mountains, where the only trees that grew there were fir and lodgepole pines. Cottonwoods didn't grow in the higher altitudes, but they were seen along the waterways of the plains and lower elevations—like the creek at the foot of this mountain. "I was fixin' to mention that we might not have to even think about goin' to Cache Valley to winter," Jug offered lamely.

Once again, they were faced with the work of preparing a camp for the coming cold weather. And since a cave was not feasible, due to the slope of the mountain, they decided they would have to build a tipi. Their major concern before they got to that, however, was for their horses. As it was, they had three more horses than they had when they left the rendezvous, again thanks to the Indians that raided their cave. They decided to build themselves a shelter, making a roof by threading small trees horizontally through the branches of two large fir trees, then crisscrossing those small trees with heavier fir limbs until fashioning a wide enough area to give some protection—and hope the roof was strong enough to support a heavy snowfall. They figured the horses would naturally gather under the makeshift roof and consequently help keep each other warm. So there was plenty of work to occupy their daylight hours between the morning and evening trapping, which had to go on uninterrupted as long as the weather permitted.

To satisfy Jug's urges, after they trapped out the streams where they first started, they followed the Judith River north for a mile or more to work the streams that emptied into it. Much to Jug's disappointment, they enjoyed extremely limited success, and that prompted Luke to offer his advice. "Next time you feel one of those urges, you'd best just go over behind the bushes and squat for a while till you get rid of it." Jug had no comeback, so he had to grin and bear it. Still, they made an honest attempt to find the busy beaver colonies until the snow began to fall and they decided to follow the streams back up into the mountains, where they were catching beaver before.

"I still think there's beaver in this river," Jug insisted. "If it weren't for the fact we'd be gettin' too far from our camp, I'da liked to go a little farther up this river. If we'da kept on followin' the river for about another fifteen miles, you coulda said howdy to Nate Jolley," Jug declared.

"Nate Jolley?" Luke repeated. "You know somebody farther up this river?"

"I sure do," Jug replied. "Nate Jolley's got a tradin' post on the Judith. Been there for twelve years that I know of."

"Is that a fact?" Luke responded, surprised to hear it. "And the Blackfeet let him run a tradin' post? How come?"

"Nate's married to a Blackfoot woman and he's got a half-breed son, name of Pike. And that boy's got more Blackfoot blood in him than anything he got from Nate. I reckon that's the reason the Blackfeet let Nate stay there. They trade with him for whiskey and powder and lead."

"I reckon it's just as well we didn't get that far up this river," Luke said. "We mighta run into some of his customers."

"We coulda just told 'em we worked for Hudson's Bay," Jug replied. "We mighta been hard put to explain why we was trappin' their beaver, though."

So it was back to concentrating on the mountain streams and ponds until they froze over and had to stop. Unlike the open plain of the Judith, there had been no real snowfall as yet, there in the mountains, but they expected it any day. The completion of the tipi they planned was the most pressing need, since they had done pretty much all they could for their horses. The framework for their tipi was built using young lodgepole pines. They covered their smaller version of an Indian tipi with the three buffalo hides they had bought at rendezvous for temporary shelter. Unlike a typical Indian tipi, which required fifteen or twenty hides, it was not anywhere near the size, area-wise, and it was not tall enough to stand in, even for Jug. But there was room to build a fire in the center of the floor and they fashioned a chimney hole in the top. Even as small as it was, there was still a sizable gap over the door, and this was patched with the hide from the deer Luke had killed. They tied the hides on securely and held the skirts down by storing all their belongings and beaver pelts around the diameter of their tipi. To complete the domicile, they chopped a good supply of aspen for firewood. It would produce a warm, smokeless fire that would warm their little tipi without burning their eyes, and just as important, would not signal their presence from afar. The grove of aspen trees was found when they were scouting out a route of escape up the mountain behind their camp. "I swear," Jug declared, "cottonwoods below and aspen above. If that ain't a sign of a perfect winter camp, I don't know what is."

"Well, if we wanted it to be really perfect," Luke countered, "maybe we could have the beaver comin' in on their own to surrender. Then we wouldn't have to wade around in that ice-cold creek."

When they had done all they felt they could to prepare their camp for the winter, there was time for other activities, along with the drying of their pelts. Well aware of the importance of exercising their horses, Luke and Jug took time to scout the mountains beyond their camp to find likely spots for their traps. They found that the mountains had numerous ponds and streams making the Little Belts prime country for beaver as well as deer, elk, and bear. The availability of deer, mule deer and white tail, inspired Luke to start practicing with his bow. It would be silent, and it would conserve his ammunition for his rifles and pistol. His efforts to interest Jug were unsuccessful, however. Jug reluctantly tried one of the two bows, shooting at a target Luke hung on a lodgepole pine. His first shot missed the whole tree. His second arrow burrowed in the dirt at the foot of the pine. He promptly handed the bow back to Luke with a huffy snort. "Dang bows and arrows is meant for ignorant savages."

Luke, on the other hand, was intrigued with the notion of killing a deer without announcing the fact to anyone who might be a mile or two away. He was encouraged to practice more with the weapon when he found that he was good at it. Now, as each day seemed to offer warnings that winter was at hand, the animals began to come down from the higher mountain meadows to seek the protection of the lower valleys. It was critical for Luke and Jug to prepare as much food as they could before the weather made it more difficult. Since the little valley they had built their camp in would seem to be one that attracted the deer or elk herds, they decided to do their initial hunting farther away from home. Their thinking was to save the food supply on their doorstep for the really hard part of the winter, when it was difficult to go searching for game. "What if we're wrong, and the game doesn't hang around when they find us here?" Luke asked.

"Hell," Jug snorted, "they won't pay no attention to us, 'long as we ain't shootin' at 'em. Then when it gets so bad you can't get outta this valley to hunt, you can just quietly pick off one or two with that bow you're so good at. And them animals won't even know what's goin' on."

Chapter 6

"They have been gone too long," Standing Elk said. "I think they have found some trouble. They should have been back before now. We have had a good hunt, and we should go back to our village before the heavy snows come." Standing Elk was the leader of this band of twelve Blackfoot hunters who came down from their village on the Missouri, close to the five great waterfalls to hunt in the Little Belt Mountains. The mountain chain had always been known to the Blackfeet as a place where the game was plentiful. His concern was for his brother, Iron Pony. He, Two Bears, and Hears the Wind wanted to scout the southern end of the mountain chain for future hunts. So they had set out to hunt on the lower end of the range. They had not returned after four days. At first thinking they had not found the game so plentiful as that found at the upper end of the range, Standing Elk expected them to return in a day or two. Now, he felt genuine concern for his brother's well-being. In recent weeks, scouts had reported seeing Crow hunting parties north of the Yellowstone River, clearly in Blackfoot territory. He feared that his brother had run afoul of one of these Crow parties.

"Maybe they did find good hunting," Lame Foot suggested, "and they have not come back because they are butchering their kill."

"It should not have taken this long to get back here," Standing

Elk insisted. "They took no packhorses with them, so they couldn't carry enough meat to take this long."

"We need to get this meat we've already packed on the horses back to the village," Lame Foot commented as he looked up at the heavy clouds overhead. There was not yet a covering of snow on the ground, but as if to emphasize his concern, a gentle shower of snowflakes began to fall.

"I must find my brother," Standing Elk stated flatly. "You are right, the meat must be taken to the village right away. But I will go in search of Iron Pony and Hears the Wind and Two Bears. You must lead the others back. Maybe we will catch up with you on your way back."

"I would go with you to find them," Lame Foot volunteered.

"No," Standing Elk said. "I would rather have you with the hunting party, in case you meet a Crow party. The village is counting on us to provide for them, so you must make sure the meat gets there safely."

"Iron Pony and the others might have been captured by the Crows," Lame Foot cautioned. "You might need help, if you find them."

"Don't worry, my friend," Standing Elk told him. "I will be very cautious. It is important that you lead the hunters back with food for our village."

"As you wish," Lame Foot said, "I'll leave right away." He told himself not to worry about Standing Elk, for there was no more fierce a fighter than Standing Elk, and no more skillful hunter than the warrior who had earned his name when he once stalked an elk. Wearing an elk hide as disguise, he was able to sneak up to a bull elk, standing at a berry bush, close enough to kill him with his war hatchet.

Standing Elk walked back to the campfire with Lame Foot to tell the other members of the hunting party of his decision. "Lame Foot will lead you back to the village. It is important that you start back right away, for it looks like the weather is going to get worse. I will stay here to look for our three missing brothers.

They may be on their way back, so we'll catch up with you when you camp tonight." Like Lame Foot, every one of the other seven volunteered to accompany Standing Elk in the search. But Standing Elk once again stressed the importance of seeing the supply of deer meat safely to the village. So they finished packing the meat on the packhorses, extinguished the fire, and started out for home.

Standing Elk watched them go, then he climbed on his horse and struck out in the opposite direction, taking the same trail Iron Pony had taken. He truly hoped he would meet the three of them on their way back, for it was forty miles to the south end of the range, where Iron Pony had talked about scouting. Unfortunately, there was just enough snow on the ground to cover any tracks that might have been useful to him. As he rode the road that circled the base of the mountain range, he passed many draws and valleys that looked interesting. But with no tracks, there was no way to guess if any of these valleys had attracted Iron Pony's interest. So, knowing he was gambling on blind luck, he continued to ride, down to the lower end of the range, as Iron Pony said he was going to do. He camped that night by the Judith River near the southern end of the range. He cooked some supper of fresh-killed deer meat and promised himself he would find some sign that would lead him to his brother.

He was awake at sunup the next morning to find his horses snuffling around in the light covering of snow, looking for grass under the cottonwoods that grew along a creek that emptied into the river. He took his war axe and hacked off an armload of small cottonwood branches and fed them to his horses. He decided to give them plenty because he knew he wouldn't see any more cottonwoods when he started up into the mountains, so he cut a few more branches. He was about to drop the branches between the horses but paused when something caught his eye. On the ground at his feet, he saw the remains of a small animal. Because of the cottonwood boughs over the bank, the remains had not been completely covered with snow. Inspired to look more closely then, he discovered more remains a few feet away, and he knew at once—trappers! These were the remains of beavers, after they were taken from the traps. Standing Elk was immediately enraged. He hated trappers more than he hated Crows. For the white trappers came into Blackfoot territory to trap the beaver and hunt the deer and elk, stealing the furs that the Blackfeet could trade to Hudson's Bay Company. Looking at the entrails and heads, he knew that they had not been there very long. Pausing to take a good look at the lay of the land and the many streams that funneled down to the river at this point, he believed the trappers were still working in this bottom. He had to wonder if Iron Pony had encountered the trappers. At any rate, he was determined to search out the streams to see if he could find the white devils.

He spent almost half of that day tracing one stream after another, searching to find fresh tracks in the snow, but finding none. Gradually, he was moving farther north beside the mountains when he passed the mouth of a small canyon and decided to ride up it a little way to see if it led to something deeper into the mountains. It turned out to be a blind canyon, however, and he was about to turn around when something caught his eye. At the end of the canyon, a steep cliff rose straight up. There was a large boulder sitting at the base of the cliff, and he realized that it hid a dark spot that looked like a hole. He rode closer to discover it to be a small cave, and not a natural one. It had been dug by someone and they had cut logs to shore up the opening. He cautioned himself to be careful, although there was no sign of life about, animal or man. He checked the load in his Northwest Trade Gun and held it ready to fire as he approached the cave. When he rode right up to the front of the cave with no challenge, he knew it was deserted. Still with his rifle cocked, he slid off his horse and went in the cave. It was a good cave, he decided, but there was no evidence that it had been used very much. The logs used to shore up the opening were still green. He felt that it had been a white trapper who had built it. Evidently, he had trapped out the streams and ponds in this section and decided to move on. That would not surprise him, for he could not trap when the streams and ponds were frozen over. Still, judging by the cave he was now standing in, it would appear that he had been planning to spend the whole winter there. What changed his mind? Did Iron Pony and the two with him have something to do with it? But there was no sign of any fight that might have happened at the cave.

There were ashes from a campfire with some half-burned sticks just outside the entrance, an inconvenience necessary since there was no chimney in the cave. He gathered some dry leaves and grass and made a small fire, enough to create a flame on one of the half-burned limbs. Then hurrying before the flame died, he went back inside. And with the puny light of his torch, he was able to see footprints inside the cave. Looking as quickly as he could, he was able to determine two different sizes of moccasins before the flame died. So there were two trappers. Perhaps a man and his woman, judging by the smallness of some of the prints. Impatient now to find some answers to his questions, he threw the smoking limb against the wall of the cave and went back to his horses. Riding out of the blind canyon, he turned north to follow a wide trail that paralleled the one he had ridden down the night before. He wondered if Iron Pony had found the trapper's cave and ridden back this way. He could have missed him, if he had. They would have passed each other, going in opposite directions, on trails no more than a hundred yards apart.

He held his gray gelding to a fast walk as he continued around the base of the first small mountain. When he came to a wide stream that cascaded down the mountain, washing over a ledge partway up the slope, he paused to let his horses drink. Then he preceded along the trail for another couple hundred yards or so, seeing no ravines or game trails leading into the larger mountains. And then the trail took a sharp turn, veering away from the direction of the trail he had ridden the day before. He soon found himself approaching a narrow valley between two large mountains and traveling in a more westerly direction. He continued to follow the trail, even though he had no idea where it might lead. Thoughts of finding his brother and his two friends were becoming fraught with frustration. He had reached a point where he could only hope that Iron Pony had taken another way back and was even now on his way to join the others. Finally deciding he had no real possibility of finding his brother, or the trapper either, he turned the gray around and started to backtrack. It was then he saw the buzzards, circling halfway up the taller mountain.

Had it been only a half dozen of the scavenger birds, he would have ignored them, but there was a swarm of them circling and swooping over something on the side of the mountain. Whatever it was, it was big enough to make him investigate, so he started the gray gelding up the side of the mountain. As the slope became steeper, he slid off his horse and led it and his packhorse the rest of the way. Close enough now to hear the raucous screeching of the competition over the object of their frenzy, Standing Elk used his rifle as a club and began flailing at some of the birds, battling his way to the edge of a shallow crevice, so he could see whatever it was that had died.

His heart seemed to stop completely when he saw what was left of the three bodies lying in the bottom of the crevice. He could identify his brother, Two Bears, and Hears the Wind, even though they were partially covered by half a dozen of the disgusting buzzards that the other vultures were trying to dislodge, so they could have a turn at the feast. Standing Elk roared out his anger and shot his gun into the crevice, killing one of the birds and causing the others to scatter briefly. He hurried to reload the smooth bore trade gun while yelling out in grief-stricken anger at the vultures. He fired it again, then fired the pistol he carried, killing two more of the birds. When the swarm was frightened away for a few seconds, he jumped down into the crevice. Knowing the buzzards would only back off for a few minutes, he reloaded his weapons, then threw the dead buzzards out of the crevice, yelling and cursing as he did. Knowing he had little time before their boldness would return, he looked at his brother. His body, already torn apart and half eaten, could not tell him the cause of Iron Pony's death. But the unmistakable bullet hole in the back of Two Bears' head and the fact that scalps weren't taken told Standing Elk that his brother had been killed by the white trapper. How, he wondered, could the trapper have gotten so close to them that he could shoot Two Bears in the back of his head? And how could he have killed Iron Pony and Hears the Wind, as well? Sick at heart, he vowed to find this evil spirit, if he had to comb every inch of these mountains. His brother and his friends could not die this way without being avenged.

He was distracted then when the flock of buzzards began to swoop closer to the crevice again. So he fired another shot into their midst, scattering them once more. Determined to stop their gruesome assault on the bodies, he did the only thing he could, and that was to bury the bodies. He climbed out of the crevice and from above it, he worked feverishly, shoving loose rocks and gravel down on top of the bodies. When he had moved all the loose gravel he could move with his hands, he started chopping the ground up with his hand axe, so he could shove dirt on top of the rocks. All this was done with the accompaniment of the raucous complaints of the buzzards, until he succeeded in covering the bodies completely. Still, he gathered rocks, anything he could lift, and continued to drop them into the crevice until he was convinced that no bird or animal could get to the remains again. When he was done, mentally and physically exhausted, he knelt on both knees, looked up at the gray skies over the mountains, and sang his death song to honor his brother. Then he made a solemn vow to seek out the devil who had done this, to search every mountain and valley, everywhere beaver could be trapped, until he found this trapper and his woman. When he found them, he would open their bellies with his knife and pull their innards out for bait. Then he would hang them in a tree while they were still alive and watch the buzzards feast upon them. Only then, could he feel some measure of vengeance. He remained there on his knees for a long time, with the vultures still screeching in the trees, until his horses began to shuffle their hooves nervously. Aware of their restlessness then, he got up and started to take them back down the mountain. He paused again, however, for there were no thoughts of hurrying back to try to catch up to the hunting party. There was only one thought driving him now, no matter how long it might take. Without a clue where to start, he decided he would search out the mountain he was on, since this was where he found the bodies. Since he was closer to the top than he was the bottom, he decided to go on up to the top of the mountain. And he chose to do it by going around and around the mountain, climbing higher with each circle until he reached the top. As he did so, he looked for any sign of a cave or cabin, making sure he didn't miss any possibility. When he reached the top, he only felt frustration for the little area he had covered. He would go back down, however, and repeat his circles until he reached the bottom. He soon realized that to find this trapper devil, he must search the creeks and streams and ponds, looking for the stakes driven into the banks that held the scented lure over his traps. If he found them, it would only be a matter of lying in wait for the trapper to come to check them.

"What the hell was that?" Jug blurted when he heard the pop of a distant shot. He paused in the scraping of a beaver pelt to look at Luke, who was also sitting up in attention.

In a few minutes, they heard a second and a third shot. Luke got to his feet and listened. "Sounded to me like it came from beyond that mountain beside this one, maybe on that mountain where I dumped those three Blackfoot. From the sound of it, I'd say it's one of those Northwest Trade Guns."

"Somebody's shootin' at somethin'," Jug insisted, immediately concerned because they had figured they were now alone in these lower mountains, since the elimination of the three Blackfeet. Shortly after his comment, they heard another shot.

"Damn," he uttered softly, now that there was clear sign that there was somebody else to worry about.

With nothing they could do about it at the moment, they just continued to listen. After a period of about a quarter of an hour, Luke stated, "Four shots, I reckon somebody ran up on somebody they didn't get along with." Like Jug, Luke had assumed they were alone in that part of the mountains, and as late in the season as it now was, they would likely continue to be alone until the spring thaw. But it was obvious that, instead of only worrying about keeping warm and keeping their horses alive, they also had the concern of another possible danger. And this one had a gun.

"I expect we're gonna have to keep a sharp eye and be real careful we don't lead nobody back to our camp," Jug said. His thoughts went at once to the same place Luke's were. "When we built that tipi, we was thinkin' mostly about keepin' warm, and not so much protection from a rifle ball."

"Yeah, I was just thinkin' about that," Luke said. "We might better build us something to shoot behind. But one thing for sure, we've got to find out who's doin' that shootin', before he finds us."

"You know, that could be somebody lookin' for them three Blackfoot," Jug suggested.

"I reckon," Luke replied, "but what were they shootin' at?"

"I'd like to know the answer to that, myself," Jug declared. "I know you're thinkin' about goin' over that way to see if you can spot whoever's doin' the shootin'. But maybe this time it'd be a good idea to make sure our camp don't get no visitors. We've got a lot to lose if somebody raids our camp now."

Luke paused to consider what Jug was saying. The little man was right. They had a lot to lose if their camp was attacked while he was out looking for the raiders. If they were a war party of Blackfoot or Crow, they could shoot the little winter tipi to pieces then take what they wanted. And that would be horses, saddles, weapons, ammunition, supplies, and a pack and a half of beaver pelts worth about four hundred and fifty dollars. "You're right," he said to Jug. "We need to get back to work on our camp." Already planning the improvements, he hustled Jug along, and they were soon riding back to their camp by the waterfall.

They made it a habit to take extra precautions when going and coming from their camp, and this time, they were even more careful when they took the game trail into the hidden grassy valley. To make sure they left no tracks to follow, they went into the water when they reached the creek that bisected the meadow until they reached the grove of trees that hid the falls. Only then did they leave the water and ride up to the camp.

After they stretched the morning's plews to dry, Jug started some coffee and cut some venison to cook over a fire outside the tipi, while Luke grabbed his shovel and hand axe and started his modification of their camp. He started by removing the floor covering of grass and setting it aside. Then he started digging up the floor of their dwelling and throwing the dirt out the doorway. When he had finished at the end of the day, he had succeeded in dropping the floor inside the tipi almost two feet, making a ledge of what was left of the original floor level. While he was working on the floor, Jug felled a large lodgepole pine and chopped it into six-foot lengths. He and Luke placed the logs in front of the tipi, using the dirt Luke had excavated as a base. When they had finished, they felt they at least had a rampart to take cover behind in the event they were attacked. They recognized the fact that the weak spot in their defense was the back of the tipi, but there was little they could do beyond cutting a flap that could be opened to shoot through. Both of them thought that, in the event of attack, it would likely come from the grove of trees at the bottom of the slope, and not from the waterfall behind the tipi. "I hope to hell we don't get the chance to find out if we're right or not," Jug remarked.

"Well, whaddaya think, partner?" Luke asked when they were standing in front of their tent-fort.

"I think I'd best go a little easy on my jug for a while, till I get used to it," Jug replied. "I might break my neck comin' in or out in the dark." He thought about it for a few moments before saying more. "Thing of it is, we don't know nothin' about that shootin' we heard. Might be Blackfoot lookin' for them three you shot. And it might be somebody just passin' through these mountains, maybe hunters, and that shootin' we heard was 'cause they run up on a herd of deer."

"If it was deer they were shootin'," Luke said, "it'd be easy enough to find out. It sounded to me like it mighta come from that mountain I dumped those Blackfoot on. I could ride up there and see if they had killed deer there."

"I reckon you could," Jug replied. "It's a good piece away from here. Reckon you could make it there and back before dark?"

"Yeah, I expect I could, since I'll just be takin' a quick look and come right back before we go check our traps." They looked at each other and shrugged. "Let me throw my saddle back on Smoke and I'll go see if they were even on that mountain." He didn't waste any more time discussing it and was soon on his way back down the creek. They both thought it was important to know the business of anybody anywhere close to their winter camp. Hopefully, it was a hunting party that was just passing close by and would soon be gone from this part of the mountains.

Chapter 7

Luke retraced the route he had taken when he led the Indian horses away from the valley, each one carrying a dead Blackfoot warrior. On that day, he had been intent upon disposing of the bodies far away from the little valley where their camp was to be located. With no horses to lead this trip, he kept Smoke to a lively pace as he followed an old game trail toward the mountain in question. When he reached the base of it, he slowed his horse down and scanned the trail before him, having no desire to suddenly surprise an Indian hunting party. He had counted on being able to see tracks in the light covering of snow, if there were new ones. But he was surprised to find there was no snow on this side of the large mountain he had just passed. He took a ride around the mountain as a precaution, but he saw no evidence of anyone having approached it from any direction other than the way he had climbed it before. There were tracks on the narrow path, but he could not extract any information from them. For he had led three horses up that path, himself, then led them back down. Maybe the gunshots he and Jug had heard had not come from this mountain after all. But he was still uncertain about whether or not there had been horses on that trail, other than those he led up there. So he decided to go up the slope just to make sure. And while he was up there, he would look to see if the buzzards had found the bodies he had left there.

As he went up the mountain, he saw no signs that would indicate a party of hunters had been there. When he approached the ledge over the crevice where he had dropped the bodies, he was surprised to find buzzard feathers scattered here and there, as if the big birds might have had a free-for-all over the fresh meat dropped in the crevice. He dismounted and walked down closer to the lip of the crevice, thinking it looked somehow different. Then he spotted what looked like a dead buzzard lying several dozen yards distant. *Maybe that was one of the shots we heard*, he thought, but he didn't go to it to see if it had actually been shot. Then he realized why the ground over the crevice looked different. He was startled to see that it had been filled in. He immediately backed away carefully, so as not to make any more tracks in the recently disturbed ground. There were many moccasin prints in addition to the ones just left by him, but they were all identical—left by one man. The story told itself. One of the members of the Blackfoot hunting party had come in search of his friends, only to find them dead in this crevice. To keep the vultures from eating them, he had to fight them off before he could bury his fellow tribesmen. *And that was what the shooting was about*, he thought.

The question to be answered now was, what would this one Blackfoot warrior do, now that he knew what had happened to his friends? Would he hang around and try to find the killer? Or would he ride back to his village to tell his people what had happened to the three? That might not bode too well for him and Jug, for that might mean a sizable war party descending upon these mountains, searching for them. When he left the crevice, he scouted the area where he had left his horse before climbing back into the saddle. There were many tracks, just as there had been on the trail up the mountain, but he found tracks of two horses continuing up toward the top. It had to have been the Indian. He took an unusual route to the top of the mountain, going round and round it as if searching every inch of it. It was Luke's guess that the Blackfoot had been making sure there was no camp on the mountain. "Eye for eye," Luke declared. "He's lookin' to avenge the killin'." It was going to be a question of who found who first. He turned Smoke back toward the camp.

Jug came out of the tipi to meet him when he came through the cottonwoods. He had been watching from inside. "Find anything?"

"I reckon," Luke declared. "We got us one hacked-off Blackfoot warrior that's lookin' to find the son of a gun who killed those three hunters." He went on to tell Jug what he had found on the mountain. "The good news is that there ain't but one lookin' for our scalps."

"Say he's after whoever killed his three friends, huh?" Jug japed in spite of the bad news. "Then, hell, he's just lookin' for you. You could save us all a lotta trouble if you'd just introduce yourself to him and maybe explain it to him that his friends was stealin' our plews and most of our possibles. Most of them Blackfoot is reasonable, if you just talk to 'em."

"What were you doin' while I was gone?" Luke asked. "You musta been suckin' on that jug again."

Getting serious then, Jug asked, "Whaddaya think we oughta do about them traps? It's time to go check 'em. You think we both oughta leave the camp at the same time? Or should one of us stay here to keep an eye on things?" The streams they were working at present were about three quarters of a mile from their camp. There were two different streams flowing down on either side of a high ridge to form a small pond where they joined at the base of the ridge. Ordinarily, they would be constantly moving their camp as they worked different areas. But this camp was set up for them to wait out the winter, and the winter was coming on rapidly. So they would continue to work out of it until the streams froze over.

"Well, we got twelve traps set and that's a lot for one man to handle in quick fashion," Luke responded, "especially since half our traps are on one side of that ridge and half of 'em on the other side. Dependin' on what kinda luck we have, it might take a while to skin 'em and reset the traps. I figure we might as well both go, like we always do, check 'em and set 'em as quick as we can. More'n likely that Indian is lookin' to find our traps, and he'll have to do that in the daylight. If we're downright unlucky, he mighta already found the ones we're checkin' tonight. So we'd best be real careful when we go, and if he ain't there, we'll get our business done as fast as the two of us can go. And get the hell back here."

"We ain't got many more days to trap," Jug said. "I reckon we'd best get 'em while we can. That's what we came here for."

With that decided, they climbed on their horses and set out in the darkness, following a tiny trail that wound around the high ridge that separated the two streams where their traps were set. At the foot of the ridge, the streams formed a small pond that fed a quiet creek that ran serpentine across a wide meadow. They were somewhat reassured when a new moon rose high enough to reflect off the snow of the grassy meadow, making it a difficult place for anyone to set up an ambush. "That's where we're gonna find the beaver," Luke predicted as he looked out across the meadow.

"Amen," Jug agreed. "We'll find out for sure in the mornin' when we get done with these two streams. Leastways, I'm pretty sure I'll move outta my stream in the mornin'." Luke wasn't sure he would be ready to abandon the stream he was working. It was still producing some good pelts. Wasting no more time, they split up to check their traps, then went into the frigid water to reset those that had caught beaver. It was a good night as far as the yield was concerned and they had no uninvited visitors. They skinned their catch and returned to their camp satisfied to find everything just as it was when they had left.

"That was a pretty good day's work," Jug commented as he sat before the fire, examining one of the firs they had just brought back. "Look at that," he said, holding the pelt up for Luke to see. "That's prime beaver. He's got his winter fir growed in real thick. That's a six-dollar plew."

Luke smiled. "They're prime, all right," he agreed, but he knew they'd be fortunate to get four dollars. And there wouldn't be many more days to work. "It's so blamed cold, I don't know how many days we've got left. I reckon you noticed that thin little crust of ice that's startin' to form along the banks."

"I noticed it, all right," Jug replied. "I don't know if we're gonna have time to run that whole creek out to the river before the winter shuts us down. We'll see what that creek looks like in the mornin'." He cocked his head to the side, which by now was a clue to Luke that he was about to hear a story that might, or might not, be totally true. "That freeze can strike without no warnin' a-tall. I remember year before last, in the Wind River Mountains, at the end of the season, I checked my traps one night, just like we just did tonight. And the next mornin' that stream I was workin' was froze solid. I had to use my axe to chop my traps outta that stream. There was a beaver on one of 'em, stiff as a board." He paused, waiting for Luke's response. When Luke only smiled, Jug went to another subject. "You did a right nice job on our little tipi. I think it's even warmer with the floor sunk like this. I can even stand up straight. Too bad your mama never told you when it was time to stop growin'."

"I reckon so," Luke replied, but Jug's remark caused him to think about his mother for the first time in many years. Georgia Ransom, a woman he really didn't know at all, because she walked out the back door when he was five years old and never came back. She ladled out a plate of grits and two sausage links and placed it on the kitchen table. She told him to sit down at the table and eat, then went out the door, and that was the last he ever saw of her. He lived with his father for a couple of years after that, but Jake Ransom was not a man suited to raise a small boy. Luke guessed he couldn't complain. His father fed him and gave him a place to sleep until he was seven. Then one night, his father didn't come home. He stayed there in that house for a week before George and Vera Spanner came to the house and said they were his aunt and uncle, and he was going to live with them.

They were fine folks. Aunt Vera was his father's sister, and she often told him what a good man his father was until Georgia Jones moved in with him. She said he had some problems, so that was why she brought Luke to live with her and her husband on their farm. She never told him what the problems were, but when he got a little older, Luke figured out his pa's only problem was him. To pay for his room and board, Luke worked hard on the farm, and when he reached his sixteenth birthday, he set out on his own, working at whatever employment he could find. When he saw the advertisement in the paper for men to keelboat up the Missouri to its end, to trap beaver for the American Fur Company, he knew that was what he wanted to do. So he really couldn't recall much of anything his mama might have told him. But he was grateful for George and Vera Spanner. They took him in after he had been abandoned and treated him kindly, and Aunt Vera taught him how to read and write. He had no complaints.

At a distance of two and a half miles away, as the crow flies, separated by two small mountains, the Blackfoot warrior Standing Elk sat cross-legged in front of a small fire. Sitting before the small shelter he had formed, binding pine boughs into the shape of a cone and covering it with a heavy buffalo hide, he contemplated his search. Oblivious to the snowflakes falling softly to the ground around him, his hooded robe of antelope hide over his head and shoulders, he, too, feared the possibility of a hard freeze. If that happened, the trapper would crawl into a hole somewhere and would be much harder to find. He had traced miles of streams that day, looking for the tell-tale little bait sticks stuck into the edges of the banks, but he found none. His frustration was multiplied by the fact that the trapper set his traps at night. So, even though he had found no traps today, the trapper might set traps tonight in the streams he had searched that day. Such was his exasperation that he wished he could stand at the top of this mountain now towering above him and shout out a challenge to this trapper to meet him in mortal combat. "I will find you, white man, no matter how long it takes," he promised himself.

They woke before daylight the next morning as usual, although they were a little later than their normal time. Jug blamed their "laziness" on the modifications to their tipi. "With that sunken floor, the fire kept the tipi warmer, made for good sleepin'." His comment rang true as soon as they went outside in the frigid air. Saddling up quickly, they rode out of their camp toward a bright moon lying low upon the hills. It was a sight meant to fool you, Luke thought, for the skies to the northwest were heavy with dark clouds. Reading his thoughts, Jug said, "It's fixin' to come up a storm." After a short ride, they came to the ridge and Jug dismounted to start his inspection of his traps, while Luke headed Smoke up over the ridge to his stream on the other side.

The harvest went about as each man had predicted. Luke was pleased to find four of his traps had been sprung, so he decided to reset those traps and leave the others for one more day. When he had done that, he started skinning the beaver he had caught. On the other side of the ridge, Jug was disappointed to find only two traps sprung, but he was not surprised. So he pulled his traps out of the stream and moved on down it to the base of the ridge where the pond was formed. Certain of beaver there, because of the lodge constructed on one side, he went to work setting a couple of his traps in the pond. Moving as fast as he could, he left the pond and followed the creek out into the meadow, berating himself for sleeping too late. "We ain't got much time before this crick will be solid ice," he mumbled. "We'll have all winter to lay around sleepin'." He wasn't sure what had happened in the next instant. He felt a blow on his shoulder that staggered him, causing him to drop the traps he was carrying. Only then, did he hear the sound, and he realized he'd been shot.

His next thought was to drop to the ground before the shooter had time to reload his weapon. To take cover from another shot, he rolled over the bank of the creek. He wasn't sure how badly he was hurt, but he was sure it was in his shoulder and not his back. The problem was he couldn't get to his rifle without coming out of the creek, but he had his pistol in his belt, so he could protect himself if the shooter came to finish him off. He began to feel a heavy numbness in his right hand as the pain began to increase in his shoulder. He pulled his heavy elk hide coat aside to reveal a bloody stain spreading on the shoulder of the antelope shirt he wore. He thought of Luke and hoped he hadn't been surprised, too, and might be lying dead with an arrow in his back. But then, he told himself he had been walking away from the ridge when he was shot, so the Blackfoot was hidin' somewhere in the meadow. He was probably in the creek, the same as he was. Luke had to have heard the shot. Jug hoped he wouldn't come running to see what the trouble was and end up shot like he was.

I should have waited, Standing Elk thought as he hurried to reload his gun. *He might have come closer if I had waited*. He had been lying there so long, hoping the trapper would come, that it had been hard to let him get closer, especially when he appeared to be contemplating wading into the water. He was surprised when the trapper rode down from the ridge and dismounted. He had not expected to see a short little man with a long gray beard. Only then did it strike him, the tracks he had read as a trapper and his woman were actually tracks left by two trappers. For surely, the other one was a big man. When it appeared the two of them were not trapping together, he had decided to go ahead and take the shot. He had hit him, but he wasn't sure how badly the man was hurt. He had rolled over the edge of the bank and had not raised his head again. Thinking he would like to finish him and take his gray scalp, Standing Elk rose up slightly from the creekbank, his gun ready to fire at the first sign of return fire. Over one hundred yards of winding creek lay between him and his wounded victim. He started to advance, slowly and carefully, wary of any sudden retaliation.

Close to three hundred yards away, Luke rode down through the firs that covered the ridge, dodging the boughs of the trees as Smoke wove his way through the heavy forest. He had dropped the pelts he was scraping when he heard the shot. Alarmed at once when he heard it, he was drastically worried now when he could not see Jug anywhere, even though his horse was standing beside the creek. A moment later, he saw Standing Elk climb up from the creekbank and advance toward Jug's horse. With only one thought, to stop him, Luke reined Smoke back hard and jumped out of the saddle. His rifle already loaded, he poured powder in the flashpan as he ran to find a clear shot. He was afraid he was a little too far for an accurate shot, but he knew he had no time to get any closer. He dropped down on one knee and took aim. As soon as he squeezed the trigger, he immediately grabbed his powder horn, then rammed another ball and patch down the barrel while still looking to see if his shot had landed true. *Gotta get closer,* he thought as he saw his shot kick up dirt just short of the Blackfoot's feet.

The shot was close enough to let Standing Elk know he was at a distinct disadvantage out in the middle of the wide meadow. There was cover in the creek, but he might be pinned down there indefinitely. Thinking it foolish to remain there until the trapper got within range, Standing Elk decided to withdraw and wait for a better opportunity. He turned and sprinted out of the meadow and into the trees on the other side where he had tied his horse.

Seeing him running, Luke's first thought was to go back to his horse and chase after him. But he thought of Jug then and the possibility he might be seriously wounded and need help right away. That being more important, he ran back and climbed on Smoke, then rode back to look for Jug. He found him on the creekbank close to the pond, his horse still standing ten yards away. "Jug!" Luke called out as he reined Smoke to a stop and came out of the saddle. "Are you all right?"

Jug peered over the bank at his partner. "That damn Injun shot me in the shoulder. My rifle is still on my saddle. I mighta got to it, but the way my arm feels, I wasn't sure I could use it. So I just sat back here and took it easy and waited for you to come get me. That's what you're good at, ain't it?"

"Well, I ain't that good at it," Luke said, relieved to see Jug wasn't in serious trouble, "'cause I took a shot at him and missed him. If you can ride, I think we'd best get outta here before he decides to take another shot at us out here in the open."

"I can ride," Jug replied. "Just gimme a hand outta this creek."

Luke took hold of Jug's good hand and pulled him up on the bank. Then he picked up his traps and helped him on his horse, and they turned around to go back the way they had come into the valley. "Ride right on up beside the ridge. I'm goin' up the other side to pick up some pelts I was workin' on, and I'll cross back over to your side."

Jug didn't wait for any further instructions and started up the slope beside the ridge right away. He was intercepted by Luke a few minutes later, when Luke came across the top of the ridge and fell in behind him. "Maybe I'd best take a look at that wound before we go any farther," Luke called out to him, afraid Jug might still be losing a lot of blood.

But Jug insisted he was all right. "Let's get on back to the camp. I think I got the bleedin' stopped. I stuffed my bandanna in my shirt. This heavy ol' buffalo coat musta helped slow that rifle ball down. Let's just make sure we don't lead that damn Injun back to our camp."

Fully expecting the trapper to follow him, Standing Elk made no effort to hide his trail as he rode through the forest of fir trees, for he intended to ambush his pursuer. When he came to a ravine leading up the mountain he was now approaching, he turned his horse into it and rode a dozen yards up it. When he was sure the horse was out of sight, he slid off his back and tied it there. Then he returned to the mouth of the ravine to set himself up for the ambush he planned. This time, the white devil would be riding straight to him. He would wait for him to come close enough to make sure he couldn't miss. He was sure the man who would be following the trail he had purposefully left for him was the man who had killed his brother and his friends. He couldn't imagine that the little gray-haired man he had shot was the killer of Iron Pony and the other two Blackfoot warriors. This man coming now must be a strong warrior, he thought. He would wait until he was sure he could place his shot where he wanted it, in the center of his chest. Then, if he was lucky, he could get to him before he died, so he could tell him that it is Standing Elk who takes his life. Then he would take his scalp while he still lived to feel the pain, and Iron Pony would be avenged.

He waited patiently, although eager, to have this confrontation he so desired, but the white killer did not come. And when he didn't, Standing Elk's next thought was that the trapper suspected an ambush. He immediately turned to make sure he hadn't circled around to attack him from behind. He hurried to the opposite side of the ravine to peer intently into the trees behind him. After a few minutes and seeing no sign, he returned to stare at the trail he had left from the meadow, finally realizing there was no pursuit. The white devil wasn't coming after him. That told him that the trapper feared him and had run away. "It will do you no good," Standing Elk declared aloud. "I have a trail to follow now." He went to get his horse from the ravine and immediately rode back the way he had just fled.

When he reached the meadow again, he paused for a few seconds in the tree line to make sure there was no one there. Certain then, he rode out to the creek and followed it back toward the mountain. He paused again for just a moment when he came to the spot, just short of the pond, where he had shot the little man.

There were plenty of tracks in the light covering of snow to tell him the bigger trapper had ridden his horse there to pick up the one he had wounded. When the tracks led back toward the ridge, Standing Elk grunted in contempt, "They run to hide now." He followed their tracks up past the pond, but then the tracks separated to climb up the slope on both sides of the ridge, holding close to the two streams that joined to form the pond. Earlier, when he first discovered the bait sticks in the bank of the stream, he had not thought to scout the creek that ran down the other side of the ridge. It wouldn't have made any difference to him, anyway, they had traps in this stream, they would come to check them. As he thought about it now, he realized this was the reason the unseen one was able to surprise him. Following them now, he had no idea which set of tracks rode out of the valley on the left side of the ridge, and which one went up the right. He would have preferred to know, for one of them was a gray-haired little man who had been wounded. The other was a big man that he knew nothing about. He would have to be wary of him. He decided to follow the tracks up the right side because that was the side he had come down when his partner was shot. To confirm it, he found the remains of the beaver Luke had skinned. Had he waited in the fir trees on that side of the ridge, he quite possibly might have gotten a shot at the big trapper. After climbing three-quarters of the way up the stream, he came to the point where Luke crossed over the top of the ridge to join Jug on the other stream. The combined tracks continued for a short distance until reaching another stream where the tracks entered the water but didn't come out on the other side. Much to his annoyance, he found that the stream joined another before he had ridden very far and he could not determine if the two horses he tracked stayed in the first stream or switched to the alternate stream. He decided that they probably switched, so he continued on in that stream, walking his horse slowly so as not to miss any sign left by the trappers' horses. It was apparent that his instincts had been correct when his sharp eye spotted one hoofprint at the edge of the stream.

The dawning of the new day began to lift the darkness up from the thick forest. It gave him hope that he would now see more signs that would tell him which way they went. But there was nothing more to give him any indication of which way they had gone. He clinched his teeth in anger when he reached a fork in the stream he was now following and realized it joined the creek that ran north of the ridge. And that was the creek that the big trapper had come down that morning. If he continued, he would wind up right back at the pond at the base of the ridge. He was struck with the realization that he had been led in a circle, outfoxed by the white men. Every muscle in his powerful body tensed in anger, and he vowed anew that he would search every blade of grass if he had to. But they must die.

Chapter 8

"I swear, if I hadn'ta knowed better, I'da thought you was lost," Jug declared when Luke offered an arm to assist him off his horse. "Danged if that weren't the most roundabout way to get back to this camp I've ever seen."

"Well, you said you were all right," Luke replied, "and your shoulder wasn't hurtin' too bad. So I thought you'd rather take the long way home, instead of bringin' that Injun back with us to get another shot at you."

"If you'd found a couple more cricks to ride up, my shoulder mighta healed up by the time we got here," Jug cracked. "Might be, we shoulda stopped and set a few traps in some of them streams."

"If it weren't for the fact we've already trapped out all those streams between here and that ridge, I mighta given that some thought," Luke retorted. Then becoming serious for a moment, he looked at Jug and said, "I believe we probably lost him. Whaddaya think?"

"I feel pretty sure we did," Jug answered. "He'd be showin' up about now, if we didn't. He sure messed up our trappin' this mornin', though, didn't he?"

"Yes, sir, he sure did," Luke responded. "Now, we'd best take a look at that shoulder and see just how bad it is. Tell you what, why don't you go on in the tipi and stir that fire up again while I take care of these horses? I'll get a pan of water to heat up, and we'll clean it up a little and decide what we can do to patch you up. I might need you with that crazy buck runnin' around out there, lookin' for us."

"I expect you might," Jug said. "Although you're the Injun killer in this partnership. I was gonna tell that Blackfoot gentleman that you're the man he needs to talk to about killin' Injuns. But he up and put a lead ball in me before I had a chance to explain it."

"What is it about you that makes Blackfoot Indians wanna shoot at you?" Luke asked.

"It's kinda the same thing that makes the saloon ladies wanna set on my knee," Jug replied, stroking his beard. "They don't get to see real mountain men as good lookin' as I am. With the Injun bucks, they're just afraid all their squaws will wanna run off with me." Luke just shook his head and started taking the saddles off the horses. "We're gonna need some breakfast, too," Jug called back over his shoulder as he walked boldly toward the tipi.

Luke shook his head and smiled as he watched the little man depart. *I was afraid I'd lost him today,* he thought. *He acts like he's proud he got shot.* His mind switched back to the cause of their joking, very much aware that the fierce-looking Blackfoot warrior he saw from a distance that morning was no joking matter. Luke was certain that this Indian was not going to give up his search for the two of them. And he didn't care how well hidden their little valley was, with whatever was driving him, revenge or pure hatred for whites, the Blackfoot was bound to stumble on their camp, sooner or later. For that reason, it was critical that they find him before he found them. *But now,* Luke thought, *the first thing to do is to see how bad Jug's wound is.* He pulled the saddles off the two horses and released them to join the others near the pond.

When he carried the two saddles into the tipi to place each one at the head of the owner's bedroll, he found Jug carefully removing his heavy buffalo coat. He had restarted the fire in the middle of the tipi and already had a strong flame going. "Let me give you a hand gettin' that shirt off," he told him and together they managed to pull it up over Jug's head while he remained as tight-lipped as he could to hide the pain. Once they got it off, they both were in a hurry to inspect the damage. "Did you get a good look?" Luke asked. "If you'd get your nose out of it, maybe I could see it, too."

"Hell, it's *my* dang shoulder," Jug shot back, but he moved his head back so Luke could see it. "It don't look too bad, but it's startin' to pain me a little. He did more harm to my blame coat—put a hole right through the fur collar and the hide coat."

Inspecting the wound carefully, Luke replied, "It's a good thing he did 'cause all that buffalo helped slow down that rifle ball. I'll bet that ball ain't in you that deep."

"I ain't sure I like the sound of that," Jug asserted. "Sounds like you're thinkin' about diggin' around in that hole, and I ain't sure that's necessary."

"Are you sayin' you'd rather carry a piece of lead around in your shoulder than feel a little bit of pain?" Luke chided. "I'll get a pan of water to heat up and we'll clean that up, so we can get a better look at it." He picked up the pan and went out to the waterfall to fill it. When he returned, he set the pan at the edge of the fire to let it sit for a while. "Is there anything left in that jug of yours?" He asked him. Jug said there was, but not enough to waste on a little hole that would heal up on its own. "Won't need but a splash of it," Luke said, "and that'll help it to not get infected. I'll put a little on my knife, too, to make sure you don't catch nothin' from those beaver I cut up this mornin'."

"Your knife?" Jug reacted at once. "You ain't gonna be doin' no cuttin' on me."

"I might be able to dislodge that rifle ball, if it ain't too deep. You druther I use my axe?" Luke was downright amazed to find the depth of the little man's squeamishness, considering his typical tough-talking persona.

In a short time, the water in the pan became hot, so Luke got some rags from his packs and cleaned the blood from Jug's shoulder. He thought he could almost see the piece of lead in Jug's shoulder. It looked as if the muscle the bullet had lodged in was already trying to reject the foreign object. He tilted the whiskey jug just enough to trickle some of the precious liquid onto his knifepoint. "Careful with that stuff," Jug cautioned.

"Hold still!" Luke warned. "I'm liable to cut your arm off." He proceeded to insert the tip of his skinnin' knife into the hole in Jug's flesh. When Jug flinched with the sudden pain, Luke pushed the knife in, until he felt the contact with the lead ball. "There it is. Just what I thought, it ain't that deep." With Jug sucking his breath sharply through his clenched teeth, Luke made one more little thrust, enough to dislodge the ball and it came out with Luke's blade.

Relaxing immediately, Jug exhaled and said, "That weren't so bad a-tall . . . dang!" He bellowed half a second later when Luke poured a shot of whiskey in the wound. "Whatchu do that for?"

Luke gave him a big grin. "I just thought you'd probably enjoy a shot of whiskey right now. I'll see if I can rig you up with a bandage for that wound." He got the rest of the old bedsheet he carried for that purpose out of his packs. "You think you're gonna need a sling to hold your arm up?" Jug said he didn't think so. "Then I reckon that's all I can do for you," Luke said. "I reckon now I'm gonna build a pot of coffee and we'll roast a little deer meat for breakfast." He picked up the pot and went out to the waterfall to fill it. When the pot was full, he remained there for a few minutes to observe the new day. He turned and looked toward the west and the clouds moving in over the mountains, and he had a feeling it was soon going to be bitter cold. He turned back to focus his gaze on the grove of cottonwoods at the base of the mountain, and the meadow beyond the trees. He still thought it the perfect spot for their camp, but he also knew it inevitable that the Blackfoot warrior would eventually find this hidden valley. Like any wild animal, he would prefer to go into his winter hibernation without the worry of a predator. "I'm gonna have to find that son of a gun, because he ain't gonna give up searchin' for me."

When he went back inside the tipi, Jug was roasting some venison strips over the fire, working one-handed, his right arm hanging limp and useless like a dead limb. "I was startin' to wonder what happened to you," he said. "Thought you mighta got out there and had heat-stroke or somethin'."

Ignoring the sarcasm, Luke responded seriously. "You know we can't sit around in this camp and wait for that Indian to find us. We've got to find him first, and the sooner the better. I ain't plannin' to sit around here all winter, waitin' for him to stumble on this valley. So after I have some breakfast, I'm gonna go see if I can pick up his trail, either where he came into that valley, or where we lost him when we were on the run. If I'da known you weren't hurt that bad, I mighta set up an ambush and waited for him to follow us. Now I'm gonna have to track him. And after takin' a good look at those clouds rollin' in over the mountains, I think there's a good chance we're gonna get more snow tonight. So I need to get back to that valley while there's still some tracks to see. Maybe I'll get lucky."

Jug nodded thoughtfully as he listened to Luke's comments about their predicament. When he was finished, Jug added his thoughts on the matter. "What you're sayin' is true, partner. That Injun has got killin' on his mind, and with a savage like that, he ain't gonna quit till he gets it done. So we need to get on his trail pretty quick. We'll split up, so we can cover more ground."

Luke paused to think about that for a moment. "Maybe so, but maybe not today. Might be a good idea if you stayed here today and guard our camp, and I'll go scout his trail while there're still tracks to be seen." Jug started to protest right away, but Luke stopped him. "Can you shoot a rifle? Can you even hold it up to your right shoulder to shoot it?"

"If I had to do it to keep from gettin' shot, I reckon I damn-sure would," Jug answered. "Ain't nothin' wrong with my eyes, I could go with you and help you track him."

"That's right, you could, but I still think it'd be best for you to stay here and keep an eye on the camp. If you needed to, you could shoot your pistol with your left hand. Reloadin' might give you some trouble, but I could leave you my pistol, too." He saw him starting to fret, so he couldn't resist japing him. "You weren't thinkin' too good this mornin' when he showed up. You shoulda stuck your left shoulder out to get shot, instead of your right one."

"I think I oughta be out there helpin' you track him," Jug insisted.

Luke sought to encourage him, "Listen, that wound ain't that bad. And I know it's feelin' stiff and painful right now. But if you take it easy with it today, you might be able to use it more tomorrow or the next day. If you don't rest it for a couple of days, it might take a whole lot longer to start healin'." He didn't really have any idea if that would be the case or not. He just thought he didn't want to have to worry about Jug getting caught in an ambush that he might have led him into. Let me go see if I can back-track his trail today. I might get lucky and find his camp. If I do, then we'll decide how best to hit him. All right?"

"Hell, I reckon," Jug replied, "if that's the way you wanna work it. Like you said, you can leave me with your pistol, too. If he gets that close to this camp, I can sure as hell handle a pistol."

"Good," Luke said. "I'll let Smoke take a little rest, he ain't been rode that far, but he'd most likely appreciate a little grass and water. While he's doin' that, I'll drink some coffee and eat some of that meat you're cookin' there."

When he was ready, he climbed up into the saddle, and he and Smoke headed out toward the creek that divided the meadow beyond the cottonwoods again. Once he was sure he had left no tracks out of their camp, he turned the bay gelding toward the mountain where they had been trapping that morning. To begin his scout, he decided he would try to pick up the Blackfoot's tracks at the point where he figured they had managed to lose him. So he rode to the cross stream where he had purposely guided Smoke close to the bank to leave a single hoofprint. If he was lucky, the Indian would not be worried about covering his tracks at that point in his pursuit and might have been a little careless in hiding his trail. A quick look told him that the hoof-print he had purposefully left had not been disturbed, so he figured the Indian had not missed it and continued on. In that case, he would have wound up back at the bottom of the hill at the pond. Luke went straight back there, hoping to pick up a fresh set of tracks from that point, which would lead him to the Blackfoot's camp.

When he arrived at the bottom of the ridge and scouted the area where the two streams combined to form the pond, he found no fresh tracks that would tell him where the Blackfoot had left that area. So the Blackfoot had not followed the streams all the way back to this starting point. But surely, he had not followed the stream in the opposite direction, Luke thought, for that would have led him straight up a mountain. *Now he's got me confused*, he thought as he turned Smoke up the stream again. There was nothing to do but follow the streams around again to try to find new tracks leaving the water. He couldn't help the feeling that the Blackfoot warrior was laughing at him right then. *You can't out-Indian an Indian*, he thought.

This time, when he got back to the one hoofprint by the bank, he paused there a few minutes to scout the bank for any sign that Standing Elk had searched for more prints before continuing on in the stream. There were none. He proceeded on another thirty yards and stopped in the midst of a large stand of lodgepole pines. There, by a bank covered with a thick layer of pine needles, was where he and Jug had left the water. While the two horses had stood in the stream, Luke had hastily gathered pine limbs and branches to place on top of the pine straw before he carefully led the horses out of the stream. He had left them waiting a couple dozen yards away while he went back and removed the branches and returned the appearance of the bank to its original. Then they had angled across the slope, through the pines, heading for home.

Returning to the spot on this second trip around, Luke was halfway out of the saddle before Smoke came to a stop. Unnoticed the first time, it now struck him that the pine needles had been disturbed since he had arranged them to disguise their exit from the stream. The Blackfoot had outsmarted him, and now, a sense of panic set in. Once they had left the stream earlier, they made less of an effort to hide their tracks until they were close to the camp. The Blackfoot assassin was on his way to their camp, even now. He and Jug had taken their usual precautions before actually entering the valley and their camp. But he was afraid the Indian would find it after their tracks led him so close to it. "Oh, Lord," he prayed, as he jumped in the saddle. "I may have set Jug up for his death." Asking Smoke for all the speed he could give him, he headed for the camp.

It had taken him longer than he would have liked, but when the tracks he followed stopped once he reached a small stream, Standing Elk sensed that he must be close to the white man's camp. He took a few moments more to look over the way before him. The stream he had now come to appeared to run down into a grassy meadow to flow into a creek that split the meadow. With his eyes, he followed the creek back until it disappeared into a grove of cottonwoods. He felt almost sure that the camp he sought would lie beyond that grove of trees. From where he sat on his horse, he couldn't see farther up the slope, so he decided he would climb up the side of the hill and approach the camp from above it. There might be a warm welcome for anyone approaching from the meadow.

As he climbed up through the forest of fir trees, he was surprised to hear the sound of a waterfall. He cut straight across the slope until he came to the falls and stopped before riding out of the cover of the trees when he saw the horses grazing beside the pond at the bottom of the falls. Farther down the slope, beside the creek formed by the waterfall, he saw the trappers' tipi. It brought a smile to his face, for it was set up to face an attack from the front. He remained there for a short while to look over the camp. There appeared to be no one there, so he slid off his horse and advanced toward the tipi on foot.

Inside the tipi, Jug pushed the back flap of their tent open just far enough for him to see the pond and the horses. It was something he did every once in a while in an effort to keep a watchful eye on the camp. But this time, he flinched when he saw Standing Elk trotting down toward him in a crouch, a Northwest Trade Gun in his hand. He almost choked to keep from exclaiming his alarm as he grabbed the loaded rifle he had by his side and poked it through the back flap. Working as fast as he could with one arm, he tried to sight it on the approaching warrior, cocked it, and pulled the trigger. The rifle failed to fire. In a real panic now, Jug reached for his powder horn. With every movement awkward because it was done with his left hand, he splashed some powder on the flash pan and tried again. This time the rifle fired, startling the Blackfoot warrior. He had not noticed the rifle barrel when Jug slid it out the flap, but the shot was far to the right of him. Thinking the shooter could not see very easily out the small opening in the back of the tipi, Standing Elk sprinted to one side and dived on the ground, rolling over and over until the angle was too much for the shooter to take aim at him. Without stopping, he came to his feet and lunged into the entrance of the tipi in time to grab Jug as he was reaching for the loaded pistol in his belt. Like a giant cat, the Blackfoot warrior attacked him, clamping an iron hand over Jug's, so he could not pull the pistol, while he trapped Jug's wounded arm to his side, rendering him helpless. He smiled in Jug's face then, his own face only inches from Jug's. "So, little dung beetle, I didn't kill you the first time. This time I'll make sure you're dead." He spoke in his native tongue, but Jug knew enough of it to understand what he was saying. Standing Elk squeezed harder and harder on Jug's trigger finger until it finally fired. With the pistol still in his belt, the lead ball tore through Jug's trousers, just missing his leg.

The powerful Blackfoot warrior, with his arm still locking Jug's arms to his side, picked up the smaller man, much like a disobedient child. Carrying his rifle in the other hand, he stepped up from the sunken floor of the tipi effortlessly and went outside. "Where is your big friend, little man?"

"I expect he's gone to your village where he's sleepin' with your wife," Jug retorted defiantly. It earned him a sharp blow to the side his face.

"The only thing big about you is your mouth," Standing Elk scoffed. "You are not worth powder and shot, so I am going to cut your guts out and let you hold them while you're dying."

"I wouldn't expect much else from a coward like you," Jug declared, still defiant.

"Little Big Mouth," Standing Elk said in disgust. Seeing a coil of rope hanging on the side of the tipi, he reached up and took it, still holding Jug prisoner with one arm. Then he released him long enough to strike him with his rifle butt, hard enough to knock him down. And while Jug was struggling senselessly, he tied Jug's hands behind his back, then tied them to his ankles. With his gun ready to fire, Standing Elk took a few minutes to look around the clearing to make sure Luke wasn't around. With no sign of the big trapper, he decided it best to find a place of cover to wait for him to return to camp. He was sure Luke was looking for him somewhere. He would wait in ambush for him. That decided, he went back to the tipi to settle with Jug, who was still lying on his side, hands and feet tied. "On your knees!" Standing Elk ordered. He grabbed a handful of Jug's hair and pulled him up on his knees. Then he took his scalping knife and cut the ties holding Jug's coat closed. Next, he opened Jug's shirt with a slash of his knife to expose his belly. "Now we will take a look at your guts, Little Big Mouth, and see how you like to wear them on the outside. First, I'll take that gray scalp." He reached over and grabbed Jug's hair again. Jug's reaction was to stare defiantly at him, refusing to give him the satisfaction of seeing him beg for mercy. He braced himself, waiting to feel the sting of the Indian's knife as he ripped the scalp from his head. But Standing

Elk grunted, his eyes opened wide in surprise and he released Jug's hair and slowly turned around. When he did, Jug saw the arrow, the shaft buried halfway in his back. Then he saw Luke, some twenty yards behind, taking aim, his bow fully drawn. A fraction of a second later, Luke released the bowstring, sending a second arrow on its way to bury with a thud in Standing Elk's chest.

The fierce Blackfoot warrior took two steps toward Luke before he sank to one knee and stared down in shocked disbelief at the shaft protruding from his chest. Knowing the life was draining from his body, he looked as if he didn't understand. Seeing no reason to let him suffer for long, Luke drew his knife and slit his throat, then pushed him over on the ground. With the execution over, he looked at Jug. "Are you all right?"

Still somewhat in between fact and illusion, Jug shook his head in an effort to clear it. When he finally answered, he seemed to have regained his normal cockiness. "Yeah, I'm all right. I'm a little tied-up right now, though. Was there somethin' you wanted?" He paused for a few seconds for Luke's reaction before demanding, "Untie me, for Pete's sake!"

Greatly relieved to see his partner was, indeed, all right, Luke replied in kind. "I don't know, I think I like you a little better that way."

"How come you used that bow, instead of just shootin' that fool Injun?" Jug asked, as Luke was untying him.

"I thought he deserved gettin' killed Injun-style," Luke said. "Maybe that'll get him a bigger tipi when he gets to the happy huntin' ground."

Jug cocked a doubting eye at him. "Nah, why did you use that bow?" He was thinking that it had been a hell of a time for Luke to be playing Indian.

"Tell you the truth," Luke said, "I used my bow because I knew I could get two shots off quicker with a bow than I could with my rifle. And at that close a distance, I knew I wasn't gonna miss. If I shot him with my rifle and it didn't stop him, he mighta shot me while I was reloadin' my rifle. I didn't have my other rifle with me, and I left my pistol with you. Bow's quicker—first arrow on the way, second arrow already notched and ready to fly."

Jug considered that for a moment before commenting, "You know, I reckon you're right at that. 'Cause he turned around after that first arrow drove in his back. You standin' out there in the open with nothin' to take cover behind, if you'da shot him with your rifle, you'da been tryin' like hell to get it reloaded before he shot you." He thought about it some more. "Hard to say, at that close range, your rifle mighta knocked him down. 'Course, I might coulda grabbed his rifle then before he got it."

"You were tied up, hand and foot," Luke reminded him.

"Yep, there's that to consider," Jug allowed. "How'd you know to come back here?" Luke told him about his tracking of the Indian and admitted that he had not been so smart in his attempts to hide their trail. "Well, don't feel bad," Jug said. "You ain't been ridin' these mountains as long as I have. There's a whole lot more to learn."

Luke grinned and shook his head. "I don't know if I'll ever get old enough to know everything you know," he said facetiously. "Maybe you've got a good idea where his camp is 'cause I need to find it. I feel pretty sure he's got a packhorse there that might be tied up. I know he wasn't carryin' much on that gray he rides. I found that gray back yonder in the woods. That's how I knew for sure he was in our camp. I'm gonna go back there and get him." He took another look at Standing Elk's body and said, "Then I reckon we'd best tidy up our camp a little bit."

Jug stood there and watched his partner as he strode back toward the forest. *Danged if that ain't another time he saved my gray old behind from getting killed by Injuns,* he thought. *Best decision I ever made was partnering-up with Luke Ransom.*

Chapter 9

Finding himself with another body to dispose of, Luke thought about taking Standing Elk's corpse back to the mountain where he had dumped the other three Indians' bodies. This one had gone to a lot of trouble to bury the bodies of his three fellow tribesmen. It might mean a lot to the Indian's spirit to go to the great beyond with his brothers. But it was only a thought. He didn't feel compassionate enough to go to the trouble. That mountain was a couple of miles away, and he sure as hell wasn't going to dig up that crevice to bury this one. So Standing Elk's body was deposited in another rocky crevice on the backside of the mountain where their camp was located—approximately half a mile from the camp.

"Did you get your arrows outta him?" Jug asked when Luke returned.

"No," Luke replied. "As a matter of fact, I didn't. I've got plenty of arrows and I got to thinkin'. If some other Blackfoot hunters come across his body, they'll think he was killed by a Blackfoot, and not a white trapper."

"That's good thinkin'," Jug responded, forming the picture of it in his head. "They might even start suspectin' each other."

Back to a subject that he was compassionate about, Luke said, "I reckon the next thing I need to do is to see if I can find this fellow's camp. He mighta left his other horse loose to graze and water, but I kinda doubt it. It'd be good if I could find him today. We've gotta set some traps tonight." He paused to add, "At least, I do, since you ain't got but one good arm. But this weather's too cold to leave a horse tied to a tree all day and all night."

"I'll go with you this time," Jug said. "I don't think we have to worry about leavin' our camp today. We ain't seen no sign of any more Injuns close around here."

Luke agreed. They left their extra horses free to graze close to the pond, thinking they would not likely wander. Their only real worry was the possibility of a bear plundering their tipi and destroying it. Their supply of meat was in bundles, hanging high up from the ground, too high for a bear to jump, and hanging from limbs on long ropes. It was even secure in the event of a mountain lion's visit. So they mounted up again and set out for the spot where the whole business with Standing Elk started. It was their intention to try to find sign of his first entry into the little meadow where he shot Jug. It was Luke's idea to take Standing Elk's horse with them. He thought there might be a chance, if they got close to the Blackfoot's camp, that the horse might naturally wander back to the camp.

Jug was skeptical. "Maybe," he allowed. "Might depend on how often the Injun moved his camp. He might notta stayed in one spot long enough for the horse to call it home."

"He might get wind of the Indian's other horse before we did," Luke argued.

"Hell," Jug snorted, "our horses will get wind of that horse before we do."

"I know it," Luke said, getting impatient. "I just think it won't hurt to have any help we can get. If we was to strike just the tiniest little sign near that meadow where the creek is, and turn that gray loose, he just might save us some time and go right back the way he had come before."

"And he might take off for parts unknown," Jug replied, still skeptical. "Horses ain't that smart, and then we'll spend the rest of the day lookin' for the dang horse."

"I'm beginnin' to think I shoulda left you back at the camp," Luke commented. "I believe I'm startin' to see how it is to have a wife along to nag me."

"I had a wife once," Jug said. "Did I ever tell you about her?"

"No, but I'll bet you're goin' to," Luke answered as he tied a lead rope to the rope reins of the Blackfoot's horse.

"She was a big ol' gal," Jug went on, oblivious to his partner's sarcastic remark, "met her in a saloon in St. Louis. I was young as you at the time. And when I say big, I mean she wasn't just heavy, she was tall as a lodgepole pine." In spite of himself, Luke found his mind making up a picture of Jug and this Amazon as Jug continued. She taught me a helluva lot that I didn't know nothin' about at that age and said we oughta get married. I weren't doin' nothin' at the time, so I said, why not? They had a regular customer that was a preacher, and he hitched us up right there in the saloon. She said I reminded her of a pony. Said when she was a little girl, she always wanted a pony. But her folks didn't have no money to buy her one. She said, 'Now I got me a pony.'" He shook his head as he thought back. "I thought she'd quit workin' the saloon after we was married. But she said, 'And do what? Live off the money you're makin'?' Well, it was hard to argue that point, since I didn't have no job."

"Here, let me saddle your horse for you," Luke interrupted. "You can't do much with that bad arm."

"Obliged," Jug said, then picked up his story right where he was cut off. "So we just made do on what she could earn. And we got along pretty good for a while till this danged French trapper came down from Canada on a boatload of furs. He was damn-near as big as my Florina and he took a shine to her. Pretty soon, she told me she was puttin' her pony out to pasture and she was headin' back to Canada with that French trapper." He finally paused there as he seemed to be back there in his mind. Luke felt kinda sorry for the little old man and was about to tell him so, but Jug stopped him. "This weren't meant to be no sad story. Florina was one of the best things that ever happened to me. I wasn't doin' nothin' till I met up with her. But after she kicked me out, I decided to go to Canada and trap for furs, myself. It took a while, but I finally made it to where I am now, an independent businessman and indentured to no man."

Luke was frankly surprised. "You started out in this business in Canada?"

"I did," Jug replied.

"Up there in Hudson's Bay territory, right?"

"Yep," Jug said. "I told you that already when we started trappin' the Judith. I started out workin' for Hudson's Bay till I got to the place where you got to in your life. I didn't wanna work for no big company no more."

"Well, when we were back at rendezvous, I don't know if I'da partnered up with you if I'd known you were a Hudson's Bay man," Luke japed. "I mean, me bein' an American Fur man for five years." He watched Jug pull himself up into the saddle using his left arm. Then he stepped up on Smoke. "You know, if you'da told that Blackfoot you worked for Hudson's Bay, he mighta let you go."

They concentrated their search around the small meadow below the fork of the two streams they were trapping just before Standing Elk attacked. There were any number of game trails leading out of the forest and onto the grassy meadow. None showed any sign of a horse or man. The only real sign to follow was along the path of Standing Elk's flight from the meadow after Luke shot at him. The sign was so carelessly left, with broken branches and disturbed logs, that they both figured it was purposely so. When they reached the ravine where Standing Elk had laid in wait for Luke, it was obvious where he had knelt, ready to take the shot. "Well, there ain't no doubt he ran here when he thought you was chasin' him," Jug commented. "But that don't tell us a helluva lot, does it? 'Cause we know where he went from here. He came after us."

Luke was thinking the same thing, but he was not convinced

he was right. He thought back over the chain of events that led to Standing Elk's finding their camp. He looked at Jug and asked, "He came right after us, but it took him a pretty good while before he found our camp. I've been thinkin' it was because I covered our tracks so well, that it took him that long to find our trail. What if it didn't take him that long to find our trail? What if he found it the first time he rode around those streams?"

"I don't know," Jug answered, not sure what Luke was getting at. "What are you thinkin'?"

"I'm thinkin' that maybe we ain't too far from his camp right now. I know I never figured it would be south of this valley. But what if it is, and the reason it took him so long to find our camp was because he went back to his camp first, for whatever reason?"

Jug shrugged. "I don't know, Luke, it'd be one helluva coincidence."

"Well, I'm gonna look around for some sign, anyway," Luke said and started scouting the mouth of the ravine. "Right here is where he left his horse." He walked over and untied the lead rope from the gray's reins, then led the gelding over to the spot where the Blackfoot had tied him. Watching in fascinated wonder, thinking he was witnessing the progression of a man in the process of going crazy, Jug said nothing but smiled knowingly when the gray horse merely stood motionless in the spot Luke led him to. "Any time you're ready, boy," Luke encouraged the horse as he scouted around and around the spot where the horse stood, each circle a little bigger than the one before. Until, finally, he found what he was looking for, a solitary hoofprint. He paused and looked back at the horse, who appeared to be as confused as Jug. Luke looked in the direction the hoofprint was pointing and starting walking through the trees on that line. To Jug's amazement, the horse suddenly started walking after Luke, but he was still convinced that didn't prove anything. Luke stopped then and waited for the horse to catch up to him. The big gray horse plodded slowly along beside him until Luke gave it a swat on its croup. The horse jumped and started to lope, but then it slowed to an easy trot, and continued on the line Luke had started out in. Luke and Jug automatically broke into a trot behind the gray, with Jug still leading his and Luke's horses.

The ground rose slightly as they approached a low ridge. When the gray approached the ridge, they heard a nicker from a horse on the other side. It was answered by the gray and received a questioning whinny from the other horses. "Well, I'll be dipped in . . ." Jug started but didn't finished when Luke looked back at him and grinned triumphantly. They climbed over the ridge to find an anxious-looking buckskin shifting its feet nervously as the gray went up to say hello. It was as Luke had feared, the buckskin was tied to a tree with enough slack to reach a small stream, but there was nothing for it to graze. And in the event of another freezing night, there was very little shelter from the lodgepole pine it was tied to. "I swear, partner," Jug commented, "it looks like we're gettin' in the horse-raisin' business. We've got a sizable herd started already."

"Looks that way, don't it?" Luke responded and went at once to free the buckskin from the tree, and it immediately ran up along the ridge for about fifty yards before returning. Most likely to get warm, Luke thought. It went with the other horses then to graze in a small clearing of grass.

Across the stream, they saw the Indian's camp, a roughly built tipi of large limbs and branches with a buffalo hide over them to shelter him from the rain or snow. It was plain to see he had not intended to be staying there for long. His one purpose for being in this little chain of mountains was to exact his vengeance upon them. "It's hard to say whether we'll get any more visitors from his village or not," Jug commented.

"If those first three were anybody really important, maybe there woulda been a whole war party of Indians comin' here to find out what happened to 'em," Luke speculated hopefully. "Seein' as how there was just this one fellow that came lookin' for 'em, might be that that'll be the end of it. They came here to make meat for the winter, and their village is probably already moved to wherever they're plannin' to spend it. I'm hopin' we're done with 'em at least till the winter's over."

"You're probably right," Jug said. He knew Luke felt responsible for the trouble with the Indians because he had killed the three that this warrior had come looking for. "Things just happen the way they do. If them three bucks hadn'ta raided our camp, they wouldn'ta got kilt. It ain't your fault they decided to fight when you went after 'em. I'da done the same as you did, so don't go gettin' ideas in your head that I think you brought all this on. All right?"

"All right," Luke replied. "I 'preciate you sayin' that."

Like them, the Blackfoot had hung his supply of fresh meat on a rope, high off the ground. Luke lowered it to the ground, so he could take a look at it and decided he and Jug could use it. With the daytime temperatures already approaching freezing, the meat would keep for a long time, and they never felt like they had too much. He pulled the buffalo hide off the framework of limbs while Jug poked around in the makeshift tipi finding nothing of value. All the Indian's weapons and ammunition had been with him on the gray. They loaded anything they could use on the buckskin and the gray, then with each man leading a horse, they returned to their camp. Both of them were convinced that it was unlikely they would see any more Indians until after the winter, with the exception of an occasional hunting party. And if they were lucky, they might avoid those hunters.

With the threat of Standing Elk resolved, they could now concentrate on collecting as many beaver pelts as possible before the ponds froze. It was going to call for a lot more work on Luke's part, since his partner wasn't much good with just one hand. And during the daylight hours, Luke decided it was necessary to build a better windbreak and shelter for their little herd of horses. What with their own horses, and the horses Luke brought back after his fight with the original three Blackfoot, and now two more, thanks to Standing Elk, they really had more than they wanted to handle. But horses were money when rendezvous time came around again, so they were inclined to hold onto them if they could.

When darkness fell over the forest beside the grassy slope next to the falls, it found Luke working to construct three walls in his evergreen barn. Using young fir trees to weave their boughs in and out of the larger uprights that he had fixed there before, he was hoping to create a windbreak for his "barn." Jug cocked his head, a little skeptical, and commented. "I ain't ever seen nobody goin' to that much work to try to keep their horses warm before. It's lookin' mighty fancy. I hope the first strong north wind don't blow it all down."

"Oh, ye of little faith," Luke quoted. "The trees around it will keep the wind from blowin' it over. And after we get a little freezin' snow fallin' on it, it'll set up solid till the spring melt. In the meantime, the horses will keep each other warm inside there."

"You know them's horses you're fixin' to put in there, don'tcha? They ain't Eskimos." Jug felt it his duty to comment further. "I've waited out a good many winters in this business and my horses always made it through. Sometimes they looked mighty poorly and shaggy in the spring, but they made it through. Even if it is too hard on some of 'em to make it, that just gives us a supply of fresh meat. It wouldn't be the first time I et horse meat."

"I thought you said your horses always made it through the winter," Luke reminded him.

"I never said it was my horse I et. It was another feller's."

"Well, I don't wanna eat none of these horses we wound up with. I rather eat deer and elk," Luke told him. "And remember what you said the first time you saw this little valley. The game will be comin' to us. Now, I'm tired of jawin' here with you. I've gotta go set our traps. It's already gettin' dark."

"I'll be goin' with you," Jug said, in case Luke might think he was going to use his wound as an excuse to sit there by the fire.

"I figured," Luke said. "You've been itchin' to trap that pond and the creek down that meadow, so I didn't think you'd wanna miss it. I'll set the traps, and you can get the bait sticks ready with some medicine for me."

"Hell," Jug replied, "I can set the bait sticks with one hand, if you're gonna be settin' all the traps."

"I just thought you might not wanna go in the water with your bad arm and all. You best keep that arm dry."

"I'll keep both of my arms dry," Jug insisted. "It's just my feet I'm gonna get wet."

Even though they were sure there were no Indians anywhere close to their camp now, still there was a feeling of uneasiness in both men as they rode out of their camp into the darkness of the firs. After the events of the last few days, it was a natural tendency to take every precaution as they retraced the trail that led them back to the ridge with a stream on each side. They took a new look at the snake-like creek that wound its way across the center of the meadow, pointing out the best spots to set their traps. The first trap was set in the pond below the confluence of the two streams that ran on either side of the ridge. Then they entered the water at the exact spot where Jug had been shot. They stayed with it until all twelve traps were set, then they returned to their tipi to warm up by the fire pit in the center of their lodge.

The next morning, before daylight, they rode back to find beaver in seven of their traps. "I knew it," Jug expounded. "I knew this creek was eat up with beaver." They saw no reason to reset any but the seven, but Jug refreshed the bait hanging over each trap. Then they quietly withdrew and returned to camp, aware now that the day seemed colder than the day before. After they prepared their plews for drying, Luke resumed the work he was doing to try to keep the horses warm. Darkness brought another trip to the creek to check their traps. It was not quite as successful as the first time, but there were four traps sprung, so they couldn't complain.

Of greater concern was the shower of snow that swept across the open meadow just as they were starting back to their camp. "That don't look too good, does it?" Luke asked. "It feels colder to me than it did yesterday."

"I think you're right," Jug said. "We ain't got many more days of this. In another week, this valley's liable to be froze solid." It was hard to argue with his prediction as they broke through the occasional layers of thin ice when they stepped into the water the following morning. It did inspire them to move quickly while re-setting the traps. After preparing the pelts they collected that morning, Luke put the final touches on his fir barn and pronounced it ready for the Montana winter. That night brought another harvest of six beaver, and they decided to move on farther down the creek with those six traps. "Maybe we can get down to the end of the meadow before the hard freeze," Jug said.

Chapter 10

Luke woke up before daybreak to the sound of the waterfall up the slope from their camp as usual, but something didn't seem right. He didn't know what it was, but something was different. He lay there a few minutes longer, listening to hear if Jug was up, but he heard nothing from the little man's bedroll across the fire from him. "Jug," he said, "you awake?" He repeated it a couple of times before his partner answered.

"I'm awake," Jug answered, sounding a little irritated at having been awakened. "I'm fixin' to get up. What's wrong?"

"Nothin's wrong, I reckon. Listen to the waterfall. Does it sound different to you?"

That captured Jug's attention at once. "Different? Whaddaya mean, different? I don't hear nothin' different." He paused and listened, then shook his head.

"Well, it's time to get up, anyway," Luke said and started pulling on his moccasins. "We can't keep those beaver waitin'." He pulled his heavy buffalo coat on and left the tipi. "I'm gonna go see 'bout the horses," he said as he went out. "It was a helluva cold night last night, coldest one we've had." He was not gone for long before he came back inside, to Jug's surprise, for he expected Luke was saddling their horses. When he gave Luke a questioning look, Luke said, "I reckon we'll be pullin' our traps outta those streams in that creek. I expect it's already froze. Our pond here is froze over. I found out why the waterfall sounds different this mornin'. It was makin' a different noise when it fell on the pond 'cause the pond is risin' up to meet it." When Jug gave him a questioning look, he said, "You'll see what I mean."

Sufficiently curious now, Jug pulled his moccasins on and followed Luke out the door. As soon as he stepped outside, he grunted, "Damn, it musta dropped twenty degrees last night. I thought it was cold yesterday, but it weren't like this." He walked with Luke up to the pond after he went back inside to get his coat. "I reckon we did a dandy job with our tipi," he saw fit to comment. "Cold as it is, I slept warm as a baby in his mama's arms." Then he saw what Luke meant when he said the pond was rising up to meet the waterfall. The top of the pond was frozen and when the water flowing from under the ice of the stream above went over the lip of the cliff, it froze when it hit the pond. The result of it was to gradually build a mound of ice on the pond. To add to the mysterious effect, spray splashed into the air around it, froze in mid-air, and showered as ice crystals on the frozen pond. "Well, ain't that somethin'?" Jug responded. "Happened pretty dang quick, didn't it? 'Course, I knew it was comin'. Didn't figure it for another day or two, though."

They stood there for a few minutes more to marvel at the sight of the water splashing down on the gradually increasing cone of ice until Luke decided it was time to go to work. "I'll go saddle the horses," he said, then paused before asking, "you are goin' with me, right?"

"'Course, I am," Jug answered. "Did you think I was gonna set here by the fire while you set them traps?"

"I thought you mighta wanted to stay here to let your arm rest up," Luke said, halfway serious. "I don't expect to be resettin' our traps. I just think we'd best get 'em outta the water before that creek freezes so solid, we'll have to chop 'em out."

"No, hell, no," Jug quickly insisted. "I was figurin' on givin' you a hand." He paused and grinned. "My good one at that," he added. They went to the windbreak in the woods and found the horses inside, huddled together. "It'd be a good idea to throw a rope on a couple of these other horses and take 'em with us. Cold as it is, it's a good idea to work 'em a little bit. If we don't, we're gonna find 'em froze to death." Luke agreed so after he saddled both their riding horses, he tied their packhorses on lead ropes. They decided the horses that had belonged to the Indians would follow the other horses, so they made no attempt to keep them penned up there while they were gone to get their traps.

"How 'bout that big gray, there?" Luke asked. "The last time we took him over to that little meadow, and turned him loose, he went straight home to that Blackfoot's camp. Reckon he might do the same thing this mornin'?"

"Nah," Jug assured him, "he'll follow the other horses."

"I hope you know what you're talkin' about," Luke japed, "'cause, if we get the rest of the horses back to rendezvous and sell 'em, I'm gonna charge you for every one that gray leads off."

"Shoot," Jug scoffed, "we'll be lucky if we've got any of those extra horses by the time we get back to Green River."

Since daylight was already upon them, they took the time to soften up some strips of smoked deer meat over the coals of their fire. They figured that would stave off their hunger until they returned to their camp later that morning. Then they rode out of camp and headed for the valley of the twin streams to recover their traps. Leading their packhorses with no packs, they were followed by the rest of the small herd they had acquired as a result of Luke's good luck and deadly aim.

When they reached the stream on the south side of the ridge, they found that, like the stream back at their camp, it was iced up heavily but still flowing. Encouraged by this, they continued on to the pond at the head of the creek, only to find the shallow little creek completely frozen over. They pulled their horses up at the head of the creek and dismounted. Luke grabbed his axe, and taking a knee on the bank, tested the ice and found it to be a pretty thick covering. Wading in the icy water, breaking up the ice as he walked, was out of the question. The ice was too thick.

He looked back at Jug, who was standing over him, and re-marked, "Partner, the fall trappin' season is official over till spring thaw." The only thing left to do now was to try to chop their traps out of the ice, so Luke set in to free the first one. Jug got his axe and went to the next bait stick to attack the ice over the trap, swinging left-handed.

When he finally freed the first trap, and realizing it was going to take a while to retrieve them all, Luke led Smoke and Jug's horses down to the lower side of the meadow and left them to scratch around in the light cover of snow for grass. The other horses followed suit. Then he went back and started in at an-other bait stick in the bank. "How you comin', Lefty?" He japed with Jug. "Soon as I chop six traps outta this creek, I'm gonna fig-ure I got my traps, and I'll meet you back at the camp."

"You oughta be thankin' me for helpin' you bust these traps out—as bad hurt as I am with my wound," he came back at him. "If it was the other way around, and you was the one with a bad arm, I woulda told you to stay in the tipi by the fire."

"You know, I thought about that," Luke replied. "But then, I thought about how much more you would enjoy choppin' up the ice than sittin' by the fire back at camp. Then, when we see the rest of the boys at rendezvous, you can tell 'em tales about havin' to chop our traps outta the creek."

"Huh," Jug snorted. "I don't expect I'll wanna tell 'em we was too dang dumb to get our traps outta the water when we oughta knowed it was gonna freeze over."

The japing went back and forth most of the morning as they worked away to recover their frozen traps. It was possible to catch beaver in a frozen pond now and again using snares, if you could find the hole where they came out of the pond to look for food. These holes were sometimes hard to find, and for moun-tain men in the business of trapping, like Luke and Jug, it wasn't worth the time for the low yield in pelts. Winter was the time to lay low, fatten up, and do whatever needed to be done to be ready when the ponds were free of ice again. And, if you were lucky, and wintered in a place where the game sought refuge from the cold, you hunted for food. Luke and Jug were lucky on this frigid morning.

"Luke!" Jug whispered hoarsely. "Look yonder!"

Luke turned to see him pointing down toward the lower end of the meadow where the horses were pawing around in the snow, looking for grass. He didn't realize at once what Jug was pointing at, then his gaze shifted to the edge of the clearing, and he saw them. At the edge of the woods, a bull elk and three cows stood, watching the horses graze. "Fresh meat just come walkin' up to bring us some tender elk cow. I told you we wouldn't have to go huntin' 'cause the game would come to us."

"You said they'd come to the meadow below our camp," Luke had to correct him. "You never said anything about this meadow."

"I meant they'd come to us, wherever we were," Jug came back. "Anyway, whaddaya gonna do about it? I'd go after 'em, if I could use my right arm."

"I wouldn't want you to hurt that arm," Luke said sarcastically. "They're too good to pass up, since they were kind enough to bring it to us." Moving slowly, so as not to make any sudden moves that might attract the elks' attention, Luke picked up his rifle. He couldn't imagine what brought the elk out of the woods to this pasture. They must be traveling with a large herd and were attracted by the horses. Most likely the rest of the herd had headed into the woods to bed down for the night. One thing for sure, he knew he and Jug were downwind of them. Elk had a sharp sense of smell and this bull would have surely picked up their scent as close as they were. "I wish I had my bow, but it's hangin' on my saddle."

"What the hell for?" Jug reacted. "You'd have to get a lot closer to take a shot with a bow."

"I don't know." Luke shrugged. "Just save powder and lead, I reckon." He didn't wait for Jug's response, knowing it would be one of sarcasm. But he wasn't quick enough to avoid hearing it, anyway.

"And it don't make no sense to try to get close enough to throw your knife at 'em, either," Jug whispered as loud as he could, thinking of Luke's altercation with Dan Bloodworth, just before they left the rendezvous.

Moving quickly out of the meadow in a low crouch, hoping not to attract attention, Luke ran into the fir trees that bordered it. As soon as he had the cover of the forest, he paused to see if he had been spotted by the elk. They were still standing at the edge of the trees, evidently puzzling over the horses in the meadow. *Good*, Luke thought and carefully made his way down through the fir trees, hurrying to get to a good position to take the shot. He was close enough now for what should be a sure shot, but he moved a little farther down the slope. *The closer, the better,* he thought, *almost close enough for the bow.* He quickly readied his rifle to fire when the bull suddenly started stamping his hooves, which caused the cows to shift back and forth nervously. Luke dropped his front sight on the cow in the middle, and as he started to squeeze the trigger, she turned her head, seeming to look in his direction. He froze for a few moments, suddenly re-membering the lone elk cow he had encountered when scouting the three Blackfoot hunters. He had spared that cow's life, be-cause the sound of the shot might be heard by the Indians, or so he had told himself. But he couldn't deny he did it because that cow knew what he was about to do and was asking him to spare her. *That's crazy,* he told himself, *that's not the same cow.* But just in case it was, he shifted his front sight to the cow behind her and squeezed the trigger. At the sound of the shot, the other three elk bolted across the meadow and disappeared in the trees. More accustomed to gunshots, the horses just milled around nervously for a few minutes, startled more by the elk running across the meadow than the sound of the rifle.

Luke moved quickly down to end the cow's suffering. He had aimed for a lung shot and had hit his mark. The cow had reared backward when the bullet struck her, then managed to run a few yards after the others before collapsing. He ended her life with his knife, and when she was still, he hoped he'd never have crazy thoughts again, like those that struck him before he shot. *Jug would think I'd gone lip-dripping loco,* he thought. The picture of the cow he spared came into his mind then and he said, "That's twice I've let you go. The next time I see you, you're meat."

While her blood was still warm, Luke decided to go ahead and hang the elk from a tree limb to gut her and let her bleed out. With Jug's help and the use of one of the horses, he cleaned the elk's innards out and left her to hang until they finished recovering all their traps. The last trap came out of the pond, and Jug was delighted to find a frozen beaver in it. "Hot damn!" he exclaimed. "I'm proud to see him. I ain't never been skunked in my trappin', and this prime-lookin' gent saved my record."

"How do you know it's your trap and not one of mine?" Luke japed.

"'Cause it's got a beaver in it," Jug answered, "and I ain't never been skunked."

With the days getting shorter and shorter, the sun was already well on its ride for the day by the time the elk and the traps were all loaded on the horses and the two trappers led their herd of horses back to the tipi by the waterfall. Using Smoke to help him, Luke hauled the elk up to hang from a limb while he skinned and butchered it. Jug built a fire close to the tree the elk was hanging from. And since they had had nothing to eat since a little bit of smoked venison that morning, some fresh cuts of elk meat, roasted over an open flame, was a fine feast indeed.

Jug stood watching the horses for a few minutes while he chewed on a hot strip of meat. "They've already got to where they'll go to your fir barn to try to get warm," he commented to Luke. "I think it helped 'em a little to get to run some, too. Maybe we won't lose too many of 'em this winter."

"I'm plannin' on goin' down the hill tomorrow and cut up a mess of cottonwood limbs and twigs to give 'em a little feed. I don't think they got much grass under that snow today."

"That's a good idea," Jug said. "I'll help you with that. Then I'm gonna make me an oven, so I can have some biscuits to go with all that meat you're gonna be killin' with your bow and arrows."

"I hope that flour we packed all the way from Green River is still all right," Luke said. "We ain't even opened it since we left there. It might be full of weevils or something."

"We didn't camp in one place long enough for me to make an oven," Jug replied, "and pan biscuits just ain't the same as oven-baked biscuits. That flour will be all right, even if there is some bugs in it. Just adds a little more meat to your supper. I noticed some good-sized rocks at the foot of that waterfall. Oughta be just right for my oven."

"Uhmm, baked biscuits," Luke commented. "Now that's to my likin'. You can go ahead and get started on your oven tomorrow. I can go get the cottonwood bark for the horses tomorrow by myself. I'm gonna have to chop down a sizable tree, to get enough bark to feed our herd. I'll take that buckskin we just got. He looks like he's a workin' horse. Let's see if he spent any time doin' farm work."

"You got a deal," Jug said. "And you'll get a chance to taste the best baked biscuits this side of the Rockies—maybe the other side, too."

"That's the reason I agreed to spend the winter in the middle of Blackfoot territory with you," Luke said. "I heard you could bake good biscuits." Although he joked about it, he sometimes wondered if they weren't both crazy to hole up all winter in territory that was definitely hostile to the white trapper. Most of the other free trappers camped together during the winter freeze, primarily for the protection of numbers. More than a few trappers wintered in a Shoshone or Flathead village, where the Indians were friendly toward the white man. More often than not, they were treated like honored guests in those villages. The same could be said for some Crow villages as well as Nez Perce. Luke thought about that and couldn't help but question his sanity again. He and Jug had started out on a risky plan, to trap beaver in not only hostile Blackfoot territory, but in Hudson's Bay territory as well. Their reason was simple, there were a lot of beaver there and the other trappers were afraid to take the risks. Admittedly, the risks were many, but the payoff in furs was worth the risks. And by wintering in the territory, they were already trapping the ponds and streams when they thawed out, while those trappers who wintered together were just starting out to their different trapping sites. He shook his head to rid it of these thoughts of doubt. Their decision was already made. *We'll just lay low and eat hot biscuits*, he thought.

The following morning, they were in no hurry to leave their cozy tipi. The fire in the center kept the lodge very comfortable, even though another morning snow shower was in progress when Luke went outside to answer nature's summons. By the time they had made coffee and roasted some elk meat over the fire, the snow shower had let up. "As much as I like sittin' here by the fire, I reckon I'd best go see about gettin' some feed for the horses," Luke finally declared.

"You sure you don't want me to help you with that?"

"Nah," Luke replied. "You'd best make your oven before the ground gets any harder than it is already. I expect it's already froze six or seven inches down."

They climbed into their heavy coats and caps, pulled on rabbit hide gloves, with the fur turned inside, and went to their different chores. Luke went to his tree-barn where the horses were just starting to move around, and he fashioned a halter in one end of a long rope. Then he slipped it over the buckskin's head. With his axe in one hand, he led the willing horse down the slope where the cottonwoods were growing. He tied the horse there while he selected a tree that was not too large for the horse to drag. When he found one that looked perfect for his needs, he set into it with his axe. In a few minutes time, it came crashing down. He untied the buckskin and led him over to the tree. He widened the loop in the rope, so it spread more evenly around the horse's withers. Satisfied that it would pull where he wanted it to on the withers, he tied the loose end to the tree and led the buckskin back up the hill. The horse proved equal to the task and pulled the entire tree up to the fir corral. Luke untied him from the tree, but before he released him, he took his axe and peeled off some of the bark and held it up in his hand for the horse to eat. The buckskin hesitated only a moment before taking all of the bark from his hand. In a few minutes time, all the horses came to him as he peeled the bark off the trunk of the tree. Before he peeled the whole trunk, the horses were biting the bark off without waiting for him.

While Luke introduced some of the horses to cottonwood bark—his and Jug's horses as well as most of the Indian ponies were already acquainted with it—Jug was working on his oven. It was necessary to use his axe on the top few frozen inches of ground, but once past that, he used his shovel to dig out a portion of the slope about a foot and a half deep. He was judging the size by the size of the big flat rocks he found by the waterfall. Weighing approximately twenty pounds each, the oblong rocks were used to form three sides of his oven. He struggled then to pick up an even larger stone to be the top. Using loose dirt to seal up the corners and cracks, he then raked dirt over the top and filled the floor of the oven with small rocks. When it was finished, he had a tight little rock-walled oven with an open front, buried in the hill. He turned when he realized Luke was standing behind him, watching him. "She's ready to go," he said. "All I need to do is build a fire in there, stick a pan of biscuits in it, and prop this thin rock up for the door. And that little oven will bake 'em just like ol' Aunt Jane bakes 'em in her oven." He stood, grinning at Luke for a long couple of moments, proud of his creation.

"When you gonna test it?" Luke asked.

"Supper," Jug answered.

Chapter 11

Ever since Luke had hooked up with Jug Sartain, whenever the subject of biscuits came up, Jug never failed to proclaim his biscuits were the best of any you would ever eat. With the construction of his oven, the day finally arrived when he was going to have to back up his claim. Holding the coffeepot in his hand, Luke watched him with a great deal of interest as the spry little man rolled out his biscuit dough on a square piece of deer hide and formed it into six large individual biscuits. He placed the biscuits in a pan to protect the bottoms from getting scorched by the fire and into the oven they went. "If those biscuits ain't no good," Luke jibed, "you're gonna be eatin' a lotta crow with 'em."

"And when you try one of 'em, you're gonna be eatin' your words," Jug replied. "You just go on back in the lodge and get that elk meat cookin'." He checked the small fire under the pan and added a few sticks from the cottonwood to keep it constant. "It ain't gonna be long before they're done, so go get the meat cookin," he prodded.

"I'm goin'," Luke replied, "soon as I get some water in this coffeepot." He went over to the waterfall then and caught a pot full of the icy water falling on the frozen pond. He didn't really think about it, but there was a feeling of peace and satisfaction that had come over both him and Jug. The hard winter had set in, and they were content to wait it out with no worries as far as hostile Indians were concerned. Their little valley was not likely to be stumbled upon until the spring thaw, and with a little luck, maybe not even then. They had already scouted a large promising area to trap without riding more than three miles from their camp. The harvest should be good.

Luke got his coffee water and went inside the lodge to cook the strips of elk meat he had prepared to roast. He was looking forward to Jug's biscuits, since their food had been nothing but meat for so long. He had a pot of coffee boiling by the time Jug came in with the pan of baked biscuits. "They look good enough to eat," Luke commented.

"They're perfect," Jug crowed. "Here, take you one and I'm gonna put the pan back on top of the oven, cover 'em with this piece of deer hide, and they'll keep warm." They both took a biscuit and placed it on their plates, and Jug went back outside to put the pan on top of the oven to warm.

"Damn, they are good," Luke had to admit when Jug returned, much to the little man's smug satisfaction. They worked on the elk strips, but soon were ready for another biscuit.

Jug graciously went back to the oven to fetch a couple more of the warm biscuits. "There's another biscuit waitin' for you after this'un," he reminded Luke.

"Those are big biscuits," Luke said. "My belly's tight as a tick right now, but in honor of this occasion, I'm gonna find room for that last biscuit." When Jug started to get up, Luke stopped him. "I'll get it. Maybe, if I take a few steps, I can shake a little more room down in my belly." When he came back, carrying the pan, he said, "I thought you meant there was one left for each of us. When did you get that other biscuit?"

Jug looked at him as if he was japing him. "What are you talkin' about? Ain't there two biscuits in that pan?" Luke held the pan down so Jug could see the single biscuit in it. Jug stared at it for a moment before grinning broadly. "I told you they'd be the best biscuits you ever et. I didn't know they'd turn you into a biscuit hog, though." He reached over and took the biscuit out of the pan. "This'un's mine. You can go get that other'n wherever you got it hid." He took a big bite of the biscuit but paused when he saw the confused expression on Luke's face. "You're japin' me, right? Where's that other biscuit?" Confused as well, now, Jug said, "You saw me put six big biscuits in that pan, and there was four in it the next time I brought it in." He was convinced now that Luke wasn't playing a joke on him.

"I don't know," Luke said, "but it looks like we've got us a varmint in our camp—possum or a coon, or a coyote, maybe one of the horses."

"Maybe," Jug allowed. "But it don't make no sense to leave a biscuit."

"No, it don't," Luke agreed. "I'm gonna go take a look around that oven and see what kinda tracks I can find." Jug followed him out the door. The possibility of an Indian raid on their camp never entered the mind of either one of them. If that had been the case, they would most likely already be dead. Daylight was fading rapidly by then, but there was still light enough to inspect the ground around the oven. There were many tracks in the snow, all of them left by Luke and Jug as they had gone about their chores that day. Luke searched carefully for the prints left by a small animal, but there was no trace of a possum or raccoon, attracted by the warmth of Jug's oven. Suddenly, Luke stopped and took a step backward, something irregular having caught his eye. He stared at one of the footprints left by Jug, easy to distinguish because they were smaller than his. Close beside it, there was a print from another moccasin, this one smaller than Jug's. He dropped down on one knee to get an even closer look at the tracks. Concentrating now on Jug's tracks, he searched until he found a clear imprint of a smaller track inside Jug's footprint.

Knowing what he was looking for now, he moved very carefully, inspecting each footprint left by Jug. Fascinated by the spell that had seemingly come over his partner, Jug remained silent but followed close behind him. Finally, when he could hold his curiosity no longer, he asked, "What is it, partner? Whatchu got scent of?"

Luke straightened up. Looking straight at the waterfall, he said, "We got company and it ain't a possum."

"Well, what the hell is it?" Jug wanted to know and dropped his hand on the pistol in his belt.

"It's either a woman or a young'un," Luke answered. "I'm bettin' it's a woman, and I suspect she's hidin' behind the waterfall. Look here," he said and pointed to one of Jug's tracks. "If you look close, you can see the imprint of another track inside your track. She musta been mighty hungry to try to disguise her tracks and steal a biscuit—pretty smart, too—'cause if she hadn't missed one of your tracks beside the oven, I wouldn'ta never caught onto what she was doin'."

"How do you know she's behind the waterfall?" Jug asked.

"Well, she might not be, but I tried to think like I figured she might be thinkin'. Figured she'd wanna try to hide her trail in your prints. So I looked till I found her walkin' in your prints when you were walkin' away from the oven. Well, you were walkin' in every direction around here all afternoon. But she picked your footprints to walk in when you were headed toward the waterfall. She stepped outta your footprints when you turned and headed toward the horses. She kept walkin' toward the waterfall."

"Well, I'll be . . ." Jug started. "She must not have a gun, else she'da been pickin' us off while we're out here in the open talkin' about her."

"Reckon so," Luke said. "You ready to go see what we can find behind that waterfall?" Jug said he was, so they proceeded on to the waterfall, aware that there was not much room for anyone to hide behind it. As a precaution, they both pulled their pistols and cocked them. At first, when they walked behind the fall, there appeared to be no one in the small dark alcove in the cliff. After a few moments, however, Luke saw the small, dark figure squatting tightly against the back of the earthen chamber. Like a fox in a trap, the woman was terrified by the two white trappers, expecting the worst treatment, but helpless to fight them. "Don't be afraid," Luke said and put his pistol away. She continued to glance nervously from one of them, back to the other. "We will not harm you." When she continued to stare at him, too frightened to speak, he assumed that she didn't speak English. So he asked, "Blackfoot?" He spoke, using their term for it. She didn't answer but shook her head. So he asked again, "Crow?"

"Absaroka," she said, in the Crow tongue and nodded.

Her answer surprised both Luke and Jug. "How did you get here, so far away from your home?" Luke asked. Both he and Jug were fluent in the Crow language. When she didn't answer him, obviously too frightened to speak, Luke said, "You must be hungry." He paused, still looking her over carefully. "And cold, too," he said. "You ain't dressed very warm to be slippin' around in this snow. Come on, we'll go inside and get you something to go with that biscuit you ate." Afraid to trust them, she still hugged the cold rock wall behind the fall. "Don't be afraid," Luke tried to assure her. "We're not goin' to harm you." Still, she did not budge.

Jug stepped in at that point, losing his patience with the woman's fear. Sounding very much like an older parent or grandparent, he scolded her. "If we meant you any harm, you'd already be hurtin'. Now get yourself up from there. Ain't no sense in all three of us standin' out here in the cold when there's a warm fire and food in our tipi yonder." His impatience seemed to have registered with the frightened woman, for she moved away from the back of the alcove at once. "There's likely to be somebody lookin' for her," Jug said to Luke. "Pretty little Crow woman like that, she was most likely took by some raidin' party."

She nodded vigorously at that. "Bloody Hand," she said, "Blackfoot war chief."

Luke and Jug were both surprised by her outburst. "So you do understand white man talk," Jug said. "Bloody Hand, huh? Where was you took from?"

"Let's get the poor woman inside where it's warm and get her something to eat while we're questionin' her," Luke said.

"Good idea," Jug said and led the way to the tipi. Once they were inside, the woman watched in wonder as the two men hustled about to roast some elk meat and pour her a cup of coffee. Caught by surprise, she flinched when Luke draped a blanket across her shoulders. Embarrassed by her reaction then, she smiled and nodded her thanks. Once they had seen to her comfort, they were ready to get back to questioning her. Of great importance to them both was how she happened upon their camp and how careful she had been in hiding her trail. "Where was you took from?" Jug repeated.

"My village camp on Yellowstone River," the woman answered, her English basic but clearly spoken. "Bloody Hand come with many warriors, kill many Crow warriors, take women, steal horses. I hide in bushes, but Bloody Hand find me. Say I his woman."

"What is your name?" Luke asked.

"Willow Blowing in the Wind," she answered.

He nodded politely. "My name's Luke. His is Jug. Both our names are short for longer names. All right if we just call you Willow?" She nodded. "So, Willow, how did you get way up here in the Little Belt Mountains? This is a long way from the Yellowstone."

"Bloody Hand lead his warriors back north to big Blackfoot village," Willow told them. I walk many miles till we come to river. Then we follow river to another river and we get close to mountains. When I see mountains, I slip out of camp at night and run up the river until I find a place to cross over to this side. Then I run to mountains to hide."

Luke and Jug listened to her simple explanation and when she was finished, Jug thought he had a pretty good picture of the Blackfoot war party's path. "Willow's people was most likely camped on the Yellowstone right where it turns south when the Blackfoot struck 'em. I expect they were in a hurry to get home after the raid, it bein' as late in the season as it is. So they set out to the northwest, till they struck the Musselshell. Then they

musta followed it west till they got close to the Judith. I reckon
they followed the Judith north. But, anyway, they was right beside these mountains then, and that's the best chance she had of
findin' someplace to hide."

"The question now is whether or not there's a big Blackfoot
war party searchin' these mountains lookin' for her, or if they just
said, 'It's already hard winter and we'd best get to hell on home."
He looked at Willow and asked, "How long ago was it that you
ran off from that war party?"

"Two nights before this night," she said.

"You've been out in this cold for three days with no more
clothes than that?" This was Luke's first reaction.

"I had to leave my blanket rolled up, so they would think I
was sleeping," she replied.

He shook his head in sympathy for her ordeal. "How did you
find this valley and this camp?" He and Jug were both confident
that their camp would be extremely difficult to find.

"I not know," Willow answered. "I afraid they follow me, so
I just go where it look like nobody goes. I surprised when I
find you."

Jug interrupted Luke's questioning then with one of his own.
"That, there, biscuit you snatched, that's the best biscuit you
ever et, weren't it?"

"Yes," she said, smiled, and nodded vigorously.

"Right," Jug turned toward Luke and gloated. "I told you,
ain't nobody bakes a better biscuit than me."

"Well, I'm glad we got that cleared up," Luke japed. "Now,
we can worry about some of the less-important things, like
whether or not we've got the mountains crawling with Blackfoot
warriors lookin' for Willow."

"I am sorry to bring this trouble to you," Willow said at once.
"I could not see any sign of a camp when I climb up the hill, not
until I came to your horses in the trees. Then I see the waterfall
and the tipi. I not know camp friend or not, but I took one biscuit. I meant to keep going, but you came out, and I had to hide."

"No, don't you go thinkin' that way a-tall," Luke replied, just as fast. "We're glad you stumbled on our camp, and mighty sorry for the ordeal you've gone through before you found us. No sense in you leavin' here now and goin' out in that snow. We got plenty of room here in our tipi and plenty of food and won't nobody bother you." He glanced at Jug. "Will they, Jug?"

Looking as if he had been insulted, Jug answered, "I reckon not, but I'm just speakin' for myself."

Luke laughed. "You just make yourself at home. We've got some antelope hides and some needles and rawhide strings. You can start making yourself some extra clothes to wear. Me and Jug will leave you alone for a while, so you can eat in peace. All right?"

"You are both so kind. I thank you for helping me. I will leave you as soon as you tell me to go."

"Fair enough," Jug said with a chuckle. "I spent half my life lookin' for a woman that would tell me that."

Willow maintained her strong resolve while she ate the food they provided. But when her stomach was full and she warmed up for the first time in three days, she began a losing battle trying to keep her eyes open. A few minutes later, like a small child, she was leaning sideways, fast asleep while still sitting upright. Luke and Jug picked her up very carefully and laid her gently on a blanket, then covered her with half of it.

They moved to the far side of the tipi, and Luke whispered to Jug. "I don't expect any more visitors tonight, but I think as soon as it's light enough to see in the mornin', I'm gonna backtrack her trail into here and maybe see if she's left a clear path right up to our door." Jug thought that was a good idea, and before very long, they both were ready to join Willow in slumber.

She awakened gradually, stirred from a sound sleep by an urgency to answer nature's call, aware that she was warm and had been sleeping a long time. But upon finding herself in the darkened tipi, lit only by the glowing coals left in the fire pit, it took a moment for her to remember where she was. Then she remembered the two white trappers who had taken her into the tipi. She looked toward the other side of the tipi to see both of them asleep. Receiving signals again from her bladder, she started to get out of the blanket she had been sleeping in. She was alarmed at once when she found her ankle was held firmly. *They have tied me to the bed! With all their friendly talk, they lured me in to eat and sleep only to hold me prisoner.* Afraid to think what plans they might have in mind for her, her first thought was to escape. Almost in a panic now, she reached for her bound ankle but found no rope around it. She realized then that she had somehow managed to tangle the corner of the blanket around her ankle while she slept and was not tied at all. She looked across the tipi to find the young one, the one called Luke, turning toward her. "Are you all right?" Luke asked softly.

"Yes," she answered quickly, feeling rather foolish. "I have to pee."

"You have to go outside," he said, then turned over and went back to sleep.

She got to her feet, and with the blanket wrapped around her shoulders, she went outside to relieve her bladder. When she returned, she found both her benefactors in the same position as before, sound asleep with their backs turned toward the fire pit in the center of the lodge. *These are good men*, she decided, again feeling regret at having suspected them of evil intent earlier. *I truly hope I have not led Bloody Hand to their camp.* This was one of many thoughts racing through her mind at the present. Thoughts of her dead husband returned to haunt her now that the panic of escape did not dominate all her thinking. Struck down by Bloody Hand's tomahawk, right before her eyes, Long Runner was slain when he tried to protect her. He was no match for the powerful Blackfoot war chief. She felt a tear run down her cheek as she thought about her husband now. They had only a few months as man and wife, not nearly enough time to know each other's hearts. The image of Bloody Hand's evil smile came to her mind then, and she immediately feared she had led the cruel warrior to these decent men. Helpless to change what could not be undone, she spread her blanket down on the deer skin as before and wrapped it around her. With all the activity going on in her brain, she found it difficult to go back to sleep, and managed to drift off only a short time before Luke awoke with the first light of day.

As quietly as he could, so as not to awaken Willow, Luke pulled on his moccasins and donned his heavy coat and cap. He was less concerned for Jug, knowing it would take a prodding with his rifle to awaken the little man. He picked up his bow and quiver of arrows as he started to leave. It had been his habit of late. Glancing at the woman, he was happy to see her sleeping, for she surely needed the rest. Outside, he took a quick look around before heading into the trees to check on the horses. Satisfied that they were all right, at least as well as could be expected under the circumstances, he made them a promise that he would cut down another cottonwood for them. Taking another look up at the clouds, he decided that there was a good possibility another snow was headed their way. There was no doubt that the makeshift barn he had labored to build for them had helped the situation some. He left them huddled together for warmth and returned his attention to the question of Willow's trail.

Her trail was readily discovered in the foot-deep snow, even in the early morning light. The placement of the small holes her feet left in the snow told of her near exhaustion as she climbed up through the trees. In the open spaces where the snow was a little deeper, he could see a faint trace left by her skirt when she dragged it as she walked. *Won't take an expert tracker to follow that trail*, he couldn't help thinking. *But why are they so far behind her?* He had to assume that she was successful in disguising her trail when she first escaped. He recalled then that she had said they were camped beside the river, and she had first run up the river to find a place where she could cross it. And if that was the case, he might reasonably assume the Blackfoot war party had given up on finding her and had gone on. *We could use another snowstorm about now*, he thought, *and that would take care of the last part of her trail leading to our camp.* He continued on, thinking to follow her tracks on down to the bottom of the slope, even though he was pretty much of the notion that the Blackfoot war party had long since departed these mountains.

The desperation of her flight was ever apparent in the confused path of her escape, first one direction, then another, ever changing as she had gradually ascended the hill. To save time, he followed the general direction of the zigzagging trail until he reached the bottom of the hill and the tiny stream that circled it. They were both startled when they met face to face across the little stream, maybe fifteen feet apart. Neither man expected the sudden confrontation, so neither man was ready to react. With no time to load a rifle, the Blackfoot warrior pulled his knife and charged across the stream with the intent to reach Luke before he had time to ready his rifle to fire. Relying on total instinct, Luke drew his knife. Taking dead aim, he waited for the charging Blackfoot to get close enough for him to hit the small target he intended to aim for. When his assailant was about seven feet away from him, Luke hurled his knife with an underhanded throw that struck the surprised Blackfoot at the base of his neck, severing his windpipe.

Luke stepped deftly aside as the stunned warrior plunged headlong into the snow, clutching frantically at the knife lodged deep in his throat. When he was sure the Blackfoot was helpless to react, Luke knelt beside him and scanned the trees around him, not sure if there were others with him. When he was certain of that, he turned his attention back to the dying Indian who was struggling desperately to breathe with his windpipe cut almost in two. He had no desire to prolong the man's suffering, but he preferred not to have a shot from his pistol heard. So he picked the Blackfoot's knife up from where he had dropped it. Then he rolled him over on his back and opened his heavy buffalo robe to expose his stomach. He thrust the knife into his belly, and when the Indian reached for it, Luke grabbed his knife and finished the job on his throat.

When the Blackfoot finally lay still in death, Luke apologized. "Sorry it had to be so rough. But with you wearin' that heavy buffalo hide, the only sure target I could go for was your throat. Anywhere else and that robe mighta kept my knife from causin' enough damage to stop you. Besides, I expect you might notta been any easier on me, if it hadda been the other way around."

Now there was something else to think about. The war party was still here. They had not gone on without searching for Willow, unless . . . He looked at the body lying there in the snow and wondered if it was Bloody Hand, the war chief who seemed to be obsessed with her, according to Willow. He decided he'd best continue following Willow's back trail, which was now the dead warrior's trail, as well. He picked up the warrior's weapons and hid them in a clump of bushes, then he resumed his backtracking. Getting farther and farther from his camp, he saw right away that Willow was accurate in telling them that she had simply run where it didn't look like a definite path to anywhere but the side of a mountain. He figured he was about three miles from his camp when he found the point where the Blackfoot warrior had struck Willow's trail. He had evidently walked up the frozen stream until he came to a point where she had crossed over it. Luke saw Willow's tracks leading up to the stream on the other side but not the Blackfoot's. Evidently, the warrior was alone in tracking her. There were no other tracks but his. Luke decided to follow the stream back toward the river to see if the war party was camped there and had not left this one warrior behind. Willow said Bloody Hand was a war chief, so it didn't make sense to him that he might have stayed behind while he sent the rest of the party home.

He didn't recall ever having followed this stream to the river before, so when he thought he was close, he became even more cautious, and in a short time, he was disappointed to spot smoke drifting up through the trees, probably on the riverbank. "Damn," he swore, for he knew he had a war party of Blackfoot to deal with. In order to scout it out completely, he left the stream and took a wide circle around the spot from which he had seen the smoke. To avoid being spotted from the camp, he made his circle deep into the forest, so that his dark form wouldn't be seen crossing over the white snow. Moving in closer from the other side then, he worked his way through the trees until he was close enough to see into the camp. It was on this side of the river. Willow had said the camp was on the far side of the river, and that could be more bad news. For it meant that Bloody Hand was determined to stay here until he found her and moved his camp across the river at the foot of the mountains.

He counted twelve warriors gathered around a big fire and wondered how many more were out scouting for Willow, or if the one he left behind him was the only scout the war chief sent out to find her. As he studied the ring of warriors around the fire, he felt sure he knew which one was Bloody Hand. He was a fierce looking man, even at that distance and under heavy gray skies, and the other warriors seemed to treat him with respect. Luke was not sure how best to handle the entire war party, if it came to that. His only option at the moment was to stay close to them to see what they intended to do when it became clear to them that their scout was not coming back. *I wish to hell I had brought some jerky with me*, he thought as he selected a better spot to observe their actions. He thought about Jug and Willow back in their hidden valley camp. Against a dozen Blackfoot warriors, the three of them were badly outmatched, especially when he couldn't count on Willow to contribute much to their defense. He feared their only chance was if their camp was too hard to find, and he could only count on that for so long, depending on Bloody Hand's determination to have the woman. He looked up again at the heavy clouds overhead, thinking how much it would help if they would go ahead and release their snow and cover his and Willow's tracks to his camp.

Chapter 12

"I think the woman may be dead," Crazy Wolf said. "She has been gone three days now and the nights are colder than when she ran away. Crooked Foot has been gone for a long time this morning. If the woman had come this way from the river, Crooked Foot would have found her trail by now. I think maybe she never made it across the river and her body is caught under the ice somewhere. Maybe we should send someone after Crooked Foot, and we should forget the woman. If more snow falls, it will make our journey home much more difficult."

Bloody Hand listened patiently to Crazy Wolf's plea to forget the woman out of respect for the older man's wisdom. But he had been struck by Willow's beauty, and his passion for her was fueled further by the fact that he had killed her husband, making her rightfully his. If she had died in her attempt to escape, then so be it. But he wanted to know for sure she was dead, for if she was alive, she belonged to him. "Your words are spoken with wisdom, and what you say is true," he said to Crazy Wolf. "We should be on our way back to our village. The snow will surely come before very long. I have need of this Crow woman, or I would not have delayed our journey. I will send Wounded Horse to follow Crooked Foot up this stream to see if he has found sign."

As Luke watched from his position behind a fallen tree, some fifty yards from the campfire, one lone Indian left the camp on foot and started following the frozen stream back toward the mountains. "He's goin' lookin' for the other fellow," Luke muttered to himself, knowing he'd be easy to find. With all the tracks lyin around, he'll see where Willow fled as well. *Might be a good idea to get on this fellow's tail*, he thought, deciding that any means available for trimming down the number of Blackfoot he had to fight better be taken advantage of. So he left his cover behind the fallen tree and circled back the way he had come, hurrying to set his pace with that of the lone Indian already trotting along beside the stream.

When the Indian was nearing the place where Willow had crossed over the stream, Luke held back a little farther, anticipating the Indian's pause to examine the tracks. It wasn't a long pause, since the signs were so obvious that Crooked Foot had left the stream there to follow the woman's tracks. Wounded Horse picked up his pace again, knowing Crooked Foot was on the woman's trail. Behind him, Luke started closing the distance between them, aware that they would soon come to Crooked Foot's body. His rifle strapped on his back, his bow ready with an arrow notched on the bowstring, Luke continued to close on the Blackfoot. He had reduced the distance between them to about twenty yards before Wounded Horse halted suddenly, stopped short by the sight of Crooked Foot's body lying in a pool of blood-red snow. He looked left and right for an ambush, unaware of the fully drawn bow aimed at his back. The force of the arrow as it drove into his back caused the Indian to stumble forward a few steps, trying to regain his balance. He turned to take the impact of a second arrow in his chest and dropped to his knees while fumbling unsuccessfully with his fusil to load it.

He ended the second Indian's suffering as he had the first. Then, although loathe to do so, he took the scalps of both and left his arrows in the one body. Just as he had done with Standing Elk, he hoped to confuse the war party, making them think they were killed by Indians, instead of a couple of fur trappers. Most important, maybe they might think there were many Indians hiding in these mountains. With no desire to keep the disgusting trophies, he found a rotten stump to cram the two scalps into. Worried about his tracks leading to the stump, he was suddenly rewarded by the gentle fall of snowflakes about him. He looked up at the clouds and expressed his heartfelt thanks.

The next problem to work on was the fact that the two bodies were partway up the hill, which would indicate the path they had been following would be a path that led to his camp. He looked up at the snow again and was grateful to see it coming down harder. If it kept up, he might get away with misleading the Indians. With no time to waste, he grabbed one of the warriors by his ankles and started dragging him back down to the creek. He dragged him across the creek and a good way up the hill on the other side. Then he went back to get the other body. When he was finished, he felt he had duplicated the scene of the killings, with the difference being they were partway up the opposite hill. *Now, if the Good Lord will do his part and cover all the tracks I've left,* he thought. Then he hurried back across the creek to climb up the hill and head to his camp. If he was lucky, the snow shower would be enough to cover everything, including the bloody patch of snow. As he hustled to climb up the slope, he could imagine Jug going crazy wondering where he was about now.

"Where the hell have you been?" Jug greeted him when he showed up to find the little man half-hidden among the lower boughs of a big fir near the horses. "I thought you mighta run into them Blackfeet lookin' for Willow and it looks like you did. I don't reckon there's a new tradin' post down that way where you coulda bought them guns." Without waiting for Luke's answer, he went on to another subject. "I told you there ain't nobody ever baked better biscuits than me. Willow wanted to know how I baked them biscuits. I had to clear the snow off my oven and mix up a batch of dough and bake her some biscuits."

Luke stared at him for a few moments, hardly believing his

ears. He had just come from killing two Blackfoot warriors, and knew there were eleven more that were going to go on the warpath as soon as they found out about the two he killed, their rifles on his shoulder. And Jug was talking about his biscuits again? Luke shook his head slowly and asked, "Are there any of 'em left?"

"Sure," Jug replied. "We saved you a couple. Willow made sure of that. She said you went off without no breakfast."

"Good, 'cause I'm hungry. What were you doin', sittin' up here in the tree?"

"Sittin' lookout," Jug said. "I was aimin' to pop the first Blackfoot that showed hisself on that rise. You was lucky I didn't shoot you."

"Oh, you interested in the Blackfoot, are you?" Luke chided him. "I thought you were just interested in your biscuits." Jug looked at him as if he didn't understand what he was implying. "Well," Luke went on, "we got ourselves a situation that don't exactly work to our advantage. There's a party of eleven Blackfoot warriors camped down by the river. There were thirteen of 'em, but one of them got killed when he came trackin' after Willow. Then another one got killed when he came trackin' after the first Indian."

"Dang," Jug grunted. "That don't sound too good. I thought them Injuns would be long gone. So they was onto her trail, huh? And it led 'em straight up the side of this hill right to this camp. Eleven of 'em," he repeated, fully aware of the problem now. "I reckon you shot the two dead ones, huh?"

"Not exactly, but I killed 'em," Luke replied. "You'da heard it, if I'da shot 'em. The rest of that war party woulda heard it, too. Their camp ain't too far away from here."

"I reckon we've got Willow to thank for that, too," Jug grumbled. "It'da been a sight better, if she coulda waited till they got a little farther up the Judith before she took off for the mountains."

"But then, she wouldn'ta had you and me to help her out, and we wouldn'ta wanted that, would we?"

"Nah," Jug replied. "We wouldn'ta wanted her to end up with that Bloody Hand Injun. She don't deserve that." He thought about her for a moment, picturing her beaming face as she watched him make up his biscuit dough. "No," he commented, "she's a keeper." Bringing his thoughts back to their immediate problem, he said, "If you killed those two Injuns where you said, then the rest of the Injuns will know they were on the way up this hill. So I reckon we'd best get ourselves ready to pick 'em off when they start up here."

"I'm hopin' we won't have to fight 'em here," Luke said. Then he went on to tell Jug how he had dragged the bodies across the creek and headed them up the hill on that side of the creek. "It all depends on if this snow is gonna keep fallin' because my tracks are all over that hillside."

"Well, then there ain't nothin' to worry about," Jug assured him. "That snow ain't even got started good. I coulda told you that. When the rheumatis in my knees start achin' like a toothache, it's either gonna pour rain or snow a blizzard."

"If that's so, then I hope your knees keep achin' all night long," Luke said. "No offense."

"None taken," Jug said.

"If we can keep that war party from findin' this camp, I'm hopin' they'll give up searchin' for the ones who killed their warriors and decide they've hung around in the cold weather too long. If that don't happen, then I'm hopin' to keep an eye on 'em and start whittlin' away at 'em till they lose too many. That's something I wanna talk to Willow about. She oughta be able to tell me what kinda weapons they've got."

Willow looked up from the antelope hide she was working on with the intent of making herself some warm clothing. Seeing that it was Luke who had come in, she smiled warmly, grateful to see his safe return. "You are hungry, yes? You go without eating anything this morning. I will cook you some elk meat."

"I am hungry, yes," Luke answered her greeting, "but I can

roast up my breakfast. Ain't no use in stoppin' what you're doin' there. And you can talk to me while I'm eatin'.'"

"I keep biscuits warm for you," Willow said and pointed to a covered pan by the fire.

"Why, I appreciate that," Luke told her, aware that she was attempting to keep a polite conversation going but was likely more anxious to hear if he had found the war party. "I hate to disappoint you, but that war party is still camped down by the river." Her face immediately showed the fear that had momentarily been forgotten. "They sent two men out to look for you, but they are both dead, although Bloody Hand doesn't know that yet." His statement caused her to draw her breath in sharply in distress, as a mental picture of the war chief's reaction when he found out formed in her mind. "We mighta got lucky with this snowfall," he went on. "Snowin' as hard as it is now, it won't take long to cover everybody's tracks. So it's still gonna take some luck for them to find this camp." He gave her an encouraging smile. "In the meantime, I'm gonna try to keep an eye on 'em. I'm hopin' you can give me a better idea of how many of those warriors have guns."

She paused to think about that for a moment before responding. "Most of them have bows," she said. "Bloody Hand has a long gun like yours and a pistol, too." She hesitated while she tried to form a mental image of the warriors in the camp as they had ridden out each morning. After another moment, she held up her hand with all fingers up.

"Five?" Luke asked.

"Five," she repeated.

He nodded. That meant there were now three armed with firearms, for both of the men he had killed on the side of the hill were carrying Northwest Trade Guns. A full stock weapon with a thirty-inch barrel, the Northwest Trade Gun was the most popular with the Indians. Called a fusil or *fusee* by the French, it was a smooth-bore weapon, which the Indians seemed to prefer over a rifle. He wasn't sure if that information would turn out to be of any value to him, but it was always good to know what you were up against. He also had to allow for the strong possibility that Willow could have easily miscounted, considering the stress she must have been under. He thanked her for her help and accepted the roasted strip of meat she offered. They sat in silence for a few minutes while he ate his belated breakfast of biscuit and elk before asking, "Where are your people, Willow?"

She answered with a sad smile and said, "My father was killed in a war with the Sioux, four winters ago. "My mother and my brother and I went to live with my mother's people in a village near the Platte River. That is where I met my husband. He took me to live with his people on the Yellowstone."

"Is that where you want to go when the winter is over? Back to your husband's people?" Luke asked.

She hesitated before answering. "There is nothing to go back to. Bloody Hand and his evil warriors killed half of Long Runner's people. They killed his mother and father. There is nothing there for me." She looked at him, waiting for his response. When he merely nodded his head but said nothing, she suggested, "I could stay and cook and sew for you and Jug. I am a good cook, and I can make your clothes and take care of your wounds."

Aware of the desperation in her proposal, Luke felt deep empathy for the poor lost young woman. He wanted to give her some comfort of mind, but he couldn't predict what might happen if the Blackfoot party found their little hidden valley. "That's a mighty fine offer you're makin'," he began. "Maybe I'd best tell you what our plans are. Me and Jug are partners in the business of trappin' animals, mostly beaver. We came up here in the fall to trap beaver, and now that winter's hit, we can't do any more trappin' till the winter's over. So we'll just hole up here like a couple of old grizzlies. And when the streams and ponds are runnin' free again, we'll go back to trappin' beaver till their fur gets too scrawny. Then we'll pack up our plews and head down to Horse Creek to the rendezvous to sell 'em. And that's what we have to do to make our livin'." He paused to add, "'Course all that might be changed, dependin' on what these dang Blackfeet decide to do." He watched her reactions throughout his whole dissertation on the life of a trapper, and she showed no emotion one way or the other. "Now that you've heard how dull it's gonna be, I'm sure I speak for Jug and myself when I say you're welcome to stay as long as you can stand it."

Her face immediately lit up at that. "Oh, thank you, Luke. I swear you not be sorry. I'm a good worker, I can skin and butcher a deer, and if you show me how to shoot, I can help you, if we have to fight."

"Well," Luke replied, laughing, "it sounds like a good deal all the way around." He finished up his breakfast and got to his feet, extended his hand, and said, "Welcome to the family." She took his hand and pumped it up and down vigorously. "I'd best go help Jug with the horses, now," he said. She was beaming brightly as he walked out.

"We got enough of that cottonwood feed till tomorrow?" Luke asked Jug when he walked up to the fir barn. "I wanna cut down another tree, but I don't wanna take a chance on somebody hearin' me choppin' a tree." Jug allowed that there was enough feed in his opinion, so Luke told him about the conversation he had just had with Willow. "I'd druther had talked to you about it before I told her she could stay, but I figured you felt about the same as I did."

"Oh, hell, yeah," Jug came back at once. "Ain't no way we're gonna turn that poor little gal out to make it on her own." He looked Luke in the eye then and cocked an eyebrow. "But one thing we'd best get straight right from the beginnin'. I ain't nowhere near as young as you two, but this is a partnership between me and you. And I'm the one who invited you to partner-up. So, if you two youngsters get to sniffin' around each other, and decide to hook up, there ain't gonna be no three-way split with the money. It's still fifty-fifty."

Luke couldn't suppress a chuckle. "Don't worry, Grandpa, there ain't nothin' like that goin' on. Hell, she's still in mournin'.

She just lost her husband. Right now, she just needs a place to get outta the cold."

"Yeah, I reckon," Jug said. "Let's try to make sure that damn Blackfoot don't get her back." He snorted in disgust and spat a stream of tobacco juice into the snow. "I swear, most of the time I have to meet a man before I get to despise him as much as I hate that Injun."

"If he finds out those two warriors of his were killed by a white trapper, I expect he'll hate you as much as you hate him," Luke responded.

Luke's remark caused Jug to pause and think about it a moment. "That ol' boy must be wonderin' about a lotta things right now, after he finds his two friends deader'n hell, scalped, and two arrows stickin' outta one of 'em. Them arrows has got all kinds of Blackfoot markin's on 'em. That's got to cause him a heap of confusion. He might hafta get him some signs made up for the rest of 'em to wear." He made a sweeping motion across his chest. "I am a Blackfoot!"

They both got a chuckle out of Jug's remarks, but both of them knew they were in an extremely precarious situation. "Let's take a look at my tracks," Luke said and walked a little way past the horses. Jug followed him and they stood looking down the slope in the direction from which Luke had returned after his encounter with the two warriors. "It's doin' a pretty good job of coverin' up my tracks," he said, "and it ain't showin' any sign of lettin' up. Pretty soon, they're gonna have to find us on their own 'cause they ain't gonna be able to follow my tracks."

Chapter 13

"It has been too long," Two Toes said to Crazy Wolf. "It is beginning to snow harder and soon it will become too dark to see anything. Still, Bloody Hand waits here. If Wounded Horse has not caught up with Crooked Foot by now, then the woman must have drowned in the river as you said." The young Blackfoot warrior obviously wanted Crazy Wolf to convince Bloody Hand to forget the woman, get off this riverbank, and find a ravine or some place to try to stay warm that night. Then start for home in the morning while their horses could still make it through the snow.

"I have already spoken with Bloody Hand on the matter of the woman," Crazy Wolf said. "I think he will surely see the folly in searching for her." He didn't have to try to talk to him again, however, for Bloody Hand called to him first.

"Crazy Wolf," Bloody Hand said as he suddenly left the campfire and marched over to join them. "I must find our warriors. Something is not right. If they could not find the woman's trail, we will have to search for her in the morning. Two Toes, you and Yellow Rock come with me. Crazy Wolf, you must stay here and keep the fire burning strong. I'll take the younger men to help me find Wounded Horse."

"As you wish," Crazy Wolf replied and stood back while the

three men climbed on their horses and started up the stream. Bloody Hand led his search party along the frozen stream while the other warriors gathered around Crazy Wolf and watched them until they disappeared from sight. Only then did one of them question the war chief's sense of priorities.

"I have fear that this Crow woman has cast a spell over Bloody Hand," Walks His Horse complained. "Two Toes is right, the woman is dead. She needed warm clothes to survive in this cold. If she is not in the river, then she is most likely lying dead in the snow. Some of us have decided to start back to our village in the morning whether he has found the woman or not. We don't want to offend Bloody Hand. Maybe he will listen to you."

Crazy Wolf nodded his head thoughtfully. "We will see what the other warriors found. Maybe he will decide she is gone and decide to leave this place. But I will tell you this, if he stays, then I will go back to the village with you." His decision seemed to reassure the other warriors.

The snow was already covering the tracks of Wounded Horse and Crooked Foot, with only an occasional spotting of a print where one of the men they followed had slipped or stepped in a hole. Bloody Hand made no attempt to hide his irritation with the weather, but eventually he was forced to give in to the solid white expanse before them. He turned to give the signal to halt brief seconds before Yellow Rock sang out, "There!" Bloody Hand and Two Toes looked in the direction Yellow Rock pointed, following a line toward the upslope of a steep hill. What at first appeared to be a rock or a clump of bushes, covered with snow, was actually the form of a human arm extended from the object. Bloody Hand immediately nudged his horse forward and came out of the saddle beside the snow-covered mound, which was twenty yards or so up the incline.

As the three warriors gathered around it, it became clear what they had found. Two objects that had appeared to be dead limbs sticking out from the clump were actually two arrows protruding from the corpse of Wounded Horse, one from his gut, the other from his back. His body was lying on its side, on top of Crooked Foot, whose throat was gaping open as if screaming out his pain. None of the three searchers uttered a word at once, such was the shock of finding this gruesome discovery and realizing at once that they were not alone in these mountains. The belated reactions of Two Toes and Yellow Rock were to look around them anxiously for signs of an ambush, even though the bodies were covered with snow and had obviously been lying there for quite some time. Bloody Hand's initial response was to rake some of the snow away from Crooked Foot's body with his foot to make sure the woman's body was not under it. "She has found some friends," he declared and stepped back a couple of steps while he considered that possibility.

He tilted his head back and gazed up the steep slope of the hill. They were no doubt following the woman's tracks up the hill. *Did she know there was something up the hill?* He asked himself, then answered it immediately. *She had no way of knowing. She was just running blindly. But now what has become of her?* He stepped back to the bodies and took hold of the arrow in Wounded Horse's back. He tried to pull it out, but the arrowhead was frozen solid in Wounded Horse's back, so he broke it in two. He stepped back again to examine the shaft. After a minute, he declared, "These markings on the shaft are Blackfoot."

"Don't they know they are killing their own people?" Two Toes asked, still looking around constantly, expecting more arrows at any second.

"Blackfoot have hunted these mountains for many years," Bloody Hand told him. "Maybe the Crows have been hunting here, too. I think our brothers were killed by Crows. Then he wondered if he had made a mistake when he thought earlier about the Crow woman wandering lost and aimlessly in these mountains. Maybe she knew where she was running to, after all. The thought only added to his desire to catch her. "Come!" He said then. "We must go back and warn the others that there are

Crow hunters here. We'll take our dead back to our camp. We must give them a proper burial."

They loaded the stiffened bodies of Crooked Foot and Wounded Horse on the horses and led the horses back to the camp where the reaction was one of total alarm. The bodies were set aside to be dealt with after a pow wow over the cause of their deaths. Bloody Hand's conclusion that the killers were Crow, seemed to make sense to the others. Evidently, they had killed some Blackfoot hunters and that accounted for the Blackfoot arrows. "It is more important that we stay here now until we find these killers," Bloody Hand said. "It is no longer a question of finding the woman. We have dead men to avenge. I think there are only a small number of these hunters. If there were more of them, they would attack our camp. But that would be suicide for the few cowards who are sneaking around in these hills hoping to attack lone Blackfoot hunters."

"What Bloody Hand says is true," Crazy Wolf said. "We must find these cowards who killed Wounded Horse and Crooked Foot. They must die." He did not say it, but he was thinking that their deaths could be directly attributed to Bloody Hand's obsession for this Crow woman. If his mind had not been filled with thoughts of the woman, they would have been well on their way back to their village, and Wounded Horse and Crooked Foot would still be alive. "It is my feeling that we should start guarding our camp at night," he continued. "And when we go to search for these Crow hunters, we should never go with less than four of us. And make sure that at least one of those four has a gun. I don't know if the Crow hunters had guns before this, but we know they have guns now, since both Wounded Horse and Crooked Foot had guns."

"As always, Crazy Wolf's words are wise," Bloody Hand said. "Let us first honor our dead." In line with the older man's advice, four of the warriors went up the valley beyond their camp until they found a suitable ravine with trees tall enough to serve as the two dead warriors' burial platforms.

After they managed to assemble the platforms for their dead as best they could under the circumstances, they returned to their camp to discuss their next move. "As for me," Bloody Hand declared, "I will not leave this place until I have found the cowards who ambushed Wounded Horse and Crooked Foot. But I cannot tell another man what to do. A man must do what his heart tells him to do."

"It would be wrong to let the deaths of our brothers go unpunished," Crazy Wolf spoke then. "And these Crow hunters need to see that they are not allowed to hunt in Blackfoot territory. I stand with Bloody Hand. We must kill these Crow devils and avenge our two warriors."

"Crazy Wolf speaks for my heart, too," Two Toes spoke then. "They must be avenged, but it is getting very cold. I think we should move our camp away from this riverbank and find a place with better protection for us and our horses." His statement was met with grunts of agreement from the rest of the warriors. So it was quickly decided to move the camp in the morning and to set up guards for their present camp throughout that night.

Back at the little tipi by the waterfall, Luke had no way of knowing, but his plan to try to persuade the Blackfoot party to think they were being attacked by some other tribe of Indians, was working. He would have liked to check to see if they had discovered the two bodies he left for them to find, but he couldn't do so without leaving a fresh set of tracks for them to follow. The snow made it difficult for him to try to keep an eye on the war party, but he felt he had to know what their intentions were. With the odds against him and Jug in numbers, he didn't care much for the idea of just sitting there, waiting for the war party to find them. His thoughts were interrupted then when Willow came to the corral in the trees to tell him she had cooked his supper and wanted him to come eat it while it was hot.

"I look through your supplies and find a sack of cornmeal,"

Willow told him. "Jug say that okay," she hastily added and paused.

When he realized she was asking if that was all right, he smiled and assured her. "Sure, that's okay. I told you, you're part of the family now. You don't have to ask about lookin' in the cookin' supplies. I reckon you saw that cornmeal had never been opened."

She favored him with a big smile then. "I notice, so I make some corn cakes to eat with your elk meat."

Luke cocked his head and grinned. "Well, now, that surely suits my taste," he said.

It obviously pleased her. "Jug say I make Johnny-cakes," she replied.

"That's right, that's what we call 'em," he said. He was already seeing the advantage of having a woman along for the winter, especially when they were waiting it out in one place. They anticipated keeping their camp right where it was now, even after the ice melted, since they found themselves right in the middle of enough potential to trap all they could manage to pack out. They were already thinking it time to create a hidden cache where they could keep their made beaver packs until they were ready to take them to rendezvous next summer. In fact, Luke already had a spot in mind, near the top of a narrow ravine on the backside of the hill their camp was located on. "Yes, ma'am," he said, "let's go try out those Johnny-cakes."

"Good thing you decided to come eat," Jug crowed when Luke and Willow came back to the tipi. "I believe I coulda finished that whole plate full of 'em."

Not sure he was japin' Luke, Willow immediately assured him. "I would make more for you."

"He's just makin' chin music," Luke told her. "If he tried to eat that whole plate of cakes, he'da blown up." His comment was good for a laugh from all three. "Ain't you gonna eat any of these?" Luke asked Willow, when she sat down with the antelope hide she had been working on, content to watch them enjoy the meal she had prepared.

"I eat one before," she replied. "I have to be sure they taste good."

"Well, they do," Luke responded. "They truly shine. Ain't that right, Jug?"

"They surely do," Jug answered, amused by the way Willow's face reflected her satisfaction for their praise. What, he wondered, were they to do with this young Crow woman, if they were able to make it back to rendezvous with their top notches still intact? Looking at the two young people, he couldn't help wondering if he might find himself without a partner next year. He hoped not because Luke Ransom was the best man he'd ever met in this business. He had not seen any signs of anything beyond polite kindness, but there was always the chance that Luke might decide to become a squaw man by the time this winter was done. Some of the boys did. It offered a lot of advantages besides the obvious one. The Indian wives he had seen were real partners to their white husbands. They cooked his meals, sewed his clothes, treated his wounds, skinned and butchered his kills, scraped and stretched his beaver plews, and more. *If I was younger, I might consider marryin' one myself*, he thought.

After supper, both men went outside to take a look around as the darkness quickly moved in to cloak the waterfall and the tipi for the night. They split up and walked the perimeter of the small clearing, searching for any sign of a visitor. When they met at the top of the circle, just even with the frozen waterfall on one side, and the corral made of fir trees on the other, they paused to talk about their plans. "I wanna start diggin' out a hole to cache our pelts," Luke said, "but I don't wanna be stuck in a hole in the ground while that bunch of Blackfeet are roamin' all over hell and creation, lookin' for this place."

"No, I reckon not," Jug replied. "I expect we'll both have to keep our eyes peeled in case they happen on our little valley. We'll need to load up all our rifles and the fusils we took from the Blackfoot, if they do show up here. We can show Willow how to load one, so we can keep shootin' in a hurry." He paused for a second or two, shook his head, and spat. "You reckon there's any chance they got scared off? Maybe decided they've lost enough with them two?"

"I don't think so," Luke answered. "I think they're gonna have to lose a couple more before they start thinkin' about headin' home. I'd like to find out if I'm right or wrong. And if they're still here, I suspect they'll move their camp, and we need to know where to. I reckon that's up to me to find out. So I'll be out of here at first light in the mornin'."

"I don't know, Luke," Jug hedged. "That sounds a little risky. If they catch you out in the open, there ain't no place you can hide in this snow. We might be better off to just hole-up in our dug-out tipi, and we oughta be able to shoot enough of 'em to make 'em give it up."

"What you say is true," Luke replied. "But even if they couldn't kill us, they could cause us a heap of damage, and not just the tipi. They could shoot that to pieces, maybe set it on fire durin' the night. But they could steal the horses and leave us with nothin' to carry our packs back to rendezvous. So I expect it'd be best if we knew where their camp is."

"You've been doin' all the scoutin' and fightin' for us, and that don't hardly seem right in a fifty-fifty partnership. I expect, if we need to know where they move their camp, it's my turn to do the scoutin'."

"Well, that is right, I reckon," Luke responded. "And I'd hold you to that if you had two good arms. But this job calls for two hands and two long legs, if I get caught in the open. And you ain't got neither one right now. So you be patient and let that arm heal up. Then, by Ned, you can chase your tail all over these snow-covered mountains, and I'll set at home here with Willow eatin' coffee and Johnny-cakes."

"I didn't ask to get shot," Jug said in his defense and rubbed his wounded arm with his other hand. "Won't be much longer and it'll be good as new." Luke suspected the arm was close to being ready right now. Jug had quit favoring it whenever he was doing any chore, but he was glad to give him an excuse. With that settled, they went back inside the tipi to report to Willow that there was no sign of the war party on the hill. "We'll be checkin' again in a little while," Jug reassured her.

Luke didn't tell Jug all the details about his plan, but when it was time to go to bed, Willow asked him where he was carrying his bedroll and a large buffalo hide to. She seemed especially alarmed when he picked up his rifle, bow, and possibles bag. "I gotta do a little chore early in the mornin'," Luke answered her. "I'm gonna sleep with the horses tonight. I think Smoke is gettin' lonesome and thinks I don't love him anymore."

He could only avoid Jug's eyes for so long before having to hear from him. The little man shook his head slowly several times before complaining. "I swear, partner, I reckon I could guard the horses just as good as you. I weren't too worried about 'em tonight. Figured it was too soon for them Blackfoot to be showin' up here."

"I figure the same thing," Luke assured him. "It'd be one helluva lucky thing for them to stumble on this camp this soon. But I got to thinkin' about the fix we'd be in if they did just happen to get up here and drive our horses off." He looked at a wide-eyed gaping Willow, grinned, and said, "Why, that would be a helluva long walk all the way to Horse Creek for a young Crow woman."

"I can still sleep with the horses tonight," Jug insisted.

"No such a thing," Luke replied. "I'll be leaving early in the mornin', anyway."

Willow looked at them, shaking her head. "You both loco."

Chapter 14

Luke was awake with the first flicker of light penetrating the branches of the fir tree he slept under. He didn't hesitate and rolled out of the heavy buffalo hide he had wrapped around his bedroll. Before moving out into the meadow, he stopped to listen for the usual morning sounds of his camp, the horses shifting about quietly, the muted sound of the frozen waterfall. Hearing nothing out of the ordinary that might cause him concern, he rolled his blankets up and stuck them on a tree limb. The buffalo robe he planned to take with him. It was warm protection, and the white skin side of it might be needed if he had to try to hide on a snowy hillside. He quickly saddled Smoke and climbed aboard, taking one final look around to make sure he was the only early riser on the hillside. Satisfied, he rode up past the waterfall, holding the bay gelding to a slow walk up over the top of the hill, since he was concerned about the horse's footing under the three-odd feet of snow. As soon as he reached the top of the hill, he guided Smoke into the thick forest of fir trees and began a very deliberate path weaving through the trees until reaching the narrow valley below. It was his hope that it would be a difficult path to discover, should the Blackfoot party come this way.

Once he was down on the valley floor, he remained in the trees until he circled back close to the place where he had killed the elk cow. He had been right in thinking the bull and his three cows were part of a herd of elk and they had bedded down in the cottonwoods below his camp. There were ample signs of the elk feeding on the cottonwoods, sprouts of other bushes and trees, even twigs and branches of firs. He continued along the edge of the meadow until he found what he was looking for, thousands of tracks left by the large animals where they crossed the snow-covered expanse of grass. With no concern for Smoke's tracks now, he could cross over the meadow and go directly back to the river and the Blackfoot camp. Directly below his camp now, even though it was not visible because of the stand of cottonwoods at the foot of the hill, he did not tarry. He held Smoke to a lope in case there might be one scout to happen to see him as he crossed over the frozen creek that split the meadow.

Once he left the meadow, he guided Smoke through the trees beside the trail that circled the mountains. The snow covering the trail had not been disturbed, which was somewhat reassuring because it meant the Indians had not ridden in the direction of his camp. It had been his guess that they would likely go in the opposite direction, since everything that had happened had come from that direction. And since they would likely find the bodies of their two warriors back that way, that would be the direction they would start looking—if they were going to stay. He still had hopes that they might have decided to head back to their village. He reined Smoke up to a stop when he recognized the fallen tree from which he had scouted the Blackfoot camp before. There was no fire and no one in sight. They had gone!

At once hopeful, he pressed Smoke forward, riding up to twenty yards or so toward the remains of the large fire in the center of the small clearing before stopping again to take another cautious look around him. Finally, he rode into the center of the camp where he could see the signs of their leaving. But the tracks did not head across the river to swing north on the trail beside the Judith as he had hoped. They led back along the frozen stream, into the mountains, the same direction they followed

Willow in, and the same direction they found the bodies of their brothers. *They are not leaving, so they must be looking for a better campsite,* he thought. *And I sure as hell didn't scare them.* The point of his scout this morning was to see what the Indians were up to, so he followed their tracks away from the original campsite.

He continued following the tracks of the eleven warriors as they moved along the stream that Crooked Foot and Wounded Horse had followed. But when they reached the foot of the hill where he had dragged the two bodies, they circled around toward the river again, instead of continuing up the narrow valley between the hills. He was not surprised. They would have better luck getting water out of the river than the tiny stream they had been following. His mind skipped back to a time before this when he had ridden along the foot of this hill. He had been riding after the three Blackfoot hunters who had raided the first camp he and Jug had built. If his memory served him, there should be a bold stream coming down this hill through a large stand of lodgepole pines. *A good place to camp,* he told himself, so he reined Smoke back to a slow walk while he decided what to do. His concern was the way the foot of the hill was shaped, like a wall of rock protruding out from the hill, forming a half-pocket that acted as a wind break. If the Indians had decided to make their camp inside that pocket, and Luke thought there was a good chance they had, he might not want to ride blindly around that rock protrusion. "Maybe we'd best find another way around that hill," he said softly to Smoke. Smoke nodded his head up and down as if in agreement, but firmer confirmation came in the form of a thin ribbon of smoke that drifted casually up from inside the pocket. He interpreted that as a sign that they had not moved during the night, but had started right at daybreak, just as he had. To confirm his thinking, the thin ribbon of smoke began to darken, suggesting a fire just starting to burn with more enthusiasm.

He turned Smoke around and rode back the way he had come, circling back between the two hills. When he came to the place where he had left the two bodies, he turned his horse up the hill, thinking Smoke's tracks would hardly be noticed with all the other tracks the Blackfeet had left. It would be highly unlikely any of the warriors would notice a single set of tracks continuing on up the slope among the pine trees. When he was about three-quarters of the way up the slope, he dismounted and tied Smoke's reins to a tree limb. Then he continued on foot, moving through the trees until he reached a spot where he could look down into the camp. With the buffalo hide draped over his head and shoulders, he slowly worked his way closer, until he could clearly see all the members of the war party. He had been correct in assuming they had only arrived at their new camp short minutes before.

The man he had assumed to be Bloody Hand before, when he had first scouted the camp on the riverbank, appeared to be even more in command as he talked to four other warriors. He seemed to be giving them instructions. One of them carried a trade gun, and when Bloody Hand was finished talking, all four nodded enthusiastically and ran to their horses. Amid war whoops and words of encouragement, the four rode out of the camp and headed back around the rock wall. *A scouting party,* Luke thought. *I'd better keep an eye on them.* It was critical for his, Willow's, and Jug's safety to know where the Blackfoot scouting parties would be concentrating. He slowly withdrew from his position directly over the camp. Then, when he had the cover of the trees, he hurried back around the hill to a position where he could see the four scouts when they rode around the wall.

In a matter of seconds, they appeared, following the trail they had made on their way to the new camp. He lingered there for a few minutes to watch them till they passed out of sight before he went back to his horse. He stepped up into the saddle and turned Smoke's head down the slope. Then he reined the horse back suddenly when the four warriors appeared between the two hills and proceeded up the little stream that ran between the hills. He assumed they were still looking for Willow, since that was where her trail had last been discovered. His next thought was that he had unwittingly treed himself right over the Blackfoot camp. He had taken the time and trouble to move the two bodies to the hill he was now on, to lead them away from the trail up to his own camp. When there was no evidence this morning to indicate they had continued on up past the bodies, he assumed they had not bit on his attempt to mislead them. He could only figure that Bloody Hand had sent them to make sure there was no one on the hill now that they had decided to make their camp at the foot of it. *I'd better get my behind off this damn hill,* he thought and started to sidle across the slope but stopped short again when the four scouts did not even glance at the spot where they had found the bodies. Instead, they turned their horses up the opposite hill, much to Luke's shock. This was no doubt in response to Bloody Hand's instructions, for they showed no interest at all in the direction Luke had sought to lead them. Instead, they were preparing to climb the slope toward his camp. With no time to think of a way to stop them, Luke sought to distract them with a plan so desperate that it had little chance of success. He quickly wheeled Smoke around and returned to the position he had taken to look down on their new camp. As quickly as he could, he readied his rifle to fire. And although he sought to catch the scouting party's attention, he took care not to waste a shot in doing so.

Some three-hundred feet below him, Yellow Rock stood in the center of the clearing, talking to Bloody Hand, who was coming out of one of the shelters at the edge of the clearing. They were both startled when Yellow Rock staggered a couple of steps backward an instant before the sound of the rifle rang out. While Yellow Rock dropped to his knees, clutching his chest, Bloody Hand dived into the bushes to find cover. All of the other warriors were not as quick as Bloody Hand. Confused by the shot, they looked around to see where it had come from. It was a costly mistake because the next rifle ball dropped another of Bloody Hand's warriors before they realized the shots were coming from the hill above them. In a matter of seconds, there were no more targets for Luke to aim at, so he quickly hurried back to see how the

four-man scouting party would react to the shots. He was relieved to see his distraction had worked, and the four of them
were galloping back to the camp. He hustled back to his sniper
position to be ready for another possible target when they rode
back around the rock wall.

His one thought now was to thin the war party down to as few
as he possibly could. So he set his sight on the first warrior to ride
into the camp. When the rider saw the two men lying on the
ground, he reined his horse to a quick stop, giving Luke an easy
target. When the riders behind him, confused by the shot, hesitated long enough to give Luke time to reload, a second target
fell victim to his long rifle. Certain now that the shots had all
come from directly above them, an angry Bloody Hand was
shouting out orders to get their horses and give chase. From the
time it took between shots, he guessed their enemy was just one
man. "After him!" He ordered as he jumped on the gray gelding
and headed up the slope.

Above him, Luke retreated hurriedly to his horse, aware that
the entire camp of Indians, which was only seven warriors now,
was coming after him. To his advantage, the warriors were all
coming up the steep slope, which slowed them down a great
deal. He was already three-quarters of the way to the top, so he
expected to extend his lead. And he planned to take them for
quite a ride. As he encouraged Smoke to make the last of the
climb to the top, he told himself that this might have been the
best thing to happen. Just a few minutes before, the four-man
Blackfoot scouting party was preparing to ride straight up the hill
that would take them to his camp—and Jug and Willow. With his
sniper action, he had reduced the enemy number by four. And
his intention now was to lead the Indians in a chase across the top
of this hill, which was the end of a range of hills that led into the
mountains. He would lead them across the length of the range
and into those mountains. From there, he would see if he could
lose them somewhere in the many valleys and canyons. The
main thing he wanted to accomplish was to make them think his

camp was in the mountains and not right next door to their camp—then hope they never became curious enough to climb the hill next to the one they camped by. His plan might have been a good one and possibly one that would have worked on most men. But Bloody Hand was not like most men.

The Blackfoot war chief had been suspicious about the location of the bodies of Wounded Horse and Crooked Foot. Bloody Hand thought it unlikely the bodies would be lying on top of each other as they had found them, so the arrows would be obvious. Standing between those two hills, he had felt he was being tricked. And he was almost certain the Crow woman he so desired had fled up the hill opposite the one where the bodies were left. That's why he had sent Yellow Hand and three warriors to climb that hill. And now, he was almost certain Willow was at the top of this hill. So he kept Crazy Wolf and Two Toes with him and sent the other four warriors to follow the man who had killed the other warriors.

On that particular hill Luke was thinking about, Bloody Hand stood contemplating a pleasure he anticipated enjoying shortly. At the top of that hill, there were now two additional concerned people. At the sound of Luke's first shot, Jug came out of the corral where he had been feeding the horses, his rifle in hand. When other shots followed, Willow came out of the tipi, alarmed. "What is it?" She asked. "Where is Luke?"

"I don't know," Jug answered her, "but that sounds like Luke's rifle. I hope he ain't got hisself in trouble." He looked at her and shook his head. "Them shots sounded like they came from that hill right next to this'un." He formed a picture in his mind of Luke being chased by angry hostiles, and he felt helpless to come to his rescue. He hesitated to run off to look for Luke and leave Willow alone, defenseless. They hadn't even gotten around to teaching her how to load and fire a gun. He couldn't leave everything they owned here unprotected, anyway. When he could think of nothing he could do but wait, he climbed up the hill over the waterfall where he could see everything from the camp, on down to the cottonwoods, and into the meadow beyond. There was no sign of man nor beast. "Doggone you, partner, you'd better not get yourself kilt and leave me to take care of all this," he muttered to himself. Ever since he had been a free trapper, he had wintered by himself. But this was the first time he had wintered in the middle of Blackfoot territory. Doing it alone didn't appeal to him.

While Jug contemplated the rest of the winter without Luke, Luke concentrated on leading his pursuers as far into the mountains as possible before he tried to lose them. Making no attempt to hide his trail, he continued across the ridge until it began to slope up where it joined a mountain. He decided it was time to try to cover his trail, not completely, but enough to make it look like he was. Heading back down now, he angled toward a canyon with a deep stream that forked to go on both sides of a small island about forty yards wide. *This might do,* he thought, decided which fork suited him, and headed for it. Finding it only partially frozen, his first thought was, *Damn! Maybe we ought to be over here setting traps.* He guided Smoke into the stream and rode up it a good way before coming out near the base of a large fir tree. The low branches of the tree were heavy with snow, so he dismounted and led Smoke carefully beneath the boughs of the trees and into the center of the island. Then he went back to the bank of the stream where he had left the water. Watching carefully where he placed his feet, he walked backward away from the stream, gently shaking the fir boughs as he retreated, causing the snow to drop onto the ground to cover his and his horse's tracks. He paused then to listen. His pursuers were catching up to him, and Smoke needed a rest, so this was as good a place as any to settle this business. He left Smoke there in the middle of the island and carefully made his way back to the end, where the stream forked. With his buffalo hide draped over him again, he knelt low and waited.

In a few minutes time, they appeared, their ponies struggling to keep from sliding down a steeper part of the ridge, but there were only four. Three had stayed behind. It offered no encouragement to Luke because four Blackfoot warriors were as much a chore as any man could ask for. Only one of them carried a Northwest fusil. They followed his tracks to the stream and paused at the fork. Then they divided up, and two followed one fork, the other two took the other fork. Luke's problem at that point was which two to attack first without leaving himself open to return fire. His problem was solved for him when Talks with Eagle pulled up to load his gun. The other two warriors proceeded to ride on down the stream on their side of the island. "Hurry," Dull Axe said when Talks with Eagle seemed to be taking too much time. He started to complain, but he was suddenly startled when Talks with Eagle's gun dropped to the ground. Dull Axe saw the arrow moments before he felt the strong impact of a second arrow when it entered his side. "Ambush!" he yelled painfully and wheeled his horse away from the stream, the arrow embedded deep in his side. Talks with Eagle still sat on his horse, unable to move as he stared at the arrow shaft protruding from his belly.

Luke moved to another position as the other two warriors wheeled their horses around and galloped back to the fork. He brought his rifle up, set his front sight on the first rider, and knocked him off his horse. That was enough to persuade the other warrior to wheel away again and head for the cover of the trees at the base of the ridge where he had seen his comrade seek cover. Luke reloaded his rifle while watching Talks with Eagle still sitting there, his eyes glazed. Luke stepped across the stream and gave the horse a good whack on the behind. The horse took off at a gallop. Halfway to the trees where the other two warriors were, Talks with Eagle rolled over to the side and fell off. To encourage the remaining two, Luke threw a rifle shot into the trees where they watched.

"Come, we go," Walking Bird said. "They are too many and you are wounded." Dull Axe didn't argue and they fled on the trail they had made moments before. The two rider-less horses galloped after them. When he was sure they weren't coming back, Luke hurried to check on the two he had shot. There was no time spent with the one he shot with his rifle. He was already dead with a hole in his chest. Approaching the base of the ridge, where Talks with Eagle had fallen, he held his pistol ready in case the Indian was playing possum. The wounded man was still alive but suffering great pain with the arrow still protruding from his gut. He made no attempt to resist as he looked up at Luke with mournful eyes almost as if asking him to hurry. To accommodate him, Luke fired a shot into his brain.

His concern now was why the other three Blackfeet had not come with the four he had just dealt with. He had been almost certain all seven of the warriors had come up that mountain after him. At a trot, he hurried back to the stream where he found the fusil that Talks with Eagle had dropped. He had no use for more of the Northwest Trade Guns, and his first impulse was to throw it in the fork of the stream. Then his natural tendency not to contaminate good drinking water caused him to hesitate. So, instead, he swung it like an axe against a tree until the barrel was sufficiently bent and the stock was broken off. Then he tossed it over in a bank of laurel bushes on the little island and went to retrieve his horse.

Chapter 15

Jug caught his first sight of them when they were only halfway up the hill. Three Blackfoot warriors, they were making their way cautiously up from the stream that ran between the two hills. "Oh, Lordy," he muttered and immediately left his perch over the waterfall to hurry down the snowy hill as fast as his short little legs could take him. He ran straight to the tipi to get Luke's spare rifle, startling Willow when he burst through the entrance. "We got company!" he blurted. "Can you load a rifle?" When her answer was an expression of frightened alarm, he said, "Never mind. I ain't got time to show you now." He picked up Luke's other rifle and started out the door. "There's three Blackfoot comin' up the hill. I'll try to stop 'em!"

"Bloody Hand!" She gasped, at once terrified.

"I reckon," he said, knowing there was no safe place for her to go. "You just hunker down here in the tipi. There's three of 'em, and I'll have two loaded rifles and a loaded pistol, and I'll make sure each shot counts. They'll have to get by me before they can get to you, and that ain't gonna happen. I gotta go now. You just stay outta sight. You can take this skinnin' knife, if it'll make you feel like you ain't completely helpless." He drew it from his belt and she took it eagerly. With no more time to waste, he hurried out the door.

With a rifle in each hand, Jug ran up past the fir corral to a barrier he and Luke had constructed of logs to discourage the horses from wandering down the steep side of the hill. When he reached it, he could see the three Indians more clearly. They had dismounted and left their horses behind when they reached the steeper part of the hill. Jug readied his rifle to fire and loaded Luke's with powder and ball and propped it on the logs beside him. He couldn't help cursing when he remembered that Willow had remembered five fusils among the eleven warriors. All three of the warriors advancing upon him were carrying firearms. *I'll let 'em get a few feet closer, then I'll introduce myself,* he thought.

When they had advanced to within about forty yards of his position, he took aim at the most generous target and squeezed off a shot. Down on the slope, Crazy Wolf howled in pain when the rifle ball struck him in the chest. "There!" Bloody Hand yelled when he saw the powder flash and immediately brought his weapon to bear on the log barrier. When Jug rose again to shoot, Bloody Hand squeezed the trigger, causing Jug's shot to go wide of his target when the war chief's shot knocked the little man on his back. Bloody Hand stood up then, confident that there was no one else to fight. He was sure there were only two men in this camp, two men responsible for the deaths of his warriors. "And now, they have killed Crazy Wolf," he said to Two Toes.

Thinking the war chief had taken leave of his senses, Two Toes warned, "Take cover!"

Bloody Hand chucked. "There is no one else to fight. The other man is running for his life toward the mountains. We will take care of these two bushwhackers who have dared to come into this territory to trap our beaver." He pointed up toward the log barrier. "Go and make sure that one is dead. I will see if there is anyone else in the hut." He would have gone first to take Jug's scalp, but he felt certain that Willow was in that hut. He knew in his heart that she had taken up with the fur trappers, and the thought of it brought the blood in his veins to a boil. He would have her, here and now, then he would kill her and tie her scalp on his scalp string. Barely able to control his excitement, he pushed on up the hill to see the frozen waterfall and the make-shift corral for the horses. With one quick glance toward Two Toes, he could see that Two Toes had not met with any opposition, so he turned his full attention to the woman he knew was crouching in fear for her life inside the tipi. There were bound to be many things of value besides the woman, as well, he thought as he reached for the door flap.

Up the hill, Two Toes approached the log barrier cautiously, alert for any tricks from the white trapper. Ready to fire at the first sign of movement on Jug's part, he paused when he saw the little trapper lying on his back, a hole in his hide coat where Bloody Hand's shot had struck him down. Looking dazed and helpless, the little man could do nothing to defend himself. When Two Toes realized that, it brought an evil smile to his face. He reached down, picked up Jug's rifle, and threw it out of Jug's reach. Thinking it unnecessary to waste powder and ball, Two Toes laid his rifle aside and drew his scalping knife. Then he knelt with his knee on Jug's stomach, causing the blood already running from the gunshot wound to increase. "This the price all you white dogs must pay when you come to trap our beaver," he spat. He then pulled Jug's cap off and grabbed a handful of his long gray hair, using it as a handle to yank the helpless man's head back, exposing his neck. Jug's eyes flickered briefly just as the Blackfoot warrior raised his arm for the fatal strike and Two Toes thought he saw the helpless man smile an instant before the lead ball from Jug's pistol exploded under his lower jaw and tore up into his brain.

Two Toes remained kneeling on Jug's stomach until Jug summoned enough strength to push him hard enough to cause him to fall over. Jug struggled to move then but found that he felt too helpless to. He knew the third member of the attacking party would find Willow in the tipi and there was nothing he could do to protect her. He hated that worse than the knowledge that, after the Indian had taken care of Willow, he would come to finish him off.

Bloody Hand paused with his hand on the flap of the tipi entrance when he heard the pistol shot. He released the flap and looked up the hill in time to see Two Toes keel over and fall on his side. Bloody Hand's initial reaction was to run to his aid, but he hesitated, watching for signs that Jug was still a threat. His concern was for the possibility that Willow might take the opportunity to run if he did so. And he was still sure that she was hiding inside the tipi. So he waited and watched the bodies he could barely see behind the logs. After a short while, he decided the trapper was dead. With great anticipation, he turned back to the tipi entrance, grabbed the flap again, and flung it open. "Now, Crow dog!" He roared out triumphantly and burst through the opening to find her standing across the fire from him, an arrow notched in the bowstring, the bowstring fully drawn. "Waugh!" He cried out in surprise and tried to put his arms up in protection, but the arrow passed through to his heart. Terrified though she was, she did not hesitate, and notched another arrow immediately to drive into his chest beside the first one. She drew another arrow from the quiver hanging close to Luke's bed and followed Bloody Hand as he staggered outside to escape the determined woman. He finally stumbled and fell outside when he was struck with a third arrow in his back. Only then, did she turn to look up the hill toward the horses, thinking Jug might be dead.

Still wary of the fearsome Blackfoot war chief, lest he suddenly jump up again to attack her, she used the bow to prod his body, harder and harder, until she satisfied herself that he was dead. She went back inside the tipi and got one more of Luke's arrows before she walked up to the corral. With it notched on her bowstring, she cautiously approached the two bodies she could now see on the ground. Immediately alarmed when she saw Jug lying stone still, with Two Toes' legs on top of his, she cried out, "Jug!"

She jumped, startled, when his eyes flickered open. He stared up at her for a few moments before he asked, "Is this Heaven?" He had not been sure if he was dead or alive, but he felt certain that she had been slain by Bloody Hand.

"You're alive!" she cried then. "I thought they had killed you!"

"I weren't sure," he groaned painfully. "They knocked a hole in me, though." He squinted his eyes as he tried to see her more clearly. "You ain't dead?"

"No," she answered. "How bad are you hurt?"

"I don't know. My whole chest hurts. I tried to move this dead Injun offa me, and I couldn't do it." Still finding it difficult to understand, he said, "That other Injun went lookin' for you. What happened to him?"

"He's dead," she replied.

"How'd that happen?"

"He found me," she said.

He continued to stare at her, amazed by what she had just said. "You sure we ain't dead?"

"I'm sure, but I not sure you not gonna be, if you don't stop bleeding. Come, I help. We take you to tipi. I take care of your wound." She laid her bow aside so she could use both hands to drag Two Toes out of the way.

"That's one of them bows Luke brought back, ain't it? Is that what you used on that other Injun?" Jug was still extremely interested to know how she had avoided being killed.

"Yes," she answered simply as she dragged Two Toes by his ankles. "Come. Now we see can you walk."

"I'll sure as hell try," he moaned, "but I ain't fit for no foot race." Doing his best to support most of the load, he got painfully to his feet with her help. Once he was up, he had to lean heavily on her to remain up. "I don't feel so good," he complained.

"You very strong," she encouraged him. "You lean on me and we walk slow down to tipi."

"We're lucky it's downhill from here," he declared, "or I ain't sure I could make it." He managed to persevere, and they slowly but surely made it all the way down to the tipi. "You was gonna make sure he was dead, weren't you?" Jug asked when he saw Bloody Hand's body lying in front of the tipi with three arrows embedded in him.

"I make sure," she answered. "Now, we take care of your wound."

She helped him onto his bed and took his coat off him, as well as his shirt and antelope undershirt. After they were off, she held them up for him to see. There was a hole in the front and another in the back of each garment. "Rifle ball go in the front and out the back," she said.

He was encouraged to hear there was no lead to be dug out of his chest, but he was surprised that the weapon had the power to go all the way through his body at that distance. "I swear, I didn't think them trade fusils had enough power to do that."

"I tell Luke Bloody Hand have rifle like his. Bloody Hand shoot you. I show you." She went outside and picked up Bloody Hand's rifle where it still lay and brought it back to show Jug.

"Well, I'll be . . . ," Jug started. "You're right, that's a Pennsylvania long rifle, all right. As close as he was, no wonder it went right through. I bled so dang much 'cause I was bleedin' front and back."

Willow heated up some water and cleaned the two wounds as best she could, then bandaged them, apologizing for not being able to search in the forest for some healing plants and moss to make a poultice because of the deep snow. Jug could not understand why he had so much pain in his chest when it seemed obvious the rifle ball had not struck any organs. He was not spitting up blood. In fact, after he was cleaned up, he was able to drink some coffee she made for him. He was not bleeding anywhere but at the points of entry and exit. Willow suggested that perhaps he had cracked some ribs.

It had been a busy morning, considering all that had happened before noontime. Luke followed the two Indians back to their new camp and from his observation point of earlier that morning, he saw no one else in the camp. So he decided he'd best find out where the other three Indians were, and his first concern was his camp. When he rode back down the side of the hill, he was alarmed at once to discover tracks leading up the hill next to it, tracks leading up to his camp. Afraid to imagine what might have happened if Jug and Willow were surprised by the three. He hoped and prayed Jug was on the alert.

He drove Smoke up the slope after finding three distinct trails going toward his camp. When a little less than halfway up, he saw a loose horse wandering alone. *Could be a good sign or a bad sign,* he thought. A little farther up, he came to the body of one of the Indians. That told him that Jug had been alert. Anxious now, he found there were two paths from that point, one heading toward the corral, the other heading toward the tipi. He naturally chose to follow the path to the tipi, pressing Smoke to hurry. The first thing he saw was the body of Bloody Hand lying close to the door of the tipi. The sight of the dead Blackfoot served to calm his heartbeat, but no one inside the tipi had taken notice of his arrival. Maybe there was no one in the tipi, he thought. With his pistol ready to fire, he suddenly jerked the flap back on the door and stepped inside. Willow screamed and Jug rolled halfway out of his bed, trying to reach for his pistol.

"Luke!" Willow cried. "We no hear you."

"That's kinda obvious," Luke replied, relieved to see both of them alive. "Looks like you two had a busy mornin'."

"I reckon you could say that," Jug said. "Sorry we ain't had time to tidy up the campsite before you got back from wherever the hell you've been. Right now, Willow is gettin' ready to fix somethin' to eat. You're welcome to join us."

"I don't know," Luke answered in kind. "If that carcass I saw lyin' outside is what you're fixin' to cook, I expect I'll just have to get by on some elk jerky."

Willow listened to the two men talk nonsense for as long as she thought necessary before interrupting. "I'm glad to see you okay, Luke. We have bad time here, but we okay now. Jug get shot."

Interrupting then, Jug said, "But she doctored me up pretty good. We was damn lucky. I was able to get one of 'em before they got up the hill." He went on to explain how he got shot and couldn't go to defend Willow. "But she took care of business when that buck came to call."

Luke looked toward Willow then. "Bloody Hand?"

"Yes," she answered. "That is Bloody Hand." She lowered her head as if ashamed.

Luke looked back at Jug then to find the cocky little man grinning broadly at him. He was obviously thinking the same thing Luke was. Luke put it into words. "That was a helluva thing you did, young lady. It took a lotta spunk to stand up to a man like Bloody Hand. When I got back here and saw those tracks leadin' up here to our camp, I was worried sick about you and Jug. I thought the three that came up here were chasin' me across the ridge. I didn't know they stayed behind to attack our camp."

"I told you she is some punkin'," Jug said, "I seen it from the first. But what's botherin' me now is the fact that you just come ridin' into camp and me and Willow didn't even know it till you walked in the door. I'm thinkin' it's a mighty good thing it was you and not some more of them Blackfoot makin' a neighborly call. And you ain't said nothin' yet about all that shootin' we heard from the hill right next to this'un. Where the hell were you all mornin'?"

"I don't think we have to worry about another attack on our camp here, at least, not from that same Blackfoot party," Luke answered. "And I expect that's because you and Willow . . ." He paused to rephrase. ". . . I oughta say Willow took care of their war chief. So now, by my count, there ain't but two of 'em left, and one of them took an arrow in his side." He shrugged and added, "Right now, we outnumber 'em."

"How do you figure that?" Jug wanted to know. So Luke told them how everything came about, starting with his following the war party to their new camp right next to their hill. He explained what the shooting was and how it had led to a chase across a string of hills and into the mountains. His part in the morning's doings brought a renewed air of optimism to both Jug and Willow. And Jug questioned him thoroughly on the total count of fatalities until they both agreed that the only remaining Indians were the two survivors of the fight with Luke. "And one of them is wounded," Jug said.

"Yep," Luke replied, "just like us. Both sides ended up with one healthy and one wounded. But we ended up with the pretty lady, so we're the winners. Right, Willow?"

She blushed in answer. "I cook you something to eat now."

"I'd appreciate it," Luke said, "but before I eat, I'm gonna take care of the bodies and the horses, especially that one right outside the door. In case I'm wrong about those two Blackfoot comin' to call, I wouldn't want 'em to think we run a messy camp here." He would check to make sure, but it was his thinking that those two surviving Blackfoot would start for home right away with the report of their tragic defeat at the hands of a couple of trappers. He and Jug and Willow should have little to fear from their village during the hard part of the winter. But when the thaws began and they would be on the move again, there was a better-than-average possibility a war party would come seeking vengeance for the village.

Chapter 16

"I know you're ready for a rest, boy," Luke told Smoke, "but I'm gonna work you a little bit more. Then I'll let you rest." He tied one end of his rope around Bloody Hand's ankles and the other end around his saddle horn, then he dragged his body to the backside of the hill and dropped it in the same deep gully that held Standing Elk's body. He collected Two Toes' and Crazy Wolf's bodies, as well, and dragged them to the same gully. "You boys oughta keep pretty well there till the wolves and the vultures find you." The next thing to deal with was the issue of the two extra horses that found their way up to his and Jug's horses. They might turn out to be a problem. He and Jug were going to have to take care of even more horses now, and that wasn't the typical responsibility for a free trapper. He'd like to think the two of them were going to need that many horses to carry all the plews they trapped this winter, but that was not likely. It would be nice to have them to sell at rendezvous. But when the ice thawed and they could go back to trapping, they were going to be moving constantly from stream to stream in hostile territory, doing their best not to attract any attention. And that was going to be hard to do while trying to move a herd of horses at the same time. *We might have to run some of these horses off,* he thought, somewhat reluctantly. And with the damage they had now done to Bloody Hand's war party, they could pretty much count on another war party coming with the sole purpose to find them. *If we had any sense, we'd get to hell outta here as soon as the ice started to melt*, he told himself. *Get back down to Wind River.* And then there was the question of Willow. That one he hadn't figured out yet, although he knew he was planning to take her back to rendezvous with them. He was hoping the answer to that question would make itself known when they got back there—*if they got back there*. He was a little reluctant to admit it to himself, but he liked having her around, and he was going to miss her.

"Come eat your food," Willow called to him when he came back to the corral.

He signaled with his hand to let her know he had heard, then he pulled Smoke's saddle off and turned him loose before going back to the tipi. "We picked up two more horses," he said to Jug. They just wandered on up to our horses."

"That makes thirteen," Jug said, shaking his head. He was obviously thinking the same thing Luke had been thinking.

"Coulda been fourteen," Luke replied. "When I got back a while ago, I passed a gray horse wanderin' loose about halfway up the hill. He wasn't with the other two up at the corral."

His comment caught Willow's attention. "Good," she said. "Don't want gray horse. Better he not come here."

Luke and Jug both looked at her in surprise. "What's wrong with gray horses?" Jug asked, but she didn't answer.

"Did Bloody Hand ride a gray horse?" Luke asked. She dropped her chin to her breast and nodded.

"Well, he's ridin' a castrated buffalo bull right through the center of Hell right about now," Jug declared. "And I expect that gray horse is glad of it."

"Jug's right, Willow," Luke said. "I know that man caused you a helluva lot of hurt, but I'd say you paid him back plus some. I expect Long Runner is mighty proud of you and he can rest easy now, knowin' Bloody Hand can't hurt you no more."

She looked up at him and nodded but said nothing. His comment caused her to experience a feeling of guilt for not having mourned her husband as she should have. They had not had the time to really know each other. She told herself that was responsible for her lack of deep-felt mourning—that and the mortal danger she had suffered through until she found Luke and Jug. Long Runner was a good man and she truly felt a heavy guilt for not caring more for him. And she had been determined to develop that deep feeling for him, given time. She hoped that he knew that now.

Sensing her concern, Luke tried to apologize. "I'm sorry if I said something I shouldn't have brought up. I surely didn't mean to make you feel sad."

"No, no, Luke," she quickly reassured him. "Your words were said with kindness. I not feel sad."

Puzzled, Jug looked from one of them to the other, unable to determine what was at issue. "What did he say? He didn't mean nothin'. He just ain't got no manners a-tall."

"Jug's right," Luke said. "I never had any manners to count for much." Back to Jug then, he said, "There's two things I wanna do, and the first one is I wanna scout that camp they set up right on our doorstep. I wanna find out what they're plannin' to do, now that there ain't but two of 'em—one, if that one buck didn't make it with that arrow in his side. As soon as those two are gone, and I expect they will be, I wanna dig a hole in this frozen ground to cache our plews in. I don't wanna have to worry about losing everything we've already trapped, if we run into trouble with another bunch of Blackfeet."

"Well, that sure as hell suits me," Jug said. "But I don't feel like I'll be much good with a shovel for a while yet."

"I swear," Luke remarked, "When we decided to partner up, I wish you'da told me about your habit of gettin' in the way of every stray shot that's fired. I see now I shoulda asked Dan Bloodworth to partner up. I think he'da been tickled to trap with me."

Reacting in kind to Luke's japing, Jug replied, "You shore wouldn'ta had to ride all the way up here in Blackfoot country to get your throat cut." Seeing the puzzled expression on Willow's face, Jug told her, "Bloodworth's a friend Luke made this year at rendezvous. Luke made quite an impression on him." He paused, then added, "With a knife."

She turned at once to confront Luke. "Is safe for you to go to ron . . . ?" She wasn't sure of the word, so she hesitated.

"Rendezvous," he said for her. "Ron-day-voo," he pronounced slowly for her benefit. "It's just what they call the place where all the trappers go to sell their plews and buy supplies for the next year. Bloodworth ain't nobody to worry about. When we get there, we'll buy you some of the foofaraw that women like, beads and cloth and vermilion and stuff." He looked at Jug and received a big smile as the little man slowly shook his head. Luke knew what he was thinking, so he frowned and shook his head in answer. He didn't know how Jug could think anything else. They couldn't just ride away and leave Willow to shift for herself. He didn't think Jug was any more capable of that than he was. His partner just wanted to jape him a little bit. Besides, Willow was a handy little woman to have around. "Well, enough of this chin rattle, I need to go see what's goin' on in that Blackfoot camp." He rose to his feet and handed Willow his empty bowl.

"You be careful," she said to him as he buckled his belt on again.

"Yeah, you be careful," Jug said, still wearing a grin.

Young Walking Bird stood inside one of the shelters he and the other warriors had constructed of limbs from the fir trees at the base of the hill. He was watching Dull Axe, who was lying on a buffalo skin he used for his bed. He didn't know what else he could do for him. He had managed to pull the arrow out of his side, but not all of it came out. The shaft had evidently broken just behind the arrowhead, and the wound would not stop bleeding. Several years older than Walking Bird, Dull Axe had tried to help him remove the arrow, obviously in great pain. And now, he seemed to be somewhere between consciousness and fretful sleep, mumbling words that Walking Bird could not understand. He frantically hoped that Bloody Hand and the others would return to the camp soon. Crazy Wolf would know what to do for Dull Axe. Walking Bird just wished they would hurry. He was afraid Dull Axe was going to bleed to death if it wasn't stopped.

He heard his pony whinny, and he immediately became excited when he heard an answering acknowledgement from a horse approaching the camp. *They were back!* He hurried out of the shelter to meet them only to find Bloody Hand's gray gelding wandering back to the camp alone. Stunned, Walking Bird almost stumbled in his confusion. He ran to the stone wall extending from the base of the hill to look for Crazy Wolf and Two Toes, but there was no one following the gray horse. *They were dead!* The realization of that struck him like a solid blow to his chest. *They had killed Bloody Hand!* He could not conceive of anyone killing Bloody Hand. The cold hard truth struck him then that he, alone, had survived this place of evil—he and the wounded Dull Axe. He didn't know what to do. He needed the wisdom of Crazy Wolf, or any of the older warriors to tell him what he should do. In desperation, he ran back to the shelter to tell Dull Axe the tragic news.

"Dull Axe!" he cried. "Bloody Hand is dead and I fear the others with him are dead, too. Only his horse returned. What should we do? They may be coming back here again!" When Dull Axe didn't respond at once, Walking Bird knelt beside him and took him by the shoulders. "There's no one left but you and me and they may be coming!" Still there was no response as Dull Axe stared up at him with sightless eyes. Then his head fell over on his shoulder, lifeless. Shocked, Walking Bird released the dead man's shoulders and backed away from him. He went outside the shelter and stood looking at the gray horse that had belonged to one he thought invincible. What should he do? He looked over at the other side of the camp at a shelter like the one Dull Axe was lying in. That shelter held the bodies of the victims of the sniper above the camp earlier that morning. They were to be taken for burial after they killed the sniper and raided the trapper camp. Now he was left to decide what he should do. His first thought was to take everything he could manage and head north to alert the village of this terrible tragedy that struck Bloody Hand's war party. But would they think him a coward? Then his conscience told him that he must take care of the dead warriors, but he wasn't sure he could take the time to bury them properly. Then he decided what the next best thing to honor their deaths would be.

He went back to the shelter where Dull Axe lay. With a great deal of effort, he pulled the body out of the shelter and dragged it across to the one that held the other bodies. He dragged Dull Axe inside, then tried to arrange his body in a dignified manner beside them. When he did the best he could to make it appear respectful, he gathered up all the wood he could find and stacked it inside the shelter with the bodies. From his war bag, he took some dry tinder and put it and some small branches under the firewood he had stacked in the shelter and set it on fire. He watched it carefully until it caught the larger limbs on fire, satisfied it would grow into the funeral pyre he planned.

As the fire gained strength, Walking Bird became more convinced that it was the right way to honor their bravery. The growing fire was symbolic of the Blackfoot warrior's fighting spirit. He stood there a long time, watching the flames fill the inside of the crude hut. When the shelter, itself, burst into a ball of glorious flame, lighting up the whole camp circle, he knew at that moment he must stay and avenge their deaths. The horses stamped nervously. Walking Bird turned toward them to discover a lone figure standing there watching him. It was a man easily recognized as a white trapper and a hated trespasser in Blackfoot country. He was instantly alarmed, yet the trapper stood almost casually, holding his long rifle in one hand, making no move to attack him. "You come here to die, white man," Walking Bird stated solemnly and started walking slowly toward him.

"I came here to kill you," Luke answered truthfully, for a few short minutes before, he had brought the front sight of his rifle to bear on Walking Bird's back. "But there has been enough killin' in this little valley. You are young like me, why don't we let this be the end of it? Take your horses and your things and go back to your village."

Walking Bird hesitated, confused by the strange white man's proposal for peace. The events of the last few days swirled through his brain. Bloody Hand had led them on a victorious raid that destroyed the Crow village, only to lead them into a murderous trap because of his obsession with the Crow woman. He and his brother warriors would be well on their way home now, had the woman not escaped. He thought of them as he stood, locked in a timeless moment, looking at the man still calmly watching him. He knew he could not accept his offer of a truce. Someone must pay for the deaths of the Blackfoot warriors who died here. He threw his head back and released a war cry, yanked his war axe from his belt, and charged across the clearing toward the hated white man.

His rifle already loaded and cocked, Luke brought it up to his shoulder and squeezed the trigger, but the rifle did not fire. With still a little time left, due to the width of the clearing, he quickly cocked it, shook some fresh gun powder on the flash pan, and tried again. This time, the flint ignited the powder and fired, catching Walking Bird in the chest when only twenty feet away. The force of the impact at that distance slammed the running man backward to land flat on his back. Luke shook his head, thinking it a useless waste of a young man's life, but fully understanding why Walking Bird had chosen to attack.

He watched the fallen man for a few moments to see if there were any signs of life, but Walking Bird lay still as a stone only a few feet from him. Luke was in no hurry to reload his rifle because he had watched the young warrior from above him on the hill as he dragged Dull Axe's body across the clearing and set it on fire. He had determined that Walking Bird was alone before he came down from the hill and stopped at the edge of the camp.

It was during that time that he decided he would make an appeal to the young warrior to leave in peace. He was unable to explain why. It just seemed like a damn waste. He stepped over and took a closer look, and there was absolutely no sign of life, so then he paused to make another decision. "What the hell? Might as well put you on the same train your friends are takin'." He put his rifle down, so he could hoist the body up on his shoulder. Then he carried it over to the funeral pyre and heaved it over into the flames. He backed away quickly, feeling he was getting scorched by the flames. His next concern was the possibility of starting a forest fire and he figured he didn't need that, now that there were no Indians to worry about. Luckily, the warriors had built their shelters close enough to the center of the clearing to get the benefit of a large fire in the center. Consequently, there were no overhanging limbs that might catch fire and spread to other trees. With a three-foot covering of snow on the ground, there was little danger of brush catching fire, as well. To be sure, however, he stayed there for a long while just to watch the fire. When it had been reduced to a blackened, smoldering heap, he deemed it safe to gather the horses and supplies and return to his camp where he was certain Jug and Willow anxiously awaited news of the Blackfoot war party.

"We was about give up on you again," Jug greeted him when he returned to the camp at suppertime. "I reckon I shoulda guessed you wouldn't miss supper."

"Not if I can help it," Luke replied. "How's he doin'?" He asked Willow.

"He doing okay," she answered. "Talk plenty good."

"It ain't too bad, long as I don't move much," Jug said. "And I ain't got nothin' for the pain, so I have to stay real still."

"Jug empty?" Luke asked.

"As empty as a coyote's head," Jug answered. "I think Willow musta been sippin' some of my medicine outta my jug." He grinned at Luke and winked, waiting for her response.

As anticipated, she stated immediately. "I not sip fire water. Fire water bad for him."

Jug laughed at her reaction. "What about them Blackfeet?" He turned back to Luke then. "Any chance we'll be gettin' a visit from them?"

"Not from those Blackfeet," Luke replied. "There ain't any of 'em left."

"I knew it right off," Jug declared. "I heard the shot. I knew it was your rifle, and I told Willow that you got the last one of 'em. Ain't that right, Willow?"

"I hear shot," she said. "I no hear you say nothing else."

"I said it, she just didn't hear it," Jug insisted. "Anyway, what happened? You was gone a long time. Was there just the two of 'em left, like we figured?"

"By the time I got there, there was just one of 'em left, and he was in the process of burnin' up the bodies of the dead ones. If the wind changes, you oughta be able to smell 'em."

"One left," Jug asked, "was that the shot we heard?" Luke nodded in reply. "What happened to him?" Jug asked.

"He went with his friends," Luke answered. "I figured it wasn't much different than stickin' him in a hole in the ground or leavin' him for the buzzards to pick apart. So I threw his behind in the fire, too." When Jug gave him a look of surprise, he said, "Hell, that's what he did with his friends' bodies, so I figured he'd want the same." Then, feeling as if he had committed some gruesome sin, he confessed. "I gave him the chance to get the horses and clear out of here, but he didn't take it, so he didn't leave me no choice. When he came after me, I shot him."

Jug recoiled in surprise with Luke's confession of mercy. "Well, I'm glad as hell that Injun didn't have any more sense than you had. 'Cause, if he had, you'd most likely be dead right now, and me and Willow would still have an Injun lookin' to find us." He grinned then. "But it all turned out all right for the right-eous, so we'll thank the Good Lord for that." Pausing then, he asked, "I don't suppose those horses followed you home, did they?" He sighed then and hung his head when Luke nodded. Forgetting his wound for a moment, he started to roll over to a sitting position, but had to stop when a stab of pain reminded him. He settled himself again, then continued with the thought that had caused him to move. "Do you know, the three of us wiped out a Blackfoot war party of thirteen warriors? And one of us is a woman." He nodded toward Willow as if to identify her as the woman. That's the kind of story you tell when you get back to rendezvous. And you know what? I don't know if I'll even tell it 'cause ain't nobody gonna believe it. Hell, I ain't sure I believe it myself."

"It wouldn't make much difference," Luke said. "If you did tell it, somebody would top it with one of their own tales."

The next day, while Luke was taking a look around the lower part of the mountain range to make sure they were in fact alone, he happened upon a deep ravine with many tall trees growing along its sides. When he decided to take a deeper look in the ravine, he discovered it to be an Indian burial ground. There were two bodies, wrapped in skins and strapped to platforms. Curious, for the skins they were bound in did not appear weathered and worn, so he cut the binding on one corner just enough to get a look at the body inside. It didn't take but a peek to tell him the body had not been there for a long time. He knew for certain that there were no recent Indians in this part of the mountains but the Blackfoot war party. These two had to be part of that party, and he was willing to bet they were the first two that were killed when they tried to follow Willow.

He tied the lace he had cut to look inside and backed away from the trees. While he gazed at the two trees holding the bodies, he thought they looked like they formed an arch. "Perfect," he uttered then and decided to dig a hole into the side of the ravine between the two trees. "Perfect place to cache our furs," he announced, "guarded by two warriors."

* * *

For the first time since Willow appeared under the waterfall, all three of them felt relief from the constant danger of discovery by a hostile party of Blackfoot Indians. As always, however, there was the need to be alert for any sign of anyone else near their camp. They figured it unlikely, but Luke took it as his responsibility to keep an eye on the neighboring mountains for winter hunters. There were other things that needed his attention, like enlarging the evergreen barn. He planned to work the horses some when he cut down more of the cottonwoods at the bottom of the hill and hauled them up to the camp. He would chop up the branches and leaves for horse feed, and he planned to use the peeled trunks to erect some low walls around the tipi to serve as ramparts in case of attack. He would search for more horse food in the many little hidden valleys throughout the mountain range where there was protection from the winds and there were branches and leaves to eat.

For the immediate time being, it was Luke's responsibility alone to take care of their needs, for Jug was slow in healing from the two holes Bloody Hand had drilled through his side. Luke jokingly accused him of purposely irritating the wounds when no one was looking, just to keep them from healing. He resigned himself to the baking of biscuits and entertaining Willow with tales of his many exploits when he was a younger man. "I was a lot taller then," he claimed. "But a man loses some height when he gets a little older, if he's worked hard all his life."

Chapter 17

It got colder. The water that flowed out of the mountain to form the stream above the waterfall froze solid before it reached the falls, resulting in a wide shelf of ice above the pond. The falls, itself, was now an ice sculpture and the stream below it turned to solid ice as well. The challenge was simply to keep themselves and their animals alive, and that was a task that Luke gave a hundred percent of himself to accomplish. As a consequence, he spent a good portion of each day outside. Luke was well aware of Jug's feelings of guilt for not helping, so he tried to maintain an attitude of cheerfulness as he went about the chores of cutting firewood to keep Jug and Willow warm, and working the horses to keep their blood flowing. One evening, the elk herd returned to the cottonwoods at the base of the hill, so he took advantage of the opportunity to stock up on their meat supply. He knew the elk would be bedding down in the trees that grew on both sides of the creek. So he positioned himself with his bow and two rifles near the edge of the trees, knowing they would be coming out across the open meadow in the morning, after they fed on the cottonwoods. As the herd came out of the trees, he was able to kill two with his bow before having to use his rifles. He got two more with one shot from each rifle before the sudden gunfire panicked the herd to run.

Willow was a willing helper in the skinning and butchering of the meat and was anxious to demonstrate her expertise in preparing the hides. They smoked-cured about half of the meat. The rest was eaten fresh-killed, with most of that cut in pieces to be kept frozen outside the tipi. With the tipi becoming cramped somewhat for space with the addition of elk hides, as well as a couple of deer hides Luke had gotten earlier, they deemed it time to rid the tipi of some of the beaver plews. Up to that point, the pelts were spread around the edges of the tipi to act as insulation and to hold the edges down. Luke had readied his secret cache, so he and Jug showed Willow how to press the individual pelts into a pack. They pressed sixty pelts in a pack which weighed between ninety and one hundred pounds. Bound tightly with elk hides to keep them dry, they would be loaded two to a horse to carry them to rendezvous next summer.

Their camp was snug and warm with plenty of wood for the fire and no shortage of meat. Jug told Willow there was nothing to worry about because, if the game became scarce, there were horses to eat. But Luke was quick to comment that the way the horses were losing weight, there might not be anything left of them to eat. "Even if they get that poorly, Willow can still make soup out of 'em," Jug said. She had already demonstrated the delicacies she could make from the marrow in the elk bones.

They joked about the condition of the horses, but that was close to being Luke's biggest concern. It was a challenge to keep them from freezing to death. Under normal circumstances, he and Jug would have a total of six horses to take care of—one each for the two of them to ride, plus two packhorses each. They had already picked up extra horses and they now found themselves with a herd of horses, thanks to those acquired from Bloody Hand's camp. When the ice melted, and the beaver were in the water again, the three of them would be on the move, trapping the streams, moving their camp every two or three days. It would be too much to have to be concerned with tending a herd of horses at the same time. He shrugged and decided there was little to gain by worrying about it. *We'll just wait and see what happens when the time comes,* he thought. "Well, I reckon I'll load that pack of plews up and take 'em to our cache," he announced as he pulled his heavy buffalo hide coat on, grabbed a corner of the heavy pack and dragged it out the door of the tipi. He walked up to the corral and decided which horse needed the exercise the most, took a rope from his shoulder and fashioned an Indian bridle in one end, then led the horse down to the tipi to load the pack of furs. Jug came out to watch him load the furs onto the horse. "Don't stand too close," Luke warned him. "I'm afraid some of this work might get on you. It could hurt a man who ain't used to it."

"You are fixin' to tell me where our cache is, ain't you, partner?" Jug japed.

"I told you, ain't nothin' for you to worry about," Luke japed in return. "I got two Blackfoot warriors guardin' it. I'll take you to see it any time you feel like you can get on a horse again."

"I was just gettin' a little worried about you, spendin' so much time outside when it's this cold. Sometimes a man loses his memory when he's in the cold too long."

"Is that a fact?" Luke came back. "Well, I ain't worried about it. Don't matter to me none." He paused and pretended to be trying to recall. "What were we talkin' about?"

The days continued to slide by slowly, one day pretty much like the day preceding it. Jug finally seemed to make a full recovery from his wounds and was helping Luke with the chores. Without either man really aware of it, Willow gradually became a part of the unit and they seemed to operate more like a family than a partnership. Although all the horses were looking somewhat poorly, none seemed in danger of dying. And then it happened—it was Willow who broke the news. "The water is running in the stream," she announced and held her pan out for them to see. "I went to get ice to melt, so I could make your coffee, and look." She swished the water around in the pan and it swirled with chunks of ice floating in it. "I don't have to use my axe," she went on. "I just dip pan in stream."

"By Ned, that's good news to start the day with," Jug exclaimed, then paused. "You ain't japin' us, are you?"

"I not jape," she insisted. "I not use axe."

It didn't happen overnight, but the days warmed up just a hair over the next few weeks, and Luke and Jug were out every day looking for signs that would tell them the beaver were out of their lodges again. Finally, there was enough sign—small trees felled, dams neatening up—telling them it was time to trap. They picked up where they had left off before the freeze and returned to the ridge where the two streams joined to form the pond that fed the creek that ran down the center of an open meadow. The meadow was still covered with snow, but the creek was running and there was beaver sign all about on both sides of the creek. The catch was as fruitful as Jug had predicted, and the beaver fur was thick and heavy. For a period of a couple of weeks, the streams they were trapping were close enough to their winter camp to permit them to stay there. There was a reluctance on the part of all three to leave a camp that had been so comfortable for them during the roughest part of the winter. But the day arrived when they decided they had trapped out the close streams. It was time to follow to wherever the beaver led them.

They moved their camp to a canyon that led deeper into the heart of the mountain range, where several small springs joined to form a wide creek where the beaver were at work replenishing a dam with fresh limbs and branches. They figured they would likely be here for a couple of days, maybe three. So Luke and Jug began bending limbs and branches over in the shape of a dome to be covered with buffalo and elk hides for a roof. They worked very quickly, having done it many times before, but then Luke thought to stop and ask Willow a question. "I know you didn't have any choice back at our winter camp, but you can have one now, if you like. Do you want us to make you a separate hut all your own? You must be sick of livin' with the two of us."

"No, is no matter," Willow responded. "Too much trouble." She would actually have liked to have her own tipi, but she didn't want to make any extra trouble to give them any reason to get rid of her. And she was aware that they tried their best to be gentlemen. "We stay same tipi, no matter."

"All right," Luke replied. "Anytime you change your mind, just let me know and I'll build you your own castle."

Willow smiled at him. "What is castle?"

"A big fancy tipi with lots of rooms in it." He chuckled then and said, "Where you could put Jug off in one corner and you wouldn't hear some of the sounds he makes when he's sleepin'."

She giggled at that. "You mean when he cough from wrong end?"

"Yeah," he answered, chuckling, "he's got a bad cough, especially when you cook beans for supper."

"We got no more beans, anyway," she said.

They both laughed after her comment, but it caused Luke to think about their supplies. "So we're outta beans, are we? Tell you the truth, when we bought supplies for this winter, we didn't get many beans 'cause we didn't think we'd have time to soak beans and cook 'em but maybe once in a big while." He gave her a grin. "We didn't know we were gonna have a cook with us. With Jug havin' to show off with his biscuits, we're most likely gettin' low on flour and lard, too." She nodded her head to confirm it. "How 'bout coffee?" He asked then, and she nodded again. "Cornmeal?"

"Gone," she said.

He realized that he had been so occupied with hunting, tending the horses, and now trapping again, that he hadn't paid any attention to their supplies. It wouldn't be the first time he had gone a long time with nothing to eat but meat. But especially with Willow along to do the cooking, he'd prefer to have something with the meat. The problem, of course, was the fact that there was no place to buy supplies. Then he thought of a possible solution to their puzzle and he walked down to the edge of the creek where Jug was watching the horses drink.

"We didn't figure we'd be drivin' this many horses with us, did we?" Luke asked when he walked up.

"We sure as hell didn't," Jug answered, "and they're already gettin' to be a problem."

"We've got another problem, too," Luke said. "Maybe the horses could help it." He went on to talk about their shortage of basic supplies to cook with. Like Luke, Jug had paid little attention to it since Willow joined them. "What about that fellow you told me about when we were trappin' the Judith? What was his name?" When Jug didn't recall the conversation he was referring to, Luke said, "You said he had a tradin' post on the Judith about fifteen miles north of where we turned around to come back here."

"Oh, you're talkin' about Nate Jolley," Jug replied.

"Yeah, Nate Jolley. You think he's still runnin' a tradin' post on the Judith?"

"I don't know." He hesitated. "I reckon. Why?"

"I'm thinkin' he might wanna trade some flour and coffee and such for a good horse," Luke said. "Does he trade horses? We might trade some of these horses we're havin' to fool with."

"That ain't a bad idea," Jug responded right away. "Nate's got a barn and a sizable corral. I think he trades with the Injuns for horses sometimes. You wanna take a ride up there to see? I reckon he's still in business. I might even be able to fill my jug." He smacked his lips thinking about it. "And right now would be a good time to do it. It's still pretty damn cold, and we're less likely to run into any big parties of Blackfoot."

"I think that's what we oughta do," Luke replied. "If I remember right, you told me that day on the Judith that his tradin' post wasn't but about fifteen miles from where we turned around. So, I bet it ain't more'n about ten or twelve from where we are right here."

With that decision made, they wondered about Willow. They

couldn't take her with them. Jolley's wife was a Blackfoot, and according to Jug, their half-breed son might as well be full-blood Blackfoot. But they didn't want to leave her alone, so Luke suggested that Jug should stay there with her and he would go alone. Jug disagreed, saying Luke should stay with Willow, because Jolley knew him and would assume he was still with Hudson's Bay Company. They were still arguing the point when they came back to the campfire. Willow listened to them for a little while before interrupting. "You both go. Take care of each other. I don't need nobody for short time you say you be gone."

They had to admit that her suggestion was most likely the best one. There had been no sign of any hunting parties anywhere they had scouted since resuming their trapping. They could check their traps before sunup, ride up to the trading post and return well before suppertime. "I scrape beaver hides while you gone," she said. That settled it. They would go the next morning.

Another good yield from their traps provided them with eight prime plews for Willow to scrape and stretch while they were gone. They debated the number of horses they should take to Nate Jolley's trading post and decided on three. Even at the rate they were trapping beaver, they had no worries about having enough horses to carry their pelts. Jug joked that when they came back next year, they'd do well to bring a wrangler just to handle the horses.

The sun had barely made an appearance over the plains to the east of them when they started out following the Judith River north. This, after Willow assured them she would be all right until they returned. They made a new trail along the riverbank through snow about a foot and a half deep, which told them no one had traveled that way recently. They spotted the trading post when still a quarter of a mile away and were satisfied to see a column of smoke coming out of the chimney. They continued on until coming to the path that led to the front of the weathered building, a path, they noticed, that was churned up by countless hoofprints. Luke noticed the barn behind the store and a small cabin a dozen yards down the riverbank. Their arrival was announced by a brown and white hound dog that came out from under the porch as they stepped down from the saddle. They walked up the four steps to the porch and went in the front door.

"Well, I'll be . . ." Nate Jolley started. "Jug Sartain," he uttered softly, then raised his voice. "Clover, it's Jug Sartain!" Then he greeted the two men. "I swear, Jug, I thought you'd gone under. I ain't seen you in a coon's age. I heard two or three years ago that you weren't with Hudson's Bay no more." He was interrupted then when an Indian woman came in from the back. "Honey, you remember Jug Sartain, don'tcha? Use to work for the Hudson's Bay folks."

"Sure, I do," Clover said. "You still carryin' that jug with you?"

"Right outside on my horse," Jug answered. "I was hopin' you might have a little firewater for sale."

"Who's this young feller with you?" Nate asked.

"This here's Luke Ransom," Jug replied. "Me and Luke have been chasin' some horses that got loose and come up this way."

"You ain't in the beaver fur business no more?" Nate asked.

"Nope, when I left Hudson's Bay, I didn't wanna see another beaver," Jug said. With Nate knowing he wasn't with Hudson's Bay any longer, it wouldn't do for word to reach the Blackfoot villages that he was trapping beaver. "Me and Luke was doin' some scoutin' for the soldiers, till they started makin' war on the Injuns. Now, we're just knockin' about, pickin' up wild horses and sellin' 'em. You still buyin' horses? I remember you useta."

"Not so much, anymore," Nate said. "There ain't nobody to sell 'em to."

"You still in the business of sellin' staples and gun powder?"

"Yeah, I reckon you could say that's about all we do," Nate answered. "That and whiskey. We do a lot of business with the Blackfoot tribe, thanks to Clover and Pike." He interrupted himself. "You remember my boy, Pike, don't you? Pike," he called out then, "you remember Jug Sartain, don't you?"

"Yeah, I remember him," Pike Jolley answered reluctantly. Luke had noticed him, sitting at a small table in a corner near the kitchen. A dark, sullen-looking young man, as far as Luke could tell, he was eating some meat out of a bowl. The corner was dark, so Luke thought he might be an Indian until Nate identified him. He made no pretense of being glad to see Jug again.

Jug didn't waste any greetings on the half-breed son but went back to the business of trade. "I'll tell you the truth, Nate, me and Luke kinda hit a hard spot in the trail. We're outta supplies, and we got no money to buy any. Which, I reckon you could say is your good fortune. We ain't lookin' to make no profit offa this deal 'cause I remember you was always square with me. We've got two fine horses out front and I'm willin' to trade you even-up for some supplies. We need flour, salt, sugar, coffee beans, dried soup beans, cornmeal, if you got any, some gunpowder, flints, and lead. You load us up with that and you get both horses."

Right away, it sounded like too good a deal to be true, so Nate said, "I'd have to look at these horses first," he said. "What's wrong with 'em? They must be old."

"You take a look at 'em," Jug said. "You know how to judge horseflesh. Take Pike, over there, with you. He oughta know horses pretty good, too." Pike didn't wait to be asked. He got up from the table and went out the front door. When the rest of them went out, he was inspecting one of the horses' hooves. "And we just come through the hardest part of the winter," Jug pointed out.

"You got three horses on that line," Nate said.

"That's a fact," Jug replied. "You get to pick two of 'em and whichever one you don't pick we'll load our supplies on him and he can tote 'em back to our camp."

The Jolley father-son team went over the three horses from muzzle to tail, forcing Nate to admit that he couldn't find anything wrong with any of the three. Well aware that he was getting a hell of a bargain, he allowed as much when he extended his hand to seal the deal. "I'll fill that jug of yours to boot," he said.

As pleased as Nate seemed to be, his son appeared to be just as strongly in the opposite direction. It occurred to Luke that Pike was looking upon Jug and him with the contempt the typical Blackfoot had for the white man. *Can't really blame him*, Luke thought, *we're most of us a pretty sorry lot.* The sullen young man left them then and took the two selected horses to the barn behind the house. When they had placed all their supplies in the bags they brought for that purpose, they loaded them on the lone packhorse. While they were tying the load down, Luke saw Pike ride out of the barn and head north along the river.

As an additional courtesy, Nate had Clover grind some roasted coffee beans in her coffee mill. "So if you're completely out, you'll have some ready to boil you up a pot of coffee as soon as you get back to your camp," he said.

They said goodbye then and climbed on their horses for the ride back to the mountains. When they were out of earshot of the store, Luke remarked. "Nate Jolley seems like a likable fellow, but that son of his is a full-blood Blackfoot. I got a real strong feelin' we ain't seen the last of Pike Jolley."

"I got the same feelin'," Jug replied. "The price of them goods we're totin' back to camp mighta gone up to be more'n them two horses we paid for 'em. We'd best get along on up this river before he comes back and gets on our trail."

"Yeah, right," Luke came back and shook his head, thinking Pike could come back tomorrow and follow their trail in the snow. But he didn't bother to point that out to Jug.

They made it back to their camp in the early afternoon, just as they had figured. When they pulled into the grove of trees by the creek, Luke was happy to see Willow emerge from a laurel thicket away from their hut. She was holding her bow and a couple of arrows, which even pleased him more. "Did you hide in the bushes with your bow the whole time we were gone?"

"No," she replied, indignantly. "I hear you come up creek, so I get in the bush to make sure it's you."

"Well, we brought you enough supplies so you can cook something to go with the meat," Luke said. "And we can have some coffee with our supper tonight." He showed her the sack with fresh ground coffee. "I might need some good strong coffee tonight, dependin' on how good we hid our trail once we got off that riverbank."

"You think somebody follow you?" Willow asked, at once concerned.

"I think they might," Luke answered. "It's just a feelin', but Jug has the same feelin'." He went on to tell her about Nate Jolley's son and the fact that they felt he might have gone to tell his Blackfoot friends about Jug and him and the fact that they had some horses.

"They might be thinkin' about our horses and they might not," Jug advised. "But I reckon we'd best be thinkin' they're plannin' to come see how many horses we've got. So, we'd do well to get set up to wait for 'em tonight and hope we was wrong."

Chapter 18

"How do you know they have a lot of horses?" Three Bulls asked.

"Because they trade two good horses for flour and coffee," Pike Jolley replied. "One horse would buy three times as much as they got for two horses. That tells me they have plenty of horses. I know I will go to see how many they have. You and Lame Coyote can go with me if you want. If you do not want to go, I'll just go alone and take the horses for myself. I would have done that, anyway, if I knew the two white men were alone with the horses, but they must have had someone watching the horses while they were at my father's store."

"Three Bulls didn't say we wouldn't go with you," Lame Coyote spoke up then. "He just asked if you knew how many horses they had. We will go with you."

"Good," Pike said. "We should go now before darkness hides their tracks. If there is no one else with the two white men, we can kill them and maybe stay in their camp tonight. When we drive the horses back to your village tomorrow, everyone will see how brave we are."

Three Bulls and Lame Coyote both liked the thought of that, so they got their horses and weapons and were soon loping along the riverbank, following the obvious trail left in the snow for them. In a short time, they reached the place where the two white men left the river and took a direct course into the Little Belt Mountains. From this point, they would have to pay attention to the tracks they followed. For, while there was snow in the mountains, the streams were not frozen any longer, and the three horses they followed rode up the first stream they came to. Pike and his friends rode up the stream as well, searching for tracks that led out of the water. They could find no trace of the horses coming out of the stream by the time they came to a fork where two smaller streams joined to form the one they had been following. Still, there were no tracks leaving the water, so they had to choose which fork to follow. One fork appeared to come from a mountain, while the other came from a wide canyon. They all agreed that the fork from the canyon was the most likely, so they followed it. It turned out to be a stream that branched off from a creek that ran down the middle of the canyon, heavily forested with willows and pines.

Lame Coyote was the first to spot it, the tell-tale stick stuck in the bank to hang over the water, with a willow sprig at the end about a palm's width above the water. He didn't say anything but held his hand up to stop Pike and Three Bulls. Then he pointed, and they immediately saw what had stopped him. Looking farther along the creek, they spotted another stick and then another. The men they hunted were there to trap the beaver. "They lied when they told my father they had come looking for lost horses," Pike snarled. "They trap beaver." The reaction of his two friends was much the same as his, for the Blackfeet held a deep hatred for the white trappers who came to their territory to trap beaver, robbing them of the trade value of the furs. There was no question now regarding the question of killing the inhabitants of the camp, or just running off with their horses. They had to be killed.

"We must find their camp and see how many of them there are," Three Bulls said, thinking of the typical American Fur Company trappers who worked in squads of at least four men but usually more.

"I think it is not much farther from here," Lame Coyote speculated, "but there are still no tracks on this creekbank. The snow has not been walked on."

"They do not walk on the bank when they set the traps," Pike said. "They do not want the beaver to get their scent and stay away from the trap."

"What do they do," Lame Coyote asked, "fly to the traps like buzzards?"

"They wade in the water," Pike answered him. "Somewhere up ahead we'll find their tracks. I think it's best that we tie our horses in the trees here and go the rest of the way on foot." The other two were in agreement with that, so they rode over into the trees and tied their horses. Then they cautiously made their way through the pines for a distance of approximately one hundred yards before they stopped when they saw a thin column of smoke drifting up through the trees ahead. Pike, the only one of them with a rifle, made sure it was ready to fire.

"There!" Three Bulls whispered and pointed to the temporary shelter nearly hidden under the trees. The smoke was coming from a fire in a small clearing beyond the shelter. "Look," he whispered again when he saw the horses near the creek. "They have many horses."

"Yes," Lame Coyote replied, "but where are the trappers?" There was no sign of anyone around the camp.

"Why don't we just go ahead and take the horses?" Pike asked. "They must be off minding their traps. We can be gone before they come back."

Lame Coyote looked at him as if trying to excuse him for his white blood. "It would be too difficult to ride up here and try to drive them back down the creek. We would be in a bad spot if the trappers came back and attacked when we were in the midst of turning their horses around. I think we must kill the white men first. Then we can make the horses do what we want. They surely will be coming in to eat before it gets dark. While we can, we should move up closer to the shelter, so when they come back, we will have clear shots and strike them down, all at the same time." Pike and Three Bulls followed him as he moved up closer in the trees.

They had no sooner gotten to their new position when Willow came out of the hut and went to add wood to the fire. "A woman!" Pike exclaimed in a whisper, already thinking of pleasures beyond the shooting of the menfolk. "We don't have to shoot her."

"We must shoot them all," Lame Coyote insisted. Judging by her dress, he said, "I think she is Crow. These white dogs insult us further by bringing this Crow trash into our lands."

At that moment, Jug appeared, coming from beyond the horses. "Willow," he called to her, "where's Luke?"

That was enough to convince Pike. "There ain't nobody else but the three of 'em! Shoot 'em!" He stood up, bringing his rifle up as he did to aim at Jug. But he grunted painfully when the arrow struck him in the back, causing him to fire his rifle up in the air. Lame Coyote spun around in time to feel the solid thump of Luke's second arrow in his throat. Luke turned to see Three Bulls stagger backward and fall, the result of Jug's rifle shot.

"That's all of 'em!" Luke called out. "There weren't but three of 'em!" He quickly moved up from his position behind them to finish off the two he had put arrows into. A shot to the head of each one, one with his rifle, the other with his pistol, then he took a look at Three Bulls, and there was no need to end his misery. "Nice shot, partner," he said to Jug who hurried over to join him. "You all right, Willow?" He turned to see her frowning face as she stood wringing her hands.

"Partner," Jug declared with a shake of his head, "I didn't know where you'd gone off to when we split up to scout the creek."

"I saw 'em when they left the fork of the two streams and headed up this way, so I just got in behind 'em and followed 'em up here to the camp. It gave me a little fright when I saw Willow come walkin' out to the fire." He turned toward her to give her a stern look. "After we told her to stay inside behind that half a pack of pelts."

"I had to keep fire going, if I gonna fix you food," she replied, still trembling. "You sure no more Blackfoot?"

"I'm sure. There wasn't but three of 'em. When I saw 'em come up the creek, I waited a little while to see if there were any more behind 'em. Then I followed 'em on up here." He looked back at Jug and said, "I reckon we were right about Pike Jolley. You wanna ride back down the river and tell his mama and papa why he ain't comin' home?"

"Hell, no," Jug replied, not sure if Luke was japing him or not. "If Nate's got any sense, he won't question anybody about it. He'll just be thankful for it."

"Well, we've got ourselves another problem now," Luke said, shaking his head.

"What's that?" Jug asked.

"We've got ourselves three more horses to add to our herd," Luke answered. "And I reckon I'd best go back in the pines and bring 'em up with the rest of our herd."

"Damn, that's right," Jug said. "They won't be no problem, though. We can use 'em for protection against the Injuns."

"How's that?" Luke wanted to know.

"We're gonna be leavin' here in a few weeks and have to ride all the way back down to Wyomin' Territory. When the Injuns see us, they're gonna come after us, so we'll just cut the herd loose and the Injuns will forget us and go after the horses."

"I know you're japin'," Luke replied, "but you might be speakin' the truth. It's gonna be hard enough as it is, just to get back to friendly country with us and our plews without havin' to drive a bunch of horses with us." He shook his head as he thought about it. "Maybe we shoulda tied up the horses we need, hid ourselves, and let Pike and his friends drive the loose horses off. They mighta been satisfied with just stealin' a few horses. I swear, though, I don't wanna just go off and leave good horses. That's like leavin' money on the table after the game's over."

"You say you know where they left their horses?" Jug asked, and Luke said he did. "Then there ain't no use in talkin' about throwin' away good money. Might as well go get 'em and bring 'em up here with the rest of the horses."

"We can use 'em to drag these three bodies away from our camp," Luke said. "I don't think we'll see any more visitors on this night, but I expect it'd be a good idea to move on to some other part of the mountains tomorrow. The two bucks with him might have families that worry about 'em."

Jug had no better idea, so that's what they decided to do. After supper, they checked their traps and reset them. Before daylight the next morning, they collected all their traps. They lingered long enough to skin and prepare the pelts before striking camp and leaving the canyon with some of their herd already carrying packs of made beaver. It was to become a familiar routine over the next few weeks, weeks that saw the gradual disappearance of the heavy snow. For the most part, they managed to remain in the mountains, moving from one valley to another, trapping the streams that wound their way down to the valley floor. To say their season was successful beyond what they had figured on would be an understatement of huge proportions.

It was the realization of the dream of a lifetime for Jug. He had always believed the Little Belt Mountains were teeming with beaver but had always been hesitant to trap them alone. They were in the heart of Blackfoot hunting country and under the control of Hudson's Bay Company, and the company depended on the Indians to catch the beaver and bring the furs to their forts. Sadly, Jug found that he was getting too old to continue many more years of the hardships of living in the mountains. He had been trying to decide if he was ready to make this season the year he would test that theory of his and set out to trap in the Little Belts. When Luke Ransom appeared out of nowhere to save his bacon from being fried by two Blackfoot raiders, he was sure it was for a reason. And the reason had to be that he needed a partner to go to the Little Belts with him, and there couldn't be a man he trusted as much as he trusted Luke.

It had turned out nearly as he had imagined it. He could almost picture the beaver fighting under the icy-cold water to get into his traps. Their plews were dark and thick with winter growth and they must have averaged two-and-three-quarters to three pounds in weight. Their packs were going to weigh heavy, and already, they had three of their horses carrying two packs each as they moved from stream to stream. There were two more packs of sixty plews each in Luke's burial-ground cache. It would soon become an issue of how many they could comfortably handle, and neither man wanted to stop when the beaver were so willing.

As far as Willow was concerned, she was not sure her two men had not caught some form of mountain fever, such was their dedication to the hunt. She did not worry, however, for she was convinced they were determined to take care of her. Her primary worry was that they were going to wear themselves out at the pace they were working, especially Jug. Luke, she felt sure, was young enough to withstand any hardship. She decided that it was time she learned to shoot a gun, so that she could be of greater help in the face of an attack.

She approached Luke one afternoon after the pelts were scraped and stretched for drying. "I think maybe you teach me to shoot gun," she suggested.

"Is that a fact?" Luke responded. "I thought you were more comfortable with your bow."

"Bow is good," she replied. "Gun is better."

He took note of the serious expression on her face then. "Yep, I reckon it wouldn't hurt for you to know how to use a gun. You never know when you might need one." When she continued to stand before him gazing earnestly into his eyes, he asked, "You mean right now?"

She nodded eagerly. "Now is good time," she answered. "You have many guns," she said, referring to the trade guns captured from the Blackfeet. "Better you teach me before they find us again."

"You're right," Luke replied. "That's a right smart idea. We shoulda thought of it sooner." He was thinking more in terms of her being able to reload weapons for Jug and him in the event they were ever pinned down somewhere, with no back door. "And now is a good time 'cause I ain't seen any sign of anybody who might hear the shots. Come on, let's go pick you out a gun to suit you."

"What's goin' on?" Jug asked when they walked past him, with Willow carrying one of the Hudson's Bay trade guns, on their way to a hill away from the horses.

"Willow's fixin' to learn how to shoot a gun," Luke answered, so Jug fell in behind them to offer his assistance. When they were about thirty yards from the hill, Luke stopped and said, "This is close enough. Now the first thing is to learn how to load it."

"I was gonna say that," Jug remarked and the two men hovered over her every move as they taught her how to load the powder, ball, and patch, and explained how the hammer caused the spark that ignited the powder that caused the gun to fire. She became very adept at it after only a few trials, so they moved on to the actual firing of the weapon. Luke selected a tree on the hillside as the target, and after showing her how to aim the weapon, told her the tree was a Blackfoot warrior coming to get her. Her first shot hit the tree, although a little lower than chest high.

"Not bad," Luke said, "not bad at all for the first time." He looked at Jug and grinned before adding, "You stopped that Blackfoot warrior all right. Maybe a little lower than where you were aimin', but you stopped him and any thoughts about what he was gonna do to you." She was puzzled by their chuckles but satisfied that she had hit the tree she was aiming at. She tried a couple more shots, and with Luke's coaching, learned to shoot a little higher. "You're a sight better than ol' Jug when he tried out my bow," Luke said. He couldn't resist japing Jug a little. He received a grunt of indifference from the little man, as he expected.

Willow was very pleased that she had performed to suit Luke. Were it not for the fact the three of them were under constant danger of being discovered by a Blackfoot hunting party this time of year, she would have wished this time would never end. She knew, however, that all good things must come to an end. The first sign of that came as a sudden warm spell that lasted for more than a week. Much of the snow melted, opening large patches of brush and grass. This made it nice for the horses, but at the same time, it acted almost as a signal to the beaver to shed their winter coats. The second sign was not as subtle. It came in the form of a gunshot.

One afternoon, after the newly caught pelts were scraped and stretched for drying, Luke decided to backtrack to a grassy canyon where he had seen deer sign when they trapped there. To reach the canyon, he rode up a mountain on one side of the canyon, and as he reached the top, he heard the shot. He recognized the sound as that of one of the trade guns the Indians favored. He rode down the other side of the mountain far enough to see into the canyon, as three more shots were fired. Then he saw them, an Indian hunting party was following the same herd of deer he was. From his vantage point high up on the mountainside, he could see the hunters, most of them with bows, riding into the stampeding herd of deer. He counted sixteen hunters.

He returned to the camp to find Jug and Willow clearly relieved to see him. "We heard some shootin' and we was afraid it had somethin' to do with you," Jug said.

"Huntin' party," Luke replied. "I counted sixteen of 'em. They were chasin' that herd of deer I was lookin' to find."

"Sixteen of 'em, huh?" Jug thought that over real quickly. "Chasin' deer. Was they comin' in this direction?"

"I can't say," Luke answered. "I expect that'll depend on which way the deer turn. I expect it wouldn't be a bad idea for us to pull up our traps and skedaddle outta here."

"I expect you're right," Jug said. "We'd best get packed up. Them last plews was kinda skinny, anyway."

At this point, they had worked their way almost to the middle of the mountain range, farther than they had been so far. They would have to head back in a more southeastern direction to return to their winter camp at the waterfall, a distance of about twenty miles as the crow flies. Realistically, they figured they could make it back to get the two packs of plews out of their cache after a full day's ride. "If we're lucky, we won't run up on any more huntin' parties," Luke said. "Willow, go ahead and pack up your beddin' and cookin' stuff. Me and Jug will go yank our traps outta the pond and get the horses ready to go."

"You no eat?" she asked. "I not cook supper yet."

"We'll move on outta here," Luke told her. "We've still got a lotta daylight left. We can cook something over the fire when we find us a good spot to camp tonight. That all right with you, Jug?"

"Suits me," Jug responded. "I don't crave to take on sixteen Blackfoot hunters on an empty stomach, so let's put some distance between us and them." The decision to quit this year's hunt was made that suddenly with no more discussion. It was time to take their pelts and leave the hostile Blackfoot country. Both men were satisfied with the results of the hunt. The challenge before them now was to pack those results safely to rendezvous.

It took them the full amount of time Luke estimated to get back to their original camp, plus a little bit more. It was already close to sundown when they drove the horses into the meadow below the cottonwood grove. The horses wanted to stop to graze there, but Luke and Jug didn't want to leave them there for the night. So they drove them on through the cottonwoods and up the slope to the waterfall where the grass was just as good as the lower meadow. After they unloaded the horses, they helped Willow get her fire started, so she could roast some of their smoked elk. In honor of their return visit to their first home as a family, Jug started a fire in his oven, which was still in very good shape, and Willow mixed up the biscuits for him. The framework they had constructed for the tipi was still intact, so they covered it again with the original buffalo hides, after Jug took a good look inside to make sure that no critters had moved in while they were gone.

There was a feeling more like a reunion or a homecoming party that settled over the three of them, as they enjoyed the smoked elk and biscuits, washed down with hot coffee. There was no mention of the hazards that might await them when they attempted to drive a herd of horses and a string of packhorses loaded with beaver plews straight through Blackfoot country without attracting attention. After supper, Luke went outside to take another look at the horses, while Jug took a couple of pulls from his whiskey jug. Luke came back to report that the horses were quiet. "Most of 'em went right back to that corral we built for 'em, just like they'd come home."

The night passed without incident and they decided to have breakfast before they started out for Luke's cache. "It's about time you showed me where your cache was. I was startin' to get suspicious about your intentions," Jug japed. "Well, I'll be . . ." He chuckled when Luke led them to the two bodies in the trees. "You weren't pullin' my leg, was you? Two Blackfoot warriors watchin' it for us." Luke went to work with his shovel and soon uncovered two packs of beaver pelts. They loaded them on the unlucky horse selected for the job, held on by the special pack harness Jug had fashioned out of buffalo hide. "Don't look so sad," Jug told the horse, "we'll switch it to one of the other horses after today."

"You still happy with that paint pony you picked out?" Luke asked Willow. "'Cause you've got a long ride ahead of ya." She had selected that horse to be hers when they moved from winter camp, and she used the Indian saddle that Pike Jolley had on his horse for her comfort.

"Yes," she answered. "He is good horse, and I think he like me."

"Well, that's the most important thing, I reckon," Luke said and winked at Jug. They left the mountains then, backtracking over the same trail they followed into them. Both Luke and Jug led three packhorses with two of those horses carrying nothing but packs of beaver pelts. Willow led two packhorses, carrying nothing but pelts. The rest of the horses were left to follow freely. Of the three riders starting out for Wyoming Territory, only one had no fears or doubts about the trek they were embarking on. And that was Willow, for she was firm in her belief that everything would be all right as long as Luke was there to take care of her. Her deepest concerns were for what might become her fate after they reached the rendezvous. They often referred to the three of them as a family, and to her, it had become a genuine feeling, but she was afraid it might not be so with the two men. Both Luke and Jug had a tendency to joke about most anything, even potential dangers—so much so that it was hard to judge their seriousness about any subject. Once again, she found herself apologizing to Long Runner for not properly mourning his death. She told herself that after her escape from Bloody Hand, there had been very little time to mourn. As for Luke Ransom, she wasn't sure how she felt about him, but the thought of saying goodbye when they got to the rendezvous filled her with a dread like none she had ever experienced before. She hoped Long Runner would understand and forgive her for the strong feelings she had for Luke. Sometimes she thought she saw signs of those same feelings in his eyes, feelings his lips were reluctant to confess. But she hesitated to approach him on the matter, afraid she might be wrong.

Chapter 19

Due to the terrain and the loads their packhorses were carrying, they walked the horses, making for a slow rate of travel. They figured, at that rate, they could plan to strike Three Forks after three full days of travel, maybe more, depending on water and grass. It turned out to be more because of the horses' need for rest and grazing. While it was too early for the growth of new grass, there was enough to sustain them. Good fortune had followed them the first few days since leaving the Little Belt Mountains. There had been no sign of Indian hunting parties or individual travelers. As they approached Three Forks, they had reason to be more concerned, for that was a favorite camping area for Blackfoot Indians because of the area's attraction for all forms of game. And this time of year, many of the tribes were moving out of their winter camps. Luke and Jug decided to wait there, about five miles north of Three Forks, and drive their train of horses through to strike the Madison River after dark.

It turned out to be a wise decision, for when approaching the confluence of the Madison with the other two rivers, they discovered a large hunting party camped on the bank of the Madison. It was close to the point where they, themselves, had left the river when they were on their way to the Little Belt Mountains at the end of the summer. They could not see the camp, but Luke thought, if they could judge the size of the hunting party by the size of their fire, it was too big for him and Jug to deal with. So they walked their horses a good seventy-five yards farther east of the rosy glow of the fire in the dark sky before circling back to strike the river. They continued on, following the river at the same walking pace, for an additional three hours before stopping to make camp for the night. Their choice of camps was influenced by the thick grove of cottonwoods they came to. So with an opportunity to supplement the horses' feed with cottonwood bark, they built their fire right there. With a clear night, there was no need for a temporary shelter, so they climbed in their blankets and went to sleep.

Awake the next morning before sunup, they hurriedly got the horses ready to go and started out again, having decided to eat when they stopped to rest the horses. Once the sun made its way above the trees that hugged the river, Luke handed his lead rope off to Jug and turned Smoke back to check their back trail. It concerned him because they left quite a trail and there was nothing he could do to disguise it. He waited there for a while longer, but there was no sign of anyone following. It would have taken someone longer than that to catch up, so he still wasn't ready to think they had slipped by unnoticed. He wheeled Smoke around and caught up with Jug and Willow where they had stopped to rest the horses and eat breakfast.

Willow was waiting to hand him a cup of coffee as soon as he set Smoke free to join the other horses. "I make Johnny-cakes," she said and held the plate out toward him with two of the fried corn cakes on it.

"I'da et 'em all, if she hadn'ta grabbed that plate outta my hand," Jug chuckled. "I tried to tell her you wouldn't miss 'em, if we never said nothin' about 'em."

Luke gave her a big smile. "Thank you, Willow. I surely do appreciate it."

"I make Johnny-cakes for you," she replied.

"Ohhhh . . . ," Jug blurted, delighted. "She made 'em for you. I reckon I was just lucky to get a couple." He chuckled again. "I reckon I'm gonna have to cut all my whiskers off, if she's ever gonna cook somethin' 'specially for me. But if I did that, then all the white ladies wouldn't find me so gol-derned handsome."

"I expect that is something you have to worry about," Luke joked. It was a subject they had joked about before, the fact that most Indians didn't trust a man with hair on his face. Hair did not usually grow on an Indian's face and they often called white men with beards, *dogfaces*.

Changing the subject as quickly as he had broached the issue of the corn cakes, Jug asked, "How far'd you go back?"

"About two miles, I reckon," Luke answered. "I swear, we left a trail that looks like a company of cavalry is riding along the river. But I didn't see any sign of anybody followin' us. It's too soon to tell, though. If we're lucky, that huntin' party might set out in the other direction."

"You're right," Jug said. "There ain't been enough time for them to catch up yet. Hell, maybe, if they see the trail we're leavin', they'll think it is a company of soldiers, like you said, and they'll hightail it for home."

"I'll ride back and take another look when we get started again," Luke said.

When they felt the horses were ready, Willow cleaned up the pan and the dishes, and the men loaded the horses again. Luke stood there and watched them until they disappeared around a bend in the river. Then he climbed back aboard Smoke and told the big bay gelding, "Let's go hope we can't find anybody followin' us." He wheeled the horse around. "And hope Jug don't run into anybody ahead of us."

He rode back about half a mile, for no particular reason except to find a better vantage point to see more of their back trail. He reined Smoke to a stop beside a large pine on a slight rise and dismounted. There was nothing on the trail as far as he could see. He was distracted after a few minutes by a disagreement between two blue jays that resulted in a noisy argument in the limbs of the tree above him. When he returned his gaze to the trail behind him, he was startled to discover the lone rider coming toward him. "Damn," he uttered softly. There was no doubt he was looking at a Blackfoot warrior, even at that distance. A scout, or just a curious observer, whichever, he was definitely interested in the trail of many hooves left along the riverbank. As he came closer, Luke could see that he was a grim-looking warrior, powerfully built. And Luke had a feeling that the warrior had already noted that of the many hoofprints he was following, there was not one that was shod. *So much for the cavalry story,* he thought. *He's thinking he's lucked on a herd of wild horses.* Luke felt sure the Indian could not see him, but he backed a little farther around behind the pine, just in case.

Still the Blackfoot came steadily onward, obviously determined to see the source of the many horses. Luke very carefully checked his rifle and propped it up close at hand, ready to shoot, if he had to. Then he took his bow off his back, thinking it would not be good for this fellow's friends to hear a rifle shot. The warrior continued and was now within thirty yards of the tree Luke was waiting behind. Suddenly, he stopped when his horse nickered an inquiry and was answered by Smoke, standing in the pines behind Luke. Luke felt every muscle in his body go tense. The warrior backed his horse a couple of yards and looked quickly to his right and left, obviously thinking ambush, Luke figured.

But Early Thunder wasn't thinking ambush. Thinking instead that the horses he had been following must have gone into the trees, or at least, some of them did. So he turned his horse off the path, as well, to cut them off, if they were thinking about turning back. His unexpected move gave Luke no choice but to drop to one knee, since he was now fully exposed standing there. Early Thunder did not look his way at once, since his attention was captured by the image of Smoke, standing in the trees wearing an empty white man's saddle. When the startled Blackfoot turned his head toward Luke, it was to discover the kneeling white man with bow fully drawn. Although quick to react, it was not quick enough to avoid the arrow that pierced his side, breaking his ribs. He grabbed the shaft of the arrow in a futile attempt to pull it out, causing him to slide sideways and fall off his horse. Luke notched a second arrow and hurried to finish the kill. When he got to the wounded man, he could see that his wound was mortal, for he was choking up blood as he tried to crawl on hands and knees. Feeling the same as he would with a dying deer or buffalo, Luke sought to end his suffering quickly and he did so with his knife across Early Thunder's throat. He took no pleasure in the taking of this man's life, and he had to remind himself that the Blackfoot warrior would not have hesitated to take his life, had the roles been reversed. *And after he did it*, Luke thought, *he would have taken my scalp and danced around the campfire tonight, singing about what a brave thing he did.*

He cleaned his knife on the Indian's shirt and relieved him of his arrows, leaving his arrow in the body, hopefully to confuse his people when they found him. He also took a fusil trade gun Early Thunder carried and the powder and lead with it. He took the reins of the sorrel horse and led it away from the pines and started out after Jug and Willow. As he rode away, he issued a word of complaint to Smoke. "Whose side are you on? When this sorrel nickered, what the hell did you answer him for? You two messed up a simple ambush and I coulda come up on the short end of it, instead of that Blackfoot." He gave the bay gelding a nudge with his heels and started after Willow and Jug at a lope.

"I see you brought us another horse to add to our herd," Jug called out when Luke caught up with them. "I don't reckon you found someplace to buy one back yonder." Although his remark was flippant, it was not without concern, for it meant that someone had caught up with them.

"I'm afraid not," Luke said. "It was just one Indian, by himself."

"I didn't hear no shot," Jug said.

"I didn't want to fire a shot, in case his partners were close by," Luke explained. "My dang horse almost got me shot." He told

Jug about his ambush and how it ended up as it did. "I brought his horse with me 'cause I was thinkin' it mighta wandered back to his friends. We can turn him loose with our other strays."

Jug nodded agreement. He figured the horse would stay with them, due to the tendency of horses to stay with a group of other horses. "Problem is, you know dang well that buck you killed ain't likely the only one of 'em that'll see that trail of horses and figure it might have somethin' to do with their missin' buck."

"You're right, Jug," Luke responded, sensing his partner's discontent with the incident. "I shoulda let the son of a gun kill me, and maybe they wouldn't have felt no need to come after us."

Listening silently at the exchange between the two men up to that point, Willow now felt the need to interrupt. "No, no, Luke, he not mean better you be killed!"

Both men laughed at that and Jug proclaimed, "The hell I didn't. That mighta satisfied them bloodthirsty Blackfeet, and I wouldn't have to share them Johnny-cakes with nobody."

Realizing they were japing again, she stuck her lower lip out like a young child and declared, "Maybe I not make no more Johnny-cakes."

"Now you see what your nonsense has cost us," Luke said. "We might have to go back to eatin' those dough-balls you call biscuits."

"Now you've done it," Jug threatened. "You ain't gettin' no more of my biscuits, and Willow ain't gonna fry you no more Johnny-cakes. Looks like you ain't gonna eat nothin' but elk jerky."

Luke could go only so long with the teasing of Willow. So he told her that he and Jug were horsing around, but they were both seriously concerned about the possibility of a party of angry Blackfoot warriors chasing after them. They were going to do whatever it took to keep her safe. And they were counting on being able to stay ahead of the hostiles until getting a little farther up the river where they would be in Shoshone territory. Underway again, they pushed on, following the winding river until reaching the mountains of the Madison Range. From that point on, they felt a little less vulnerable to an attack. For a party of Indians would be as restricted as they, with the mountains crowding in upon the riverbed to leave little room for a broad charge.

Able to travel only as fast as the horses carrying the load of pelts, they worried about the slain Blackfoot's friends catching up with them. But it finally reached the point where Luke and Jug were forced to call a longer halt to rest the horses. Faced with the prospect of being overtaken while trying to urge their pack-horses forward, they decided there was no choice but to find a suitable ambush spot and wait for the Blackfeet to catch up.

They knew it was the perfect spot when they came to it. Where the river had formed a bend between a steep mountain-side and a high, cliff-like bluff, the narrow riverbank was partially blocked by some fallen rock. There was no room left between the rocks and the water, but a thin bank of sand, leaving just enough space for one rider and his two packhorses to pass at a time. When Luke passed through, he pulled up on the other side of the rocks and waited for Jug to come through. When Jug cleared the passage, Luke merely gave him a nod. Jug nodded in agreement, and they signaled Willow to continue for about seventy-five yards where it appeared the mountain slope was gentler. "There's grass the horses can get to up there and wood for a fire," Luke said to Willow as she rode on by him. She nod-ded and said nothing, but her eyes were questioning the early stop for supper. "We've gotta rest these horses," he explained.

Jug and Luke looked the rocks over and picked the spots they planned to use as firing positions. "We can have Willow set right down here between us and reload our rifles," Jug said. "I don't care how many of 'em there are, we can make it pretty dang costly for 'em."

"You know, we don't even know for sure if there's anybody comin' after us a-tall," Luke said.

"That'ud be even better, wouldn't it?" Jug responded. "But I got an itch under my left arm that's tellin' me somebody's comin'."

"More likely tellin' you it's time you took a bath," Luke said. "But I'll unload these packhorses, and then Smoke and I'll backtrack a ways to see if we're lucky or not. Smoke ain't hardly tired a-tall, since he ain't done nothin' but walk all mornin'."

"Couldn't hurt," Jug replied. "If there is a bunch of redskins on our trail, it'd be a lot of help to know how many there are and how soon they'll likely get here."

So, once again, Luke rode back over their backtrail, with Jug watching his departure, knowing absolutely why he had never ventured into the Montana country by himself, and wondering if he hadn't gone just a little bit loco to do it with just one partner. He began to speculate on what he would do if Luke got jumped by a Blackfoot war party. Even if he could manage to get Willow and himself away from them with their lives, he wasn't sure his spirit wouldn't be broken for good, if he had to dump the pelts and run. To finally get into those mountains he always knew held such a treasure in beaver fur—and prove it by trapping all he could carry—then to lose it all to the Blackfeet, might be enough to scramble his brain for good. He shook his head and spat to rid his brain of thoughts he had no control over, then turned his horse to follow after Willow.

"Do you want me to cook food now?" She asked when he rode up and dismounted.

"No. Why don't you wait till Luke gets back and see how long we're gonna be here," he told her. Might be, we'll be here all night, dependin' on what he says."

He couldn't have ridden three miles before he caught sight of them in the distance. He counted six riders and they were pressing forward at a trot. Obviously Blackfoot warriors, just like the one he had killed. He knew they would soon catch up to them.

He quickly turned Smoke around and loped back to warn Jug and Willow.

Jug saw him coming and knew from the way he was pushing his horse that he wasn't bringing good news. He called to Willow and told her to bring her gun and his extra rifle. By the time Luke loped past the fallen rocks, Jug and Willow were busy loading weapons for their defense. "How many?" Jug yelled as Luke went by.

"Six," Luke yelled back and rode Smoke down with the other horses.

"Six," Jug repeated to Willow, "we can handle six." He checked the load in his Pennsylvania long rifle and laid it on the rocks beside him while he took his other rifle when Willow handed it to him. In a matter of seconds, they were joined by Luke, carrying both his rifles. He took his place on the other side of Willow and quickly checked his weapons. "How long you figure?" Jug asked.

"Any minute now," Luke answered.

He had no sooner uttered the words when Willow cried out, "There they are!" The warriors came into view, riding two abreast.

They were still over two hundred yards away but within the effective range of the long rifles, so Luke and Jug decided to send the Indians a message. "Best let 'em know what kinda fire power they're up against," Jug advised casually. "Maybe they'll change their minds and go chase buffalo instead. I'll take the one on the left, you take the one on the right. All right?"

"All right," Luke said. "Lemme know when you're ready and we'll shoot at the same time." He figured if they fired at the same time, that would prevent the target beside the first one from ducking and spoiling the second shot.

"I'm ready," Jug said, and Luke counted to three and they both fired, knocking the two leading warriors off their horses and causing the other four to scatter to look for cover. "Now we'll see if any of 'em is carryin' a long rifle." It took only a few moments for the remaining four warriors to realize where the shots had come from. The question concerning the range of their weapons was answered when a couple of shots were fired from the foot of the mountain. The bullets plowed a couple of ridges in the ground a dozen yards short of the rocks protecting Luke and Jug. And the familiar sound of the Hudson's Bay trade guns confirmed the fact that it was not an error of not aiming high enough. The shots provided an additional helpful clue as to where the shooter had taken cover, when the powder flash indicated a pine tree near the foot of the mountain. Luke lined his sights on the pine tree and waited. At that distance, it was not easy to see clearly. But when he saw something that looked like a bulge appear on the side of the tree, he squeezed the trigger. The bulge jerked straight up and cried out.

With three of the six dead upon arriving within two-hundred yards of the horses they had been following, the remaining three decided to retreat. On foot, and using their horses for cover, all three ran back out of sight of the fallen rocks. "Whaddaya think, Jug? You reckon that'll be enough to turn 'em back?"

"Hard to say, ain't it?" Jug responded. "Mighta just made 'em mad enough to try to get some revenge for us killin' those three."

"If they are thinkin' about revenge," Luke speculated, "I'd guess the next thing they'd do is climb up this mountain beside us and try to get in behind us." He backed away from the rocks to take a look up the steep mountainside. "Maybe come over that ledge right there." He pointed to a rocky ledge about one hundred feet above them. "That'd put 'em right over us, so maybe we'd best back up to where the horses are 'til we see what they're gonna do." Noticing Willow standing there as if all ears, he thought he'd give her a word of encouragement, so he said, "You did a good job there when we were shootin' at those Black-feet."

She looked puzzled. "I do nothing," she said.

"Sure, you did," Luke insisted. "You reloaded the rifle I shot the first time. I just didn't get another shot with it." When she looked skeptical, he added, "You were right there with powder and ball, ready to keep us shootin' if they hadn't run." She shrugged in response.

They retreated back to their horses to decide what to do. It was early afternoon still, too early to camp for the night. Ideally, they would rest the horses for a couple of hours, then load them up again and drive them five or ten miles farther up the river before going into camp. The problem, however, was having no way of knowing what the three surviving Blackfeet were going to do. Jug expressed it first. "We really need to know what those three bucks are thinkin'."

"I reckon I can try to find out," Luke volunteered. "The only way to do it is to go up this mountain and get over that spot they crawled back to."

"It ain't right to ask you to stick your neck out every time there's some dangerous scoutin' to be done," Jug muttered. "I reckon I could do it this time."

"It's better if I do it," Luke replied. "It'll have to be on foot 'cause the side of this mountain is too steep to ride a horse up it, and your legs ain't long enough."

"I reckon that's a matter of fact," Jug confessed reluctantly. It wasn't as embarrassing to him as admitting he was getting too old to go mountain climbing. "And I done give up thinkin' they might still be growin'."

"You're the brains of this partnership," Luke remarked. "I can't have you wastin' your time doin' the little things I can do."

"Well, you watch your topnotch," Jug warned. "These boys play dirty."

"I'll do that," Luke replied. "Now, I'd best get goin', or they're likely to wind up over here."

Willow stood astonished as she listened to the exchange of conversation between the two. *They make crazy talk,* she thought. *Luke the smart one. I don't want him get killed.*

* * *

Thinking his long rifle was not the best choice for what he had to do, Luke strapped his bow over his shoulder and carried his shorter barrel shotgun and his pistol as he started up the gentler slope where the horses were grazing. Stretching his long legs, he didn't waste any time getting up to the steep part of the mountain because he wanted to reach a point over the three warriors before they decided to do the same thing he was doing. When he had climbed high enough to reach the ledge he had seen from the trail below, he followed it around the mountain to reach a spot directly over the fallen rocks he and Jug had used for cover. Moving very carefully at this point to prevent a surprise confrontation with the three Blackfeet, he continued through the heavily forested mountainside. He estimated the Indians had been about two-hundred yards away when he and Jug had shot the two leading them. If they hadn't moved, they were still that far from where he now was. Maybe he might reach a position over them in time to see what they planned to do. Hopefully, it would be to take their dead and withdraw.

"Hurry!" Red Feather exhorted the two Blackfoot braves behind him as they climbed the mountainside. There was no verbal response to his urging beyond the labored breathing caused by the steepness of their climb. After the fatal demonstration of the enemy's superior firepower, Leads Pony and Little Bear were of the opinion that they should withdraw and take their dead brothers back to the others at Three Forks. Then, they argued, the whole hunting party would become a war party and they would come back to avenge the dead. But Red Feather had insisted that it would take too long to do that. The shooters and their herd of horses would be much farther into Shoshone territory. "We must not let them go unpunished for the killings," he said. "I will go, if you will not." So out of a feeling of guilt, they followed him up the mountain, not sure how many they were stalking. There were only three shots fired at them, but all three hit their target. Now, they were concentrating on getting within the effective range of their weapons and preferably behind those who shot at them. Shoshone, Crow, or white trappers, they weren't sure. All were enemies.

It would be difficult to determine who was the most startled when suddenly rounding a boulder, the two men came face to face. It happened in the flash of an instant, although it seemed much longer to the two men involved. It was also impossible to judge who was the first to realize what had happened. But there was no question about which man reacted the swiftest, for Luke emptied one barrel of his shotgun in Red Feather's chest before the stunned warrior got his trade gun halfway up to aim at Luke. Holding his shotgun right where it was, Luke waited for Red Feather to drop, exposing an equally stunned Leads Pony still fumbling for his gun. Luke unloaded the other barrel of his shotgun, cutting him down as well. Little Bear, the only one with no gun, had his bow in hand, but made no move to react when Luke dropped his shotgun and pulled his pistol from his belt. The shocked warrior knew he could not notch an arrow and draw his bow before Luke pulled the trigger, so he stood waiting for his doom. Luke pulled the trigger, but the pistol did not fire. Both men were struck dumb for a moment until Little Bear slowly smiled, notched his arrow and drew the bow, only to be stunned once more when Luke's knife struck him just below his Adam's apple. He dropped his bow and grabbed the knife with both hands, straining to pull it out of his throat. While Little Bear grappled with the knife, Luke hurriedly measured out fresh priming powder and pulled the trigger again, this time successfully. The pistol fired, just as Little Bear managed to free the knife from his throat, putting a hole in his forehead.

Finding it hard to believe he was still standing, Luke hurriedly checked to make sure all three men were dead. *I reckon I'd best thank my lucky stars for the way this turned out,* he told himself. There were three chances for him to go under and he was wise enough to know it was pure luck that he didn't. Before he checked the bodies for anything of value, he took a few minutes to think about how easily it could have gone the other way. Then he picked up the two trade guns, as well as his weapons, turned around, and went back the way he had come.

Jug met him halfway up the gentle slope. He looked relieved to see Luke walking back to the valley floor, carrying an armload of weapons. "Luke!" Jug called out excitedly. "We heard the shootin'! What happened? I figured they musta come over the top of that mountain with the same idea you had. I swear, you had me worried. I didn't know who was gonna end up walkin' down this side of the mountain." He waited then while they made their way back down beside the river. "Well?" He finally said when they got there. "What happened?"

"They're dead," Luke answered.

"All three?"

"That's right," Luke said. "We won't have to worry about those three anymore. What I don't know is whether or not there'll be any more comin' after all six of 'em don't come home. So I'm thinkin' we'd do well to put some more distance between us and that bunch at Three Forks, just in case they do."

"Well, you won't get no argument from me on that," Jug declared. "I figure the horses can make another ten miles or so today, so why don't we get 'em started and get to hell outta here?"

"Fine by me," Luke replied, "but first I've gotta go back down the river a piece. They most likely tied their horses somewhere, and I wouldn't wanna ride off and leave 'em tied to a tree."

"I swear," Jug blurted, "I forgot about the horses. We got more horses to fool with." He sounded truly disappointed.

"That's a fact," Luke said, "six of 'em, if ain't none of 'em run off." He looked over at Willow, who was standing, holding her Hudson's Bay smooth bore trade gun by her side, listening to their conversation. "You look like you were ready to help Jug out, if those fellows came chargin' down here," he teased.

"I do what I have to, if you not come back," she replied. "Those Blackfoot dogs never get me no more."

When he realized how stone-cold serious she was, he said, "As long as me and Jug are alive, we ain't gonna let that happen. Are we, Jug?"

"That's God's truth," Jug answered. He looked back and forth from one of them to the other. *It's just a matter of time*, he thought. *Be a shame if it don't happen.* "Six more horses," he blared then, when his mind promptly left the two young people. "What the hell are we gonna do with six more horses?"

Chapter 20

They stayed there at the site of the ambush until they rounded up the six new ponies to add to their growing herd. They were operating on the principle that these new horses would do as the other captured horses had and follow along with the herd. The principle seemed to be working, because all six followed along as expected. "If we make it to Cache Valley with all these horses, everybody's gonna think we're in the horse business for sure," Jug commented. "Too bad there ain't some more mares in the bunch 'cause this beaver business ain't gonna shine forever."

"Why not?" Luke asked. "People ain't gonna quit wearin' hats."

"Reckon not," Jug replied. "But the way we've been trappin' these mountains, the mountains are gonna run outta beaver. I expect folks would learn to make hats outta somethin' else."

"You might be right, but that's hard to believe," Luke said.

For the next two days, they followed the river, with Luke riding back every so often to check their back trail for signs of pursuit. There was none, however, and by the time they struck the Snake River and traveled a short distance to strike the Green River, they were no longer worried about the Blackfoot hunting party behind them. This deep in Shoshone territory, it would be unlikely to encounter other Blackfoot parties, as well. Unlikely, but not impossible, so Luke and Jug maintained a cautious eye for the not impossible. After the winter just past, it was difficult to acquire a carefree manner. Luke figured it was going to take the rendezvous to relieve the tenseness in his mind and body.

They had decided to follow the Green River at least as far as Horse Creek before crossing over the mountains to the west and continuing on to Cache Valley. With the rapid warming in the past few days, they weren't really sure just what month it was, May or June. So they followed the Green River to see if anyone was arriving for the rendezvous. As Jug had suggested, "If the companies are startin' to pull in and set up for business, what's the use of us drivin' these horses over into Utah territory? It ain't gonna be that long before we turn 'em around and drive 'em back up to Horse Creek. And it ain't no question about the weather no more, so there ain't no need to go to Cache Valley."

"Well, that makes sense to me," Luke agreed. They had not reached Horse Creek yet, but they were already seeing plenty of fresh tracks along the river trail. And a great many of them wore horseshoes. "Wouldn't hurt to be early, anyway," he went on. "We could pick us a spot to set up our camp for our horses to graze and water before everybody else shows up."

"I think that's just exactly what we oughta do," Jug said, "now that we've got a ding-busted herd of horses to graze." So the decision was made. They wouldn't bother to drive their horses down to Cache Valley. There was always a threat of attack by hostile Indians, if it was too early for the start of rendezvous, but both Jug and Luke felt they had seen enough tracks to indicate they were not the first to arrive.

Willow listened with great interest to the discussion between her two white friends, and since there was no mention of her, she finally got up her nerve to approach Luke when he was checking a worn spot on his saddle to make sure it wasn't irritating Smoke.

She didn't say anything when she first walked up to him, but he could see that something was troubling her. He asked, "What is it, Willow? Is something wrong?"

"You will camp for rondy . . . ," she started, still having trouble with the word.

"Rendezvous," Luke pronounced it for her. "That's right. We'll be pullin' in there tomorrow, about dinnertime."

She hesitated to ask but finally summoned the nerve. "What are you going to do with me?"

Her question took him by surprise, for he hadn't prepared for it. "Whaddaya mean?" he asked, not sure what she wanted him to say. "Whaddaya want me to do with you? There's always a big bunch of Crows at these things. If you're wantin' to go back to your people, I'll help you get together with 'em, if that's what you're thinkin'." He looked at her, questioning, but she seemed uncertain. "I told you on the first night you showed up at our camp that you could do what you wanted. We were glad to help you out. I meant what I said, so what do you wanna do?"

She dropped her chin and pleaded softly, "I want to stay with you."

He still wasn't sure if she meant by that what he hoped she meant, and he was afraid he might jump to the wrong conclusion. He asked, "You wanna stay with Jug and me?"

She raised her head up to look directly into his eyes. "I want to stay with *you*," she repeated with emphasis on the last word. "I like Jug very much. He is nice man, but I want to stay with you."

There was a strong hint of desperation in her voice that was not there before, and he did not want to respond to her in any fashion that would be presumptuous on his part. He was reluctant to suggest the first thing that came to his mind. So instead, he said, "You don't have to worry about bein' alone. I'll take care of you, and that's whether Jug and I stay partners or not." He paused to watch her reactions, then said, "I expect we'll still work as partners next season, but I don't know if we're headin' back up in the same territory or not. If we do, I don't feel like it's the safest place for you. I want you with me," he confessed, "but I don't wanna put you in danger again."

"I go where you go," she stated simply.

With that, he felt they were of a like mind, so he said, "I reckon by now you've already figured out how weak-kneed and speechless I get around you." She looked totally confused, with no idea what he meant by that, so he finally spat it out. "Willow, will you marry me?" Her response was immediate and just short of violent, for she threw her arms around his neck in an exuberant embrace, causing him to take a step backward to keep from losing his balance. When he regained his stability, with Willow clinging to him as if to never let him go, he asked, "Is that a yes?"

"Yes, yes!" she gushed. "You never be sorry. I make you happy. I cook your food. I clean your clothes. I butcher your elk. I give you babies!"

"You better, or he's gonna whup you with a pine limb," Jug blurted as he walked up to join them, having overheard her acceptance of Luke's proposal. "It's about time you two young'uns got together. I swear, I was beginnin' to think I was gonna have to ask her for you." He walked up to them and gave them both a pat on the back while they were still locked in an embrace. "I reckon this means we're gonna be buildin' a honeymoon tipi 'cause I don't want no hanky-panky goin' on when I'm tryin' to sleep."

"We ain't gonna worry about that, till after we're officially married," Luke declared. He cared too much for Willow to have her climb into his blanket like a rendezvous camp girl. He gently untied her arms from around his neck and held her by her shoulders while he talked to her. "When we get our camp set up, I'll look for someone to marry us, official-like. Then, if you want to, we can go to one of the Crow camps when they get here and let them marry us, too. I want you to know how much I think of you. And I want everybody to know that you are an honorable woman and not just some Injun woman that jumped into bed with a beaver trapper." The gleam in her eyes told him that she had not expected such a demonstration of devotion on his part. She felt a tear welling up in her eye when he said, "When I asked you to be my wife, I meant forever." She and Jug could not know that he was making that commitment largely because of the memories he had of his mother and father and their abandonment of him when he was a child. He had learned from his Aunt Vera that his mother and father were never officially married, and she figured that was one of the reasons she had found it easy to walk out on him. Thinking of all this was the main reason he intended to make his marriage legal. It was important to him that Willow should know that he took this marriage seriously.

To celebrate this special occasion, Willow made Johnny-cakes with the last of their cornmeal. The last of the dried beans went into the pot with strips of venison after soaking in a jar of water all day. All three of the travelers were hoping to find some of the merchants at the rendezvous site early, so their stores of supplies could be replenished. It was a pleasant evening with no real fear of trouble any longer. They had managed to avoid serious attacks from the Blackfoot hunters, but Luke was superstitious enough to keep watch over their horses and their furs until they had made camp at the rendezvous and their plews were sold. Willow came out to sit with him while he drank the cup of coffee she made for him. Sometime after midnight, Jug came out, carrying the dregs of the coffeepot, and insisted that Luke should go on to bed. He assured him that he would remain awake until breakfast. "I got a little shut-eye," he assured Luke. "I'll stay awake till breakfast." He nodded toward Willow, who was fast asleep, her head resting on Luke's shoulder. "Better carry her over and put her in her bed or we're liable not to get no breakfast."

As gently as he could, Luke lifted the young woman in his arms. Like a sleeping child, she put her arms around his neck, content to lay her head on his broad shoulder and dream, her mind free from the worries of previous days.

Chapter 21

It was a little past noontime when Ike Hopper paused in the filling of his pipe with tobacco to watch what appeared to be a brigade of trappers for one of the fur companies approaching. "They're startin' to come in now," he said aside to Zeke Singleton. A few moments later, he said, "They look like they're turnin' those horses on over by the creek, and that ain't where none of the fur companies are gonna set up their headquarters. I don't see but three riders. They mighta had some Injun trouble. Reckon we oughta go tell 'em American Fur is settin' up their post a mile and a half from here, and the other companies are below them?"

"Hell, it ain't up to us to tell 'em where to camp," Zeke replied. "They'll find out pretty quick that they're movin' in with a bunch of free trappers." Interested in the party now, he walked over beside Ike. "They got a lotta horses. That's why they're headin' to that grassy area by the creek." He continued to stare at the column of horses and packs for a long time, unsure of what he was seeing, until they were close enough for him to be certain. "Well, I'll be go to hell," he mumbled under his breath. "Ike!" He exclaimed then, "That's Jug Sartain and Luke Ransom!"

"Nah, it ain't," Ike responded, finding that hard to believe.

He took a step closer in that direction while straining to make his eyes focus. "Who's the other feller with 'em?"

"Danged if I know," Zeke answered, "looks like an Injun. Let's go find out." He didn't wait for Ike and took off across the valley floor on foot at a trot. Ike didn't hesitate, hustling off after him.

About one hundred yards away, Luke saw them and called to Jug, "Looks like we've been spotted." He pointed to the two men running across to intercept them.

Jug turned to look in the direction Luke pointed. "Hopper and Singleton," he said. "Can't think of anybody I druther see." He was eager to see their response to the load of plews and the extra horses he and Luke came back with.

They picked a spot to set up their camp and dismounted. By the time Ike and Zeke caught up with them, they were unloading the horses, and Willow was gathering wood to start her cookfire. "Hot damn!" Zeke exclaimed. "Looks like you boys did all right partnerin' up." He and Ike were both counting the packs of plews. "You picked up some horses, too."

"Howdy, boys," Jug greeted them. "Glad to see you made it back to another rendezvous with your top-notches still under your hats." He looked at Luke and winked. "I reckon we had a fair hunt. Coulda come back with a lot more plews, but we said we wasn't gonna take nothin' but heavy winter fur. You boys do all right?"

"Fair to middlin'," Ike answered. "Looks like you done some other trappin', too," he said and nodded toward Willow, who was busy starting her fire.

Before Luke could reply, Jug quickly introduced her. "Let me acquaint you gentlemen with Mrs. Luke Ransom. At least she will be, just as soon as they can find somebody to tie the knot for 'em. Ain't that right, Luke?"

"That's right," Luke said at once. "Her name is Willow, and she's accepted my proposal of marriage." He turned toward her.

"Willow, this is Ike Hopper and Zeke Singleton. They're friends of mine and Jug's." She looked up and smiled at them but continued with her preparation of food.

With the prospect of selling their pelts foremost in his mind, Jug asked, "Have you boys sold your plews yet?"

They both answered yes at the same time, and Ike continued. "Sold 'em at your old company," he said to Luke. "American Fur, they're payin' as much as anybody is, but that ain't but three dollars a pound. And if that ain't bad enough, they're sayin' beaver won't bring hardly that much next year." That was disappointing news to Luke and Jug. "I don't reckon there's much we can do about it, so I'll be trappin' again next year. Maybe they're wrong about the prices. But if they ain't, you and Luke musta been thinkin' about it when you started collectin' horses. How'd you come by so many horses?"

"Horses are just like saloon women," Jug answered. "They're just naturally attracted to me. We just picked 'em up here and there when we saw we was gonna need more to carry our packs," he japed.

"Blackfoot country?" Zeke asked and nodded toward Willow again.

"A man would have to be plum loco to go to Blackfoot country to steal horses," Jug said, "and dumber than that to trap beaver there."

"I know what you're thinkin'," Luke said then, "but Willow ain't Blackfoot. She's Crow. Her people live in the Absarokas. Blackfoot country is where you go to get your scalp lifted, not to look for a wife."

"I reckon you're right about that," Ike said.

"You say you sold your plews to American Fur Company?" Luke asked, changing the subject. He turned to Jug then and asked, "Whaddaya think, partner? You wanna go talk to them?" Before Jug answered, Luke asked Ike, "Is Axel Thompson still the buyer at American?" Ike said that he was, so Luke looked at

Jug and said, "Axel has always been pretty fair with me and the crew I worked with at American. You wanna talk to him about our plews?"

"Good as any," Jug replied. "The quicker we get it done, the better. I'm tired of guardin' 'em."

Back to Ike then, Luke asked, "They in the same place as last year?" When he was told they were, he looked at Jug and suggested, "Let's eat some of whatever Willow's cookin' over there, and then go sell our plews."

"That suits me just fine," Jug said. "How 'bout you boys? You want some smoked elk? I expect that's about all Willow's got left to cook." They both declined, as he expected, but they stayed to talk while Jug and Luke ate. "I've et so much elk and deer," Jug burst out again, "I know what I've got a cravin' for now. Is the Chinaman back yet?"

"Yep," Ike replied. "He's back. He was back before we got back."

"Good!" Jug exclaimed. "That's gonna be one of the first places I spend some of that beaver money."

While Jug was smacking his lips at the thought of The Chinaman's, Zeke leaned close to Luke. "I reckon you'd find out sooner or later," he said to him, "but maybe I oughta tell you before you go to sell your plews, so you won't get surprised. Your old friend at American Fur made it back here this year."

That captured Luke's attention at once, knowing he was referring to Dan Bloodworth. "Oh? Is that so? Well, I reckon I'm glad I didn't kill him, him bein' a company man and all."

"He couldn't make it with the bunch he usually trapped with, so he missed the whole season, but he's back this year with the company. I reckon he's got enough vinegar in his veins to keep him from dyin'." Zeke shrugged. "Anyway, I thought it best that you knew."

"I 'preciate it, Zeke," Luke said, "but I've got no business to attend to with Bloodworth. I told Lonnie Johnson that when I helped him put Bloodworth on the wagon. I don't know if Bloodworth could hear me or not, but I told Lonnie to tell him that's the end of it. He's supposed be a friend of Bloodworth's, so I hope he told him I ain't lookin' for no trouble from him."

"I hear what you're sayin',' Zeke said. "But you'd best be careful 'cause we ain't talkin' about a man with a helluva lot of common sense. Might be wise to do your fur tradin' with Rocky Mountain Traders."

"Like I said, I 'preciate it, but I know Axel Thompson will treat us right, and I didn't come here to the rendezvous to hide from Dan Bloodworth or anybody else."

"I expect Bloodworth's learned his lesson by now," Zeke said. He exchanged a knowing glance with Ike, both men having the same thought. Bullies like Dan Bloodworth never learned their lessons. And the previous trouble with Luke would never be considered over to Bloodworth—not after having missed a year's work trapping because of Luke's skill with a knife. Seeing Luke and Jug return after an enormously successful season for themselves would only drive the nail of resentment deeper into Bloodworth's heart. Having witnessed the brief, but deadly encounter between Bloodworth and Luke, Zeke felt certain the only lesson Bloodworth had learned was a shot in the back was his best chance to avenge himself.

"Me and Ike was fixin' to go to Red's Place for a drink of likker when we saw you pull in," Zeke declared. "When you get done sellin' your pelts, come on by and we'll help you celebrate."

"Sounds like a good idea to me," Jug responded. "Whaddaya say, partner?" Luke nodded his approval. "It's liable to take us a little time, though," Jug couldn't resist pointing out, since there were a lot of plews to weigh.

After Zeke and Ike left, Luke and Jug prepared to lead their packhorses down Horse Creek to the buyer's tents. Willow had watched silently while Luke ate the meat she had cooked, and finally spoke when he came to tell her he and Jug would be gone for a while. "You don't have to be afraid here at rendezvous," he assured her. "There won't be any Blackfoot war parties coming in here. So I'm sure you'll be safe till I get back. With our camp-fire burnin' and our horses grazing, everybody'll know there's somebody usin' this campsite." He looked into her eyes to try to determine her true feelings. When he wasn't sure, he said, "Or you can go with us, if you're not sure about waitin' here till I get back."

"No," she said. "I wait here." He smiled at her, then bent forward and kissed her forehead. She took his hands in hers and gazed up at him. "I hear the talk with your friends," she started. "You never talk me about that man, Bloodhound. Why Blood-hound after you?"

"Bloodworth," he corrected her. "He's nothin' for you to worry your pretty little head about." He attempted to put her at ease, but she continued.

"Those men said you need to be careful," she insisted. "They say he not forget what you did to him."

"We ain't even married yet and you're already frettin' over some loose talk," he said with a chuckle. "Dan Bloodworth ain't nothin' for you to worry your pretty little head about," he re-peated. "Me and Jug will go sell our plews, and then you and I are gonna find us a preacher to marry us. I know there'll be one here somewhere. Last year, a preacher came to the river and held a Sunday service every week. He was still here when we left last fall. Wasn't he, Jug?"

"That's a fact," Jug said. "I saw him when we left Red's that mornin'." *He was comin' down off a four-day drunk on a cot Red let him use behind the bar,* Jug thought but didn't share.

"Is that right?" Luke asked. "You never said anything about it to me."

Jug shrugged his shoulders in response. "You never said you was thinkin' about gettin' married."

"Maybe he's back here this summer," Luke said to Willow. "We're gonna find out pretty quick 'cause I've gotta get you hitched up before you change your mind."

She blushed when she said, "I not change my mind." She had hesitated to suggest something to Luke that he apparently had no knowledge of. She decided she would tell him now, since he had so much concern about being honorable about his commitment to her. "In Absaroka village, when man marry woman, he move in her family tipi, they married. I have no tipi, but you move in here." She placed her hand over her heart. "We already married, just not white man married."

Her simple declaration left Luke speechless for a moment, but Jug responded right away. "Well, I'll be . . . That is right. I shoulda thoughta that." He enjoyed a hearty chuckle over it.

Then Luke grinned and shrugged. "It makes no difference. We're still gonna find a preacher to marry us by white man's law, so nobody can say you ain't legally married."

"Howdy, Luke," Axel Thompson called out in cheerful greeting when they walked in the front tent next to the American Fur Company's trading post. "I see you and your partner made it back again." He hesitated, obviously trying to recall Jug's name.

"Howdy, Axel," Luke quickly replied. "You remember Jug, I reckon."

"'Course, I do," Axel replied then. "Jug Sartain, last year was the first year you traded with us. I'm glad to see you fellows back here this summer. Did you have a pretty good year? Some of our men with the company didn't have the year they were expecting."

"That's why we came to you," Jug claimed. "We was afraid you might notta got the prime furs you were lookin' for. And me and Luke have got the best lookin' winter plews you'll be lookin' at this year."

"Is that a fact?" Axel replied. "Well, seein's believin'. We'll take a look at 'em."

"They're out back of the tent," Luke said, "but there's one thing that's kinda worrisome to me. We were talkin' to some of the other free trappers. And they said you weren't payin' but three dollars this year. I surely hope that ain't what you're payin' for top quality, prime beaver like you're gonna see in our packs."

"Luke, you know I ain't gonna lie to ya," Axel replied. "What those fellows told you is true. The whole beaver market is down, and it's gonna keep goin' down." When Luke questioned the cause of the poor market, Axel said, "Silk, they're makin' hats outta silk over there in Europe where they used to make 'em outta beaver fur."

"How can that hold up?" Jug asked. "No hat made outta silk can last as long as one made outta prime beaver fur."

"Maybe you're right," Axel allowed. "I don't know about that, but I have to tell you, ain't nobody payin' more than three dollars a pound. And that's the God's honest truth." He paused and shook his head when he saw the disappointment in their faces. He had a fair idea how they had probably risked their lives day after day in the cold rocky streams of the mountains, counting on the payoff for their efforts. "Look here, let's go look at your pelts. If they're as prime as you claim, I might be able to go three-ten, or maybe three-fifteen, but they'd have to be mighty damn good."

Luke and Jug exchanged looks of disappointment, but they knew they were not likely to get a better price anywhere else, so they followed Axel out the back flap of his office tent to the long rows of storage tents and the weighing station. "You weren't jokin' when you said you had a lot of 'em, were you?" Axel remarked when he saw the string of packhorses waiting there.

"We weren't jokin' when we said they were prime beaver fur, either," Luke answered.

It didn't take long for Axel to realize they had not exaggerated when touting the quality of their pelts. Each pack of sixty pelts he opened was as high in quality as the one before it. Axel was truly impressed. "By Ned, you boys landed in a hot spot. I don't reckon there's any chance you'd care to say where the hell you were trapping."

"There's two chances," Jug replied quickly, "slim and none."

It took some time, since the pelts were many and they weighed heavy. When they were all finished, Axel made out the bill of sale and accompanied them to the cashier's wagon where they received their money. "It was a pleasure doin' business with you fellows," Axel said. "I hope to see more of what you brought in next year." They shook hands and Jug started rounding up their horses.

Luke lingered a moment to ask a question. "Do you know if there's a preacher here at the rendezvous this year?"

The question took Axel by surprise. "A preacher?" He exclaimed loud enough for one of the men hauling the pelts to the warehouse tents to hear him. "I don't think so, Luke."

"There is one, Axel," the man loading the pelts spoke out. "I couldn't help overhearin'. I don't know what kinda preacher you're lookin' for. But he's a Mormon. Got him a little alter-like setup in his wagon. He was preachin' sermons down in Cache Valley, and he said he was comin' to the rendezvous."

"Have you seen him since we got here?" Axel asked. The man said that he hadn't. "Well, there you go, Luke. Maybe you can find him. A man preachin' out of a wagon oughta be easy to find."

"'Preciate it," Luke said to Axel and nodded his thanks to his helper, then he went to help Jug take care of the horses. They led their small herd of horses back to their camp by the river and released the tired animals to graze and drink water. Then they sat down on the ground and counted out the money to split fifty-fifty.

"Now, I'm ready to go visit with the boys at Red's," Jug announced. "I need a shot of likker so bad, I'm a-feared I'm gonna turn to pure rust inside my gut." When Luke didn't respond in similar fashion, he asked, "You ready?"

"You go on ahead," Luke said, "and I'll be along directly."

"Why?" Jug asked, not sure anything could be more important at this particular moment. "Whatchu gonna do?"

"Well, it took a little longer to grade all our plews than I thought it would," Luke answered with some reluctance. "I was thinkin' about Willow waitin' back here all that time. She ain't ever been to a rendezvous before. I expect she mighta been a little bit scared when we left her alone right at the start." When he said that, they both turned and looked at the little Indian woman, kneeling by the fire, but looking toward them and the horses. "I kinda hate to leave her alone again and go off to the saloon. We really ain't set up our camp yet. I oughta at least do that first."

Jug looked at a loss for a couple of minutes as he considered the situation. He had grown awful fond of the little Crow woman over the winter, even encouraged Luke to take a romantic interest in her. Now, he wondered if that might have been a mistake. It looked like his young partner might be getting tangled up in the little lady's web. The first thought of any mountain man on the first day back to rendezvous oughta be a drink with the boys who made it back. Finally, he suggested, "Hell, bring her with you. There'll most likely be some other women there."

"You think I oughta take her with us and set her down with the whores that work the saloons?" Luke asked, pointedly.

"No, I reckon not," Jug replied. "Red might not allow Injuns in his saloon, anyway." Then he had another thought. "We can take her to The Chinaman's for supper. She oughta like that." Luke was hesitating again, but Jug didn't give him a chance to argue. "Chinaman usually feeds everybody on one table, but I bet for a dollar more, he'd set the three of us up at that little table he uses when the big table fills up. Be like our own little private party. She could set there in one of his rockin' chairs out front and wait for us to go have ourselves a drink with the fellers."

"I'll see what she says," Luke told him. "I ain't ready to leave her here by herself till she gets to feelin' safe." He promptly went to her to see her response to the idea. He was surprised when she told him she would enjoy eating at The Chinaman's. When he told Jug she agreed to it, he suggested that he should go on ahead and make the arrangements with Lee Wong. Luke said he would also have time for a drink or two before he and Willow got there. "I gotta make one stop by the American Fur store on the way. Then we'll be right there for supper."

"All right," Jug replied, happily. "Where's my jug? I'll get right over and set it up with Lee Wong. He's gonna be tickled to see me again." He didn't waste another second before picking up his empty jug and heading out. He was thinking that maybe he had time for more than a couple of drinks before he went to The Chinaman's for supper.

"I look okay to you?" Willow asked when he led their two horses up to the partially finished tipi.

"Pretty as a picture," he answered. It occurred to him then. "I need to buy you a mirror, don't I?" He hadn't thought of it before. He guessed she had used her reflection in the stream for a looking glass. "We'll pick one up for you tomorrow when we buy all the other supplies we're out of. I'm just gonna make one quick stop on our way to supper tonight, though." He lifted her up on her horse, then climbed up on Smoke, and they rode directly to the store. When they got there, she remained in the saddle. He held his hands up for her. "Come on, I need to have you with me."

"Howdy, Luke," John Dean sang out cheerfully. "Axel told me you and your partner had brought in the best-lookin' lot of furs he's seen in a long time. I hope he gave you good money for 'em."

"Howdy, John," Luke returned. John had been clerking in the company store for as long as Luke had been with American Fur. "I think he did the best he could for us." Luke turned aside so John could see Willow, who was standing behind him. "This is Willow. I need a ring to fit her finger." It would have been difficult to decide who was the more surprised when he said that, John or Willow.

"What?" John responded. "Oh," he recovered. "Well, I oughta be able to fix you up. I've got plenty of rings."

"I ain't lookin' for any of your cheap trade rings," Luke said.

"I'm lookin' for a weddin' ring. I know you don't carry any expensive jewelry, but you might have something like a plain silver band."

"Right," John recovered, "I think I can find you just the right thing." He went to a corner cabinet, on top of which were a couple of large wire hoops, filled with cheap rings of all kinds and colors. He opened a drawer, pulled out a heavy cloth pouch, and returned to the counter. "This might be what you have in mind," he said as he opened the pouch and exposed two rows of silver rings. One row was plain, the other had a faint design. "Will one of these do?" Willow's eyes were answer enough for Luke, and he nodded to John. "You just have to start tryin' 'em on till you get the one that fits your finger," he said to her.

She looked first at Luke for his permission. "Go ahead," he told her. "Pick the one you want." She hovered over them for a few moments as if they might fly away if she touched them. Finally, she tried one on her forefinger and Luke shook his head. "Un-uh, you wear it on this finger." He touched the ring finger of her left hand.

She quickly pulled it off and put it on her ring finger. It was too big, so she tried two more before settling for the second one. She admired it for a couple of minutes, then started to take it off. "Cost too much," she said.

Luke caught her hand and stopped her. He looked at John. "How much?"

"We have to get twelve dollars for those rings," John answered. "They're pure silver."

Back to Willow again, his hand still holding hers. "You like it?"

She nodded her head vigorously and said, "It's beautiful," in the Crow tongue. Then, using Luke and Jug's terminology she said in English, "It shines."

He smiled at her and released her hand. "You can't ever take it off."

"I never take it off," she responded.

While Luke counted out twelve dollars, John looked from one

of them to the other. "I didn't know you had taken a wife, Luke."

"I ain't stood up in front of a preacher yet," Luke said. "That ring is my promise that I'm goin' to, just as soon as I can find a preacher to make it legal."

John almost made the mistake of asking why he would bother waiting for a preacher. Quite a few of the mountain men he knew had taken Indian wives. He didn't know of any that had actually made the union legal under the law. Instead, he said, "Well, let me wish you both the best of happiness." He paused, then said, "You know, there's a Mormon fellow drivin' around here in a wagon, who says he's a preacher."

"Yeah, I heard about him. I hope we run across him." He gave Willow a reassuring grin and declared, "We'll find him."

"Whatever you say. I be your wife," she responded happily.

"That sounds like a good start for a weddin'," John Dean commented. "Reckon you'll find out how long that'll last before it's whatever I say." He chuckled good-naturedly.

"I reckon," Luke said and winked at Willow.

Chapter 22

"Luke Ransom!" Lee Wong greeted them when Luke and Willow entered the huge tent the Chinaman had erected this year. "Come in, come in. Jug Sartain tell me you bring your special lady to The Chinaman's to eat. I fix small table for you, so you not be disturbed by noisy guests. You follow, please." He led them past the long table of heavy eaters to a table barely big enough to seat four, but just right for this occasion. When they were seated, Lee Wong asked, "You eat now, or you wait for Jug?"

"We'll go ahead and eat," Luke said. "There ain't no tellin' when Jug will show up, once he gets to drinkin' with that crowd of trappers. I want you to bring the lady a cup of tea, but I want coffee." He had to capture her attention, for her eyes were as big as saucers as she looked all around her. "Is that all right with you?" He asked her. She said nothing but nodded her head excitedly.

Lee Wong was back to the table very quickly with two plates of food. A tiny Chinese woman came with him, carrying Willow's tea and Luke's coffee. She smiled shyly at Willow as she poured her tea in a China cup and motioned toward a small sugar bowl beside it. "Sugar for your tea," Luke said when Willow looked puzzled. He motioned for her to put some in her tea. Lee Wong told them the name of the entrée he served them, but Luke had no idea what it was, just that it was good eating and Willow seemed to enjoy it as well.

The young man with an Indian woman did not go unnoticed by the collection of trappers and hunters at the long table. There were a few comments that brought some chuckles, but none loud enough to give cause for offense, not even noticeable to the young couple, in fact. One of the diners found special interest in the couple, however. He made no comment, but Lonnie Johnson did not take his eyes off the couple, as he stuffed his mouth with Lee Wong's special of the day. *Wait till ol' Bloodworth hears about this*, he thought. The object of his attention was seated with his back toward the long table, unaware that Lonnie was there.

They were finished with their supper and having more tea and coffee when Jug finally made his appearance. It was obvious that the little man was more than a little unsteady on his feet as he stumbled back to join them. "I swear," he blurted as he plopped down in a chair, "I've drank a little too much on an empty stomach. I need to get some food in my belly."

"I reckon," Luke said. "You ain't lookin' too good—a little green around the gills."

"We got to drinkin' and I swear I almost emptied my jug before I realized how much I'd had," Jug confessed painfully. "You folks ready to eat?"

"We've already finished our supper," Luke replied. "It was mighty good, too. Weren't it, Willow?" She murmured a soft yum-yum and nodded. Grinning at Jug's distress, Luke looked at Willow and said, "Firewater."

"Firewater," she repeated. "No good for you."

At that moment, Lee Wong brought a plate heaped up with food and placed it on the table in front of Jug. Jug took a deep whiff of the steaming mixture of vegetables and meat and backed away from it immediately, knocking his chair over in the process. Holding both hands over his mouth, he stumbled toward the entrance and disappeared outside. Willow was immediately concerned. "We need to go to him?" She asked, obviously afraid he was in danger of dying. "He look very bad."

"He's just gonna heave up some of that rot-gut he's been drinkin'. If you're through with your tea, we'll go find him and take him back to camp. He'll straighten out in a little while after he empties his gut. He'll likely want something to eat then, but he'll do a lot better with some jerky and coffee. Then he's gonna wanna go to bed and sleep it off." He shook his head and laughed when he said, "In the mornin', he'll feel all right again and he'll be crowin' about what a good time he had tonight." They got up to leave then, and as they filed by the long table, Luke shoved the empty chair Lonnie Johnson had occupied back out of the way. He paid Lee Wong for all three suppers, apologized for Jug's reaction to his food, and explained it was whiskey that caused the reaction.

"Too bad you didn't go to eat with me at The Chinaman's," Lonnie Johnson said. "You missed a chance to say hello to an old friend of yours."

"I don't eat that slop they serve in that place," Bloodworth reacted typically. "What friend? I ain't got no friends. Who was it?"

"Luke Ransom," Lonnie said as casually as he could manage. As expected, it was akin to shoving a stick of dynamite in Bloodworth's gut. While Bloodworth was too enraged to speak, Lonnie continued. "He was dinin' with a sweet-lookin' little Injun woman, settin' off at the edge of the tent at their own private little table. That ain't all. A couple of fellers settin' at the long table said him and that sawed-off runt he partners with brought in a mess of prime beaver they're all braggin' about at the weighin' station. And it weren't at Boutwell's or Rocky Mountain Fur. They sold 'em at our company." Bloodworth still said nothing, but he continued to sit there like a pot on a hot stove, boiling angrily. Lonnie imagined he could almost see the steam rising from the top of his head. "I just thought you'd wanna know he made it back this summer. You remember? After he stuck that knife in your gut, he told me to tell you he was done with it, and to tell you to just forget about it, if you lived." He was intent upon seeing how angry he could get Bloodworth.

"Shut your mouth," Bloodworth finally spoke. "I know what he said, but he didn't think I was gonna be here this summer. He's a dead man. He just don't know it yet. He made a mistake comin' back here 'cause all he did was save me the trouble of havin' to go huntin' for him." He was making the threats, but he hadn't decided how he was going to satisfy them. He was determined to make Luke pay a price for the trouble he had caused him, and he wanted it to be as painful as he could make it. "You say he's got an Injun woman with him?"

"Yep," Lonnie answered. "And a feller settin' at the big table said he was gonna marry her. All I know is she surely is a pretty little thing. I expect he'd be pretty tore up if anythin' happened to her."

Bloodworth didn't respond until he thought about it for a few moments, then, "What is she? Blackfoot? Crow? Shoshone?"

"Hell, I don't know," Lonnie replied, "she's an Injun. Don't make no difference, does it? He quits the company and comes back here showin' off all them plews—him and his half-pint partner. I'll bet that woman told 'em where to find them prime plews and that's why he's treatin' her like a royal princess."

Bloodworth let that sink in while he formed a picture of it in his mind, and he thought he could feel a sharp pain in his belly where Luke's knife had been driven. "Is he still at The Chinaman's," he asked.

"I don't know," Lonnie answered. "He was still there when I left, and they didn't look like they was in no hurry. Why? What you fixin' to do? You teased that cat two times already and he damn-near sent you up the river for good."

"Maybe this time, I ain't gonna give him a chance to play all his tricks," Bloodworth said, still thinking out his best option. "Maybe I'll just shoot him down before he knows what's what."

"That'ud do the job all right, but you might get a shot in the back from Jug Sartain or one of them other free-trapper friends of his," Lonnie warned him. "The company might not be too tickled with you, either, even if he did quit 'em to go on his own. They was pretty good to keep you hired on when you couldn't go with us this past winter." He could see that Bloodworth was giving serious thought to what he had said, but he knew the simple brute would not let Luke Ransom go unpunished. After a long pause, Bloodworth finally seemed to relax the tenseness in his face enough to permit a slight smile to appear. "Whaddaya thinkin' now?" Lonnie asked.

"Nothin' much," Bloodworth responded, "maybe take a little ride to settle my belly after all I et for supper. Get a few things ready for tomorrow. I'm thinkin' about goin' huntin' for some deer meat."

"Goin' huntin'?" Lonnie exclaimed. "You ain't said nothin' about goin' huntin. Where you goin' huntin'?"

"I ain't decided yet."

"You want me to go with you?"

"Hell, no, I wanna go by myself. That's why I ain't said nothin' about it before."

Lonnie shook his head impatiently. "I swear, you do beat all. We got plenty of meat, smoked and salt cured."

"We ain't got no fresh deer meat and that's what I've got a hankerin' for," Bloodworth insisted.

"You do beat all," Lonnie told him. "I'm goin' to bed."

They waited in front of The Chinaman's for Jug to return from the bushes behind the wagons to see if he was going to need any help getting back to camp. In a short time, he appeared, looking slightly disheveled. "I swear, I believe Red is sellin' some of that rot-gut stock to his good customers. I believe I fought off death this time, however. I think I'm gonna make it. I told Zeke and Ike I'd bring you back with me for one drink. They said to tell you your likker was on them. Dang cheapskates, they know you don't ever drink more than two shots of whiskey."

"What do they wanna buy me a drink for?" Luke wondered aloud. He didn't express it, but he was suspicious that it might be because Jug was bad about telling heroic tales about him. "I think me and Willow are ready to call it a night. Right, Willow?" It was already beginning to get a little noisy in the clearing on the other side of Red's Place where a bare-knuckle boxing match was in the making. "I don't wanna take Willow over to that saloon."

"The boys will be disappointed if you don't have a drink with 'em," Jug said. "Willow can set right here on this bench and wait for you. I'll set here with her. She'll be all right."

Luke started to protest, but Willow interrupted him. "It's all right, Luke. I stay with Jug. You go drink one drink."

"There," Jug crowed, "you hear that? The missus says you can have one drink. Then you'd best get your tail back here."

Luke looked at her and laughed. "All right, Sweetheart. I'll have one drink and that's all." He gave her a little squeeze and stepped off the porch and walked across the clearing to the saloon.

"He ought not be too long with you waitin' out here for him," Jug told her. "I don't know if I've ever told you, but you've got yourself a good man there in Luke Ransom. I know you two are gonna make it."

She bowed her head and smiled, so pleased that he would say that, and grateful for his faith in her. She heard a sound she could not identify, and when she raised her head again, it was to see Jug falling to the ground. She started to scream, but it was muffled by the heavy burlap sack pulled roughly over her head and lost in the noise of the fist fight across the clearing. She stood up but was immediately swept off her feet by one huge arm around the sack, locking her arms to her sides. Helpless to resist, she was carried around to the back of the big tent where a horse was waiting. Her captor still held her in one arm as he stepped up into the saddle, laid her across the horse's withers in front of him, and rode away into the night. The nightmare returned of her abduction by Bloody Hand, and she was terrified by the realization that she was bound to relive it. At the point when her life had seemed to have fulfilled her fondest dreams, she was not sure she could survive the fate that was cast for her now. She struggled in an effort to slide off the loping horse, but the hand held her clamped down so hard she was unable to move.

Back at The Chinaman's tent, Jug struggled to clear his head as he found himself lying on the ground, with no idea how he got there. He pushed himself up on his knees and started to get to his feet but found that he couldn't without feeling dizzy and weak. Thinking it still the whiskey that had cast this awful sickness on him, he attempted to apologize. "I'm sorry, Willow, I reckon I got into some bad likker." His head was splitting with a massive headache, but he tried to get to his feet again. This time, he remained upright, aware only then of a wetness on the back of his neck and collar. He felt it with his hand, and when he drew it back, he realized it was blood. It occurred to him then that Willow had not answered him when he apologized. Taking care not to fall, he slowly turned around to find that she was not there. It struck him then, like the impact of the hand axe that had struck the back of his head. She had been taken! Seized by panic, he staggered across the clearing like a drunk man, calling Luke's name.

One look at Jug when he stumbled in the door of Red's Place was enough to send Luke into immediate alarm. He dropped the shot glass he was holding and rushed to meet him. "Willow?" He cried out desperately, knowing at once that something had happened to her

"They took her!" Jug gasped. "Caught me from behind."

"Who took her?" Luke pressed frantically as he guided Jug to a chair.

"I don't know," Jug groaned, the whole back of his shirt wet with blood. "I never saw 'em. When I come to, she was gone."

Luke looked around him desperately. He had to go after her, but Jug was in serious need of medical attention. Zeke Singleton stepped up to help. "You go," he said to Luke. "We'll take care of Jug."

"I'm obliged," Luke gasped hurriedly, then back to Jug, he said, "You hang in there, partner. Zeke's gonna take care of you."

Jug grabbed Luke's arm. "Go get her, Luke. I'm sorry, I never saw 'em. They got the jump on me."

"It wasn't your fault," Luke assured him. "You just let 'em fix up that cut on the back of your head. I'm goin' after her" He ran out the door, oblivious to the raucous noise of the spectators watching two men exchanging rights and lefts in the middle of the circle. His, Willow's, and Jug's horses were still standing at the rail in front of The Chinaman's, but there was no one outside the tent.

She was gone, and he was at a total loss as to what happened to her. His thoughts of panic were penetrated then by a high-pitched voice behind him. He turned to see a young woman, who was obviously a camp follower, staring up at him. He was about to dismiss her in a hurry when she spoke again. "I said I saw who took that Injun woman."

"You saw 'em?" Luke responded anxiously.

"I saw him," the woman replied. "It weren't but one man, a great big man. He walked up behind that feller with the woman and knocked him in the head with an axe. Then he threw a sack over the woman's head and picked her up like nothin' a-tall. I yelled when I saw him do it, but nobody paid me no mind. They was all hollerin' at them two fellers fightin'. I woulda told that feller that got knocked in the head, but I thought he was dead. Then he got up and started runnin' to the saloon. I tried to tell him then, but he just ran right by me, hollerin' for somebody in the saloon." She paused then before adding, "I reckon that musta been you."

In total desperation moments before, Luke felt as if he had been granted a miracle. "You say he was a big man?"

"Yessir, bigger'n you, maybe not taller, but bigger everywhere else. He picked that woman up with one arm."

"Did you see which way he went after he grabbed her?"

"Yessir." She walked a few feet toward the corner of The Chinaman's tent and pointed. "He went around the end of that tent and got on a horse and rode off yonderways." She paused to watch his intense reactions to her report. "That Injun woman, was she somebody you know?"

"She's my wife," Luke answered.

The young prostitute didn't reply at once, just nodded her head solemnly. "Oh. Well, I'm mighty sorry for her. I hope you catch up with him."

"Thank you for tellin' me what you saw," he said to her. "If you hadn't, I wouldn't have even known which way to start." He started to leave, but then thinking of her profession, he reached in his pocket and peeled off a five-dollar bill and pressed it in her hand. With no time to waste then, he ran to the horses.

"I didn't want no money for that!" She yelled after him. *I wouldn't charge that much if I spent the night with him*, she thought.

"Say a prayer that I catch him," he yelled back. "You're a good person. It might count comin' from you." He was already certain he was chasing Dan Bloodworth. Too many clues pointed to him. He knew Bloodworth was not going to back off from his passion for revenge, and he blamed himself for not thinking Bloodworth might go after Willow. And he couldn't rightfully blame Jug for not protecting her. He knew the little man would have given his life to protect her.

He climbed on Smoke, grabbed the reins of Willow's horse, and started in the direction the woman had indicated. It was already getting too dark to follow any tracks, especially across an open valley filled with tracks now. But he did pause when he started to cross a small stream that flowed behind The Chinaman's and dismounted to inspect the sandy bank. He was rewarded by finding the clear tracks of one horse where it entered the water and where it came out again on the other side. He faced the direction in which the tracks led. *If they continue in that direction, they'll lead me straight to the American Fur Company's campsite, where all their men are camped,* he thought. Now that he was sure where he was heading, he turned Smoke toward his and Jug's camp first. When he got there, he hurried to get his extra rifle and decided to take his bow, too, thinking he might as well be heavily armed for whatever he might run into. He hung the rifle and bow on Willow's horse. Ready then, he climbed back into the saddle and headed for the American Fur camp.

Chapter 23

It was a familiar-looking campsite Luke rode into. He had camped in one just like it for several years before the year just past. The American Fur Company provided tents for their men during the rendezvous. Luke had shared a four-man tent with the other three members of his team—Tom Molloy, Fred Willis, and Charlton Lewis. Lewis was now the only member of that team who was still with the company. Luke thought of Charlton Lewis as he rode into the meadow where the tents were arranged in a semicircle pattern, all facing the creek. There was little sign of life, which was not unexpected, for most of the men would be spending their money at the various places of adult entertainment available at rendezvous. He pulled Smoke to a stop and looked at the herd of horses grazing downstream from the tents. There was no way he could tell if there was one that had just been ridden into camp. He was still going on the assumption that Bloodworth had returned to camp with his captive. He rode on into the circle of tents and stepped down at the first one he came to with someone in it.

"Hey, Luke Ransom, what are you doin' here?" Hiram Jones asked as he looked out of the tent, surprised to see him in the camp.

"Hiram," Luke replied. "I didn't have any idea whose tent

this was. I'm glad it's you. I need an honest answer. I'm lookin' for Dan Bloodworth. Which one of these tents is he in?"

Hiram wasn't sure whether he should give Luke that information or not. "Luke, I've always found you to be a level-headed man, and never a troublemaker. I know about all the trouble there's been between you and Bloodworth, but I hate to see you still carryin' that on your mind. Why don't you just stay clear of him. He ain't nothin' but trouble, and I'd hate to see you wind up dead because of him."

"I 'preciate what you're tryin' to tell me, Hiram, but I ain't got any choice in this. I've tried to stay clear of him, but he won't have it." He quickly told Hiram why he was looking for Bloodworth and why his need to find him was urgent. "So, if you'll just tell me which one of these tents is his, I'll thank you for your help and not bother you further."

"Damn," Hiram exhaled upon hearing the foul deed Bloodworth pulled off. "Your wife! Everybody knows what a lowdown dog Bloodworth is, but I didn't know he could do something as bad as that. He stays in a tent near the back with Lonnie Johnson. Come on, I'll go back there with you." He stuck his pistol in his belt and came out of the tent.

"I ain't sure that's a good idea, Hiram. Bloodworth's got it in his mind to settle with me for good and all. He might start shootin' as soon as he sees me, and I'd hate to see you wind up shot in the process."

"There ain't very many of us that don't know what a sorry excuse for a human being Dan Bloodworth is, and that goes for Lonnie Johnson, too. If he's got your wife back there, after kidnappin' her, I wouldn't hesitate to shoot him, myself. Let's go!" He didn't wait for Luke but started toward the back row of tents.

When they got to the tent, Luke held his rifle ready to fire and Hiram didn't wait for him to announce their presence. "Bloodworth! You in there?"

"Who's that?" A question came back.

"Hiram Jones," Hiram said, still in charge. "That you, Lonnie?"

"Yeah, it's me. Bloodworth ain't here. Whaddaya want with him?"

"Where is he?" Luke asked, impatient with Hiram's questioning.

"Who's that?" Lonnie asked, not recognizing Luke's voice.

"It's the man who's gonna gut you like a chicken, if I don't get some straight answers outta you!" Luke threatened. No longer patient with the question-and-answer game, he grabbed the tent flap and plunged through the opening to find Lonnie sitting on the floor pointing a pistol toward the flap. Reacting at once, Luke kicked Lonnie's hand sideways, causing Lonnie to shoot a hole in his tent when the gun went off. He grabbed Lonnie by his shirt collar, yanked him up on his feet, and spun him around to hold him from behind. Before Lonnie could try to free himself, Luke's knife was resting on his throat. "Where's Bloodworth?" Luke demanded.

"I don't know where he is," Lonnie cried. He struggled in vain to free himself from the powerful arm locking his arms to his sides.

"That ain't the right answer," Luke said. "If I have to carve the answers outta your sorry hide, that's what I'll do. So make up your mind. Where is Bloodworth takin' my wife?" He put enough pressure on the knife to draw a little blood.

Lonnie almost sagged to the ground in response. "Your wife? I don't know nothin' about that. Bloodworth said he was goin' deer huntin'. That's all he told me."

"That's another wrong answer," Luke said and bore down a little harder on the knife. "If anything bad happens to my wife, I will kill you and Bloodworth. Do you understand that?"

"I swear," Lonnie pleaded. "He didn't tell me nothin' about grabbin' your wife. He just said he felt like he wanted to go huntin' for deer."

"All right, if you can't help me find him, then I ain't got any reason to keep you alive." He put the blade in a position to pull it straight across Lonnie's windpipe.

"Wait, wait!" Lonnie screamed. "I might know where he took her! I swear he didn't tell me he was gonna grab no woman. All he said when he left here this evenin' was he felt like goin' deer huntin'. Summer before last, we built us a little lean-to shed, east of here in the foothills of the Wind River Mountains, by a little pond we trapped for beaver. The deer used to show up there damn-near every night. I bet that's the place he took your woman. If it ain't, I ain't got no other idea of where he's goin'. And that's the God's honest truth."

"How far is it from here?" Luke asked, and Lonnie said twenty miles. "If I find out you lied to me, I'll spend the rest of my life, if I have to, to track you down and kill you."

"I ain't got no reason to lie," Lonnie pleaded, convinced that Luke meant what he said. "I ain't got no part in whatever Bloodworth's got in mind. He didn't tell me nothin' more than what I already told you. He ain't said nothin' about no woman. Said he had a hankerin' for some fresh deer meat."

"All right," Luke said, "get your bridle. You're gonna show me the trail you follow to get to this huntin' spot you're talkin' about." Stripped of all his weapons, Lonnie caught his horse while Luke and Hiram watched. "You ain't gonna need your saddle, if the start of this trail is as close as you say it is," Luke said.

While they watched Lonnie fetch his horse from the herd grazing there, Hiram posed a question. "You think this might be part of a plan for you to ride into an ambush? He's sayin' stay on this one trail and it'll lead you straight to Bloodworth. No cross trails, no forks, no creeks, just stay on this trail. How you know ol' Bloodworth ain't settin' behind a rock somewhere just waitin' for you to show up on that trail?"

"I don't," Luke answered. "But I'll be surprised if he ain't, and disappointed, too. Bloodworth's come at me twice with a challenge and I've tried to avoid it. But this time he's gone too far when he goes after Willow."

Hiram was still concerned about an ambush when Lonnie led his horse back to them, but Luke climbed back into the saddle, ready to go. "You want me to saddle my horse and go with you?" Hiram was inspired to ask.

"No, I don't," Luke answered flatly. "And I'm sendin' Lonnie back as soon as he shows me the trail to follow. This has to be settled once and for all between Bloodworth and me. I don't want anybody else to get hurt in it. But I appreciate your offer to help."

Still not wholly trustful of Lonnie, Hiram asked. "What if Bloodworth's ol' pal, here, puts you on the wrong trail?"

"Now, why would he do that?" Luke came back. "He's wantin' Bloodworth to drygulch me, ain't he? And he knows, if he don't put me on the right trail, I'll come back and kill him."

Hiram thought for a brief second. "Yeah, there's that, I reckon." He looked at Lonnie and the look he got in return was not a friendly one. The thought entered his mind then of the possibility that it could be Bloodworth to return, instead of Luke. He didn't like the thought of that, he told himself. He wasn't the only one in camp that would welcome the departure of Lonnie and Bloodworth. "You be careful, Luke," he said when they parted. He watched them ride out, then decided to see if Jim Frazier, or any of the other men were in camp. He thought it would be a good idea to let everybody know what was going on between Luke and Bloodworth. And he was not anxious to face Lonnie Johnson when he returned after showing Luke the trail to the deer camp. He figured he'd be a great deal more comfortable if Lonnie thought the rest of the men felt the same as he.

Riding bareback, Lonnie led Luke a quarter of a mile to the north until reaching a sharp turn in the Green River. He rode to the outermost point in the river bend and into a stand of pine trees, then reined his horse to a stop. "Yonder it is," he said and pointed toward a game trail that ended at the river. It was barely visible in the gathering darkness. "You follow that trail and it'll take you right up to some foothills and a little valley with a pond in the middle of it."

"How far?" Luke asked.

"'Bout fifteen or twenty miles, I ain't sure."

"Are you sure this is the trail?" Luke asked. "Your life depends on it."

"I'm sure," he answered. He knew Luke was serious. He sat there while Luke wheeled his horse and rode into the pine trees. Wishing he had a weapon at that moment, he folded his hand to pretend it was a gun and aimed his forefinger at Luke's back, and softly uttered, "Pow." He sincerely hoped that Bloodworth was waiting for Luke to come after him. "Doggone it, I plum forgot to tell him about that little deer shack, and why we liked it so much—how you can set up there high on that hill back of the pond and see the deer comin' on that trail three or four hundred yards away. Then you just wait for 'em to get in range." He pointed his imaginary gun at the now empty trail and shot another imaginary bullet after Luke.

He had not been lying when he told Luke and Hiram that Bloodworth didn't confide in him about any plan to kidnap the Indian woman. He was as surprised as anyone when Bloodworth decided he wanted to go deer hunting in the middle of the night. Now he allowed himself a little chuckle when he thought about Bloodworth snatching Luke Ransom's sweet little Injun wife right out from under his nose. "He sure found a guaranteed way to get ol' Ransom riled up, and he'll be comin' up that deer path, right where Bloodworth wants him." *Maybe I oughta go back and have a little talk with Mr. Hiram Jones, now that he ain't got his bodyguard to protect him,* he thought and turned his horse back toward the camp.

It was impossible not to think that Lonnie might have sent him off on a wild goose chase, but he had no choice other than to accept it as the truth. It was the only clue he had of Willow's whereabouts. As he followed the narrow deer path out of the shadows of the pines and across stretches of open, moonlit, valley, he tried to concentrate on the trail, itself, and not what might

be happening to Willow. He felt that he was to blame for her abduction, that he had failed to protect her. *I should have slit that maniac's throat when I had the chance,* he told himself. *Keep your mind
on the trail you're riding,* he lectured himself. Just because Lonnie
said it was twenty miles to that hut, it didn't mean Bloodworth
wouldn't wait in ambush short of that.

As much as he wanted to hurry, he had to hold Smoke to an
easy lope, broken up by stretches of a fast walk, so as not to tire
him out. The big bay seemed to sense what his master wanted
and almost set the pace himself. It was a long ride to this place
Lonnie had described and it was going to be late that night when
he got there. It would be better to get there in the morning,
when he could scout the whole area to determine his best approach to Bloodworth's camp. But he could not delay another
moment in his panic to reach Willow. He would stop when about
halfway to make sure Smoke and Willow's horse were rested.
There were no thoughts of rest or food for himself. He didn't
bring anything to eat, even if he had an urge to eat it. He could
think of nothing but the torment Willow might be suffering
while he plodded along an empty deer trail.

As the time dragged slowly past, and he rode farther and farther from the rendezvous camps, he just naturally became more
cautious, telling himself he was of no value to her if he blundered
into an ambush. Up ahead, he saw a line of trees that evidently
lined the banks of a stream or creek, and the path continued
straight toward it. His instincts told him it was a perfect spot for
an ambush, even though he was still some distance from the
foothills of the Wind River Range. He didn't waste any more
time to make a decision, turning Smoke off the game trail, and
angling across the valley at a lope to intercept the creek about
seventy-five yards to the south. When he reached the narrow
creek, he drove his two horses into the border of fir trees, down
into the water, and crossed to the other side. Then, counting on
the darkness of the shadows to disguise his movements, he
walked the horses slowly back toward the game trail.

When he was about forty yards from the game trail, he tied Smoke and Willow's horse in the trees and proceeded on foot, his rifle loaded and ready to fire. He had not walked twenty yards more when he suddenly dropped to one knee, stopped by the sound of movement among the bushes ahead. Horses, maybe, or someone moving from one spot to another, he couldn't tell, but someone was there. In the darkness of the creekbank, he was afraid he would not be able to see where Willow was, and he couldn't risk a shot until he knew. Anxious to confront the loathsome Bloodworth, he had to caution himself to remain calm as he slowly advanced toward the noises he had heard in the bushes. He took one firm step at a time, so that his moccasins would make no sound as his feet followed the contour of the creekbank. Although moving silently, he was suddenly startled by an explosion among the laurel bushes at the water's edge when half a dozen deer sprang up and bolted from the thicket. His natural reaction almost caused him to shoot at one of them. Frustrated, he could only stand there thinking of the time he had wasted. A picture formed in his mind of Willow lying helpless, bound hand and foot, and he wanted to cry out to her to hang on. He would come for her, no matter what.

Approximately five miles from the creek crossing, Willow lay at the back of a roughly built, three-sided shelter, her hands and feet tied behind her back. Her face was swollen and bruised, the result of her captor's means of getting her attention. It had been her misfortune to be a victim of this treatment once before when Bloody Hand's Blackfoot raiders captured her. She had refused to cry then, and she refused to cry at the hands of this man now, which seemed to infuriate him. All she knew about her captor was that he held an intense hatred for Luke and that he was using her as bait to draw Luke into the ambush he had waiting for him. "If things happen the way I think they will," Bloodworth told her, "your husband will come ridin' up that trail I'm settin' here lookin' at. And I'm gonna knock him outta the saddle before he gets to the foot of this hill. Then, if I'm lucky, he ain't gonna be dead, so I'll have to kill him real slow." He turned to leer at her. "Maybe he'd enjoy watchin' me strap you on a time or two. I ain't partial to rollin' around with a damn Injun, but I'd do it to entertain your husband. Put a picture in his head to take to hell with him."

He continued to leer at her for a long moment. "You are a pretty little thing, though. Don't you worry, me and you are gonna get it on, whether your husband comes after you or not. But I'll promise you this. When I'm done with you, I'll throw your ass in the same hole with what's left of him. How's that? That'ud work out, wouldn't it? You and him can go to the Happy Huntin' Ground together. He ain't gonna be in no condition to do much huntin', though."

She tried to turn a deaf ear to his endless boasting, but he droned on and on. Sitting on an upside-down bucket at the front of the shelter, he had his Kentucky long rifle beside him. The open front of his shelter was concealed behind a row of mountain laurel bushes. So he had to make a little hole through the bushes to keep a constant lookout on the trail leading up to the pond. He had had thoughts about some pleasure at the expense of his captive, but he could not risk interrupting his constant watch on the game trail. She had known in her heart that Luke would come for her and had prayed that he would hurry. But when they reached the hill, and she saw the setup Bloodworth had planned for Luke's arrival, she prayed he would not come. For to come would certainly mean his death, and she could not bear the thought of that. She wiggled the ring finger of her left hand and came close to breaking her vow not to cry when she felt her ring move. She felt that she had come so close to a perfect marriage. Why was it to be denied? She could not understand.

Another thought entered Bloodworth's mind then, so he questioned her. "Where was Ransom and Jug Sartain trappin' last winter?" She didn't answer, so he asked, "You want me to come over there and knock it outta ya?" She still did not answer. He started to get up, but thought better of it, afraid to lose his vigil of the game trail. "You're probably the one who told 'em where the beaver were. That's most likely the reason he married you, so you'd tell him where to trap. You tell me where the beaver are and I might let you live. Whaddaya say? Hell, I might even marry you." That thought caused him to chuckle.

The thought of it made Willow feel sick to her stomach. She spoke for the first time since her abduction. "I don't know beaver. Luke have beaver before he find me."

"So you can talk white man talk," he responded. "And you know that's a damn lie. You know where they trapped those beaver, so you might as well tell me. Luke ain't gonna be around to trap no beaver next year and neither is that little runt, Jug Sartain." He turned to glare at her for a few seconds before one final threat. "I got ways to make you talk. We'll just wait till I take care of Mr. Luke Ransom. Then I can give you all my attention. You be thinkin' about that."

"Well, Smoke, that's gotta be it," Luke spoke softly to the bay gelding as he gazed far up ahead of them at the first hill before the mountains. Had it been in broad daylight, he could have easily seen the pond that was supposed to be at the base of that hill. Staring at it now in the dark, he could tell that the trail he had been following went straight up the hill, just like Lonnie had said. What was obvious to him was the fact that anybody, anywhere on the slope of that hill should be able to see a rider coming up the path. There was no sign of a hut or anything else man-made. If he were to believe Lonnie Johnson, he would have expected to see the three-sided structure he described. *I might as well just shoot myself in the head, instead of riding up that trail*, he thought. He looked north and south, and picked south again, as he had when he circled around the deer. The southern slope of the hill was heavily forested, which suited his purposes, especially since the first light of the new day was beginning to filter down upon the path. He turned his horses off the path and began a wide circle that would take him to the south slope of the target hill. He figured he was almost back to the game trail when he got a glimpse of the pond through the trees ahead of him. He dismounted and tied the two horses there, having already decided his best chance was on foot. In line with that thinking, he decided for stealth and quickness, so he would fare better with his bow, with his pistol and knife for backup. The long rifle was not handy for close combat, and he just might find himself in that situation. As an afterthought, he decided his shorter barreled shotgun would have been the weapon of choice, but it did him no good to think about that now. Besides, he thought, the bow was silent, and it somehow seemed more fitting for Bloodworth to die as the result of an Indian arrow.

Once he was satisfied that his horses were all right, he grabbed his bow and continued his scouting of the ambush he felt sure was awaiting him. As he carefully made his way through the forest of firs, he was aware of the wind in the boughs of the trees, the only sound in the deep silence that surrounded him. And then he heard it, a sound that didn't belong, and he identified it as the crude guttural chuckling of Dan Bloodworth. He at once had to fight the urge to charge recklessly toward the sound, telling himself that the odds would be good that he would be shot down immediately. And what good would that do Willow? From the direction the sound of the chuckle had come, he figured he was a little uphill and still a couple of dozen yards away. He continued his path through the firs until he finally got a glimpse of the pond down the hill. He didn't see the three-sided shelter at first, but when he took a few steps closer, he saw the crude structure wedged between two small trees. He figured he was about ten feet above it and he could now see why the hut wasn't visible from the trail. There were several laurel bushes hiding it.

The problem to be solved was the fact that he could not see Bloodworth, for the shelter was facing the other way. Bloodworth was no doubt sitting inside the shelter, watching the trail, waiting for him to appear. He could see no sign of Willow, so he had to believe she was inside the shelter, too. As the first light of morning began to penetrate the thick forest, he caught sight of Bloodworth's horse, hobbled near the pond. There was just the one horse, which told Luke that Bloodworth had carried Willow all the way to this hill on his horse. Back to his problem then, he thought, *I might have to wait for him to come out to answer nature's call.* Then he had to wonder if Bloodworth was so crude that he might not bother to leave the hut for that purpose.

Inside the shelter, Willow tried to shift her position in hopes of easing the pain in her back and hips after lying tied hand and foot all night. She could now see bits of light through the cracks in the shelter, and the fact that Luke had not appeared was the one thing she could be thankful for. There was a part of her that she could not deny, however. She had hoped that he would come for her, even though he would have likely paid for it with his life. Then her thoughts returned to her fate and she once again hoped that he would make it quick, since his plan to torture Luke with acts of cruelty upon her might not materialize. Her thoughts were interrupted then when he complained.

"What the hell are you doin'?" He barked and looked sharply at her. Stumped by the question, she didn't respond and that only served to irritate him more. "Knock that off!" He barked again.

"I do nothing," she finally spoke.

"The hell you ain't," he responded. "There you go again. I don't know what kinda tricks you think you're up to, but all it's gonna get you is a good whuppin'."

She realized then what was bothering him. She had been so engrossed in her thoughts of what horrors lie in wait for her that she had paid no attention to the little sounds of limbs or cones falling on the roof of the shelter. Still, she couldn't understand why it caused him to react so violently. Maybe he was losing his nerve, waiting for Luke. Then she heard what sounded like a large cone bouncing off the roof. He was glaring right at her when it hit and realized that she was not the source of the noises. Still irritated, however, he got off his bucket, stepped outside the shelter, and stood up to look at the roof. He went over backward when the shaft of the arrow drove through his neck, causing him to land on his back in the laurel bushes in front of the shelter. Luke notched a second arrow and walked around the shelter to find Bloodworth struggling to pull the arrow out of his neck. He drew the bowstring back and released the second arrow, this one driving into Bloodworth's abdomen just below his rib cage. Then he rolled off the bushes and dropped to the ground in front of them. Luke hesitated for only a moment to make sure he was finished before he called out, "Willow!"

"Luke!" She answered. "I'm here."

He looked in the rough shelter, saw her lying at the back of it and hurried to her. He took his knife and cut the ropes binding her feet and hands. As soon as her hands were free, she threw her arms around his neck. He carried her out of the little shelter, clinging to him like a small child, as he carried her in one arm, walking in a crouch due to the low roof. As he came out of the shelter, he encountered the monstrous hulk of Dan Bloodworth, the two arrows still embedded in his body. Like an enraged grizzly, Bloodworth clawed at the laurel bushes to pull himself up the hill. With Willow still clinging to him, Luke reached down and picked up the long rifle still lying beside the bucket and pulled the trigger. When the gun fired, it knocked Bloodworth back down the hill, this time for good.

Chapter 24

He carried her in his arms down to the small pond at the foot of the hill and sat her down beside the water. "I'm gonna leave you here for a minute. I'll be right back."

"Where are you going?" She asked at once, almost in panic.

"I'm just gonna walk back up the hill a little ways to get the horses. Won't take a minute. I've got a clean cloth in my saddlebags. I'll clean up your face a little bit. Get some of that dried blood off. I'm sorry I didn't bring any food to cook, but I didn't wanna take the time to pack up a lotta stuff. Took me long enough to get here as it was." She still looked worried, so he said, "I'll be right back, then I'll clean those cuts and we'll head back to camp."

She grabbed his sleeve when he started to walk away and looked up into his eyes. "Luke, you not ask, but I wanna tell you. Marks on my face, only place he hurt me. He not hurt me no place else." She looked at him as if begging him to believe her.

He realized then what was worrying her. "Oh," he reacted. "I'm real glad to know that, but it wouldn't have made any difference in how I feel about you. You're my wife, now and for always. All right?"

"All right," she said, but held onto his sleeve a moment longer. "I knew you would come for me."

"You can count on it," he said and gave her hand a squeeze. "I'll be back in a minute."

After he cleaned the bruises and the broken skin on her face, using whiskey from a bottle he found in Bloodworth's saddlebags to kill the germs, he went through the rest of the deceased man's possessions to see if there was anything they could use. This was in spite of Willow's protests that she didn't want to keep anything that had any connection to the evil man. Luke figured Bloodworth's horse and saddle might still belong to the American Fur Company. He hadn't been with the company but a couple of years and Luke remembered that he was with the company for three years before Smoke and his saddle and rifle were deemed his personal property. So he saddled Bloodworth's horse with the intention of turning it over to American Fur. He decided Bloodworth didn't rate a hole dug in the ground by him. He would tell Lonnie Johnson where he could find the body, if he wanted to go bury him. For the time being, he thought Bloodworth could serve a useful purpose as buzzard feed. He had a notion to try to pull his arrows out of the body. But on second thought, he decided Bloodworth looked good with two Blackfoot arrows sticking in him.

They rode straight back to their campsite at the rendezvous with only stops to let the horses drink. Jug was waiting anxiously for their return and greeted them wearing a large bandage on the back of his head. When he saw them coming across the valley, leading Bloodworth's horse, he started jumping up and down excitedly, blurting out, "I knew he would do it! I told you he would get her back!" He continued to repeat it as he watched them approach the camp, even though there was no one there but him. It struck him then that Luke had taken no food of any kind, so he grabbed up the coffeepot and ran to the creek to fill it with water. Luckily, they had some ground coffee, so he fixed up a pot and set it on the fire. They were only about fifty yards away by then, and his jubilation took a turn toward worrisome. For he laid full blame on himself for Willow's abduction. He worried now about what she might have suffered at the hands of that evil monster.

As soon as they pulled the horses to a stop, Jug came forward to meet them. Passing right by Luke, he hurried to Willow's horse to help her down. "You poor little punkin," he cooed when he saw her bruised face. "I'm awful sorry. It's all my fault for lettin' that no-account maniac slip up on me." He turned to look at Luke, and Luke smiled at him. He turned back toward Willow then and said, "You don't know how glad I am to see you back here in one piece."

Anxious to dispose of any doubts or suspicions, she quickly informed him, "Only hurt on face. No hurt anywhere else."

"Thank the Good Lord for that," Jug responded, feeling the lifting of a great weight of guilt from his shoulders.

"I look at wound on back of your head now," Willow said.

"After you folks drink some coffee and eat some jerky," Jug insisted. "I didn't have no idea when I'd see you again, or I'da cooked up somethin'. I ain't sure what it'da been, since we ain't had a chance to go to the store yet." He gave Luke a sheepish grin and added, "Bloodworth kinda messed up our plans."

"I cook some elk jerky," Willow said.

"Lord knows we got plenty of that," Jug replied. "You get you some coffee. I'll take care of your horses. What about that gray, Bloodworth's horse?" He was eager to help any way he could, even though he was most anxious to hear the story of how the gray's saddle became empty.

"Right now, we'll take the saddles off 'em and turn the gray out with the rest of our horses. All three of 'em could use a rest. I'll talk to Axel Thompson over at American Fur to see if he thinks they have a claim on Bloodworth's horse and saddle."

"Right," Jug responded and started pulling the saddle off the gray. When Luke unsaddled Smoke and Willow's horse, they led the three horses toward the other horses a little way before releasing them to continue on their own. That was as long as Jug could contain his patience. Well out of Willow's earshot, he grabbed Luke's elbow and stopped him. "If you don't tell me what happened when you caught up with that sorry piece of trash, I'm gonna bust!"

Luke paused and looked at his fiery little partner. He started to relate the incident as it happened, but he hesitated, unable to resist an alternate version. "Well, I found him. He was right where Lonnie Johnson said he'd be, settin' up on the side of a hill watchin' the trail that led to him. As soon as I spotted him, I raised my hand and told him I came to talk, so we talked. And the more we talked, the more he came to see he was in the wrong about the whole thing and he wanted to apologize for everything he'd done. I said he had nothin' to apologize for as long as Willow had not been seriously harmed. He said he was awful sorry he had lost his temper once and hit her and left those marks on her face. He said she had already forgiven him for that."

"Well, I'll be . . . ," Jug started. "I'da never thought . . ." He didn't finish either sentence, amazed as he was to hear of the miraculous turnaround of a maniacal mind. Staring after the three horses they just released, it struck him then. "But what happened to him? That's his horse, ain't it?"

"Oh, well, yeah, that's his horse all right. When he was bringin' Willow down the hill to me, he slipped and broke his neck." Luke shook his head sadly. "Awful sight it was, awful."

Completely taken in at first, Jug's facial expression changed from wide-eyed wonderment to indignant disgust when it struck him. "Damn you, Luke Ransom, you oughta be shot. I've got a good mind to tell Willow the story you just told me."

"No, you don't," Luke said at once. "I'll tell you what happened, every detail, but you gotta promise me you ain't gonna say nothin' to her about me japin' you about it. There ain't nothin' about this thing she wants to joke about. And it sure wasn't a joke to me. I don't know what I woulda done if anything had happened to her." He told Jug all about the execution of Dan Bloodworth then, but only after he got Jug's solemn promise that he would never tell her that he had japed him at first.

After hearing all the events that happened after Luke left Red's Place the night before, Jug still had questions that concerned him. "From what you're tellin' me, it sounds like Bloodworth's pal, Lonnie Johnson, was in it up to his neck, since he's the one who told you where to go to find Bloodworth."

"I'm sure he was," Luke agreed, "but it was Bloodworth's show, just like it always was with Lonnie. He just did Bloodworth's errands, so I ain't worried about him causing us any problems. I am a little worried about Hiram Jones, though. He went with me to find Lonnie and Lonnie wasn't too happy with him about that. I expect I'll need to talk to Lonnie. I made some pretty serious threats on his life that he wasn't very happy about. I figure they'll all be at Berman's Saloon tonight, so I'll go over there and talk to him and Axel Thompson about Bloodworth's horse."

The three of them went to Boutwell's store that afternoon to buy the supplies needed to sustain their camp for the rest of the summer and the coming trapping season. Willow had already informed them, in no uncertain terms, that she was going to be with them right through the season. Luke didn't put up much of an argument, since he didn't like the thought of being away from her all winter. Jug wasn't about to argue. It meant having a cook and a hard-working hand with the pelts. With that decided and now stocked with new supplies, Willow was pleased to cook them a big supper. When supper was over, Luke decided to go over to Berman's to catch the American Fur Crew and get that issue settled. "Maybe I oughta go over there with you," Jug suggested.

"No need, partner. I ain't gonna be gone long. I'm just gonna say my peace and whatever Axel says is fair, I'll agree to. We don't need the extra horse, anyway. You stay here and finish the coffee." Jug went out with him to saddle Bloodworth's gray while he saddled Smoke.

"You be careful, Luke Ransom," Willow told him. "I save you some coffee."

"Yes, ma'am, Mrs. Ransom," Luke replied, gave her a light peck on her bruised cheek, and stepped up into the saddle. "Tomorrow we go find that preacher."

As he had figured, most of the American Fur Company's crew was in their nightly session at Berman's Saloon when he pulled up at the hitching rail and tied the horses there. Armed only with his pistol and his knife, he walked into the noisy saloon. Moments later, a blanket of silence fell over the room when he was recognized. Luke paused only a moment to look at those gathered at the large table at the back of the room, most of whom he recognized, having worked with many of them for five years. He did not see Lonnie Johnson, but he saw Axel Thompson, so he walked on back to the table. "Luke," Axel acknowledged.

"Evenin', Axel," Luke replied. "I came to bring Dan Bloodworth's horse, saddle, and his weapons back. I didn't know if they belonged to him or to the company. Figured you'd know. Bloodworth won't be comin' back." There was a low buzz of mumbling at that. "I don't see Lonnie Johnson here," Luke continued. "I was gonna tell him he has nothin' to fear from me. Bloodworth was my only target, and now I'm done with it. I worked five years with your company, and I hope there ain't no hard feelin's because of this. That's all I've got to say on the matter. What's your decision about the horse and tack?"

"Well, Bloodworth hadn't worked off the cost of his horse and saddle yet," Axel said. "The weapons were his. I appreciate your honesty in the matter. Let me tell you this, though. Every man here knows what Bloodworth did, and nobody can fault you for going after the man who abducted your wife." Again, there was a buzz of mumbling among those standing there, this time a vote of approval. "I'll tell Lonnie what you said, and we wish you good luck, you and your wife."

Luke was frankly touched. He nodded and said, "'Preciate it," as he looked around the table, pausing when he met Hiram Jones' gaze for a moment.

"You wanna stay and have a drink on me?" Axel asked.

"Thank you just the same, but I told the little woman I'd be right back." His comment drew a round of chuckles. "You know how it is with us old married men."

Standing in the doorway at the back of Berman's Saloon after having stepped outside to return some of the beer he had imbibed, Lonnie Johnson listened to the conversation between Luke and Axel. He had no desire to come face to face with Luke Ransom again. And from what he heard, he was considered of no consequence to Ransom or Axel and American Fur. Everything had gone wrong, it was supposed to be Bloodworth who returned to the camp, so he elected not to go back inside and risk the possibility of having to face Luke in front of the others.

When he heard Luke leaving, he walked around the saloon to the front corner and watched for him to come out. In a moment, Luke appeared and walked to the hitching rail to untie his horse. Lonnie realized Luke had no idea he was there, as he stood at the rail, his back to him. *It was there before him, the opportunity to kill the man who had shamed him*. He would never get another opportunity like this, he told himself. His hand shaking, he drew the pistol from his belt and checked to make sure it was ready to fire. Luke went around the rail, his back still toward Lonnie as he walked up to grasp his saddle horn, preparing to mount. Lonnie raised a shaking hand and forced himself to hold it steady enough to take aim. He screamed in surprise when the .54 caliber rifle ball struck him in the chest, knocking him backward, his pistol firing straight up in the air.

Startled, Luke was at once confused. The first shot sounded to have come from some distance in front of the saloon, but it was followed instantly by a shot directly behind him. When he turned back toward the saloon, it was in time to see Lonnie hit the ground. Thinking maybe he was caught in a crossfire, he pulled his pistol and dropped to one knee, searching for the source of the shot that downed Lonnie. In a few seconds, he heard the shooter. "Don't shoot, Luke, it's me."

"Jug?"

"Yeah, it's me," Jug answered and came out from behind a large pine tree. "He was fixin' to cut you down. I figured you needed some backup."

Still surprised, Luke was speechless for a few moments while he replayed what had just happened in his mind. When he finally spoke, it was to say, "Partner, I ain't never been so glad to see you before." They walked over to look at the body. There was no question, Lonnie Johnson was dead, shot through the heart. "I don't know where he came from," Luke said. "He wasn't in the saloon."

Jug told him Lonnie had come from behind the saloon and was taking dead aim at his back. "I was fixin' to go in there if you didn't come out pretty soon, but I saw that snake sneakin' around the corner. I'm glad I had my rifle with me. I mighta missed with a pistol."

By that time, after there were no more shots fired, the men inside the saloon decided it safe enough to come out to see what was taking place. One of them, Hiram Jones, was not at all surprised to find out Lonnie had attempted to shoot Luke in the back. And it was fairly obvious to the others when they saw the pistol still in Lonnie's hand, having just been fired. "I expect we'd best take our leave now," Luke said to Jug. "Partner, I'm sure glad you decided to come lookin' for me." Jug was glad, too. He didn't tell Luke that he was there because Willow had asked him to go after him, in case Luke got into trouble.

"I make new coffee, so you both have some," Willow greeted them when they returned. "I make more Johnny-cakes, too." It was a pleasant evening with another full moon, and no one worried about the extra coffee keeping them awake, especially Luke and Willow. They had not slept at all the night before. They made themselves comfortable sitting there by the fire, and Luke seemed to be the first to submit to the call for sleep. There was a lull in the conversation that lasted several minutes before Willow interrupted it. Speaking softly, so only Jug could hear, she said, "Look, he sleeps like baby." She reached over and gently removed the cup from Luke's hand.

"He's been pretty doggone busy for the last two days," Jug whispered. "But so have you. You need to get the both of you to bed."

"I'm okay," she said. "I not bother him right now." She gazed fondly at her sleeping husband. Then she reached over to pat Jug on his hand. "You are good friend to Luke. Thank you for going to look for him tonight. He say you save his life."

"I shoulda thought to go after him, myself," Jug said. "I wanted to go, but he said stay here. You heard him."

"He not always do what's best for him," Willow said. "But he always say Jug good friend to him." She gave him a warm smile, "And to me, too." Jug was deeply touched. He felt like he was family. Willow continued to gaze upon her sleeping husband for a while. Then a question occurred to her. "Jug," she pronounced. "Why you called that?"

"It's because I like to drink my likker outta a jug," he answered.

"I know that, but when they start calling you that? You don't drink fire water when a little boy."

"No, that just happened after I growed up a little. I took it on as my regular name on account I didn't like the name my mama gave me."

"What name your mama give you?" She asked, really interested at this point.

Jug shook his head. "I don't never tell nobody that name. I don't want nobody callin' me that. Luke asked me when we first partnered-up. I wouldn't tell him."

His reluctance only served to increase her curiosity. "You can tell me. I promise, I not tell Luke, or nobody else."

He hesitated. His given name was a secret he intended to take to the grave with him, but he had come to trust Willow's honesty and integrity. He bit his lower lip as he tried to decide, then he took another look at Luke, sleeping, exhausted. Finally, he leaned over closer to her and whispered even more softly, "You swear you won't tell Luke or nobody else?"

She whispered back, "I swear, I no tell nobody."

"Carmen," he whispered, and when Willow seemed puzzled, he went on to explain. "My mama heard that name somewhere and thought it sounded good, so she stuck it on me. Come to find out, Carmen's a girl's name. I caught plenty of hell over that name till I left home and took on Jug."

"Carmen," she repeated softly. "I not tell."

"I know. I trust you. I wouldn't tell nobody else in this whole world but you." They sat there by the fire for a long while until Jug decided he was going to have to turn in for the night. "You gonna need any help gettin' your husband up from there and into your hut? You'd most likely do just as well throwing his blanket over him right where he is. He'd probably sleep right there till mornin'."

"Maybe I do that," she said. "I'll see after I clean cups."

"All right, then," Jug said. "I'll see you in the mornin'. Good night."

"Good night," she returned.

"Yeah, good night, Carmen," Luke spoke out. "See you in the mornin'."

"Damn you, Luke Ransom!" Jug cursed. "I wish I'da let Lonnie Johnson shoot your lowdown ass! Wipe that smile off your face!"